TILTSTONE,
GEM AND TOMBSTONE

TILTSTONE GEM AND TOMBSTONE

Part Three of
THE TILTSTONE TRILOGY

by

DONOVAN LEAMAN

My Family, Past and Present
Nurserymen and All Who Depend on the Soil for Their Daily Bread
Dreamers of Dreams
Dry Stone Wallers
Those Born to be Teachers, Preachers and Spinners of Yarns
And the late John Fisher, my Teacher of English who inspired in me a
Lifelong Appreciation of our Literature and Language,
Etymology and Elocution.
Benedicamus Domino, alleluia. Deo gratias agamus.

Copyright © Donovan Leaman 2018

First published in 2018 by
Scotforth Books
Carnegie House
Chatsworth Road
Lancaster

British Library Cataloguing-in-Publication data

A catalogue record for this book is available from the British Library

ISBN 978-1-909817-39-5

Printed and bound by Jellyfish Solutions

Acknowledgements

In gratitude, I thank all the patient followers of the life of Daniel Tiltstone Greensward aka Damnit, who demanded that I complete the Tiltstone Trilogy. I hope the thirteen year wait will be worthwhile.

'Tiltstone' was written in eight months:

'Tiltstone Fire and Brimstone' in thirty two months:

'Tiltstone Gem and Tombstone' has taken eighty eight and a half months from start to finish.

How time flies when you are having fun with a pencil and India rubber.

Thank you to a leading forester for his advice on the subject of 'Biomass.' I hope that for you 'T.G.&T.' will be as unputdownable as 'T.F.&B.' Your beauty sleep is important.

Thank you, Jackie Warden who so enthusiastically embraces the storyline even when having to decipher/translate my manuscript – of which I am not proud – and commit it to disk. You bring such grace and good humour to a painstaking task and it must come as a relief to you that I have not been persuaded to proceed from a trilogy to a tetralogy – yet.

The proofreader of the full Tiltstone Trilogy, Lesley Evans, has moved home to Buckinghamshire before she could teach me the dark art of proofreading. So even at a distance I humbly and thankfully acknowledge her expertise in spotting and correcting so many little and some glaring errors in my script. She knows full well that writers know their own tales too well and skate over their mistakes with insouciance. It is a great comfort to me that Lesley and I understand the same language – Latin.

There would be no book to read without my publisher, Scotforth Books, who make the whole process a pleasure. My special thanks go to Anna Goddard, Lucy Frontani and Srishti Kadu whose dedication to their Fine Art has brought forth a book that is pleasing to hold in one's hand and so attractive to the eye of the beholder. The cover says, 'Read Me!' Thank you.

And most important of all, Carol, my precious wife of over forty years, and still standing, who humours me and copes with my occasional ill-mannered and ill-timed flights of authorial fancy. Even now, 'My broken dreams are still yours to mend'. Thank you.

Contents

A Random Selection of Vegetable and Mineral Items of Some Importance.

A Bramble bush of 1947 vintage
Fragrant roses for a sad lady
Lavender
Raspberries
Birch trees and others of many genera
Ash trees by the thousand and Moses
Grass and weeds
'Sam's Diamond' A gem of a Lime tree
'Ezekiel Keld' English Field Maple. An upright tree for an upright man.

Mount Etna
Rock and stone
Water
Various cars
Money and the Bagalog currency
Tiltstones (3)
Rubies
Phoenix House and Lambkinfold Farm
Weedkiller
A Kinnon Fountain with accompanying 'Bottle'
The Bethdan

Live, Dead, Ghostly, Mythical and Legendary Characters in order of first mention.

Final Chapter (LVIII) of Tiltstone, Fire and Brimstone

1. Daniel Tiltstone Greensward (Damnit)
    A churchwarden of Saint Michael the Archangel, Tupshorne.
    Sometime director, Rolls Royce research.

2. Albert Prince (d. 5/2/2000)
    Master locksmith of Gorrington, Cambridge.
    Mentor of Daniel and renowned raconteur.

3. 'The Prof' Tobias
    Retired professor of engineering and Principal
    Curator of the National Museum of Engineering.

4. Aidan Ferrers
    Cumbrian blacksmith. Creator of 'Ferrers', the
    gigantic shovel designed by John Smith of Latvia.

5. Athene Hope
    Portrait artist of Preston.

6. Vulcan
    Ancient Roman God of Fire and Forge
    (and metalworkers).

7. Bethan
    Daniel's sister and her husband Gerald – both deceased.

The Chapters of Tiltstone, Gem and Tombstone

8. The Reverend Samuel Bone (a.k.a. Sambo) deceased.
   Headmaster of High Ashes Preparatory School. Noted
   classical scholar and 'Double Blue' from Cambridge.

9. Silas Kinnon Beaune (Skinny)
   On first encounter, a cherubic schoolboy.

10. Katharine Kinnon, (dec) wife of Marcel Beaune
    (whereabouts unknown)
    and mother of Silas.

11. General Charles de Gaulle (dec).

12. Mrs Askey. Drama teacher of High Ashes (dec).

13. Lorna Greensward
    (formerly wife of the late Matthew Swann). Wife of Daniel.

14. Colin Blunden
    (Married to Carolyn). One time colleague of Damnit
    at Rolls Royce.

15. The Reverend Jacob Drake (Jake)
    Married to Martha. Damnit's closest friend. Recently retired.

16. 'Uncle' Jonah Drake (dec)
    Reverend father of Jake.

17. Henry Royce and Charles Rolls (dec)
    Once of Knutsford.

18. Miss Wynn (dec)
    Historian of Knutsford.

19. Mr Snowdrops.
    Galanthophile and brother of (62). (Husband of Harriet, dec).

20. Douglas Swann
    Married to Dr Rachel Rosenbaum, née Ross). Lorna's son. Oilman.

21. Timothy Welsh
    Married to Muriel. Churchwarden.

22. Violet Rose
    Church Treasurer.

23. John Smith
    (Janis Kalējs of Priedsne, Latvia) deceased.
    Hero of 'Tiltstone, Fire and Brimstone.'

24. Bert 'The Bells' Alderwood
    Married to Freda. Bellringer.

25. Professor Brendan O'Driscoll (a.k.a. Bod or Sod)
    Suicide. Eminent Plant Toxicologist.

26. A Venerable Archdeacon.

27. George Greensward (dec)
    Great-grandfather of Daniel and father of Absalom (dec).

28. Jim and Emily Greensward (dec)
    Parents of Daniel and Bethan (dec). Jake's 'Uncle Jim' and 'Aunt Em.'

29. Nic the Vic
    (a.k.a. Lucifer Liquidator). Suicide. A rogue priest.

30. Freda Fazackerley
    A mythical Blackburn character responsible for any strange 'goings-on.'

31. Mrs Herbison
    'Her next door' to Violet Rose.

32. Baggins and Rauch
    The Greenswards' two beautiful black bitch Labrador
    retrievers. Both young.

33. Miss Bindle
    The Drakes' beautiful black bitch Labrador retriever.
    Not so young.

34. Eleanore Bormann
    Widow of Heino (35).

35. Heino Bormann
    Killed accidentally by (23).

36. Otilija Kalējs. (dec)
    Mother of (23) and stillborn Willams.

37. Zigrids Kalējs. (dec)
    Latvian blacksmith.

38. Lutz (Ludwig Kaltmann)
    S.S. sniper who murdered Zigrids. Killed at Stalingrad by
    Janis Kalējs who at the time was in the process of burying
    his own father Arvids.

39. Max Herrick
    English teacher, cricket coach and collator of the stories
    of John Smith (23).

40. Aino
    Wife of Zigrids Kalējs.

41. The Reverend Reuben Ossian
    of the Church of Saint Thomas, Ravensrigg.

42. Minerva Jemima
    Wife of Reuben Ossian.

43. Helen Ossian (b.1992)
    Vicarage kid.

44. Troy Ossian (b.1995)
    Vicarage kid.

45. The Reverend Stanley Freeborne
    A visiting priest.

46. Stephanie Potts
    Church organist and choirmistress.

47. Mr Nathan Ross (geboren Rosenbaum)
    Eminent physician. Father of Rachel Swann.

48. Miss Cirponis
    of the Latvian Embassy.

49. Demelza Heniot
    (née Trelawney) Widow of Herbert Heniot.
    A landlady of Tamarel, Cornwall.

50. 'That Foul Fiend'
    Priest-in-charge of Saint Barnabas, Tamarel.

51. Mrs. Kent
    A landlady of Wrensdown, West Sussex.

52. The Reverend Hazel Mears
    of Saint John the Divine, Wrensdown.

53. Roland Mears
    Husband of Hazel. Maitre d' B&B.

54. Sprottle
    Douglas Swann's 'Hairy Lurcher'.

55. The Right Reverend Bishop of the Diocese.

56. Barney Hammond
    Marine engineer. Owner of S.C.A.M.P.S.

57. Harold Miller
    of Lambkinfold Farm. Retired.

58.   Ajax Achilles Agamemnon Ossian
      A 'Triple A' rated baby.

59.   A lady gas service engineer.

60.   Frank Flint
      Principal of the Yowe Quarry Company.

61.   'Tell' William Taylor
      Prep school contemporary of 'Damnit', responsible for telling
      Sambo that Daniel Greensward had 'swored' and so earning
      both boys their nicknames.

62.   Ezekiel Keld
      Elder brother of Samuel Keld. (19)

63.   Luke Drake and Family
      Jake and Martha's son.

64.   Benbo Beaumont
      A young man of Skipton, and Bilbo Beaumont his handsome
      black Labrador, the sire of Rauch.

65.   Two wedding guests in search of a wedding venue in
      Tupshorne.

Genesis: Tiltstone (In the beginning was the stone)

An extract from Part One of the *Tiltstone* Trilogy

Daniel was born in Tupshorne in the autumn of 1934, the son of James Greensward a prosperous agricultural engineer whose forebears had been blacksmiths. His mother Emily, the daughter of a railway engineer from York, had been a teacher of mathematics prior to her marriage. On the occasion of his christening in Saint Michael the Archangel, the vicar at the time, the Reverend Raphael Manley asked the reason for the boy's middle name, 'Tiltstone.' Mrs. Greensward provided the answer. Her great-grandfather Joseph North was born in a village near Darlington in 1821, the only child of very loving but very strict parents who truly believed in such sayings as 'Spare the rod and spoil the child,' 'Children should be seen and not heard,' and 'Whom the Lord loveth he chasteneth' (Paul's letter to the Hebrews). When young Joseph was about eight years old, so it was told, he quite unintentionally managed to break a pane of glass in the conservatory by kicking at a loose pebble which flew in the wrong direction. This so incensed his father that by way of punishment Joseph was shut in the cellar overnight and only let out at breakfast time the next morning. He never forgot the horror of being in total darkness with no means of escape and in some ironic way such an experience was to shape his whole life. He grew up to become a famous architect, noted for his designs of fine mansions, all of which, from the earliest plans had light and airy basements with provision for at least two windows where no child could be confined in blackness. Then one of his most influential, not to say wealthy, patrons insisted on having a house built without any natural light reaching the cellars. Joseph refused the commission and explained to his client the reason why he would not exclude light from any house which carried his name as the architect.

An argument ensued between the two stubborn men, the upshot of which was that the patron told the architect that a personal problem dating back to childhood was no concern of his and if Joseph wished to design the mansion and earn his fee – and he as the potential owner still wanted Joseph to design it – then surely he could work out an alternative way of escaping from a dark cellar other than by the door, which once a child had been incarcerated was locked behind him. In brief, Joseph was ordered to use his ingenuity. His architect's fees for such a commission would be considerable and he recognised that his reputation within the Profession demanded of him that he should maintain a certain lifestyle in keeping with that reputation. He needed the money! He thought back in time, with much anxiety, to when he was that young lad in the cellar – no key to open the lock from his side of the door and perhaps the door was bolted anyway – no axe on hand to chop his way out and no form of light to work by. Then an old saying, surely of biblical origin, suddenly pierced the fog of his contemplation. 'You only need to look upwards for inspiration.' In a black cellar it is no use looking up because you cannot see anything, but you know the ceiling is there and if you can touch the ceiling then a means of escape should be within the reach of an architect. For an eight year old boy to reach the ceiling, there must be some kind of mounting block in place which can be located in the darkness. The mounting block could be built into the foundations. The ceiling had to move. He had the answer to his problem. At the drawing board, he designed a stone ceiling slab for the cellar which served as a floor slab in whichever room was above the cellar. This slab was mounted on an iron spindle allowing it to oscillate on its axis just enough to allow a body to climb out from the cellar. The slab would be secured in place in the cellar by a simple but substantial latch or catch, operable only in the cellar, and when the prisoner had passed into the room above then the stone would automatically resume its place with the latch re-engaging. There would be no provision made for moving the slab from the room above by anyone wanting to enter the cellar, except by the usual door and steps down into the 'dungeon.'

Joseph North called the device his Tiltstone and he incorporated it into all his buildings from that time on, whether or not the cellars were lit by natural light or as black as night. In much the same way that the famous landscape gardener Lancelot Brown became known as Lancelot 'Capability' Brown because he would look at a landscape, weigh it up and state that it had 'capabilities,' Joseph became known as Joseph 'Tiltstone' North.

'So, vicar, James and I decided to have him baptised Daniel Tiltstone Greensward just in case there might be a touch of genius in there somewhere. Don't worry, vicar, we won't lock him in the cellar to test the theory.'

The Final chapter of the Second Book of the 'Tiltstone Trilogy,' Tiltstone Fire and Brimstone.

IGNICULUS ALIBI
(Somewhere else – a spark)

It was noon, precisely, in British Summer Time as at one o'clock in Sicily, Daniel relinquished Albert's ashes into the care of Vulcan, working away in his smithy under Mount Etna.

At that same moment, in the room which housed the Prince Collection of the locksmith's art at the National Museum of Engineering all the light bulbs exploded and the room was plunged into darkness. Later the strange phenomenon was explained away as being due to a sudden surge of power from the national grid. 'Prof' Tobias could never understand why only the Prince Collection took the hit.

A coachload of engineering students were on an educational visit to the National Blacksmiths' Museum. On entering the foyer, their tour guide for the day, Mr Aidan Forrero, brimming over with infectious enthusiasm, as part of his introductory *spiel* brought the students to admire Athene Hope's magnificent painting 'Vulcan, Ancient Roman God Of Fire And Forge, Creates The First Woman, Pandora, Out Of Soil.' As they were all gazing in some awe at the huge picture, one student remarked, 'How in Hades did the artist know that Vulcan was such an ugly bru...?' The smoke and sweat-grimed face of the Divine Smith in the portrait broke into a grin, followed by a knowing wink. None of the students saw the facial changes – after all, to them it was a grand day out away from run-of-the-mill lectures. But Aidan Ferrers saw what had happened and marvelled. After fifteen years, the portrait of Vulcan, the God of Metalworkers, had come to life. Wonders never cease.

Tupshorne in Yowesdale was luxuriating in the traditional flaming June sunshine beloved of the tourism industry. This day the heat was tempered by the gentle southwesterly breeze sauntering in from over the Pennines and down the dale.

The mid-summer sun beamed down on the Church Hall of Saint Michael the Archangel, seeking out the clear glass chink of a pane in the cellar door and so unlocking the latent power hidden in the crystal water jug which Damnit had given to Bethan and Gerald on the occasion of their wedding. The heat was on.

A faint blue tendril of smoke arose from the newspaper on the old table.

Vulcan, Ancient Roman God of Fire and Forge, was at work – with a grin and a wink.

Daniel Tiltstone Greensward stood on the summit of Mount Etna – two missions accomplished.

The Third Book
Of The
'Tilstone Trilogy'

Tiltstone,
Gem And Tombstone

CHAPTER I

Prooemium Audivi Illum Canentem

(I heard him sing)

It was mid-January 1947 and the beginning of the Lent term at High Ashes Preparatory School in Derbyshire. The Headmaster, The Reverend Samuel Bone, M.A. (Cantab), an outstanding sportsman when in his prime with First Class Honours in the Classical Tripos, did not include in his list of attainments the title of Weather Prophet. The Lent term was destined to go down in meteorological records as one of the most bitter winter periods of the twentieth century. Snowdrifts as high as telegraph poles were the norm in the neighbourhood of High Ashes and for some weeks it was necessary to collect essential food supplies by toboggan from the nearest town.

Ten days after the start of term a rather unusual new boy arrived who spoke little English, and that, only when spoken to. Yet his command of French, especially his accent, was so good that if the French teacher was indisposed then the latecomer, even allowing for his limited vocabulary of a typical eight year old, was quite capable of taking a French class – provided the class was prepared to listen to *le petit pain* in the neck. Schoolboys of a certain age can sometimes be capable of tactless cruelty. Silas Kinnon Beaune was the only son of an English mother, Katharine Kinnon, and a French father, Marcel Beaune, a Commissioner with the International Refugee Organisation, working under the auspices of the United Nations.

One of the several peculiarities associated with the residents of High Ashes was the high incidence of nicknames. It was an affliction common to staff and pupils alike, starting at the very top with Sambo, the Headmaster, and eventually reaching down to the latest arriving new boy. Silas, in name only, disappeared within days, replaced by 'Skinandbone' which quickly gave way to 'Skinny.' It mattered not a jot that 'Skinny' was a roly-poly pudding of a boy, fair-haired and blue-eyed. He looked like a cherub, sang like a little angel, yet for all the overall impression of chubbiness visible to an observer he had inherited from his mother the long slender hands of an artist. To the staff he was forever Beau and never to be confused with their revered Headmaster.

For a boy of only eight years old Silas was nobody's fool. Born on New Year's Day 1938, a Paris suburb was his home until late-May 1940 when Marcel Beaune, anticipating the fall of France to Nazi Germany, fled the country to Switzerland with his wife and young son before enlisting in the Free French Army led by General Charles de Gaulle. For the next five years, at times living in considerable deprivation, Katharine Beaune reared her son in the absence of his father, always mentioning his name as if he was expected to come home on the morrow. Doubt never entered her mind, and her unfailing optimism was mirrored in Silas's attitude to life. Living on her wits for a few years called for some base cunning at times and Silas even as a little boy was well aware that his mother had a talent for being manipulative when it suited her to be so. As a well qualified linguist fluent in several European languages it was as a teacher of English that Katharine survived the War years, and the one child who received true one-to-one tuition was her son Silas. Katharine was also an accomplished musician, both a pianist and a soprano singer, which all went to explain why her son, at eight years old, spoke and understood English perfectly well and could sing folk songs in three languages. He was clever enough to notice that when his mother needed time to think before answering a question, she would either ask for the question to be repeated or pretend that her knowledge of the language was not secure enough to grasp the question. Silas imitated his mother, developing a fine impression of total puzzlement as and when it suited his plans. He could be devious.

The final week of the Lent term at High Ashes was one which featured two highlights of the school year. On the last evening before leaving for the Easter holidays the drama department staged a performance of a show titled, 'Hyperhistrionics.' This theatrical vehicle was a means of allowing any boy in the school to appear solo on stage to speak a 'party piece' of his own choosing. Histrionic behaviour to the nth degree was positively encouraged in an attempt to give the youngsters an opportunity to release their pent up emotions. In such a way did Mrs. Askey, the drama teacher, identify many a promising actor or orator.

Two days prior to 'Hyperhistrionics' saw the culmination of the term's athletics events, the Age Cross Country Championships. This was a handicap race over a roughly oval shaped three mile course running through the fields of the four farms that were contiguous with the High Ashes estate. The handicapping system resulted in those boys who were in their final year being required to cover the full distance while those in their first year started the course with only two miles to run. The boys of the intermediate years were handicapped at levels between two and three miles. The 1946 Championship had been won by an outstanding schoolboy athlete who was confidently expected to beat his own course record in his final year. If betting on the outcome of the Championship had been permitted at High Ashes, any wise bookie would have been on holiday quoting the weather as an excuse for his absence.

On the day, however bright the sunshine, the snow-melt threatened to turn the form book upside down. Mud, slush and the remains of snowdrifts in north-facing hedgecops negated all thought of a new record time. The reigning champion appeared to be oblivious to the conditions underfoot, picking his sure-footed way, shod in his seemingly magical spikes, through all the hazards until having left behind all his contemporary competitors, as he clambered over an elevated stile he caught sight of HIS Championship Trophy glinting in the sunshine standing on the trestle table by the finishing tape. He had a half mile to go and he exulted in the knowledge that he could easily run down the few junior stragglers left in his sights. Then, approaching an open gateway he became aware of a fat eight year old French boy snared in a bramble bush. Skinny Beaune had slipped in the mudslick by the gatestump and landed on his back in the prickly thicket. Between his sobs of pain and frustration Silas displayed a remarkable command of the English language. Overcoming his surprise at Skinny's vocabulary – hidden until now – the Champion, a boy known for a 'safe pair of hands' whatever the circumstances, stripped off his running singlet and, binding it round his hands, used it to free the little French canary. As the sun slipped behind a cloud, the shine on the Championship Trophy died away. The Champion donned his vest again and gently shepherded Silas to the finish, uncaring now if he was to come in last. The incident went down in High Ashes history. The Champion's course record of 1946 was to last another fifty years but he himself chose to forget the Age Cross Country of 1947. Silas Kinnon Beaune never forgot either the day that a bramble bush loosed his English tongue or the Champion who, in his innate compassion, had thrown away his Championship.

CHAPTER II

Et Uxor

(And wife)

Honeymooners Daniel and Lorna Greensward peered through the aeroplane window as the big silver bird lifted off from Palermo Airport en route for Manchester.

'That's quite some heat haze,' remarked Daniel. 'I don't suppose that there will be a matching phenomenon visible on the Cheshire plain as we make our approach in a few hours' time.'

'And I don't imagine there's any risk of fog either in the middle of June,' replied Lorna. 'At least we can't bump into Mount Etna at that end, or ditch in the sea. Mind you, it would seem a bit strange if we arrived home to find there had been volcanic activity during our absence, would it not? By the way, did you know that in the good old days Manchester Airport used to be in Cheshire. It's not the sort of fact that I would expect a Yorkshire-man to know. But of course, most of your working life was spent in Cheshire, and some of that at the time before the county boundaries were altered – so maybe you do know.'

'Actually,' said Daniel, a trifle pompously, 'I am fully conversant, as they say, with that particular situation on account of the fact that Colin Blunden was born in Styal and you can't get much closer to the airport than that. To him it has been and always will be 'Ringway,' first and foremost, and 'Ringway Airport' at a pinch. His father trained there as a paratrooper, one man among thousands, at the beginning of World War Two. They used to practise dropping into Tatton Park and occasionally into Tatton Mere just on the outskirts of Knutsford. There is a very fine memorial stone in the parkland dedicated to the Allied servicemen who dropped out of the sky to land in the area where it is erected. Just a word of warning at this point. When Colin picks us up at the airport, for heaven's sake don't mention the subject of airport names – he's very sensitive about such matters. When he was my second-in-command at Rolls he even organised a sort of ginger group calling itself R.I.C.A. – Ringway Is Cheshire's Airport. He also turned himself into a very knowledgeable if amateur Rolls Royce historian.

Don't be surprised if, as he drives us to his Sandbach home for our overnight stay, he chooses to take a minor detour through Knutsford. He likes to keep an eye on two particular houses there – both in the same road. Henry Royce lived in a delightful villa on the north side of the road while, so it's said, one of Rolls' relations, perhaps by marriage, occupied a lofty seven-bedroomed Victorian semi not many yards away from Royce on the southern side. Legend has it that the chatelaine of the seven bedrooms – apparently they had no children, and just as well by the sound of things – ruled her husband with a rod of iron. Rather apt for an eminent engineer you might think. Anyhow, it seems that at breakfast one morning her unfortunate husband spilled a drop of coffee on the tablecloth, which one presumes must have been immaculate in that household. When the wife had finished berating her dearly beloved, he never uttered a word either by way of mitigation or retaliation but calmly and deliberately picked up the coffee pot, black coffee surely, and proceeded to water, or coffee, the whole table before going to pack his bags and quitting the marital home to live in the offices of his engineering company based in Trafford Park. I don't know if the building still exists today but it was said that after the poor fellow died, his ghost walked the works' corridors when the moon was full. Colin can quote you chapter and verse on little nuggets such as that.'

Lorna laughed. 'I like it, legend or otherwise! Just think – if Colin hadn't been in a position to intervene and summon medical help when you suffered your heart attack in 1989 you could be haunting Rolls Royce, Crewe, even now. I'm no termagant though, and I don't see you as an unquiet spirit. We can change, I suppose. It strikes me though that any troubled spirit that's around is that of dear old Albert Prince, your beloved mentor, whose ashes we relinquished into Mount Etna just a week ago. Do you think he'll leave you to your dreams now that you have carried out his wishes as expressed in his will?'

Daniel prevaricated. 'I'm not sure. I had rather got used to his presence in my dreamworld when it suited me to look him up in bedroom number seven of my fantasy mansion. We both heard his voice on Etna just after I'd tossed the paper bag containing his ashes into the fiery furnace. You heard him say, "Thank you for coming," and I heard him say, "See you in the Prince Collection, not bedroom seven." It's obvious that he'll be there if I need him. What puzzles me now is, did he mean me to visit the Collection to consult his ghost in my physical body? Or was he inviting me to dream my way to the

National Museum of Engineering where his Collection is housed? I'm almost duty-bound to check it out – when we get home.'

'I'd rather you didn't,' said Lorna, disapproval in her tone. 'I do hope you're not playing with fire, my love. I'd hate to see you burn your fingers unnecessarily. All this tinkering with the spirit world ill becomes any churchwarden, never mind a husband of mine.'

Daniel shivered, imperceptibly. 'You've just echoed some words of Jake, uttered on the morning of our wedding. I had burnt my fingers in a most disturbing manner. I may as well explain now, why you will find a refurbished horseshoe hanging over our front door at High Ash.'

And then he told Lorna the story of how Janis Kat js had appeared in a complex dream and instructed him to find an antique horseshoe beneath a stone beside the gateway into Jake and Martha's cottage garden.

'I waited until Jake, Martha and I had breakfasted before walking the short distance to their front gate Sure enough, there lay the stone and sure enough under the stone was the horseshoe. My disquiet was akin to horror as I held it in my hand. Horripilation was the order of the day and I swear every hair on my body must have stood on end until I summoned up one of my life's mottoes. *"Aequam servare mentem"* "PANIC NOT", took a deep breath and went indoors to confess it all to Jake. He listened grimly but with total composure as I should have expected. After all is said and done, as they say, whoever THEY may be, Jake and I were in the same form at High Ashes when we were all taught, *"Aequam servare mentem."* Anyhow, his words to me were, "You really have burnt your fingers." Then, in as a matter of fact voice as you could wish for, he told me that everything would turn out for the best once I'd got the wedding over, and by the time we arrived home from our honeymoon he would have the horseshoe sanded, cleaned, lacquered, blessed by the Bishop and hung over the High Ash front door. Now you will understand why Sambo considered Jake and me to be each other's *alter ego*.'

'That's most intriguing,' said Lorna. 'Obviously, I am quite aware that you and Jake have been close friends from boyhood. I've known you for over forty years but he must have known you for more than sixty. I think perhaps you may have told me that already but put it to the back of my mind. Was there any one defining moment, looking back, when you might have said, "As of now we are brothers?"'

Daniel replied immediately. 'Oh yes! But Jake and I have never mentioned the occasion since. It just happened as it must have been preordained to happen. Now that you have become my better half you may as well know the details and then you will understand why Jake and I could have been called David and Jonathan.'

'I don't understand already,' said Lorna. 'Why David and Jonathan?'

'Just a biblical allusion, dear,' said Daniel. 'David and Jonathan were such good friends in their time. I wonder which of us will go first?'

'For Heaven's sake,' expostulated Lorna. 'You've only just got married. That's dangerous talk.'

'Sorry,' said Daniel with a little smile. 'I always remember my cardiac consultant telling me that the human heart is a bit like an elastic band. How long it lasts depends on the quality of the rubber. I digress. Back to Jake and me. As a child, Jake never cried – in my presence at least – but once. His mother was killed in a road accident when we were both at High Ashes. It was Michaelmas term 1944, mid-November when his father, who became my "Uncle" Jonah, took him home to Yealingden for his mother's funeral. A week later he returned to school and his first night back crept into my bed after lights-out and sobbed himself to sleep. Such a friendship, born out of tears and nurtured on laughter was never in danger of faltering. Mind you, it's been an added bonus that Martha and I have always "got on", perhaps because we both have had Jake's best interests at heart.'

Hardly had Lorna dropped off to sleep before the pilot announced that he was making his approach to Manchester Airport and would passengers please fasten their seatbelts. Clearance through airport security went without a hitch and both travellers were heartened to see Colin Blunden awaiting them at the barrier in the arrivals hall. Greeting Lorna with a kiss before turning slightly to shake hands with Daniel, he was unaware of the broad wink she gave Daniel before speaking.

'It's lovely to see you, Colin. I just love Manchester Airport so much as an international hub of comings and goings, and as a research historian I am thinking of writing a comprehensive account about it, beginning with its very origins.'

In a flash, Colin's genial welcome turned to frozen-faced horror before Damnit exploded into a great guffaw of laughter at his friend's obvious discomfiture at Lorna's heresy. 'She's having you on, Colin, and it is I who all unwittingly put her up to it. Not long into our flight home, I warned her of your well founded obsession with Ringway and that it might be wise to avoid mention of this particular International Airport. I'm not at all surprised that my advice has been ignored so soon. But rest assured, my good friend, your leg having been pulled for one good, if purely sentimental reason – Lorna is on your side. Before she snoozed off, she confessed that in 1963 she enjoyed more than one late-night romantic tryst at this airport. In those happy times, so she told me, you could park in a nearby field, without charge, and wander into the cafe to do a spot of courting over a cup of coffee and a bun. How times have changed in nearly fifty years. For a Blackburn girl, Ringway is still a happy memory.'

Lorna laughed and then extended her hand to receive a mock slap on the wrist. 'If I wasn't hanging on to my new husband's arm I might suggest meeting you later this evening, Colin. A shame I can't afford the parking fee these days!'

On exiting the airport for the M56 motorway, Colin turned to his passengers and asked them if they would mind if he made a brief detour through Knutsford. He had heard a rumour that some building alterations were in progress at the one time home of Henry Royce in Legh Road, and as self-appointed amateur chronicler of the Rolls Royce legend it was imperative that he take a look. It was his earnest hope that the current owner of the cottage had not been forced into installing electronically operated gates together with all the associated security so much in vogue.

'Is it necessary?' asked Lorna.

'Sadly, I think it probably is,' replied Colin. 'For many years now, the cottage has been a centre of pilgrimage from all over the world for those who worship at the altar of Rolls Royce. I know for a fact that, as well as the formal visits of coach touring parties and private appointments for individual pilgrims, the owner does, from time to time, encounter total strangers wandering round the gardens at their leisure. They are mostly American, extremely polite, and talk about Royce as if he was still alive. Maybe the whole scenario has become too much of a good thing. Can we just check it out?'

'By all means,' said Daniel. 'We're in no rush unless Carolyn is expecting you for a deadline. I was telling Lorna about the Hon. Charles Rolls' connection in the same road. Are the two houses close?'

'Not really close. Perhaps one hundred yards apart, on different sides of the road. The Rolls one is a towering Victorian semi with seven bedrooms. The old lady, Miss Wynn, who told me the story of the coffee pot incident thought that it was Rolls' sister who was left to rattle around the house when her engineering husband left to live in his Trafford Park works. I think her tale was very probably based on fact because she herself lived to ninety seven with her powers of memory undimmed, and Knutsford born and bred in 1881, she remembered Queen Victoria at the inauguration of the Manchester Ship Canal on 1 January 1894, as clearly as if it had happened the day before I had audience of her.'

Carefully driving his way through the traffic congestion that is the twenty first century Knutsford, Colin soon found his way to the one time home of Henry Royce and was relieved to see the road frontage unaltered even if several other mansions in the same road resembled fortresses in a garrison town except for the absence of razor wire round their perimeters.

'That's all right then,' said Colin. 'It's ages since I played tennis here, so it's good to see the court is in use this afternoon.'

He drove the short distance along the road and drew up opposite the red brick Victorian semi of the coffee pot incident.

'I wonder what became of that coffee pot,' said Lorna as she surveyed the house. 'Maybe it's buried in the garden awaiting a metal detector. No, no – I bet it was a choice piece of Wedgwood.'

'Miss Wynn didn't know the answer when I posed the same question, said Colin. 'It could have turned up – who knows – it must have been about 1970 when she told me that story, over thirty years ago. There must be many coffee jugs with a tale to tell.' Colin continued 'While we are parked here, you see that wide grass verge the other side of the road, between the kerb and the footpath next the garden wall. If you were to drive along here in late-winter you would witness a veritable sea of snowdrops. The local taxi drivers have the location on their itineraries for tourists at that time of year. The little bulbs were planted by a Knutsford galanthophile some time in the 1960s, so I understand. Someone once told me that he had moved to your area in the 90s – could have been Wensleydale. Turned his hand to writing, apparently.'

'You're a proper mine of information, Colin,' said Lorna. 'Do invite us back next year at snowdrop time. You weren't to know it, but I have "a thing" about snowdrops. I wonder if the plantsman is still alive. I'll leave Ringway history to you and see if I can trace your Mr Snowdrops and his ancestry as my next project.'

'Damnit, man,' said Colin, full of admiration, 'It's one feisty wife you've found after such an extended bachelorhood. I hope she lives long enough to finish the project. Mr Snowdrops' family had lived in Knutsford since Napoleon was a lad and he was the last of the line.'

Daniel smiled before speaking. 'Lorna, dear, I hope you abort the project before you open a can of worms. If you do carry on with such a hair-brained scheme, you will be bound to spend a lot of time here, in and around Knutsford and as Colin knows very well, as the crow flies, it's only a few miles to Manchester International Airport. I rest my case. Perhaps your Mr Snowdrops kept his sanity by moving to the Yorkshire Dales or maybe he had grown tired of Cheshire cheese. For all we know, he may even be in Yowesdale. Now that's real cheese.'

Colin snorted. 'Leave Ringway to me. When rocket travel succeeds air travel and genetically modified pigs have dragon's wings, Ringway will return to being prime farm land and Knutsford will become Cranford all over again.'

'But the snowdrops will still bloom here in this beautiful road as each winter turns to spring,' added Lorna. 'That's for sure.'

'Amen to that,' said Daniel. 'Now drive on cabbie, I'm looking forward to afternoon tea with Carolyn. Does she still bake yummilarious chocolate cake you used to bring in your lunch box and sometimes shared with me? I wonder if she could be persuaded to part with the recipe.'

Within half an hour, they arrived at the Blunden home in Sandbach to be greeted by Carolyn wearing a kitchen apron and pushing a Dutch hoe through the circular rosebed in the front lawn. 'What splendid timing,' she said. 'It's not many minutes since I took my famous chocolate cake out of the oven.'

'If it's that good, I'd better have the recipe, if you'd be so kind,' said Lorna, prompted by Daniel.

'Now that is what I call telepathy,' stated Damnit, 'Or even a bloomin' miracle.'

'Oh no, it isn't,' answered Colin. 'I placed the order before leaving for Ringway to meet you.'

After being cocooned in the Blunden's garage for two weeks while the happy honeymooners were in Sicily, Trollop was relieved to hear her master's voice and gave an impromptu hoot on her horn. In the excitement of homecoming and the exchange of greetings nobody heard the solitary sound.

CHAPTER III

Flamma Fumo Est Proxima

(No smoke without fire)

The following morning Trollop the Toyota Rav4, with Damnit at the wheel, left the Blunden's Sandbach home anxious to complete the one hundred and forty mile journey home to Tupshorne before lunch. Apart from a few days spent in the opulent surroundings of the car sales showroom, she had never been garaged under cover and after two weeks of incarceration in Cheshire was longing for the blissful open air that is Yowesdale all the year round.

'Sicily in June was simply beautiful,' said Lorna, 'but I'm dying to get home to Tupshorne.'

'Don't die until we arrive there,' growled Daniel. 'I have driven most strange car conversions in my time but up to now I'm not an accredited hearse chauffeur.'

'Feeble witticisms do not become you, and I suspect – in fact, I'm sure – that even an old stick in the mud which you may be in danger of becoming is excited at the prospect of arriving home after two weeks away. Speaking as one with experience in such affairs, honeymoons are not to be dismissed lightly; but coming home again safely is as good as the icing on the wedding cake. I can't wait to see and hear the dogs' welcome – that is if they remember who we are. Sprottle always used to remain stand-offish for several days if I was away for over a week. Yet when Douglas returned from Nigeria after several years' absence to reclaim her, the welcome she gave him was amazing. Except for bedtime and meal times, she followed him everywhere, her nose just about tucked into the hollow at the back of his knee. We coined a phrase especially for her, "Sprot walks to knee". Perhaps it's a lurcher trait.'

'Maybe Sprot just preferred men,' offered Daniel 'If my memory serves me correctly, and generally it does, she was much at ease in my company when you introduced me first, back in 2000. I'm sure that Baggins and Rauch will give us a suitably riotous welcome within the limitations of being a more laid-back breed than Douglas' Hairy

Lurcher. Talking of Sprot possibly favouring men, do you remember back in February 2000, when I came to see you in Cambridge, shortly before Albert Prince died?'

'How could I forget?' said Lorna. 'Looking back now, I think it was probably Albert's death that brought us close so long after our undergraduate years. Our joint discovery of his body after breaking into his cottage was a powerful shock to the system. No wonder we clung to each other, however briefly, at the time. What brought Albert and Sprot to mind?'

'Well, Albert had never owned a dog in his life, yet when Sprot was introduced to him she made an inordinate fuss of him as we sat at table having our lunch. You commented, at the time, how unusual it was. I remember the exact words of Albert's reply. "Got an eye for an antique haven't you, girl?" as he fondled her ears like a dyed-in-the-wool dog lover. We both remember how a dog which had never howled before howled your house down at the precise time of Albert's death. When the police surgeon put the time at between six and eight o'clock in the morning, Sprot had already told us it was 7:45. Quite uncanny. Did you ever tell Douglas the tale of his psychic dog?'

'He wouldn't have believed me,' said Lorna. 'He has yet to experience that kind of happening.'

Daniel went quiet for a few minutes as he concentrated on his driving in the build up of heavy traffic on the M6 approaching Junction 34. On the slip road, he spoke again. 'Trollop's been running very smoothly all the way. I wonder if Colin's been busy under her bonnet while we've been away. I wouldn't put it past him and of course he wouldn't think to mention it if he had been tinkering. His sixth sense for tuning a motor was almost on a par with that of John Smith who even now must be tuning the heavy roller on the heavenly cricket ground.'

Trollop gave a discreet cough.

Daniel continued 'If we stop for a bite of lunch in Caton I can refuel at the petrol station opposite the cafe. I know Trollop's keen to get home but not on an empty tank.'

'You and your empathy with the internal combustion engine,' said Lorna. 'No wonder I ditched you when we were undergrads all those years ago.' She laughed. 'I have never told you this before, but my mama was quite desolate at the time, thinking you were a fine catch. In fact, I think she fancied herself as your doting mother-in-law. It took her some time to appreciate the entirely different qualities that Matthew brought to bear and which persuaded me to change from being a Fairchild to Swann. In one of her rarer moments of humour she remarked how glad she was that I hadn't become Lorna Duck.'It was Daniel's turn to smile. 'You were never born to be the Ugly Duckling. "Lorna Greensward" has a certain ring to it. Just be happy that I'm not Daniel Lawn!'

Their inconsequential, good natured banter continued in the same vein all through their lunch in the Caton cafe and the rest of the journey back to Yowesdale. And then, having come through the outskirts of Tupshorne and with the High Street and Market Square just hoving into view, Lorna suddenly gave a startled half smothered cry of disbelief.

'Daniel! The church hall's gone.'

At that moment, Trollop was about forty yards away from where the church hall had stood when they had set off on their honeymoon. A few seconds later, as the car passed the hall site, Daniel remarked, with no hint of excitement or emotion in his voice, 'So it has.'

How he managed to suppress the huge sense of elation which he felt, he never knew.

Lorna cut into his momentary introspection. 'You don't seem remotely surprised, almost as if you knew already.'

'How could I?' observed Daniel. 'We've been away for two weeks, incommunicado in Sicily, so no one could have contacted us by telephone. Looks like fire to me. Mind you, you know that I don't "surprise" easily. It dates back to my prep school days – one of my classical headmaster's favourite Latin maxims *"Aequam servare mentem"* was programmed into me. "Panic not". I think all High Ashes old boys were encouraged to live by that eleventh Commandment of Sambo, the head. Jake's another. But you may remember Sambo. Didn't you meet him after the Varsity match when we beat Oxford?'

'I remember the occasion well, but although I can't put a face to the man any longer the sound of his voice made a lasting impression. *"Aequam servare mentem"* has served you well. Incidentally, I know all about your "A.S.M." You've forgotten that you mentioned it on our return flight when you were regaling me with the story of the horseshoe of your dreams. Never mind m'dear. Put it down to advancing years. Do you want to stop and inspect the damage?'

'Whoops! Sorry about the repeat of "Panic not,"' said Daniel. 'I'm a bore.' He paused. 'But, no. Let's get home and unpacked first. It's too late today for me to start the rebuilding. It looks as if we are in for a fine evening, so if we have an early supper, when we have eaten we can stroll back through town and weigh up the situation. I will make a few telephone calls – Timothy Welsh and Violet Rose, churchwarden and treasurer, for a start. I suppose we may have several messages on the answerphone already. Wait and see.'

Two minutes later Trollop nosed her way into the High Ash drive only to be blocked by another car about to make an exit. Two minutes later and the welcome home committee of two, Jake and Martha, would themselves have been on their way home in the upper reaches of Yowesdale at Middinside.

The porch of High Ash was festooned with multicoloured balloons surrounding the main entrance door which carried a large placard with the lettering 'Welcome Home, Damnit and Lorna', highlighted with glitter. A highly polished horseshoe gleamed in the sunlight. Both cars drew to a halt, bonnet to bonnet, and all the occupants seemed to spill out simultaneously. Damnit and Lorna, Jake and Martha, and three very excited black Labrador bitches, the Drakes' Miss Bindle, Daniel's Baggins and Lorna's Rauch all came together in one scrum. 'We really intended to be gone before you arrived,' said Martha, 'but the dogs were playing some kind of canine hide and seek game in the garden and were not to be easily rounded up. Just move Trollop and we'll leave you lovebirds in peace.'

'Baggins would have known we were getting near, said Lorna. 'She always seems to sense when Daniel is in the offing.'

'And Trollop isn't to be shifted until after tea, so when the dogs have calmed down we can all go in and put the kettle on,' added Daniel.

'That's not fair,' said Jake, putting his oar in at last as the dogs lost interest in the new arrivals and went to wait for the front door to be re-opened. 'To quote from an ancient ditty, we've only laid out "Tea for two."'

'Yorkshire style and appetites, I bet,' chipped in Lorna. 'That being interpreted would indicate enough for four. We won't take "no" for an answer, will we Daniel?'

'Bow to the inevitable, Jake,' said Martha. 'The car stays put until this happy couple lets us go.'

'Sensible girl, and you can tell us about what has happened to the church hall of Saint Michael the Archangel of which August establishment I am a churchwarden,' said Daniel Tiltstone Greensward with mock gravity, 'prior to an evening inspection.'

'All right! All right! All right!' said Jake. 'At least it means that I get to taste my own home-made cheese scones. They are from the recipe that Aunt Em, your mother, Damnit, gave me when she taught me how to cook after my mother died. It was probably about 1945 or 46, judging by my distinctly childish writing. I wrote it down under Aunt Em's beady eye and I remember even now how she insisted that the vital ingredient, mature Yowesdale cheese, be written in capital letters. Happy days! You've the door key in your handbag, Martha. Open up and let Damnit carry his bride over the threshold.'

Martha obliged, the dogs rushed into the house, Daniel picked up Lorna in a fireman's lift and Jake and Martha brought up the rear.

It was left to Lorna to raise the subject of the church hall, once the highlights of the Sicilian honeymoon had been revealed.

'So tell us all you can about the disappearance of the parish hall. Was it arson? Daniel remarked that it looked like fire was responsible as we drove past the remains!'

'It only happened a few days ago – June 6, to be precise – I suppose that is ten days,' said Jake. 'Middle of the day by all accounts. We were at home in Middinside so we did not hear about it until we saw a report on the evening television north-east news. The next day, rumour ran rife as you might imagine. I spoke to several of my ex-parishioners – well, those who live within a stone's throw of the site. Arson was mentioned but personally I doubt it. Apparently the building burnt out as if hit by an incendiary. Before the fire brigade arrived, the earliest bystanders reported that they had heard a succession of muffled explosions which gave rise to the suspicion of sabotage. The forensic team were very quick to point out the shattered paint cans and the shards of glass from a large bottle of turpentine – hence the explosions.'

Damnit broke into Jake's narrative at this point, quietly observing that he was personally responsible for buying the wherewithal to redecorate the hall once he was home from honeymoon. 'I left all the materials for the whole job, including my own collection of antique paintbrushes, on a couple of old tables in the hall cellar. The paint was the cheapest I could buy. I've kept the receipt, so presumably new paint will be covered by insurance. Pity about my brushes though.'

He paused. 'Sorry to interrupt, Jake. Do continue.'

'There's not much else to add, really,' said Jake. 'Not being vicar since the end of September last year, I felt sidelined and not particularly inclined to ask too many questions. "No mine business, no longer, no how," as John Smith would have said. Just what or who started the fire is still a mystery. Timothy Welsh wondered about a possible electricity fault until Violet Rose pointed out that the place was re-wired not that long ago and only recently had been granted a safety certificate. Not to put too fine a point on it, in spite of all the theories that have been propounded since the hall burned down, God only knows what set the paint alight.'

'I'm sure He does,' said Damnit, drily, 'and I expect that He will keep the information to Himself and leave the matter as an impenetrable mystery like the Church of England in general.' Lorna glanced sharply at her new husband and was not amused to see something of a rather self-satisfied smile flit across his face.

'And you a churchwarden of longstanding,' she said. 'I hope you haven't offended Jake with your minor heresy, never mind the accompanying smirk.'

'Don't worry on Jake's account. He knows when Daniel is in teasing mode,' said Martha. 'And, even with his priestly long service he isn't blind to certain shortcomings in the way that the C. of E. can fail to address its problems. Which reminds me, Daniel – is there any news on the interregnum front? It's nine months since we left the parish.'

'Applications for the vacancy were to be in a week ago,' replied Daniel. 'I'm hoping that Timothy and the Archdeacon might have been busy in my absence and produced a shortlist for my perusal. That's if anyone has bothered to apply. You never can tell. St Michael the Archangel in Tupshorne, although a plum parish within the diocese, only attracted a single worthy applicant last time, in spite of extensive advertising of the post. The other two worthies after the job weren't up to scratch.'

Then came the grin to cancel his earlier smirking comment.

'How else do you think Jake got the job? The choice was unanimous of course. Well, two votes to nil. I, with my lifelong association with him, was barred from voting.'

Martha joined in the joshing – with a vengeance. 'You and your imagination, Daniel. You overstep the mark. I know the truth because we hadn't been many weeks in the vicarage when Timothy came with some paperwork for Jake to check. He was out so I persuaded Timothy to stay for a cup of tea accompanied by a little chat. Confidential, it was. That was how I learned that Damnit had, quite literally, destroyed the two candidates, other than Jake, with a line of questioning that must have raised doubts in their minds about their own fundamental beliefs. "Brutal" was the word that Timothy used. I wasn't altogether surprised. It brought to mind an occasion many years earlier –

probably post-Cambridge – when I made a complimentary remark to Jake relating to Daniel's apparent sangfroid. I don't suppose you can recall your answer, Jake, but it might interest Lorna. You said that Daniel had a violent temper which he had learned to curb to the extent that he could turn it on and off at will, as and when it suited him to do so. I think Timothy must have witnessed something similar – a time that suited you to be thoroughly objectionable, Damnit.'

Only Daniel was aware of the faint flush in his features, veiled by the light suntan acquired in Sicily. Martha's seemingly innocent barb had found its mark and he needed to release it before the homecoming became clouded by unintentional poison.

Utterly composed, he addressed the only person present who might be dismayed by Martha's revelation – Lorna. 'Martha's memory, I wouldn't presume to query – we've been the best of friends since Jake presented you for my approval Martha, dear. I don't think he would have suggested that I was given to violence. In fact…'

Jake butted in. 'In fact, I think what I really meant to say was that you with your copper hair in those days had the potential, but I never saw the potential realised, I must admit. Your temper simmered without boiling over, such was your self control. I am the one who once upon a time had the short fuse. Then training for the priesthood taught me how destructive anger can be. Supposed to be one of the Seven Deadly Sins in Christian tradition but that didn't stop Jesus from venting his fury on the money changers in the temple. Must we truly suffer fools gladly? It's not easy.'

'You're preaching now,' said Martha with a smile of indulgence, 'and that can be infuriating. I mean, I've lost count of the number of saucers I've thrown in my time and never hit the target.'

The teasing nature of the conversation had returned and continued in light-hearted vein until it came to teatime for dogs. The impromptu tea party broke up and the Drake family were allowed to leave High Ash to drive home to Middinside. It was too late in the day for a gentle stroll to inspect the church hall ruins.

As Damnit was accompanying Jake to his car, Jake had a final thought to convey to his one-time churchwarden of St Michael the Archangel, Tupshorne. 'Keep me in the picture when it comes to appointing the next lucky vicar, Damnit. I may have a little bit of strictly covert wisdom to offer.'

'Now that, I call telepathy!' replied Damnit. 'I was just about to ask. *Aere perennius.*'

CHAPTER IV

Hoc Erat In Votis

(This was among my prayers)

'Are you happy to unpack the cases?' asked Daniel. 'I feel I should ring Timothy and fix up a site meeting at the hall at the earliest opportunity. And he can tell me if he and the Archdeacon have produced a shortlist of likely new vicars for us at the same time.'

'Sure,' said Lorna. 'No doubt, you'll also need to involve Violet as treasurer. The sooner you can summon the whole P.C.C., the sooner the way forward will become clearer. Violet will have all the relevant insurance policies at her fingertips by now, you can be sure.'

'Good old Violet,' said Daniel. 'It was her idea to burn down the church hall in the first place.'

'No!' said Lorna, in utter disbelief.

'Perhaps I didn't phrase that statement too well. But I think, in her fervent prayers, it was her wish that something of the sort might happen to the place. At the emergency meeting of the P.C.C. held after John Smith accidentally set light to the church cellar she very coolly informed the committee that she was sorry that the fire hadn't gutted the hall instead of smoking out the church. I wasn't surprised at all because when I went to see her immediately after the fire to ascertain that our insurances were in place she said that had the blaze occurred under the church hall she would have taken her pair of bellows to help things on. She must be thrilled that her prayers are answered, and so soon. It's only about nine months since that P.C.C. meeting and she confirmed back then that all church building insurance policies were in force. She may be eighty-odd but her monetary policy brain remains sharp. If I give her a ring, would you like to come with me when I visit? Violet's Award Winning Shortbread Biscuits are a powerful excuse for dropping in. I can ask her how she managed to arrange the hall bonfire. She'll love that!'

'It's a good thing that she shares your sometimes warped sense of humour, Daniel dear. I shall congratulate her on achieving her goal in your absence, just to show that we are all on her wavelength. Yes, make your 'phone calls and I will unpack our things and put a wash on.'

Two calls later and Daniel had set 10 o'clock Monday 18 June, as a time to meet Timothy at the hall ruins, followed by an 11 o'clock tryst with Violet to talk finance.

Daniel and Lorna gave church a miss the next day as they quietly settled into High Ash after their honeymoon, and assured the dogs that life had returned to normal with a strenuous walk on the moors between Tupshorne and Skipton. Then on the Monday Damnit set off for the church hall and his ten o'clock meeting.

Churchwarden Timothy Welsh could shed no further light on the subject of the church hall fire except to say that Bert "The Bells" Alderwood wondered if any of Damnit's garden chemicals that he used to control weeds around the church and the hall might have been involved. He knew for certain that there was a time when he'd heard mention of sodium chlorate, as recommended by Damnit.

'Bert's a bright lad, remembering that,' said Damnit. 'But if I was minded to set fire to something, sodium chlorate would no longer be my choice. It is sold now with an additive which prevents the spontaneous combustion that used to make it such a handy explosive. I know all about it Timothy, as it so happens, because a friend of mine from my National Service days had taken a First Class Honours degree in Horticultural Chemistry at Reading University. His knowledge of plant poisons and poisonous chemicals, including those with explosive habits, was encyclopaedic and I managed to pick up a few tips from him. We treated him with great respect. I kept in touch with him for some years after our service but when he became a professor of Plant Toxicology at an American university our paths finally diverged. The last I ever heard of him was that, still comparatively young and in his prime, he developed some rare kind of wasting disease, couldn't face the prospect of a lingering death and killed himself with one of the lethal plant toxins he had discovered in the course of his research. So terribly sad. Even at a distance by then, and separated by time and years, I felt an enormous sense of loss. His name was Brendan O'Drisoll – known as Bod – but I always called him Sod, such was his love of sod chlorate. As Sodit and Damnit we were a dangerous duo on occasion!'

'So now, any news on the next vicar front, in my absence?'

'Absolutely,' answered Timothy. 'The Archdeacon and I sifted through the nine satisfactorily completed application forms. When I say "satisfactorily completed" I really mean those which seemed most likely to fulfil the particular requirements of this highly desirable Yowesdale benefice. We picked out one candidate from Sussex, a lady; one from Cornwall, a chap; and another chap from Northumberland. Not a tyke in sight, I'm afraid. I've brought the details of all three, in this envelope so you can cast your eye over the written word – fairly soon if possible – then we can arrange interviews on a day to suit the Archdeacon. The Arch has pencilled in, provisionally, Tuesday 10 July.'

'Good, good,' said Damnit. 'I knew you'd find the sifting process easier with me away, and I promise to be very courteous to the chosen trio when they come. Yesterday evening I was reminded, quite forcibly, by Martha Drake that when we interviewed Jake and the two other contenders for the post, last time, you told her that I had destroyed the also-rans with an interrogation severe enough to make them doubt their vocational beliefs.'

'Whatever,' said Timothy. 'At least you made quite sure that the right man got the job. Jake has been an outstanding pastoral priest.'

'Just like his father before him,' observed Damnit. 'As you know already, he was my courtesy "Uncle" Jonah. It was well before your time in Tupshorne, of course, but Violet can remember him coming to St Michael's as a guest preacher on several occasions when Jake spent so much of his school holidays with my family after his mother's death. Give me forty eight hours and I'll get back to you when I've decided which one is right for me! Only joking. I'm off to have a word with Violet next. If it's all right by her, can we hold an emergency meeting of the P.C.C. this Wednesday. That's two days time. I'm presuming that you will be available.'

'Yes. That's fine by me. When you let me know that the date suits Violet, I will summon the rest of the crew – at least those who are available to make a quorum.'

'Splendid,' said Damnit. 'Lorna's meeting me at Violet's at 11 o'clock. The pair of them get on like the proverbial house on fire. Of course, I'm only going for the shortbread. I suppose insurance might get a mention at some stage. She must be so pleased that the church hall is gone. Her naughty prayers are answered. It's just struck me. Why didn't I think of it before? You ought to come with me. Violet can rustle up another cup and saucer without straining her housekeeping resources and we three can talk finance while Lorna admires the cottage garden. That is unless you think she might have any useful input. A quick co-option, temporary like, and we don't need to tell anyone. Having been P.C.C. secretary in her last parish in Cambridge she knows when to keep quiet!'

'Right,' said Timothy, briskly. 'I'm with you. I haven't spoken with Violet since church yesterday, so the gossip will not flag as long as the tea flows.'

Within ten minutes, there were four people sitting round Violet's garden table enjoying the warm sunshine and the perfume of her carefully nurtured roses.

Once the niceties of the giving and receiving of hospitality had been observed, it was Violet who introduced the reason for the meeting with the words, 'Now about this providential blaze. For what it's worth, I think myself it was a spot of arson.'

'Well,' said Damnit, with a grin, 'is this a confession? It's in P.C.C. minutes that you would rejoice if the hall went up in flames. The mystery is, how you achieved it, young lady.'

'I'm not telling,' answered Violet, smothering a chuckle of mock umbrage at Damnit's little dig. 'At eighty-odd, I don't think they'll send me to clink, will they? But I still reckon it was arson. I can't explain why – it's just a feeling in my old bones. Whoever managed it must be someone to be reckoned with if forensics have drawn a blank. In fact, Daniel, were it not for your being on honeymoon in Sicily, I wouldn't have put it past you. You could be devious as a child – even when I was babysitting for your mother.' She winked at Lorna. 'You need to watch him, Lorna. His waters run deep!'

Lorna laughed. 'If I really need to check him out, I just ask Jake who knows everything about my new husband. He's in the clear in this instance, barring long range miracles.'

'Back to business,' said Timothy. 'After the unfortunate fire in the church cellar, Violet, you made it clear that all our insurance policies were in place. Is that still the case? Silly question but one that has to be asked.'

'Silly question, easy answer,' said Violet. 'The policy on the hall allows for a complete rebuild in the event of fire destroying the whole thing. Then there is a funny little sub-clause stating that any new works must be with the approval of the owner of the land.'

'How very convenient,' murmured Damnit. 'Church land of Saint Michael – let's start next week.'

Violet dropped a delicious bombshell into the discussion. One that she had been hiding until she could keep it a secret no longer. 'It's not Saint Michael's.'

'It must be,' said Timothy and Lorna, simultaneously.

'You're pulling our legs,' said Daniel. 'If it was, in fact, arson, the fire raiser could not possibly have known that.'

Lorna glanced at Daniel as he spoke, detecting a slight hint of certainty in his assertion. 'Arson or not, it doesn't matter either way,' she said. 'What really does matter in the context of rebuilding, is who owns the ground. Violet is obviously quite beside herself with excitement as she is the only person here in the know and, as for me, I am agog. Take your time, Violet, but please don't overdo it.'

'Well,' said Violet. 'This is the eureka moment of my time as church treasurer and I can't resist prolonging it, as you three hang on my every word.'

'Come on, Vi, for Heaven's sake, get on with it,' said Timothy. 'The suspense is unbearable.'

'You know that I don't like being called Vi,' whispered Violet. 'No more shortbread for you, "Mothy" until you apologise.'

At this exchange, Lorna broke down into a gale of laughter that turned into a fit of the giggles which being infectious reduced all four to tears. Giggles had been her speciality since childhood.

'Right! That's it,' said Damnit, struggling to control himself. 'I can't remember a sort of half-emergency P.C.C. getting so out of hand...'

Eventually it fell to Violet to call the meeting to order by dint of banging on the garden table with a trowel which she had spied, hiding under her garden chair. Eyes were wiped and noses were blown before she spoke. She was unhurried as she began her explanation.

'Tell me, Daniel, why we all presumed – you in particular – that the hall was church property built on church ground?'

'Simple,' replied Daniel, confidently. 'The plot was given to the new church, as it was at the time, by my great-grandfather George Greensward the year after the church was completed. Family legend has it that after years of being without issue, as they might have called it in those times, my great-grandma produced my grandfather Absalom. That was 1866. George was so overcome by the occasion that to mark the advent of a son and heir, an answer to his prayers, he presented the piece of field, such as it was then, to the church by way of a thanksgiving. He was a very devout Christian, so nobody was surprised. He called grandpa, Absalom, after the son of King David because after waiting so long he would have died for his son, just as David said. It wasn't necessary, but it means "bringer of peace", and as far as I know grandpa was something of a disappointment being somewhat of a choleric nature in Shakespearian terms. So that is why I would confidently bet our house on the safe knowledge that the ground belongs to the Archangel Michael.'

'You've just made yourself and Lorna homeless,' stated Violet. 'But don't give up hope too soon because you have grounds for much optimism. You are the undoubted and sole owner of the plot on which the hall used to stand. How's that for a revelation?'

'How on earth can that be?' asked Lorna, 'after Daniel's so confident history lesson. I know that you wouldn't invent such an unlikely tale.'

'I took the trouble to look into the church archives – I really don't know why I felt the compulsion to do so after so many years as treasurer. What an eye opener! Daniel was right – George, his great-grandfather, fully intended to gift the land to his local church, but even in 1866 you had to sign the appropriate transfer document, assigning the property by deed to another owner. He never did. So it's been a presumption all along the way and down the years. Even the diocesan authorities are ignorant on this particular front. What happens next is entirely in your safe pair of hands Daniel. Perhaps Jim and Emily should have called you Solomon. You'll need all the wisdom you can muster. This present problem is no longer just about money and insurance policy payouts. Land and its ownership raises the stakes even though I know you are not a betting man. I do have only one serious suggestion to make, Daniel – consult Jake. That way you'll get divine guidance. With Jake comes Martha – King and Queen. You already have the Ace…Lorna.' She chuckled at Damnit before finishing. 'I think you are well up to playing the Knave and as I look into my own crystal ball the cloud is clearing and I see a Trump card approaching – a very tall person with immense charm and a voice to match.'

'Come on Violet. Snap out of it. You're not a gypsy fortune teller,' said Timothy, rather brusquely. But Violet had fainted away before he spoke and was slumped across the table. Lorna was quickly off her own chair and round to Violet's quadrant of the circular table almost before Timothy had finished his sentence, and as she grasped Violet's wrist to feel for a pulse the would-be clairvoyant stirred and came to.

'Now where was I?' asked Violet. 'I must have nodded off. An age thing perhaps, but I was dreaming of playing cards. It's years since I played Bridge.'

The meeting broke up with an enormous triple-strength sigh of relief from Damnit, Lorna and Timothy. Violet, unaware of the fright that she had given them, was all smiles as she waved them off at her garden gate. Her parting shot, aimed at Damnit, was a testimony to the power of dreams. 'The choice of Trumps will be down to you, Daniel, but may I suggest Diamonds – a girl's best friend!'

Lorna was as mystified as Daniel at the incredible turn of events. Life in Tupshorne was becoming complicated.

CHAPTER V

Audi Alteram Partem

(Listen to the other side)

It was only a few minutes' walk from Violet's cottage to High Ash but enough time for Daniel and Lorna to discuss and reach agreement on what to do next. Lorna began. 'I'm not altogether convinced that Jake is over bothered about replacing the church hall just at the moment. When we came home, I had a feeling that there was something else on his mind, taking priority. The fire seemed more like a sideshow – exciting and exercising the imagination but not the main attraction. What do you think, dear? My feminine intuition doesn't often play me false. I suppose as the ex-vicar, the hall is no longer his concern.'

'Spot on,' said Daniel. He's more worried about his successor at the vicarage than any rebuilding programme. Whether he will change his mind when he finds out who owns the hall site, I can't say. I doubt it. He is a "people" chap as against "bricks and mortar". We'll soon see. When we get in, let's ring the Drakes and either invite ourselves to lunch with them or invite them to eat with us. We owe them a meal, at the very least, for dog sitting while we were in Sicily. Spur of the moment stuff – we can go to the Ram, it's only a few yards for them to walk.'

'Nice thought, but Martha might have a dish in the oven already,' said Lorna. 'We can but try.'

Once again, Lorna had seen the future except that the future was cold. Earlier in the morning Jake had taken his fishing net down to the Yowe and returned with enough crayfish to satisfy four middling appetites. A quick trawl of the garden yielded a rich variety of salad plants; anything from American land cress to yellow early zucchini. Martha's culinary skills were matched only by Jake's expertise in the preparation of Yowesdale cheese soufflé. Aunt Em Greensward's tuition during school holidays had resulted in Jake being able to hold his own in most kitchen situations, but shellfish was Martha's domain.

At the outset, Damnit complied with Violet's instructions and in very low-key manner told Jake the outcome of her delving into the ownership of the church hall ground. Then he followed that announcement with a statement which mystified Lorna who was party to Violet's suggestion that he should consult with Jake and get some divine guidance on the way forward with regard to the future of the church hall, and the ground which he now owned.

'I'm not in any rush to tackle the problems of hall or ground redevelopment. But I am confident that if I don't receive any help from on high, I am bound to dream up something. In fact, this dreamer can hardly wait. So that's item one disposed of.

Item two, Jake. You wanted to offer some sage counsel on the matter of your possible successor at St Michael's. Now's your chance – and I'm sure it is immaterial as to whether or not Martha and Lorna are privy to your thoughts.'

'As a matter of fact,' said Jake, 'they could be highly material, as you might say, Damnit. I would prefer to say that they are germane to my machinations. Let me tell you a true story. None of your dream sequences about this. I'll try to be brief but really I could write a book about it. When I was training for the priesthood, my theological college fellow men were as motley a bunch as you might meet in a day's march, with only one thing in common – we had all passed through a fairly rigorous selection process. Apart from myself, whom you will remember as something of an actor, from my school Hyperhistrionics, Damnit, to my triumphs with the Cambridge Footlights – Captain Hook was my zenith while treading the boards – only one other trainee ordinand fancied himself as a thespian. He did not impress me as much as he must have impressed the selection board. Once, I came across him preening, and polishing his delivery and his facial expressions in front of a mirror. Perfectly acceptable, normally, for an actor but just for that brief moment I caught a glimpse of the man behind the facade. At a distance, I followed the career of that flawed priest to its bitter end several parishes later a trail of utter destruction. The point that emerges is interesting and it goes against the rationale of believing in the honesty of personal references. If a so-called priest-in-charge antagonises his unhappy parishioners so much that they make his life hell and he opts to seek pastures new, he can expect something approaching a glowing reference for the relief of easing his departure. So – when a fresh parish congregation welcomes its newly inducted vicar and there is not a coachload of his former parishioners present to wish him well, know that you have trouble brewing. Unfortunately it is not *de rigueur* to investigate the track record of a potential new shepherd for your flock, so unless the fraud commits a gross misdemeanour – I won't go into lurid details – he can stay in the vicarage as long as it suits him.'

Martha intervened. 'The same goes for a woman priest, Jake. Don't automatically presume it's a man.'

'Of course,' said Jake. 'I was just telling of my own experience which happened to relate to a male. You know how much I am looking forward to seeing the first woman bishop – at least before, hopefully, I am called home to higher things.'

'Good for you,' said Lorna. 'Personally, I doubt if I will last long enough to witness an "Archbishopess", but it would be nice. In the meantime, what are we to learn from your intriguing story? And as you were talking of the man's bitter end, what happened to him? A thunderbolt perhaps?'

'Last question, first answer. His final parish was in mid-Cornwall. The day came when his two long-standing, and long-suffering churchwardens found just the right moment to inform him that after two years as their parish priest he had acquired a rather formal nickname. No pun intended. Nic the Vic had become Lucifer Liquidator. He must have looked in the mirror once more and finally have seen himself as others saw him. It was too much. Later, that same day, he drove his car to the nearest seaside village and hired a little fishing boat. The boat was found eventually, floating offshore at Sennen Cove. Lucifer disappeared.'

Damnit spoke quietly. 'I remember many moons ago, someone telling me that drowning was as quick and painless a way to leave this world as any other method. An easy exit, once you've inhaled the first lungful but make sure you're on your own.'

'How horrible,' said Lorna. 'Presumably he was a bachelor carefree, careless and caring for no one. Your story reminds me of a great friend of Matthew, my first husband, who was a churchwarden of a Devon parish. Their old vicar had to retire on grounds of ill health and was replaced eventually by a priest from Essex whose credentials and references were indicative of a certain saintliness. He broke, or rather shattered, the parish in less than a year before falling from the church tower. Hold on! I'm sure I've told you this tale not that long ago. Sorry about that – old age creeping on, I fear. Now you can address my first question, Jake.'

Jake pursed his lips before replying. 'The lesson to be learnt is, when appointing a new priest-in-charge, disregard etiquette; in racing terms examine the form book and send in the investigators – incognito. Prepare to open a can of worms.'

Daniel looked puzzled. 'Are you suggesting that we, or I as churchwarden, use a detective? I hate wasting money, as you know. Timothy would have to be involved.' His face brightened. 'Maybe he would cough up!'

'No need to go that far,' laughed Jake. 'I'd do the job for nothing were it not for the undeniable fact that when I attend any church, sporting collar and tie as opposed to wearing my clerical dog collar, any cleric worth his salt or even a keen churchwarden would smell me a mile off. I suppose I could disguise myself as a part-time chef with a dab of garlic behind my ears. However, two heads, or sleuths, are better than one and I nominate Martha and Lorna as our Holmes and Watson. Martha deserves a break away from me and I'm sure Lorna would appreciate a little rest away from her newly beloved. How about it, Damnit? They're a natural double act.'

Lorna looked at Martha and Martha looked at Lorna before, as one, they burst out laughing. Lorna spoke first. 'Do you know anything about this, Martha?'

'The Nic the Vic plight?' said Martha. 'Yes, although I never met him, Jake would mention him occasionally. I suppose it would have been on seeing a fresh appointment announced in the press as Nic moved up and down the country and from diocese to diocese, leaving shattered church communities behind him. Daniel would have heard Jake inveighing against Old Nic once in a while, I'm sure. But the idea of you and me being a couple of private eyes looking for skeletons in vicars' vestry cupboards is certainly news to me. But is it Christian?'

Damnit re-entered the fray having taken in very quickly the notion that investing in such unusual tactics could reap important dividends. It was obvious that Jake had given much thought to his scheming plan, perhaps over some time. He did recall him mentioning Nic the Vic a few years earlier at the time of Nic's disappearance, when the Church covered up the incident as best it could. The final damning comment on the affair by the Reverend Jacob Drake was, 'I bet Lucifer's congregation are praying like fury that he's safely stowed in Davy Jones's locker. For fury read Hell.'

'Christian? Christian? I think not. More like the Wisdom of Solomon if you ask me. Christ could well be on earth today if a private investigator had blown the gaff on Judas before he joined the band of twelve disciples. It's a marvellous idea, Jake – you can come and cook for me while they're away. Basic rate of pay and all the food you can eat. Seriously, though, it does make sense just so long as these two lovely ladies can carry it off – that is if they agree to the assignment. How about it, girls?'

'I can't wait,' said Martha. 'We'd need to go in disguise never mind incognito. I'll need to dig out my theatrical makeup kit if I can find it. I've not seen it since the parish pantomime of 1999. It may have been lost in our moving house. Lorna, how do you fancy going the rounds of these clerics we are set to investigate, dressed up to the nines and made up like candidates for a harem? Oodles of rouge and stacks of mascara!' She chuckled mischievously. 'We could put on a different act for each church. How many parishes would you like us to visit, Daniel?'

'It's three,' interjected Lorna, quickly, ahead of Daniel, before joining in Martha's infectious giggle. 'If I am to be a participant in this deception, such as it is, and I must confess that it greatly appeals to my sense of the ridiculous, then I see myself as the back-end of a pantomime horse. Daniel does not know that in my last year at school I played Lady Godiva – brilliantly at the time so I believe – but I always envied the two lads playing the horse, especially the rump end comedian and his habit of leaving black puddings on stage. Never failed to bring the house down. Yes, I'm all for it, Martha. May I suggest that one church could benefit from a visitation by a couple of nuns, and for another a pair of heavily veiled and highly perfumed widows wearing the appropriate weeds. Minimum makeup for nuns and veiled widows, and then we can really major on the concubine front using the same powerful scent we used on the widows. I really fancy smoking a pipe as well. Will we be allowed to swear?'

Jake's shoulders were heaving with laughter. 'I think you two ladies can be given a free rein, *carte blanche*, to play it to the hilt. What's more, maybe you should take a covert cameraman with you to capture the performances. Oscars beckon!'

Damnit called the meeting to order with one simple word. 'Time.'

'What now?' asked Jake.

'It's something we don't have much of,' said Damnit. 'The archdeacon has booked, provisionally, Tuesday 10 July for interviewing the three shortlisted candidates.' He paused and carried out a speedy bit of mental arithmetic before continuing. 'That means that we have a mere twenty two days to gather information from Cornwall, Sussex and Northumberland. Those are the counties that Timothy mentioned.

And what is more, one is a woman. She is the Sussex contender. I wonder which of your disguises you will choose for her benefit?'

'We'll expect to be paid, you know,' said Martha with mock seriousness. 'Clandestine work doesn't come cheap these days and even less so at such short notice. Perhaps we should indulge our little girls' love of dressing up by cross-dressing when we investigate the lady. What do you think, Lorna?'

Lorna had been thinking quietly and with some concentration since Jake had said that she and Martha should have a free hand, all the while taking in what Daniel and Martha were saying, and now she came out with her own observations. 'Shall we just settle for expenses like accommodation, drink and tobacco? If we explain it all to Violet, she is bound to be able to hide the outlay in her accounts somehow. That's what treasurers do all the time. I actually think she'll revel in the idea – might even want to come with us. I wonder which garb would appeal to her most – mother superior, old tart or wealthy, flirtatious widow. Timothy Welsh will have to know what we're up to and that will involve him in putting Muriel in the picture. The rest of the PCC don't need to know, and the archdeacon must not know, although we can expect the truth to emerge eventually however hard we try to conceal it. Anyhow, I'm ready for the challenge but only if you fancy it, Martha. I think, in view of the time element, we need to make up our minds now and get organised.'

'I can't wait,' said Martha. 'Since it is Jake's cunning plan and I am a classic example of the dutiful wife who always obeys her husband, I have to go whither I am bid.' She smiled sweetly at her husband.

'Well, this is a first,' said Jake, leaning back in his chair with his hands clasped behind his head. 'Next thing you'll be asking me to tell you what to wear for this espionage assignment. Any thoughts about that, Damnit?'

'Not really. Just keep it simple, if you can,' replied Damnit. 'You're the actor, Jake – or rather you were – and you were at your best and brightest when dressed to kill. Captain Hook was never more colourful. However, if the wardrobe department was down to me I'd settle on one outfit only for all three venues. The first two church visits would then be rehearsals for the final performance. Correct me if I'm wrong.'

'I'm sure you're right, Daniel,' offered Martha, 'but I think you underestimate our acting abilities. Personally, I'd go for all three – or could we combine two of the characters to make it all a bit more exciting, not only for us but for the three congregations we shall be finding ourselves a part of? What do you reckon, partner?'

'I reckon,' said Lorna, choosing her words with care, 'as Daniel says, two practices would be helpful. I like the suggestion of not overcomplicating things but it's jolly tempting just the same.' She paused. 'It has suddenly struck me that it is important that we aren't rumbled. If we play at being a couple of nuns on the loose, our targets will be suspicious and wary from the start. So nuns are out. But we would make a wonderful pair of liberated widows in search of some extramarital bliss – if you get my gist. A bit of gross misdemeanour is quite the thing in church circles at the moment, so I'm told.'

Jake laughed louder than the others at Lorna's final statement. 'I can see you've been reading the wrong newspapers on your honeymoon. Too much Sicilian sun, I suspect.'

Lorna spoke again: this time to introduce some reality into the jollity. 'I have to admit a personal interest at this point. You see, I know what it means to play the grieving widow, at least until Daniel managed to persuade me to tread a happier path. I never acted the merry widow then but I'm sure I can do it now. After all, it's only make believe. With lots of makeup and heady perfume, we'll slay them in the aisles, Martha. What a brilliant duo! Think Morecambe and Wise, Martha and Lorna.'

'Slay them in the aisles, indeed! It makes it sound as if we are planning a production of "Murder in the Cathedral,"' said Martha. 'We'll need pseudonyms, do you think? In case anyone craves an introduction to such a ravishing pair of beauties. Three churches, one set of clothes. Three different names or just one? What do you think, Daniel?'

'As before,' said Daniel, 'keep it simple. I see you as sisters-in-law who married brothers. That gives you the same surname. Make it short – easy to remember – and then choose some exotic Christian name. Jake can dream up the surname. I'll give you twenty seconds, Jake.'

'Waters,' said Jake, without blinking. 'Then Martha can be Virginia and perhaps Lorna could be…'

'Soda or tonic?' volunteered Lorna, with something akin to a giggle. 'No, no! Lavender will fit nicely and I will be profusely perfumed as one fragrant widow.'

'That's going to be very hard for you, dear,' commented Daniel. As long as I've known you, you've never used any perfume other than "Aphrodite," and lavender is one of my pet hates.'

'Come, come,' teased Lorna, 'you know how expensive my tastes are. That is why I have to buy my own subtle perfume. I refuse to waste it on potential priests for St Michael's. Lavender in plenty will leave a lasting impression on whoever comes close to yours truly. Just you see. Mind you, if Violet is to be in charge of our expense account perhaps I should answer to Rose Waters, and I do have a rather smart pastel pink outfit I could wear, free of charge. Can't you imagine Virginia and Rose Waters, aromatic beyond belief, genuflecting and crossing themselves at every available opportunity, then giving the sermon a miss to go for a quick fag in the church porch. If we are outrageous enough we might even merit a mention in the Church Times. Three parishes at different ends of the country, three successive weekends and three bravura performances by the same pair of very attractive widows. So, Virginia and Rose it is.'

'Steady on,' pleaded Jake. 'Somebody – even the C.T. might put two and two together. And you can't avoid the sermon – that has to be a part of your penance. Go to sleep by all means: snore if you like. But you ought to listen, while remembering sermons in isolation count for nothing, unless the preacher has bought a copy of my best-selling book of riveting sermons in which case you may note the wisdom of the man in the pulpit. Martha will recognise the stamp of Jacob Drake in the humour and phraseology emanating from the pulpit. After that it is all down to the ability of the actor's delivery. Don't be fooled by the apparent quality of a sermon any more than you should take personal references at their face value. In my humble experience, just about the most damning words I have heard when referring to a priest-in-charge are "at least, he preaches a decent sermon". It usually means that he – or she, of course – can be pretty clueless or useless when it comes to the pastoral values expected of a parish priest. I say no more. Perhaps I have said too much already and should leave the stage to you, Damnit, as a churchwarden regnant.'

'Amen to that,' said Damnit. 'I will square things with Timothy this evening – in other words, a.s.a.p. Something else has just occurred to me with regard to Mr. T – he took our wedding photographs. You two ladies could take him and his camera along with you to capture the moment, whatever that might mean, on film. He'd need to be anonymous, incognito and entirely discreet. It'll depend on Muriel as to whether or not she will release him, and I will need a quick answer on that question. I must say, it would be quite delicious fun to present the next vicar with a photographic record of the lady detectives at work. No need to record a sermon, having received Jake's opinion about such things.'

'We're very short of time, Daniel,' said Lorna, interrupting his flow of thought. 'How do you think we should tackle that problem? There's more to this expedition than just getting dressed up for a Sunday service. We need to be very quick off the mark.'

Jake broke his self-enforced silence. 'There is no cause for worry, girls. I, better than anyone, know Daniel's superb organisational skills. From our early school days, he earned a reputation as a safe pair of hands whatever life threw his way. No one is more committed than he to *"aequam servare mentem"*. I can hear his brain from here, slipping into overdrive.'

'Please, not that again,' begged Lorna.

'Nonsense,' said Daniel. 'It's only my preference for having things cut and dried, if that is possible. So here goes. I suggest the following approach. Can you jot it down for me, dear? I'm sure Martha can find you a suitable back of an envelope.'

It was Jake who produced an A4 notepad from his desk.

'Point one, use Lorna's old Volvo,' said Daniel. 'It has an "A" registration plate, not a "Y" like Trollop. So our inspectors will not be linked to Yowesdale by any inquisitive churchwardens.

Two. It's Tuesday tomorrow. I undertake to arrange all holiday accommodation at or near the three locations to be visited, and pay for it – in case Violet isn't minded to see it my way. I really don't expect that Timothy will fancy a trip to Cornwall and Sussex – Northumberland perhaps. I'll see. Will you two ladies be happy to share a room?'

'As you're stumping up, Daniel, I must insist on a single,' said Martha with a surreptitious glance at Lorna, before bursting into laughter.

'There's your answer for both of us,' said Lorna. You can expect us to be up half the night comparing notes anyway, if we are to do the job properly. How long do you require us to stay in each parish?'

Daniel dug his diary out from an inside breast pocket of his sports jacket and thumbed his way through to June. 'Let's see now. The whole exercise needs treating as if you were taking three weekend breaks with three nights B and B, arriving on a Friday and leaving the following Monday. It's a wearisome long way from here to Cornwall if you're driving, so I suggest doing the Cornish parish first but take two days to get there. At a guess, it might be between four and five hundred miles, depending on whether it is north or south Cornwall. Before the motorways were built, it was understood that Tupshorne to Land's End was a neat five hundred miles.'

'I can share the driving,' said Martha. 'I'm insured for all that kind of thing. So to arrive on the Friday we would need to depart on Thursday morning and so break the back of the journey on day one. Bristol is not that far off three hundred miles from here, I think.'

'That gives us two days to choose our wardrobes,' said Lorna. 'Only just enough time for us two handsome widow women.'

'No need to be frivolous,' said Daniel, smiling. 'Then it would give you all of four days to motor from Cornwall to Sussex taking in the sights or calling in on old friends as well as writing up your Cornish findings. Let's hope parish number two is in West Sussex, as near to Chichester as possible. Hastings is nearly a hundred miles further east.

Then you can repeat the B and B routine, Friday to Monday and so homeward again. The Northumberland leg will follow on the third weekend. Let me just check the diary to see if that all fits in with the archdeacon's intent to have the interviews on Tuesday 10 July.

Cornwall leg 22–25 June

Sussex 29 June–2 July

Northumberland 6–9 July

That's a bit tight for time. We'll need the day of Monday 9 to examine the reports before the Arch descends on us the next day.'

'No,' said Lorna. 'It will be manageable at the last because we can come back to Tupshorne from anywhere in Northumberland on that Sunday evening. It's not long distance stuff like getting to Cornwall – and back. And Martha might have got the hang of driving the Volvo by then.'

'Nice one,' said Martha. 'You did say that you wanted to do all the driving, didn't you?'

Jake looked at Damnit. 'Maybe we should go along for the ride as well to keep these lovely "widows" in order. They'll demand another holiday when they get back home, claiming stress related time off.'

'What a lovely idea,' said Lorna to Martha. 'Do you suppose our husbands might wish to accompany us. We could cover the same itinerary, flaunting our "new" husbands in the churches we've been inspecting. Act Two, so to speak.'

'I think that's quite enough, thank you,' said Damnit. 'One honeymoon a year is my limit. It looks as if Lorna may have managed to make some brief jottings from our wide ranging discussion. One final thought from me. You could ring me or email me with the Cornwall and Sussex information, immediately it is gleaned. Then I can chew it over with Timothy. The results of your final parish health check can wait until the day before the interviews. How you go about gathering such information, I will leave to your feminine guile and intuition. It seems a shame that you will play no part in the appointment when it happens but the homework that you will have done will be invaluable in unearthing the next gem to shine from the pulpit of St Michael's – even if the oratory fails to electrify. As Jake suggests, we can arrange to leave a large tome of specially selected short sermons, [Editor in chief, J. Drake] on the mantelpiece in the new vicar's study. Find me the right book, Jake, and I'll pay for it.'

'Please can we go home now?' said Lorna. 'I think we've all had about enough laughter and excitement for the time being, don't you agree Martha?'

'Don't be so sure,' replied Martha, tongue firmly in cheek. 'I suspect we're in for the time of our lives over the next few weeks. What a blessing you and I have such shapely legs. They say short skirts are back in fashion. Roll on Thursday.'

'I'll sort things out with Timothy in the morning,' was Damnit's parting comment.

CHAPTER VI

Forsan Et Haec Olim Meminisse Iuvabit

(Maybe one day it will be a pleasure to recall even such things)

On reaching home after lunching at the Drakes', Damnit rang Timothy to arrange a meeting the following morning. Tuesday in Tupshorne was Market Day, ever an occasion for the great and the good, and the neither so great nor good, from the town and surrounding villages to congregate in the Market Place to pass the time of day, set the world to rights, moan about the weather and gossip about any local scandal, be it current, past or even brewing.

At Damnit's invitation, Timothy brought Muriel along with him and they met for coffee and biscuits in as quiet a corner as they could find in the Ram and Raddle Inn, a pub down a narrow ginnel leading off the Market Place.

From the outset, Damnit made it very clear that anything he said in connection with the next incumbent situation was to go no further, explaining that the only other people privy to any scheming were Lorna, Martha and Jake. Without quoting Lorna's words, he emphasised the belief that the fewer who knew what was about to happen the better. Certainly the archdeacon had to be kept in the dark at all costs, and any mention of Jake as a source of sound advice should be disregarded.

Then, without any hint of the hilarity that accompanied the discussion at the Drakes' and making full use of Lorna's notes, he explained the details of the plan to check on the truly pastoral qualities of the three possible, one of whom was destined to succeed the Reverend Jacob Drake.

Damnit kept his presentation, such as it was, as short as possible. Hardly into his stride, he was quick to realise that Timothy was having reservations, particularly with regard to the intended breach of etiquette in the search for Jake's successor; until he heard the salutary tale of Nic the Vic who had become Lucifer Liquidator. Muriel, on the other hand, was very taken with the idea of employing two lady sleuths on holiday as a means of checking on pastoral credentials, and even was moved to wonder what Raymond Chandler would have had to say about such carryings-on. For a moment, Damnit thought she was about to offer to accompany Lorna and Martha on their journey of discovery – a possible expensive complication.

Timothy, to Damnit's relief, suddenly changed tack altogether and announced that he could see quite clearly the benefits of researching the background of the three selected for interview. It had occurred to him, independently of anything that Damnit might have had to say in favour of probing the parochial potential of all three applicants, that in particular the two who had the furthest to travel could have any number of awkward reasons for wishing to leave their present flocks in search of pastures new.

Muriel had come to the same conclusion as Timothy but from an entirely different angle. Both Walshes had been very involved with the Guide Dogs for the Blind Association when they had lived in Bolton before retiring to Yowesdale. They had been responsible for the early training and puppy-walking of numerous guide dogs over many years. Muriel knew the importance of the breeding programme in relation to the production of successful adult dogs. Canine family attributes over several generations count for a lot if man is looking for special characteristics in his best friend. The potential is all in the genes, be it a police dog, sniffer dog, border collie or guide dog. All animals, including man, have a background worthy of investigation. The racehorse trainers of Middleham all knew the importance of track records. Muriel reasoned that you could use the same criteria for the appointment of a new parish priest and she said so.

When the question of funding the operation came up, Timothy favoured Damnit's idea of not troubling Violet with a request for church money. Also he fully agreed that it would be for the best if the number of those in the know be limited to the six who knew already. He and Muriel could be trusted to keep a secret.

Muriel was starting to appreciate the humorous side of the plot even before it began to unravel. Here was Daniel Greensward, a man of undoubted integrity and a highly respected churchwarden of his local church, newly returned from honeymoon and now keen to send Mrs Greensward on a further holiday break. Daniel smiled at her teasing, hinting that he would like to have included her in the investigation team but his finances did not stretch that far and he knew that Timothy would be lost without her, to say nothing of his frowning on such frivolity. After all, it might have cost his fellow churchwarden money.

During the banter between Muriel and Damnit, Timothy was indulging in a rethink concerning the exclusion of Violet from any knowledge of the plot. He reasoned, and Damnit had to agree, that if anyone would be likely to smell a rat about the proceedings it would be Violet. She would be the person to quiz Damnit, in her finest inquisitorial mode, as to why Lorna was holidaying again so soon after returning from honeymoon. Damnit would not be able to disguise the fact that Lorna was to be accompanied by Martha and their destinations were to be Cornwall, Sussex and Northumberland. Violet knew the diocesan roots of the chosen three and in spite of being church treasurer for at least a generation could well put two and two together. Muriel joined in by stating that sooner or later Violet would certainly stumble across the truth and even if the church finances had not been involved in the expense, she would be disappointed if not downright angry that she had not been taken into their confidence. Also, Muriel wondered about the wisdom of Daniel funding the expedition off his own bat, suggesting that perhaps she and Timothy, if Timothy was in favour, could go halves on the expenses. In her opinion, the two doughty churchwardens of St Michael the Archangel should both be ready, not to mention willing, to face the flak if the archdeacon ever discovered the lengths to which they had gone to examine the bona fides of each contender for the vacant post. She also pointed out that a decent parish welcome party for any new vicar could be as costly as the organisers cared to make it. Violet would be well aware that an entry in the accounts that mentioned caviar for the party could possibly have been coloured cod's roe. With a little juggling or creative accounting, such differences in expenses, as between caviar and cod's roe, would go a long way towards funding the investigation by the two lady private detectives.

And so it came about. Daniel, Timothy and Muriel agreed that Violet should be told and so become the final member of the Saint Michael Magnificent Seven. The sensitivity and security of the operation would not be compromised in any way. Violet's skills which she had for so long brought to bear on St Michael's finances had always been full of imagination and inventiveness. The parish purse strings were hers to control and she knew when to be generous and when to be tight-fisted in the manner of a Yorkshire woman who appreciates the value of a bit o' brass. But, just as importantly, she knew that 'tight-fisted' went hand in hand with 'tight-lipped,' a classic mixture of metaphors that she expected to see in some form on her tombstone when the time came.

At Muriel's suggestion, the task of telling Violet of her expected involvement in checking out the three hopefuls fell to Daniel. Muriel reasoned that as Violet had known him since his birth she would appreciate being put in the picture by him. Violet thought that she could read Daniel like a book on account of their lifelong association. Yet she was mistaken. Nobody, not even Lorna, was privy to the devious inner machinations of Daniel's mind. When the situation suited him, he could be full of Christian forgiveness but as for Christian forgetfulness, forget it, and he had the memory of an elephant.

CHAPTER VII

Fide, Sed Cui Vide

(Trust, but be careful in whom you trust)

After leaving the Ram and Raddle, Damnit walked home to High Ash and over a light lunch briefed Lorna on the details of his meeting with the Walshes and intention to ring Violet to check that she was at home and prepared for a visit from a churchwarden bearing important exciting information.

Lorna asked him to repeat every detail of what had transpired in his conversation with Timothy and Muriel. It exercised her analytical mind just how they had come round to agreeing with the plot after their initial reservations. Their opinions had changed and she wondered why. It was at this point that Daniel realised how important it was that a proper record should be kept, in précis form, of the planning and the execution of the stratagem that had been set in train. To preserve the integrity of the Magnificent Seven themselves, proper names and places would become fictitious.

'What do you think, Sweetheart?' He put the question to Lorna. 'Would you agree that it would be a good idea to log the progress of our underhand scheming until it all comes to fruition? All seven of us involved need to speak with just one voice. The timescale we are operating under is so short that any whiff of dissent must of necessity abort the whole mission. The record could be destroyed at any time to suit us, and certainly be shredded in the final analysis. Personally, I would not wish the intrigue of Saint Michael the Archangel to become a blueprint for any other parish to use.'

Lorna was quick to respond. 'The situation has the stamp of a short story by Somerset Maugham. I'll write the story, using a pseudonym, as a work of fiction. All characters will have a name change. Call the church after another archangel – Raphael sounds well – and Tupshorne in Yowesdale positively invites one to use one's imagination. We can ask the other five for their take on alternative family and place names. Though I say it myself, as an historian with a certain reputation to uphold, I think I could manage a decent short story, possibly shot through with a shaft of history.'

'You never cease to amaze me,' said Daniel. 'I mention the simple topic of keeping a diary of events and before I can say "Cakes and Ale", you've produced a Maughamesque short story. It serves to remind an old stick in the mud like me of the youthful enthusiasm of our undergraduate days. Your *joie de vivre* remains undimmed.'

'Just leave it to me,' whispered Lorna, 'and I shall craft a tale to captivate the readers of the Church Times. What's more, in my crystal ball I see an anagram in the Daily Telegraph cryptic crossword. The clue reads "Search light firms diversify to produce something worth owning." The mist is clearing to reveal the answer. "Film rights"'

'Come back down to earth,' chuckled Daniel. 'I've yet to run it all past Violet. She may be a dear, sweet, old lady but when it suits she can be an awkward cuss. If, for some reason, she thinks we are wrong in our skulduggery, she'll say so. And that will be the end of Archangel Raphael. Until I've spoken to her later this afternoon, I fear that we can't count her among our hatched chickens.'

'Hold on,' said Lorna. 'Should Violet wield the veto, we still have the bones of a rollicking good yarn. If I let my imagination take wing, I could even end up with a full length blockbuster novel involving all the archangels.'

'Steady on,' chuckled Daniel again. 'You're getting carried away. And I must draw the line at Archangel Uriel. He sounds just a bit too like a privy for me.'

'Perhaps I ought to accompany you on your visit to Violet,' said Lorna. 'From what I have come to know of her, I think the absurdity of the situation will appeal greatly to her wicked sense of humour. I know she has taken to me since our very first meeting, and I also recognise that you could be the son that she never had. So if we approach her together, your charm is guaranteed to win the day. What do you think? Ring her now.'

Daniel smiled. 'As usual, you're right – or rather, half right on this occasion. My job is to phone her but I won't tell her that I am bringing you with me. You can come as my secret weapon and it will be you, my love, who charms her.'

'Flatterer,' said Lorna.

'Charmer,' replied Daniel. 'Violet can be as rude to me as she likes if the mood takes her. I don't mind. "Water off a duck's back," as far as

I'm concerned. In your presence, she'll be as nice as pie – all sweetness and light.'

'Now you are counting chickens,' cautioned Lorna. 'I bet she can be as fickle as Freda Fazackerley if the mood takes her.'

'Freda Fazackerley?' queried Daniel, looking mystified. 'Where on earth have you dug her up from?'

'Oh, she was Blackburn's mythical equivalent to Dublin's Molly Malone or Durban's Little Audrey, so my mother told me. Whenever anything strange, whimsical or untoward occurred that could not easily be explained, it was laid at Freda's door. In my mother's opinion, Freda was responsible for everything from government blunders to vagaries in the weather. I'm sure that Yorkshire has its Freda and if it hasn't, then we can invent her. How about Penelope Pontefract or Henrietta Halifax?'

'Sounds like a parlour game to me,' said Daniel. I'm not sure that Violet will appreciate being linked with a Lanky lass. We'll find out shortly. I'll give her a bell now and tell her we're inviting ourselves to tea. Tuesday morning is her baking time and so with a bit of luck we will be able to sample her quite excellent scones.'

Violet greeted her visitors with a most unusually woebegone face. The faint whiff of smoke, detectable on the outgoing draught when she opened her cottage front door to let in Lorna and Daniel, betrayed the fact that Violet had suffered a King Alfred moment – her famous scones had burnt. Apparently she had been having a neighbourly natter with Mrs Herbison from the next door cottage, conducted over their party fedge, and totally forgot the batch of scones in the oven. As omens go, this one would be classified as 'inauspicious.'

Lorna sized up the situation immediately, sympathising with Violet's obvious distress, and seized the moment to reverse the state of affairs by insisting on providing tea at High Ash. Then Daniel chided Violet for allowing her penchant for a good gossip to override her innate sense of culinary timing and it was his gentle teasing that restored her customary good humour, bringing an indulgent smile to her careworn features.

'When you reach my age, Daniel,' said Violet, 'you will understand that although love makes the world go round while money oils the wheels, it is gossip, preferably of a scandalous nature, that provides the spice of life. Surely you must have been aware of Tupshorne tongues wagging when your lovely Lorna here took up residence at High Ash without the benefit of matrimony. All good-natured, to be sure. And yes, Lorna, dear, I'd love to come to tea. Daniel tells me that your scones are the equal of mine.'

'That's not what he tells me,' laughed Lorna. 'According to him, it's Jake who is King Scone and he uses Daniel's mother's recipe.'

'That's rich,' said Violet. 'Guess who I got my recipe from. Emily Greensward could have baked for England. In fact, she was responsible for masterminding "Cuisine According to Saint Michael the Archangel", a fund-raising effort back in the year dot. My copy is falling to bits now but if you do find one anywhere, grab it. Maybe it is time the Archangel issued a revised, updated edition. A little job for you Lorna?'

'Sounds like a bit of fun,' said Lorna. 'If by chance Jake has a copy, I could combine the two, presuming his is also in as parlous a state as yours, Violet. My problem would be in converting the weights from pounds and ounces into the gram equivalents. There's something you can do for me, Daniel.'

'Thanks a lot,' said Daniel. 'I shall need to see my name in the list of credits. Meanwhile let's get to High Ash and defrost a few of your scones. I'm sure Violet's never had a frozen scone in her life.'

'You'd be surprised,' laughed Violet. 'I'm a freezer fanatic when it comes to the preservation of excess food. Cooking for one is no joke when so many recipes state "serves four."' She frowned. 'You've yet to tell me what it is that you want to discuss with me. Must be important or top secret if you come here at such short notice. Urgent, is it?'

'Yes, yes and yes,' declared Daniel. 'Highly classified and very confidential in fact. High Ash has thick walls and two fine guard dogs for security – so let's go.'

'If I must then,' sighed Violet. 'I can't wait for the dogs to welcome me in their customary boisterous fashion. Guard dogs, indeed!'

A short time later, over tea, scones and lemon drizzle cake Daniel, with the occasional tactful interruption from Lorna, laid before Violet the plan for checking the parochial suitability of the three candidates for the vacancy at the Vicarage of St Michael the Archangel. As the Shakespearian proverb would have it 'Since brevity is the soul of wit', Daniel, not a man of many words, was as brief as possible and quite witty – at least in his own opinion. Violet sat and listened, stony faced and steely eyed until it came to the question of disguising the cost of the adventure in a bill for caviar. At which point she could keep up the pretence no longer and dissolved into tears of laughter. Lorna, for all her discreet comments, had been watching Violet's face with growing dismay, and finally when the mask slipped she gave a sob of sheer relief. But Violet was not finished with her teasing. 'Daniel,' she said, 'surely you don't expect me to apply my culinary expertise by cooking the books, without some serious involvement in this deception. May I suggest that Lorna and Martha drop the wealthy widows pretence and do their convent sisters act, then I can tag along as their Mother Superior. I fancy myself in a wimple as a member of the "Three Wise Nuns". And if I am to cook books for two, one more in a stew of this tasty nature would improve the flavour no end. "In for a penny, in for a pound," as they say. On reflection though, there's too much going on in the garden just now and a lot of jam to make. I'll make sure you have a jar of my "World's Best Jam", Lorna, dear, when it is ready in September. This year I'm thinking of jellying my ten different berries and designating it as "Violet's Verry Berry Jelly."' She paused. 'But I digress. Of course, I'll play my part in this delightful charade. Rest assured, the accounts will not reflect the enormity of what you are asking of me. The idea of being a member of the Saint Michael Magnificent Seven appeals to my sense of the absurd. This honorary treasurer gives her blessing. Now, if I might have just another small sliver of your lovely lemon drizzle, Lorna, I'll call it a day.'

'Right,' said Daniel. 'I think that means that all our arrangements have, quite conveniently, fallen into place. Thanks, Violet. Your endorsement of the plan will prove to be an important chapter in Lorna's fictional novel, suitably embroidered to protect the innocent.'

'Novel? What novel?' asked Violet.

'Well,' said Lorna, 'subject to approval from the full meeting of the Seven, I thought I would keep a record of how we go about finding a replacement priest and then turn that record, radically embellished, into a novel – crafted under a pseudonym, of course. What do you reckon, Violet?'

'I reckon,' said Violet slowly, 'you'll need to spice things up somewhat to capture the *zeitgeist*, as they say in Berlin. For a start, might I suggest two young and definitely flirtatious widows when it comes to weighing up the credentials of a potential new vicar? The possibilities are endless, given some imagination. Oodles of gross misconduct. You can't beat that.'

'You're incorrigible,' laughed Daniel. 'You've been reading the wrong kind of magasine. Dangerous at your stage in life – so much excitement.'

'No, no, Daniel,' said Lorna. 'Violet's got the right idea. I can turn the whole story on its head with lots of saucy side issues to obscure the central thread of what we are about to attempt. Perhaps you would like to name the characters for me, Violet. How about the honorary church treasurer being the Hon. Cherie Blossom?'

'Miss Lavender Bouquet would be more apt in my case. Or even Lavender Bagg,' giggled Violet. 'Not all roses are fragrant.'

Gradually, the facetious chatter petered out and Violet asked to be taken home. At which point Lorna suggested that she might like to stay and join in the Greenswards' evening meal.

'I'd love to, thank you,' said Violet. 'There's nothing worth watching on television on Tuesday evenings and you're such good company.' She smiled. 'You and I can discuss character naming, Lorna, and Daniel can consider character assassination in case we invent too many. I promise not to overstay my welcome.'

'Just say when you've had enough of us,' said Daniel, 'And I'll run you home.'

The telephone rang. Martha was calling to ask that if she was to share the driving, with her being unaccustomed to Lorna's Volvo, would it be possible to alter the itinerary and complete the short leg of their journeying first. To Northumberland and back was just the right distance to enable her to familiarise herself with any little eccentricities of Swedish engineering. Could Daniel perhaps rearrange their accommodation even at such short notice? He most certainly could and did. Not without reason did his prep school headmaster's final report in the summer of 1947 state 'A safe and sensitive pair of hands in all situations.' Ten simple words that defined the man he was to become.

CHAPTER VIII

Cum Finis Est Licitus, Etiam Media Sunt Licita

(The end justifies the means)

By noon, the next day, Wednesday 20 June, Damnit had managed to rearrange the 'widows' selection tour schedule. However much he despised the loathsome telephone, he had to admit that once in a while it had its uses. It was, after all, his own failure to answer his office 'phone when suffering his heart attack in August 1989 that had alerted Colin Blunden to the realisation that something was seriously amiss.

The 'widows' holiday programme now read as follows

1. Northumberland parish of Ravensrigg. Alnwick area. Church of Saint Thomas.
   Depart Friday 22 June and return evening of Sunday 24.
2. Monday 25 June. A day of rest and recuperation back in Yowesdale. Submission and discussion of preliminary report on the Northumberland weekend.
3. Tuesday 26 June. Leave Tupshome for Cornwall, breaking the journey overnight at Worcester. Reach Cornwall Wednesday 27 in time for lunch. Parish of Tamarel, near Bude. Church of Saint Barnabas.
4. Leisurely investigation of Cornish parish matters until Monday 2 July when leaving for Sussex. Destination now confirmed as Wrensdown, West Sussex, close to the county border with Hampshire. Overnight break at Salisbury. Tuesday 3 July, arrive West Sussex. Midhurst area. Church of Saint John the Divine.
5. Return home late on Sunday 8 July, to report to the Magnificent Five on Monday, 9 July.

After returning the telephone to its cradle, he sat at his desk for a while, Baggins and Rauch stretched out in slumber either side of him on the floor. It had all been too simple: a few reasonably brief telephone calls were all it took to put the travel arrangements in place. Suddenly, almost as one, the two dogs were on their feet as if startled by some sound not audible to the human ear.

'What's up, girls?' Damnit enquired of them. 'Something disturbed your doggie dreams? The mistress won't be home until teatime – gone shopping.'

They lay down again and tranquillity was restored. Neither dog had raised a growl. The brief episode gave Damnit pause for thought. Just as the dogs had been awakened by something unexpected and beyond human ken, so he wondered what chance was there that his seemingly so carefully contrived plans might be upset by fresh circumstances outside the control of the Magnificent Seven. For all their undoubted enthusiasm, and without for one moment questioning their acting skills, how would the two 'fragrant widows' cope with the itinerary involved in covering well over a thousand miles of driving in a mere seventeen days, start to finish. Was there a way of lightening the motoring burden? The various distances between the three target destinations could not be shortened significantly. He had to face the fact that neither Lorna nor Martha would celebrate their sixty sixth birthday again. Upon examining the planned schedule once more he identified the most demanding part of the journey – the return from West Sussex to Yowesdale, late in the day of Sunday 8 July, would be very tiring. Perhaps the 'widows' should skip Evensong and set off for home after the morning service. He had no idea if the morning worship would take the form of a Eucharist, matins or even a songs-of-praise-parish-knees-up. Being the second Sunday in July, Evensong might be sung at afternoon teatime or be absent altogether. The thought crossed his mind that any one or all three of the priests under scrutiny could be on holiday. If such a situation as that were to obtain, he realised that God was mocking his efforts. Turning the problem over in his mind and experiencing a total lack of inspiration, he glanced down at his two Labradors, still either side of him like a pair of black bookends except that both were splatted out like kippers, flat to the ground with their heads between their paws. They could have been at prayer, he thought. He thought again before taking the obvious hint. It was intended that he should pray; and pray he did. The answer was swift in coming – send Jake down by train to West Sussex two or three days before Lorna and Martha would be due to drive home. There was no need for Jake to attend church or to queer the 'widows' pitch in any way, just as long as he showed up when they wished to depart.

He rang Jake with his new proposition which was welcomed with alacrity, largely because, unknown to Damnit, in the past few months Martha had developed a distinct aversion to driving in the dusk. Jake's immediate concern was for the care of Miss Bindle during his absence, a concern easily resolved by Damnit's insistence on having her join his two black bitches. After all, Miss Bindle had put up with Baggins and Rauch while the Greenswards were in Sicily on honeymoon. One good turn…

Lorna and Martha returned to High Ash in time for tea and were joined by Jake. The 'widows' had taken their forthcoming tour of inspection as an excuse to visit the Oxfam Charity shop in Harrogate where the range of first-class second-hand clothing was extraordinary. Limiting their purchases to an outfit each for a modest outlay gave them both a great sense of satisfaction if not downright virtue. Damnit was unsurprised when, tongue firmly in cheek, Martha asked him if the Oxfam receipts should be presented to Violet or him for reimbursement. He replied to the effect that the budget for the annual parish pantomime could be relied upon to swallow the expense of two sets of widow's weeds even if it meant writing into the script two roles for ladies of a certain age. This facetious exchange of financial fiddling brought Jake into the conversation. He wondered how long he would be required to reside outside Tupshorne before he would be allowed to take part in the pantomime. A fine actor in his time, his public stage appearances while vicar of St Michael the Archangel had been restricted to the pulpit. Damnit came up with the answer immediately. The lead in 'Beauty and the Beast' was just the part for Jake, requiring the minimum of makeup to render him unrecognisable while not leaving the audience in any doubt as to who was not to be confused with Beauty. For a fleeting moment, Lorna could have sworn that a Drake tongue was pointed in the direction of a Greensward.

Returning to serious discussion, the four considered Daniel's fresh arrangements and agreed that unless intervention arrived by way of a higher authority such as an act of God or, God forbid, a thunderbolt, by the time of the key meeting with the archdeacon they could expect to have in their possession a helpful dossier, however brief, on each of the candidates. If he had not done so already, Jake was appointed to look into Crockford's Clerical Directory to see what could be gleaned from the form book in the most recent edition of that worthy tome, and to inform the Magnificent Six in due course – after the return of the two investigators.

Gradually, the conversation changed emphasis and more mundane matters came to the fore. Lorna excused herself from further chat as she decided, once the dogs had been fed, to prepare an evening meal for all four. Martha joined her in the kitchen a short time later with the intention of helping her with whatever might have been on the High Ash menu, and was mildly surprised to find Lorna sitting at the kitchen table, elbows down, hands up and chin on palms in a position of serious contemplation.

'Do we have a problem?' enquired Martha gently. 'You're a million miles away.'

'Not a problem as such,' said Lorna, coming to. 'All Daniel's planning appears to be straightforward enough and even if we encounter an occasional obstacle in our path I'm confident in our joint ability to cope. In fact, I rather hope that something might happen to test our resources and, or, our intelligence. Whatever may be in store for us two well preserved "widows", we are in for some fun however serious the underlying reasons for our journey. No! What was surfacing from my brief meditation as you came into the kitchen was the extent to which you and I will be bearing the responsibility for the appointment of the next vicar here.'

'Tell me more,' urged Martha, 'at least before we leave tomorrow.'

'Well,' said Lorna, 'I reckon that if, with the maximum amount of subtlety, we can paint an accurate picture of what we find out on our travels you won't find such a picture in Crockford's – if you get my drift. I've never been recruited as a spy until now and I'm not sure that I shall relish the power it will give us over the new appointment. Having said that, I do hope that we shall discover something or things of importance that will either damn or bless those we are about to put under scrutiny: otherwise I shall feel cheated in our endeavours. I'm not accustomed to playing the judge <u>and</u> the jury.'

'You're not having second thoughts at this eleventh hour are you?' asked Martha. 'Because if you are and you feel like resigning your commission, you'd better say so right now. Otherwise I'll be left at the church door like a jilted bride. I'm in no doubt that I could manage on my own perfectly well but it wouldn't be half the fun without your company.'

'No, no, no,' said Lorna. 'I'm sorry if I sounded as if I was hinting at withdrawing. It'll be a somewhat unusual holiday for both of us. Our undercover investigation may be underhand in some way but we are, or will be on a mission in search of honesty and integrity. Who was it said, "The end justifies the means," or was it the other way round? Sounds like Karl Marx.'

'If you really want to know, it was another German, about two hundred years before Marx: a theologian with the wonderful name of Hermann Busenbaum. Latin, you know, it read, *"Cum finis est licitus, etiam media sunt licita."* In translation it means, when the end is allowed, the means also are allowed.'

'I am impressed,' murmured Lorna. 'For all Daniel's love of Latin phrases and proverbs, I bet he doesn't know that one. My only contribution to such a nugget of learning is to tell you that Busenbaum, in literal translation, means Bosomtree as in the family tree or the bosom of the family. You know that already of course.'

'Of course,' laughed Martha. 'Now let me peel the spuds. Duty calls. Our men must be getting hungry and the joys of a shopping spree always sharpen my appetite. And just think – no more domestic chores for ten days.'

While dining, the four tried very hard to leave any talk of the tour out of the conversation. Only at the post-meal coffee stage was serious mention made of the 'widows' departure the next morning, Friday 22.

'I do hope we shall be comfortably kennelled after all Daniel's efforts to rearrange our schedule,' said Martha. 'At least I know Lorna's Volvo will guarantee a gracious passage around the country.'

Lorna spoke quietly. 'As long as I get a decent night's sleep I'll be content. I think our Sicilian honeymoon has disturbed my sleep patterns.'

'First time I've heard about it,' said Daniel. 'Why didn't you tell me?'

'I just expected to return to normality as the days passed by, but it doesn't seem to be happening just yet. We've not been home many days and while you're snoring away in the Land of Nod I'm not inclined to moan.'

'So why do I detect a little moan now?'

'It just sort of slipped out when Martha mentioned the comfort of my Volvo. No doubt the problem will sort itself out given time. Once I'm asleep, I'm fine. Getting to sleep is a different matter.'

'Right,' said Daniel, 'now I know I will soon settle you down, starting at bedtime tonight. Doctor Greensward will have you in the arms of Morpheus before you switch off your bedside light. His method requires no drugs and when it comes to infallibility is more reliable than the Pope.'

Shortly after half past nine, Daniel and Lorna waved the Drakes off and away to their Middinside cottage and, having settled down the dogs, departed for bed themselves.

Lorna was quick to switch off her bedside lamp and in so doing deprived Daniel of making good his boast that he would have her in dreamland before she could do so.

'You meanie,' said Daniel. 'You did that just to spite me, didn't you?'

'Not really,' replied Lorna, an unseen smile hidden in her voice. 'I just thought I'd bring your morpheotherapy to bear that much faster. Persuade me into the private world of your dreams. How do we begin? Which side do I lie on for a start?'

'I don't know,' chuckled Daniel. 'I've never tried this on anyone else before. We'll just have to see if you can follow my whispered instructions. Here we go. Lie on your left side and tense as many muscles as you can and then relax them – this while you are straight. Make sure your palms are flat and spread out. Now gently curl up, still totally relaxed, and, if you wish, back into my embrace. We need to do this together. Comfy?'

'Very comfy, very relaxed, thank you,' murmured Lorna. 'Pray, continue. I'm cuddled up and snuggled down.'

'Now,' continued Daniel, whispering quietly as in a daze himself, 'I am at the wheel of your Volvo, and we are setting off to inspect a rather grand country property with a view to buying same.' He paused. 'There is a good chance that I shall be asleep before you and in that case you will need to continue the commentary in your own mind – whisper if you like. We have just passed through an imposing gateway and are driving down a long avenue of what appear to be beech trees – or they might be hornbeam – underplanted with scarlet rhododendrons in full and brilliant flower. At the far end of the avenue, can you glimpse the house, just coming into view on the left? And I don't recall a mention of that ornamental lake in the sale particulars. What a view from the front door! Good heavens, Lorna – we never expected to see a family of Black Swans. Can you count how many cygnets there are?' Lorna was asleep.

Three cheers for Morpheus, Ancient Greek and Roman God of Dreams!

CHAPTER IX

Festina Lente

(Hasten slowly)

Starting in on his breakfast next morning, Daniel asked if his dear wife had enjoyed a good night's rest.

'Miraculous,' said Lorna. 'In fact it was a complete revelation, you might say.'

'As regards my technique of getting you off to sleep,' said Daniel, 'have you any recollection of the last piece of commentary you might have heard from my lips?'

'Just, how beautiful the rhododendrons were before we caught sight of a lake.'

'What then?' said Daniel. 'Was it oblivion or did something else happen? I have to know. So many dream sequences are totally forgettable and thus forgotten.'

'You will find this hard to believe, but you stopped the car and told me to get out and walk the rest of the way. I couldn't believe it.'

'Go on,' said Daniel. 'This is promising.'

'Why I didn't protest about your uncharacteristically ungentlemanly behaviour is beyond me. Anyhow, out I got, started to walk further down the avenue and a most handsome house appeared as if out of a mirage or heat haze. Now here's the rum twist.'

Daniel interrupted. 'Your powers of recall are amazing. Are you sure you haven't been practising? A twist, you say?'

'Yes. I met a gardener who was busy spraying the roses in a rosebed, kidney-shaped it was, set in the drive in front of the main entrance. He was wearing not a gardener's apron but one made of hide such as a blacksmith might wear. Suddenly I realised that this man was your Latvian friend, John Smith, whom I had never met in real life although I have heard you talk of and about him so much.'

'Did he tell you his name?' asked Daniel. 'Otherwise I don't understand how you could know.'

'I suppose it's possible that I may have seen a picture or photograph of him, but by no means sure. You once described to me your first encounter with him at Rolls when you became director of engineering research. "A huge man standing in front of me, Desperate Dan to the life," were your words. Well, when I reached him he was slightly stooped as he used the sprayer, and on seeing me he straightened up to his full height before speaking. He was a colossus.'

'Did you feel frightened or intimidated?' asked Daniel.

'Not a bit. Perhaps because he greeted me with a beaming smile, addressing me in perfect German with "Guten Morgen, Gnädige Frau." How could he have known that I am fluent in German?'

'And then?' said Daniel, prompting her.

'Then, before I could reply to such a courteous greeting – you wouldn't know, but it means "Good Morning, Madam, or Charming Lady," – he inclined his head towards mine and spoke in English. I was conscious of his almost indigo eyes boring, seemingly into mine. He was very blonde – film star handsome I'd say.'

'Could you understand what he said?' queried Daniel. 'John's pronunciation of English needed some getting used to.'

'His gutturals served to reinforce my original idea of his identity but I needed to ask him to repeat his one brief sentence.'

'Which was?' said Daniel.

'He said, "Go and tell my story to Aino". Rather rudely, I said, "What?" Again, a little more slowly, he said, "Go and tell my story to Aino." Then he vanished and I was left with the perfume of the roses.'

'Did you wake up at that point or was that the end of a dream?' asked Daniel. 'You can't go on much longer – my coffee is getting cold.'

'So drink it, dear Daniel, dear Daniel. Drink it!' sang Lorna. 'I'm almost through. After the disappearing act which I have to admit rather threw me, I gathered myself together and walked to the front door. As I raised my hand to grasp the ornate brass knocker, the door was opened by none other than Albert Prince. "Hello, Lorna, dear," he said. "You've picked up the message. Check it out." Then he was gone as well and my revelation was at an end. Your tactic for putting me to sleep would appear to have stirred things up. Can you even begin to interpret what I have told you or shall I consult a Freudian psychologist?'

'Oh dear, oh dear,' sighed Daniel, an air of resignation in his tone. 'I wish John had warned me about this before he popped his clogs. When he set out to walk home to Latvia he had no idea what he was going to find there in his own village. When the S.S. took all men and boys, who were physically able to handle a rifle, and pressed them into service in the interest of the Third Reich he, aged only fifteen, began a new life and cut himself off completely. He never wrote a letter home to his mother and I know, because he told me, that the last news he ever learned from home was in a letter that he found on the dead body of his father when he stumbled over the corpse in a field outside Stalingrad.'

Lorna gave an involuntary shudder which did not go unnoticed by Daniel. 'What a truly ghastly shock that must have been for a teenager, however physically mature he may have been.' She stopped, abruptly, before going on. 'Surely, his mother would have written to John, as well as his father. Or did she presume that they were serving in the same S.S. unit?'

'It seems not,' replied Daniel. 'Very rarely did John even mention his wartime exploits and then it was most likely to have been when we were sharing a drink – beer for me, schnapps for him, and no one else in sight. In fact I can only recall one occasion when he let slip any item of note. He had been awarded a medal, the Iron Cross no less, for gallantry under fire when he retrieved the body of an injured soldier – except in his case there were two men to bring back. Once he had told me, he clammed up almost as if he was ashamed of his action and yet he had every reason to be proud. Can you imagine that giant of a man staggering around a battlefield with an S.S. stormtrooper under each arm?'

'Not really,' said Lorna. 'It must have been a miracle that all three were not mown down and cut in half considering the size of the target. It's funny that you never spoke about that incident before. Mind you, I'm not surprised. I've long been aware that there are times when you choose to withhold the truth from me without resorting to downright lies.'

'Ouch!' groaned Daniel. 'If that is so, and I can't dispute your observation, my intentions are well meant to spare you worry or distress. Sorry. You also know me to be secretive, never betraying a confidence.

Would you like another cup of coffee? This dream interpretation is taking longer than expected.'

'Yes please,' said Lorna, and then I'll pack my case before Jake brings Martha over. Cut the cackle.'

Fresh coffee provided, Daniel continued. 'Now that John's gone, I don't feel that I am letting him down by filling in some of the legend that he carried around with him like an invisible cloak.

'To "cut the cackle" as you so neatly put it, while the kettle was coming to the boil I remembered John's final letter to me, lodged with his solicitor and accompanying his will. I had tucked it away in my bureau. Here it is. As an accomplished speed reader you'll soon be through it.'

Lorna accepted the letter and began to read.

'Damnit Man!'

If this letter of mine ever reaches you, then I will be beyond your reach, having travelled from my cradle to my grave. If you never receive it, then I will have seen you to your grave. Yet, in my own mind, I am confident that you have it in your hand right now.

I have a premonition that my destiny precludes my ever setting foot on continental Europe again. I may be wrong – in which case you may cheerfully disregard this letter, John's last epistle! In a nutshell, if I make it over the North Sea and die somewhere there, – say my own country or one I have yet to walk across – then I will be its problem, not yours. That leaves just Baggins the Beautiful to be considered. If this letter takes a long time to reach you, Bags may have been assigned to a new master and be happily settled with him, (or her) or she may have been put down, God forbid! In which case, Amen. However, should you be reading this shortly after I have died, Bags is yours if you want her but you will have to take the necessary steps to claim her, quarantine her and bring her to High Ash. I know she would be happy in Tupshorne with her Uncle Damnit. As for me – I couldn't care less! Perhaps I should say, I'll be past caring!

In some sort of a more perfect world I would like to be buried alongside my father outside Stalingrad where I dug his grave. Even after almost sixty years, I know I could find the exact spot, so vividly does the memory live on. Perhaps the farmstead there has been built on by now and his remains scattered to the four winds. Who knows? And no one would have been able to identify his body anyway because, as you know, I kept his personal effects and his dog tags, one of which adorns Baggins' dog collar. So Stalingrad is out and if the authorities that find me wish to feed me to the lions in the nearest zoo, again I say AMEN.

However…my dear friend for so much of my life – if my premonition is correct, things are different and Baggins will still be this side of the North Sea. I leave her, Ferrers my super shovel, my Pregnant, my giant backpack and its contents, AND ME to you to dispose of as you wish. I shall be in no position to argue. Our mutual solicitor, Mr. Stint, will take care of the arrangements

57

concerning the disposal of my estate. Consult with him if necessary – I know you value his friendship as well as his legal expertise.

It seems odd, after all these years, we have never discussed a life hereafter. Maybe we recognised that our beliefs on such matters were diametrically opposed and so not open to argument. I wonder. It must be as a result of my experiences of war in all its vicious horror and brutality that I cannot discern the hand of a good and loving God at work in my life since the SS took away my innocence. It seems to me that there is a case to be made for the existence of two Gods and one is called the Devil, perhaps referred to in Trinidadian parlance as De Evil One, responsible for the pain and terror which Creation endures. So make no effort please to hand over my remains to the tender mercy of any God, lest I end up in the everlasting arms of the wrong one. If I have a soul, set it free of my human frame by letting me be consumed by fire. That done, I ask of you one last favour. I lay on you the duty of strewing my ashes under the chestnut tree we planted at the National Blacksmiths' Museum. I'm sure that will put a smile on the portrait of Vulcan, hanging in the foyer. No doubt you can remember people's reaction when the Museum opened – the question, open-mouthed, Who is that? when first seeing the God of Fire and Forge. After you've scattered what puff of dust I'm reduced to, the visitors will look at the painting and say, Whoever that chap is in the picture, I wish he'd share the joke with me. It should make a good pub sign for The Jolly Blacksmith. Don't ask anyone – just do it.

Since we first met, Daniel, we have shared some hairy, scary moments and more than a few secrets. Now that my mortal coil has been shuffled off, as the Prince of Denmark might have said, I think it right that you should know why I decided to walk home to Latvia toting Pregnant, the biggest pack you ever saw, topped with Ferrers, the massive shovel, and spurning the shelter of anything better than a roofless, ruined barn. (Except for the time you lured me onto the Bethdan when I was at a physical low ebb without any resistance to the dreaded drink you plied me with!) You know that it was Eleanore Bormann who suggested that I should go home. I'm not sure that I ever told you why I had been so devoted to her and her family since my early months in the SS. If not, then it was because it was my guilty secret, established in the most bizarre circumstances. To be brief, I killed her husband Heino during a routine bit of harmless barrack-room horseplay. He hurt me, quite accidentally of course, so I picked him up and threw him through a window. Death must have been instantaneous and, on my part, absolutely unintentional. No SS man ever messed with me after that – I had earned my nickname, Janis der Jähzorn, or in your language, John, The Fiery Temper. (I'd rather have been called Damnit.) The incident went down in SS records as an 'accident in training' but I, in my own chivalrous, naïve mind – I was, after all, only in my mid-teens at the time – decided to call on the man's widow in an attempt to explain how the tragedy had come about and to express my personal remorse. I was quite prepared to face any verbal or physical abuse which Eleanore might have thrown at me. However unlucky had been the accident to Heino, the guilt I felt was unbearable – it is, even today. Ready as I was for an onslaught, I was totally undone by the beauty who opened the door to me, listened to my pathetic self-introduction as a comrade of her late husband and then, without an opportunity for me to say why I was there, led me across her sitting room to a low table on which was displayed the citation for valour awarded on the battlefield where he lost his life. The SS had lied to her and so the truth was locked away in my heart for ever – or so I thought. I stayed with her for several days and, like a foolish youth, fell in love with her, her little girl and the unborn son she was carrying. War can make a man so cruelly vulnerable in so many ways. I'm sure you will understand that along with the guilt I carried, so my love would have to remain buried. But we remained truly loving friends from that time, corresponding over the years more like brother and sister than lover and lass with a heigh and a ho and heigh nonny no. Shakespeare would have made a fine tragedy out of such an unlikely plot. You already know that from that impossible, implausible start I had always sent her gifts of money to help with her family finances – no questions asked. Somehow the arrangement worked and in some small way my conscience was salved until, after fifty eight years, FIFTY EIGHT, (can you believe it?) the inevitable happened when she encountered another SS man who had been party to the rough-house brawl in which Heino had died. He remembered Janis der Jähzorn, that giant Latvian, all too vividly. Our friendship was smashed in a flash of enlightenment and, although she understood why I had done what I had done for her and her family for so long, I should think of her as dead. Then she told me it was time I went back to Latvia, on foot. She was never to know how hard the SS tried to frustrate my search for her. Yet I'm still glad I found her.

If this letter ever gets to you, you will know how far I have travelled to my journey's end.

But I carry a double burden of guilt on my shoulders like a heavy yoke.

Once again, you already know my rather unlikely tale of how I buried my father in the countryside outside Stalingrad. That story was gospel. In short, I fell over his body and then buried it. In an artist's terms, what I told you was only a part of a much bigger picture altogether, which I will now endeavour to reveal to you – a picture tucked away in the cellars of my mind since I uttered a brief prayer over my father's grave. Those were the days, I suppose, when there must have been a good God looking out for me, guarding my every step.

I had a vision as I looked at my father's lifeless corpse. I saw a gravestone that told me that my loving, beautiful mother Ottilija had died in childbirth along with my infant brother, Willams. There was no one alive now to welcome me home to my village.

Going back further in the story of my life, again you know how I was forcibly conscripted into the SS after witnessing the cold-blooded murder of my Uncle Zigrids by a Scharfsch tze, a sniper, while we were all lined up in the village street. The senior officer of the conscription unit was, I still think even now, appalled by the target practice perpetrated by his sniper comrade whom he named as Lutz, and promised that in due course he would be disciplined for his crime. Some hope, or fat chance you might say nowadays! The officer was trained to play by the rules, however unfair they may have been: whereas Lutz, a trigger-happy, sadistic sniper crackshot recognised no rule book and considered himself to be above the law and untouchable. He was never punished.

I cannot begin to explain or excuse the strange manner in which I took to life in the SS as a fifteen year old conscript – how I gloried in the iron discipline and power of the brotherhood. I had been adopted into the SS family when at an age ready to respond to the challenge of men already in the prime of manhood. When the SS hierarchy told me that I was part of the most fearsomely efficient warrior force the world had ever known, I believed it. It took a few years for me to understand that the Death's Head emblem of the SS was no fancy insignia. The letters D E A T H on an SS officer's cap said it all. The murderous activities of the Allgemeine SS quite were the antithesis of any imaginary crusading zeal exhibited by my Waffen SS. A brutal war may have produced an untold number of heroes, yet the idea of war itself was an invention of the devil – unheroic in the extreme. The awful truth eventually dawned on me. I had cut myself off from my Latvian roots for nothing, nothing. And there was no road home for me, the brutal SS stormtrooper that I had become.

I made it my business to find out the name of the murderer of Uncle Zigrids – not so much out of any desire for revenge, although there must have been that element present in my thinking. No, part of my intention was concerned with self-preservation in that I would not want to cross the path of such an undoubted psychopath if I could avoid it. He was called Ludwig Kaltmann – a small, insignificant man with the kind of beady eye one might expect of the holder of medals for shooting at the Berlin Olympic Games of 1936. I was to meet him once again at Stalingrad in the guise of my senior *officer, still a small man but now dedicated to discipline – you might say he had become a 'proper little Hitler!'*

What follows now, as I look back, reminds me of the grand tale of David and Goliath except that in this case I was the giant, armed with a humble shovel, while little Kaltmann had the drop on me with a Luger revolver. He knew that I was a Latvian and I knew that he hated having to look up to me when issuing orders. His record relating to service in Latvia was never open to inspection and I chose to follow my own wise counsel, not disclosing the name of my home village and certainly never mentioning how my uncle was picked off by some sniper just known as Lutz. The one and only time he managed to talk down to me was when he found me standing in the trench which I was digging out to provide a grave for my father's body using a heavy iron shovel I had found in the ruined buildings of the farmstead nearby. Hard at work, about four feet down, I was unaware of Kaltmann's stealthy approach until he spoke. He asked precisely what was I doing. The ensuing conversation seems surrealistic even now. I was at his mercy if he wished to dispose of me in a classic case of 'He dug his own grave.'

I replied that I was digging a grave for the soldier's body which he could see lying the other side of the pile of earth which I had dug out already.

He pointed out that I was going against orders. After the removal of any identification all our dead were to be left for the Russians to bury. It was demeaning for the mighty SS to bother about corpses. Then he enquired, with a steely note of sarcasm, why I had chosen to disobey strict orders.

At that point I was beginning to get emotionally upset, searching for the right German words to express the mental turmoil in which I had become embroiled. I tried to explain that the corpse was that of my father whom I had not seen since the two of us had been 'grabbed' from our little village in Latvia and conscripted into the SS. Surely he could understand that I could not leave my father's body for the Russians to abuse – as they most surely would have done.

He didn't understand. In chilling tones he ordered me to fill the hole again – immediately.

I reminded him of my nickname, Janis der Jähzorn, first of all, before suggesting that it might be unwise to try to stop me in my sad task – 'a matter of family honour' were my precise words.

Kaltmann still appeared to be oblivious to my increasing agitation because he responded by pouring scorn on my supposed reputation and then coolly informed me that the SS was my family. Was I threatening him, he asked.

In the brief time we had been confronting each other – perhaps I should say talking up and down, me in the grave, he above me – I was becoming chilled after my digging exertions. To defy an officer in the SS, I well knew, was asking for instant execution. Nevertheless, I invited him to try to force me to fill in the hole.

As I recall now, Kaltmann smiled – almost gleefully. He was actually beginning to enjoy himself. He pointed to the Luger at his belt, indicating without any question that he had me at his mercy but this would not be a moment for such a nicety. His smile hid the murderous intent behind his sniper's eyes.

I was now in a mood to give genuine substance to the myth of just how I earned my nickname. My skin was cold and clammy, my mind was stone-cold but in my heart I was incandescent with rage, (one of my favourite English phrases – a supercliché). 'Furious' doesn't begin to describe how I felt.

I'm sorry to be so longwinded about this, but I have a compunction to dredge up the details of such a climactic, definitive event in my early life which has been a burden of guilt ever since. I think I will feel purged when I have finished the outpouring of my secret to somebody after all these years. They say that's what friends are for!!

So, – slowly lifting the iron shovel up and out of the grave, I insulted him, pooh-poohing his pathetic show of strength with the revolver and calmly telling him I'd pull him to pieces with my bare hands and, being kind, I'd save him (or the bits of him!) from the busy Russian gravediggers by dropping him in with my father.

Even in the gloom, at last I detected a flicker of fear in those killer's eyes. But I had driven him too far already. I tried to suggest we should forget what had transpired; he could let me bury my dead and no more said. He could even join me in prayer over the grave. Then I made a mistake, revealing my own weakness; – I said (again my exact words, so clear to this day) 'I take no pleasure in killing.'

There was to be no going back. The fear in his eyes gave way to blind rage as he made his move. The Luger was hardly clear of its holster before that massive heavy shovel scythed through the gap between us as I swung it with all my furious might. It nearly cut Kaltmann off at the knees and he pitched forward into the grave beside me. A wild shot from the revolver passed through the material of my right trouser leg, furrowing the calf muscle but in all the excitement I scarcely felt it. My Uncle Zigrid's murderer lay crippled at my feet and his Luger had gone flying. I finished him off. My rage died with him as I buried him with father but it was only the dying light which intervened to prevent me from tearing him limb from limb as I had promised. Pragmatism finally won the day.

And so, my friend, you will now understand why I undertook my last walk home the hard way, carrying my heavy shovel on my back and with a Luger revolver at the bottom of my pack. I didn't mean to kill either Heinrich Bormann or Ludwig Kaltmann. Heino's death was purely accidental; the assassin got what he deserved only because he aroused my fury in self-defence. But still I am confused, knowing now that by attempting to punish myself I have not succeeded in washing away the blood guilt which has stained my life since my teens. I am beyond redemption.

Now I am gone, it matters not who knows what I have told you in this letter and perhaps Max Herrick, who has a collection of my stories to publish sometime, should be aware of its contents. He could never tell the difference between fact and fiction when he was recording my tales, so you can safely tell him now, that Eleanore is still alive, (I think) and Scharfsch tze Lutz is very dead.

On re-reading what I have written so far, I appear to be going round in circles. Old age I suppose!

In summary, perhaps Ferrers should return to Aidan who made most of the implement under my instruction.

Pregnant can go back to the makers for archive material if they would like it.

Keep the Luger if you can – it is not licensed and the safety catch is OFF – and isn't it lucky for you that my boots are your size!

As for Baggins – brush up your Latvian dog commands! She never appreciated having to learn English. She's a remarkable dog and now she's yours.

Given one wish, it would be for an after-life where we would meet again, tune our beautiful engines, play the glorious summer game, and together with our dogs walk the high hills of the Lake District. That's five wishes – five slices of pie in the sky. I'm getting maudlin, damnit! My innings is over. Is there a God somewhere to catch me?

P.S. If you feel I may have missed mentioning something of importance in this letter of explanation – use your imagination. See you in your dreams. J.

Lorna sank back in her chair and gave out a sigh of relief. John's final prophecy had come true – but in her dreamworld and not that of Daniel.

'What a man,' she said. 'At last I can understand and come to terms with the enormous mutual respect and affection you had for each other. But who might Aino be? There's no mention of his name in this last letter. Heino Bormann, yes. Aino, no.'

'I had to let you read the letter first,' smiled Daniel. 'It provides John's home background. And you're absolutely right – he never did mention his aunt Aino, the wife of uncle Zigrids. He must have presumed that she was long dead. Now you know she isn't. So what do we do next, Mrs Greensward?'

'Damnit, man! Check it out, of course,' said Lorna echoing John's words: she who had never called him any name other than 'Daniel' in nearly forty five years.

CHAPTER X

Suaviter In Modo, Fortiter In Re

(Gentle in manner, resolute in deed)

Hardly had Lorna and Daniel finished their cups of fresh coffee, than Martha and Jake arrived – earlier than expected.

Lorna rushed away to complete her packing while Damnit explained to the Drakes how his attempts to interpret Lorna's vivid dream of last night had resulted in them taking longer than usual over breakfast.

Jake was unamused by the excuse offered and he expressed his disapproval in no uncertain terms as one good friend may do for another good friend when pointing out the error of his ways. Telling the honest truth can often be hurtful and painful, and Damnit, stung by the vehemence of Jake's criticism, flushed with anger. In trying to justify his elucidation of Lorna's dream, he suggested that belief in another spirit world was surely a fundamental part of Christianity. Jake, even less amused now, agreed but stated bluntly that Damnit was manipulating for his own ends his well-documented method of getting off to sleep and it was a dirty trick to involve Lorna. He reminded Damnit of his dream of finding a horseshoe which had indeed come true and how it had caused him so much agony of mind. Damnit protested that when he led Lorna down the path to a decent night's sleep he had no idea or intention of involving her in his own well-documented dreamworld. Martha intervened, trying to pour oil on the troubled waters which were flowing between Jake and Daniel. With a twinkle in her eye, she asked if Daniel knew his way to Latvia.

Lorna reappeared, suitcase in hand, just as Martha posed her question and knew intuitively just what had been the subject under discussion while she was packing. Without time, as yet, to give any serious thought to the strange situation that had arisen, she suggested that the first step might be a visit to the Latvian embassy armed with any scraps of information that Daniel could dredge up with regard to the existence of Aino. Failing that, said Lorna, it might be possible in the last resort to access S.S. records of recruiting activity in Latvia in 1941. She knew that in spite of the frantic efforts of the S.S. High Command in the immediate aftermath of the war to burn all the carefully chronicled deeds and misdeeds of both wings of the S.S., Waffen and Algemeine, Simon Wiesenthal's Jewish Documentation Centre in Vienna had amassed an enormous amount of information to do with Nazi war crimes.

Daniel delivered the final words on the subject by stating that any investigations would need to be delayed at least until after St Michael the Archangel had a new priest in his pulpit. Jake merely nodded his approval secretly praying that that would be the end of the matter.

'Time to go,' announced Lorna. 'Would you be kind and put my case in the car for me, dear? Martha's as well, while you're about it.'

'I'll bring Martha's,' said Jake. 'Its a bit on the heavy side for Damnit. He'll need all his strength to cope while you're away, Lorna. I expect you'll be beavering away at church, inside and outside, tarting the place up before the interviewees come face to face with the judging panel, eh, old friend.'

Daniel laughed. 'You've obviously forgotten that you're staying here while Martha's away. Walking all three dogs and creating culinary delights for the satisfaction of my ravenous appetite will be your lot while, as you say, I shall be beavering away. If I dress you up in disguise you can help me as well by polishing the brasses. You'd have to play mute, otherwise Muriel would rumble you.'

'Come on, Lorna,' said Martha. 'Take me away before our men get too far out of hand. Will they ever grow up?'

As the Volvo moved away down the drive Damnit called out. 'Remember – plenty of lavender perfume.'

Just after noon, Martha at the wheel, the two lady investigators arrived in Ravengrigg, a town of some three thousand souls, five pubs, three major denominational churches and one post office. The car came to a halt a few yards inside the town boundary sign and Martha turned to Lorna.

'What are we going to do now?' she asked. 'I'm thinking it's a long time since breakfast.'

'In that case,' said Lorna, 'let's find our B and B, unpack as best we can and then find a bite to eat before we go looking for the church. "Saint Who" is it?'

'Saint Thomas,' said Martha. 'Hang on – that road over there on our right calls itself Church Road. Could be what we are looking for. Turn right when we move off and we can check out the building.'

One hundred yards down Church Road stood the church of St Thomas and in the roadside gutter stood a line of eight 'police – no parking' traffic cones, spaced out, three yards apart from each other.'

'I've had a wicked thought,' said Lorna. 'And you're hungry.'

Martha laughed. 'I know what your wicked thought is. I'm not so ravenous that I can't see the hidden possibilities of a funeral when it comes to the provision of a hearty snack. My veil is the top item in my suitcase. Where's yours?'

'Easily accessed,' replied Lorna. 'We'll find our lodgings after the service. There must be a quiet corner reasonably near where we can make ourselves presentable as well as parking the car. The church looks as if it is up to date enough to have a loo if we get desperate.'

'It's fortunate,' said Martha 'that without being in collusion before setting off this morning, we are both soberly clad for this time of year. Let's hope that the deceased left instructions such as "Please – no black." I do hope that he or she approved of lavender perfume.'

On entering the church, they were offered a beautiful service sheet, specially printed for the occasion, by a sidesman tall enough to look down on the above average mortal. Lorna was struck immediately by the timbre of the gently modulated voice as he welcomed the two fragrant ladies and offered to escort them to a pew of their choice. Martha meanwhile was aware that despite the disparity in their heights they were under scrutiny by two sapphire blue eyes set in a craggy face that seemed to be composed entirely of laughter lines. For a moment she wondered if their veils were giving a high enough degree of opacity to preserve their disguise.

Once they were seated, Lorna leant towards Martha and whispered. 'What do we do if by some unkind act of God this funeral is to be conducted by a guest vicar and it is our man's day off? It may not be a good idea to ask the sidesman. Is the name of the officiating priest on the service sheet? Yes. There it is. The Reverend Reuben Ossian. Did you happen to see the name on the church noticeboard by the lychgate as we came in?'

'Same name,' said Martha, 'followed by a string of qualifications or the initials thereof. They don't mean a thing, of course, idiocy and genius can be unidentical twins. Let's hope he's married at least. That would mean his feet are on the ground – family wise. I'm not sure that it was such a good idea after all to send us on this mission without being fully briefed on the personal details of the three candidates we are due to observe. I suppose it means that we are truly unprejudiced – that is to say we are working in the dark and exercising our famous feminine intuition in search of enlightenment. We'd better stop this idle chatter. Looking around us I see that the church is about two thirds full. That's either an indicator of a dutiful shepherd of the local flock or a pointer to the esteem in which the deceased was held. We're about to find out. Here comes the funeral director leading the pall-bearers and the chief mourners, with the Rev. Reuben bringing up the rear.'

'I wish we had a mini-tape recorder, said Lorna. 'I bet we miss something important.'

'Never mind,' said Martha, 'we'll manage between us, that's for sure. Let play begin!'

A host of late arrivals, delayed by the search for a car parking space within reasonable proximity to Saint Thomas's Church, surged in so quickly following the vicar that by the time he reached the well known quotation from St Paul's first epistle to Timothy, 'For we brought nothing into this world, and it is certain we can carry nothing out,' the church was full.

The service itself was a clever blend of the traditional and the modern; solemn reverence with an undeniable sense of celebration of a life well lived. The two veiled visitors were silent as they returned to the Volvo, both aware that they had been chance witnesses to a special occasion in the parish life of the St Thomas's faithful. Before uttering the closing prayers, the vicar drew the attention of the congregation to the final paragraph on the service sheet in which it was stated that it was the earnest wish of the bereaved family that, following the private burial in the church graveyard, all those who had gathered together in church to make their farewells to the late Patriarch, should repair to the Saint Thomas's Church Hall to continue the celebration of his life over a light buffet lunch. Lorna and Martha would have been prepared to miss out on the beanfeast to avoid any awkward questions concerning their joint presence at the funeral, but hunger decreed otherwise and they resolved to avail themselves of any hospitality that was on offer before beating as seemly a retreat as possible. After a hasty discussion they decided that if asked to explain their presence at the funeral they would infer that in actual fact they were researching their family background in the belief, mistaken or otherwise, that an ancestor of long standing had been laid to rest in the church graveyard when they became caught up, so to speak, in the excitement of a burial of the moment. Christian solidarity demanded that they should attend the funeral service and the farewell buffet but the brief interment rites were an optional extra that they chose to forgo.

Saint Thomas's Church Hall, no more than a brisk two minute walk from the church, turned out to be of ultra-modern construction; light and airy with the potential to be turned into a small concert hall when such an amenity was required. The high quality buffet indicated the presence of excellent catering facilities coupled with a dedicated team of parishioners, accustomed to producing all kinds of meals from tea and buns to a full-blown banquet.

The two fragrant ladies found their way to a small table in a corner of the hall furthest away from the main door, from which vantage point they could observe the various patterns of behaviour of a good number of the folk who had attended the funeral. Lorna estimated that perhaps some eighty people from a congregation of over three hundred had chosen to take up the offer of hospitality from the family of the deceased and one of the eighty was the Reverend Reuben Ossian who proceeded to work his way around and through the assembly in the same way that a seasoned political campaigner might.

'What a performance!' breathed Martha in admiration. 'You'd think he was related to the lot of them, he seems so at ease. All we're short of is a few babies for him to kiss and then he can count on my vote. Do you think we should make our getaway before we appear on the Reverend's radar?'

'I'm not sure,' murmured Lorna. 'This is too good an opportunity to miss to showcase our acting skills and unless I'm mistaken Reuben has just got wind of our perfume. Here we go.'

'Sorry,' said Martha, 'I'm not ready for this. The "Ladies" is my refuge in the passage to our right. You're on your own, luvvy.'

'Coward,' hissed Lorna, 'we can't fall at the first hurdle.' But Martha was halfway to her destination before she could make any further comment and the Reverend Reuben was laying a gentle hand on her shoulder. From her position, seated at the corner table, she looked up into the eyes of the quarry that she and Martha were hunting down. Safely behind the anonymity of the veil, she noted the pale blue Sapphire intensity of Reuben's eyes which reminded her of Richard Widmark, her favourite American film star, acting the role of Colonel Jim Bowie, inventor of the eponymous knife, who was killed at the Siege of the Alamo. He spoke, a whimsical smile playing between his mouth and his eyes.

'You are not of my flock or I would know you. Have you come a long way to attend Herb's funeral?'

Lorna crossed her fingers before replying, in no way savouring the thought of telling the proverbial pack of lies, even in pursuit of finding out the truth.

'As a matter of fact, vicar, my sister-in-law Virginia and I are what you might call accidental mourners in that as we are researching the ancestry of our late husbands in the graveyards of this part of Northumberland we pitched up here today, just in time for what, if I might say, was a very fine funeral. We are not ghouls I can assure you but since we were widowed we find some small solace in sharing in the efforts of others to address a family loss.' She paused, anxious not to embellish her story too much, ahead of the inevitable return of Martha who would have no inkling of how their presence had been explained.

'I'm pleased to see that the solemnity of the occasion has not spoiled your appetite in any way,' remarked the vicar, drily. 'Our church catering committee are equal to any challenge and post-funeral fodder is their forte. I trust that you made a suitable contribution to the funeral collection before leaving the church. This organic stuff doesn't come cheap so they tell me. Pardon my facetiousness. You are very welcome in Saint Thomas's, and your sister-in-law, who I see approaching, for any reason you may choose. And if you are still in the area on Sunday, I shall hope to see you in church again. Choral eucharist begins at eleven o'clock, followed by coffee and a biscuit for those who may wish to linger. If your researches throw up any ancestral revelation there's a chance you might meet a distant relation. Now that would be exciting. And I can also arrange access to the parish archives if need be.'

'I am a believer in miracles, vicar, chimed in Martha, who had returned in time to hear his last few sentences. 'And we both find great comfort and joy in a sung eucharist, don't we Rose, dear? Judging by the way the funeral congregation sang, your choir must be worth hearing. Is that charming sidesman who greeted us in church a choir member? He certainly can sing and we caught your tenor as well.'

'He is indeed,' replied the vicar. 'If I catch a really nasty cold I can rely on him to sing my responses. In fact I've learnt an awful lot from him over so many years. But he will be away on Sunday on an important scouting mission.

Now if you will excuse me, I must go my pastoral way. See you on Sunday, perhaps?'

'Definitely,' replied Virginia and Rose Waters, as one.

Hardly had the vicar resumed his tour of duty when the two lady investigators decided that it was a suitable moment for them to leave. Martha was keen to use the side door as a means of avoiding any unnecessary confrontation, whereas Lorna, having survived her first audience with the Reverend Ossian, was ready and bold enough to face any further chance meeting with confidence.

'Leave the talking to me, Virginia dear,' ordered Rose, 'nod your head and murmur in agreement. Your chance to engage will come on Sunday.'

Martha could only listen in admiration as Lorna made their farewells with such phrases as 'so uplifting an occasion', 'those comforting words from the vicar' and 'what a privilege it had been to be present at Herb's send-off.' Leaving behind them a waft of lavender perfume lingering in Saint Thomas's Church hall, they soon found their way to their B and B where they were able to unwind over a relaxing cup of tea provided by a genial landlady.

'Time to take stock, I think,' said Lorna. 'Have we seen already enough of our Reuben in action to allow us to go home early? At this point, I have to admit – I am impressed. Do we really need to stay until Sunday? We'd save Violet a few bob if we cut and run tomorrow.'

'Well,' said Martha, choosing her words carefully, 'first impressions aren't always to be relied on and part of our remit must be to play the devil's advocate, don't you think? Our B and B still has to be paid for the two nights that Damnit booked, so Violet's accounts won't show any change whether we opt to go or stay. We might witness a different performance altogether on Sunday. Meanwhile there's all day tomorrow for us to gauge local opinion of the Rev. Reuben. I suggest that we make as early a start as possible, depending on what breakfast is served, then off to Bamburgh, an easy drive – a bracing walk along the shore to blow the cobwebs away – then back to Ravensrigg for mid-morning coffee prior to wandering round town picking up any vibes we can, starting with our landlady.'

'Agreed,' said Lorna, without a second thought. 'But we can start with our landlady at breakfast. And before we go to Bamburgh we ought to check if there is a "coffee morning" event at Saint Thomas's. You never know – we might meet that lovely sidesman again. I'm sure he had his eye on you or maybe it was your perfume that was getting to him.'

Martha laughed. 'He would have been disappointed if I had removed my veil. Mind you, I suspect that he treats all the ladies with that charming courtesy – just like Daniel.'

During breakfast next morning they gently quizzed their landlady on the subject of Saint Thomas's place and status in the community. From her personal agnostic point of view, she spoke in glowing terms of the body of folk responsible for the church's wellbeing and its Christian outreach beyond the confines of the parish buildings. Then, without any prompting from her guests she admitted that if ever she was to be tempted to affirm her baptismal vows it would be because of her admiration for the Reverend Ossian, a shining example of a practical, practising Man of God. Sensing that there was more to this wavering agnosticism than mere disinterest in matters spiritual, Martha dared to ask if there was a reason or even several reasons. The reply astonished Lorna and Martha. Their landlady, in her strange way of thinking, was a septannocredic, believing that the power of seven was paramount and that a seven year cycle was more than just an itch for married men to scratch. It appeared that the Reverend Ossian's predecessor had taken seven long painful years to reduce the congregation of Saint Thomas's Church, Ravensrigg to a dispirited rump of Doubting Thomases many of whom, the landlady among them, had laid aside their steadfast faith. It had taken nearly seven years of dedicated shepherding by Reuben to restore the church community to robust health. When his full seven years were fulfilled, then the landlady would return to the fold and reawaken her dormant faith, because it suited her.

Lorna wondered what would happen should Reuben fall short of the magical seven year stint and be chosen to fill Jake's pulpit in Tupshorne. Did he have an Achilles heel? Why should he wish to leave now?

'Can you pinpoint any particular reason for his success, as you see it?' asked Martha. 'A secret weapon perhaps?'

'Oh yes,' answered the landlady with a broad smile. 'Her name is Minerva Jemima – a goddess in her own right. Mrs Ossian.'

The rest of the day passed without incident. The walk along the Bamburgh shore proved to be an excellent lead-in to the half hoped for coffee morning that materialised in the church hall in aid of an Indian orphanage, linked to Saint Thomas's. The vicar was conspicuous by his absence this time, an absence explained when the coffee waiters cleared everyone out of the hall before midday. The caterers required the main room for the wedding breakfast to be served at four o'clock. Reuben was ironing his ceremonial cope as he practised his wedding address – no notes for him – he believed in concentrating all his thoughts on the couple kneeling before him.

Nothing of any significance came to light from their quiet socialising at the coffee morning, mainly because the overwhelming majority of the coffee drinkers were tourists and not Ravensrigg residents, but knowing that a church wedding was imminent they discussed the possibility of attending the event as curious bystanders.

'I'm inclined to give this wedding a miss,' said Lorna, 'and we certainly can't invite ourselves to the reception in the same way that we gatecrashed the funeral buffet.'

'You're right of course. Three days on the trot, being seen in the same church might well raise suspicions in the wrong quarters,' Martha replied. 'We know that Reuben is expecting us tomorrow, so let's be content with that. We'll need to keep the lowest of profiles and not engage with the congregation beyond "Good morning" and "Goodbye". If Minerva Jemima happens to be there we'd better stay clear of her if we can because, as a vicar's wife, she is the most likely person to see through our veiled pretence.' She paused for a moment before continuing. 'We don't know if there are any Ossian offspring, do we?'

'No, we don't,' said Martha. 'Nor if they have a dog. It crossed my mind this morning when we were walking along the sands at Bamburgh, what extra fun it would have been if we'd had our dogs with us. Our landlady will have the answers if we but mention the subjects *en passant* at breakfast time tomorrow.'

'That's all right then,' said Lorna. 'We'll make a speedy getaway after church and with a clear run be home for lunch. I'll ring Daniel this evening and enquire what's cooking.'

Martha grinned at her. 'I think, Lorna dear, you have forgotten who is the High Ash chef in your absence. Let me speak to Jake about the menu while you are updating our report.'

Their final morning was one of anticlimax. The vicar had come down with a touch of summer 'flu and the choral eucharist was celebrated by a very confident lady curate. Acting on some rather sketchy information gleaned from the landlady the two veiled investigators were able to identify Minerva Jemima Ossian and the vicarage kids, Helen and Troy.

'It would appear that Reuben and Minerva enjoy showing their shared sense of humour when it comes to naming their children,' Martha remarked as they began their journey home. 'Judging by her present silhouette it can't be long before they consult Homer's Iliad again.'

'Well, there are plenty of characters to select a name from,' said Lorna, 'as long as they don't settle on "Horse". But how lucky we were to drop in on Friday's funeral and see the man in action, never mind actually meeting him face to face. The only knowledge we've been able to glean from today's no-show is based on the ambience we experienced in church. I don't know about you but I felt almost at home, so warm was our welcome.'

'Absolutely,' said Martha. 'As a loyal wife I can't help but compare any other church I attend with those where Jake has been vicar. This one is remarkable. Even with the curate in charge, that choral eucharist was a magnificent celebration of Christian harmony, never mind the lovely music. Did you pick up on anything else of note?'

'I think so,' replied Lorna, 'and I hope that as a vicar's wife you will agree. I was struck by the obvious concern that the whole congregation had for their absent priest even if it was caused by a spot of 'flu. If their prayers are answered he'll be back in his pulpit in time for Evensong.'

'There must be a flaw in the man somewhere,' said Martha. 'Makes me wonder why he fancies leaving his flock for pastures new.'

'Perhaps we'll never find out,' was Lorna's final comment, 'unless he's just one more septannocredic.'

CHAPTER XI

Altissima Quaeque Flumina Minimo Sono Labi

(All the deepest rivers flow by the quietest)

It was Sunday 24 June and Churchwarden Damnit Greensward was carrying out his wardenly duties prior to the Sunday morning Communion Service, putting up hymn numbers on the board, sorting out the readings and gospel for the day in the lectern bible and generally ensuring that everything should flow smoothly for visiting celebrant, the Reverend Stanley Freeborne. Timothy Walsh meanwhile was busy checking the lists of those parishioners who would merit mention in the prayers of intercession, perhaps on account of current ill-health or the anniversary of a death in the community. Stanley Freeborne arrived fifteen minutes before the appointed time that the service was due to start and was followed closely into church by another man whom Timothy took to be a friend of the celebrant. He greeted both of them but was surprised when Stanley, well known in Saint Michael's, walked straight down to the vicar's vestry while his apparent companion found his way to a pew just a few paces away from the choir stalls.

As Damnit and Timothy passed by each other in a side aisle Timothy remarked quietly that the visitor sitting close to the choir must be a tourist anxious to sound out the reputation of Stephanie Potts' choristers. He was only partly right. As the service proceeded, the stranger joined the choir in their singing of everything but the anthem, and he did it all without the use of words or music. Seated at the organ, Spotty Potts was impressed. She had been praying for some years that a decent tenor might find his way to her choral realm and hardly had she finished playing the retiring voluntary before she was off the organ stool and bearing down on the new arrival – surely heaven-sent. Her opening question was direct and not open to equivocation.

'I'm Stephanie Potts, mistress of the choristers and general musical dogsbody of St Michael the Archangel. If you're here in Tupshorne for a while, however brief, would you care to join us?' She looked him up and down, a suspicion of a smile flickering in her eyes. 'We might need to lower the hem of our longest cassock to accommodate you or add a frill if you would rather. We're the finest church choir in this dale – some say in the Dales – but tenors like you don't grow on trees. You should have asked for a copy of the anthem as an instant enrolment form.'

'Thank you,' answered the visitor, 'I take that as a compliment.;' Then rather peremptorily, 'I am here for only a few days but my movements are very vague, I'm afraid. I'll let you know. A 'phone number perhaps?'

'I'll write it on a service sheet for you,' said Spotty.

'No need. Just sing your number and I will memorise it,' was the reply.

Six notes later and he was on his way out of church moving quickly as if on a mission, and he bumped into Damnit. The collision looked to be accidental but it caught Damnit off-balance and he all but fell over.

'Steady,' said Daniel, 'you can't be that keen to escape the clutches of our director of music, surely?'

'I'm sorry, the sun shining through the window blinded me for a moment. I should have been more careful,' replied the visitor. 'The organist was in no way to blame, I assure you. In fact, she offered me a place in the choir for as long as I happen to be in the area.'

'Good for her,' said Daniel. 'She certainly knows her musical onions, and I heard you singing as well. You can trust Stephanie's judgement – unlike me, she's blessed with absolute pitch, whatever that might mean.' He paused. 'So are you here for a while?'

'Just a brief visit, I'm afraid. A week at most. I can always come again, depending on how much wildlife I find. Birdwatching is one of my hobbies, in a very amateur way.' It was the visitor's turn to pause before continuing. 'You have the air of a churchwarden about you. Am I right? If I am, you must be a very busy man as I understand it in the current interregnum.'

'Right on both counts,' said Damnit with a wry smile. 'Luckily I'm not alone in carrying the load of responsibility. You've met Timothy Walsh as you came in. I'm Greensward.'

'Interesting name,' mused the visitor with a quizzical glance. 'Can't be many Greenswards to the square mile, I imagine. You're only the second I've come across. Does "High Ashes" mean anything to you by any chance?'

'My prep school was High Ashes and "High Ash" is the name of my house,' observed Daniel. 'Why?'

'Bullseye!' chuckled his inquisitor. 'You'll remember Sambo, Mrs Ashley and Hyperhistrionics – and Queenie, the matron, then.'

'Sure. Happy days, no responsibilities, marvellous time of life and remarkable people,' replied Damnit. 'So should I know you?'

'That depends on your memory for childhood trivialities and the importance you place on them. Do you remember a fat little French boy arriving in early-1947?'

'Vaguely,' said Damnit, somewhat puzzled. The penny had yet to drop. 'It was a long time ago.'

'Well, you should remember me. I was Silas Kinnon Beaune, that chubby lad you extricated from a bramble bush – or it could have been a wild rose – when you were on track to retain your trophy in the Age Cross Country Championship that Lent term. You threw away the chance of athletics glory to free and comfort a very tearful and unhappy little new boy. I could never forget that. Heroic, it was. Now do you remember? I was nicknamed "Skinny."'

'"Skinandbone," of course,' laughed Daniel, having picked up the thread of the questioning at last. 'Let's see – 1947–2001 – fifty four years to change from a roly-poly pudding to a lanky, not to mention skinny, senior citizen. I suppose we ought to shake hands on the strength of this coincidental reacquaintance.'

As they shook hands, Damnit looked up into the face of this stranger, now revealed as a childhood school fellow, and wondered for one fleeting moment if he detected a flicker of amusement in the pale blue eyes that met his gaze.

'I'm afraid I'll have to cut short this impromptu trip down Memory Lane if you'd excuse me while I say goodbye to our visiting priest. We must meet up again before you leave the area. You probably remember me as "Damnit", but I can't call you "Skinny". Enlighten me.'

'My mother never called me any other name but Silas. That'll do. Do you always answer to "Damnit?"'

'Yes, since 1942. But I too was "Daniel" to my mother and father, and my wife. Otherwise "Oy, you", guarantees my attention. Now, how are you fixed for lunch today? I'm sure we can set another place.'

'It's a nice idea, thank you, but I'm booked in already at a pub in Hawes.'

'Here's an offer you can't refuse then,' said Damnit. 'Church here next Sunday followed by lunch at High Ash where I can promise you a big surprise. I know another of Sambo's old boys living further up Yowesdale. I'll see if he would care to join us.'

'Sounds great fun to me,' said Silas enthusiastically. 'I'll be here. Would you ask Miss Potts to find me the longest cassock in the wardrobe?'

'Consider it done,' said Damnit. 'Spotty will be thrilled.'

'We might bump into one another during the week – you never know,' said Silas. 'Meanwhile I look forward to next Sunday.'

They shook hands again on parting and Daniel set off for the vicar's vestry only to meet Timothy in the process of escorting Stan Freeborne to the door. Both churchwardens saw Stan safely to his car so completing the proper courtesies extended to all visiting preachers.

Spotty had left church several minutes earlier, humming cheerfully the tune of 'Someday he'll come along, the man I...'

When Jake realised that Lorna and Martha would be home in time for a late-lunch he reasoned that if he could convene the remaining members of the Magnificent Seven round the dining table, then the Ravensrigg report would be heard, hot off the press. Thus it was that Daniel, Violet, Timothy and Muriel walked together from St Michael's to High Ash in good time to welcome Lorna and Martha, after an incident-free drive back to Tupshorne.

Jake had prepared a buffet style meal based on various sliced cold meats, even more various salad plant leaves, brightened up with a fiery red dish of tomato, red pepper and onion vinaigrette. At Violet's suggestion, on a lovely warm June afternoon, the dining table was abandoned in favour of a couple of garden tables and over a leisurely lunch the two lavender laced ladies retailed their findings.

'Sounds good,' said Timothy.

'Sounds too good to be true,' was Damnit's comment.

'I like the sound of the family,' said Violet, 'as well as the loving concern for his wellbeing that you sensed in the congregation when he was off poorly. And as for the children, Helen and Troy – that's some sense of humour. As for the one to come, I've always liked Agamemnon or Clytemnestra – good for a spelling test.'

Muriel joined in the discussion. 'You've not mentioned any vicarage animals so far. Did your landlady have any info on that front? Children's pets perhaps?'

'Not even a hamster as far as she knew,' said Martha.

'I said he sounded too good to be true,' repeated Daniel. 'As Martha said earlier, there had to be a flaw in the man somewhere.'

'Steady on,' said Timothy, 'that's a bit harsh, Damnit. We can't expect everybody to be as keen on dogs as we are.'

'Quite right,' said Muriel, 'we're mad about dogs in Tupshorne, never mind being keen. They might have a pet in mind when the youngest starts school a few years hence. If they do land up here, one thing's for sure, they'll not be short of advice in that department.'

'In that case, we must look elsewhere for a potential flaw. I'm suspicious of apparent perfection,' grumbled Daniel. Jake said nothing as conversation died in the wake of Daniel's voiced misgiving.

Violet broke the hiatus and changed the subject. 'Well, I think our investigators have made an excellent start and merit a well-deserved day of rest tomorrow. By the way, Daniel, who was that stranger that you were chatting to after service? It looked like quite an animated conversation to me.'

'You don't miss a thing, do you?' said Daniel, before addressing Jake directly. 'Do you remember Lent term 1947 when that rotund little French boy arrived at High Ashes? We called him "Skinny."' Jake pursed his lips and looked thoughtful for a moment until a flash of recognition lit up his features. 'That winter! Of course I remember. We even helped ourselves to slices from the cheeses in the larder using Tell's long bladed sheath knife and reaching through the open window. Never tasted better Cheddar after we'd toasted it on the brazier in the lavatories. As for Skinny, he was the star of Hyperhistrionics that year, the first year actors were joined by singers. Voice of an angel by Mrs Askey's reckoning. Are you saying it was Skinny in church?'

Damnit laughed. 'It was and it wasn't. His puppy fat is long gone, he's as thin as a rake and tall as a beanpole but as Sambo said in our Latin lessons that term "*Audivi illum canentem,*" I heard him sing.'

'We all heard him sing, this morning,' stated Violet with sarcastic emphasis on the word 'all', 'So Daniel, how did he roll up at St Michael's?'

'He's on a birdwatching holiday for a few days. If you want to know any more about him, come to lunch next Sunday. I've invited him. Spotty has persuaded him to sing with the choir so we're in for a treat. By the way Jake, I haven't mentioned you by name, just that there is another High Ashesian living updale.'

'I suppose you're expecting me to cook for you again,' grumbled

Jake. 'Well, you can light the brazier and I'll toast the cheese, but I don't think we need to eat in the loo after all these years.'

'Next Sunday is a non-starter for me,' said Violet. 'Bert and Freda Alderwood have invited me out to lunch – a rare event in their calendar, so I daren't cry off.'

'We're also absent then,' said Muriel. 'It's the Yowesdale Society's Summer Lunch Party up at Middinside. I'm surprised you're not going Jake, what with you and Martha becoming Middinsiders now you're retired.'

'I would have gone if it weren't for the fact that I'm contracted to cook for Damnit, damn it – and Martha will be away with Lorna on their fact finding tour. Can't do with Damnit starving can we? Perhaps you should invite Spotty if Skinny is going to sing for her.'

'I think not,' said Daniel. 'Three "Old Ashesians" would be altogether too much for her.'

'By the way,' asked Jake, 'what does Skinny do for a living?'

'Never thought to enquire,' replied Daniel. 'We'll find the answer to that question with our toasted cheese next Sunday.'

CHAPTER XII

Aut Non Tentaris
Aut Perfice

(Either do not attempt or finish the job)

Monday 25 June had been decreed a day of rest for Lorna and Martha, the two Tupshorne contender inspectors. Their report on the state of affairs in Ravensrigg had been received and adopted by the five stay-at-home members of the Magnificent Seven with approbation and some good measure of admiration. 'Chutzpah' was Timothy's word for their gatecrashing antics when they had seized the opportunity to see their quarry in action at a funeral.

Jake was quietly grateful that their B and B landlady had been such a mine of information, despite her professing to be a septannocredic, a word unknown to him. As a true Cambridge blue Classical Scholar he felt bound to question its authenticity. As a falsely construed word it had to rank with Hyperhistrionics, invented by the Reverend Samuel Bone, his High Ashes headmaster, and Mrs Askey his English teacher. Hyperhistrionics, half Latin and half Greek, had restored his sanity following the sudden death of his mother in November 1944. But the concept of Hyperhistrionics had been the brainwave of a ten year old schoolfriend, a certain Daniel Tiltstone Greensward.

Daniel himself wondered if their scouting endeavours had been blessed with a little too much providence. Had it been too easy as a first time exercise? The next two visits would be bound to be more testing surely. He made a mental note to telephone Lorna at least once a day while she and Martha were away to reassure her that the backup from Tupshorne was solidly in support. Ever the optimist, he had to admit that trying times might very well be on the way even if not imminent.

While Lorna was indulging in a siesta after lunch – the day was flaming June at its best – Daniel made a call to Aidan Ferrers in Ravenstonedale to arrange a meeting of the trustees of the National Blacksmiths' Museum in Preston at the museum itself for Wednesday

27 June. At such short notice, no other trustee was invited or even expected to attend. A meeting over lunch was swiftly agreed.

A second telephone call followed hard on the first. Daniel made an appointment to see Mr Nathaniel Ross, the Preston physician consulted by John Smith before he set out on his doomed epic walk home to Latvia. On instruction from Mr Ross himself, his secretary was able to alter the afternoon schedule to accommodate Daniel. It would not have been the first occasion that an eminent specialist had made time for a distinguished engineer and, after all, his beloved daughter Rachel was Daniel's stepdaughter-in-law.

Nathaniel's innate Jewishness demanded that family ties and values be honoured – with or without step – and Damnit was in his estimation a most estimable fellow. He would enjoy carrying out a medical MOT on the one time director of engine research from Rolls Royce.

Neither telephone call lasted longer than two minutes and Daniel was surprised when Lorna entered the sitting room, refreshed from her snooze, and enquired who had been on the line.

'I was talking to Aidan,' said Daniel. 'It appears there's a meeting at short notice, of the N.B.M. trustees, or at least those who can make it, on Wednesday. He says we have a high-ranking Canadian visitor intent on setting up something similar to John's N.B.M. brainchild over the pond and wishing to see how we operate and no doubt picking our brains such as they are. It shouldn't take long – with a bite of lunch thrown in – and then, while I'm in Preston I'm going to drop in on Nathaniel for a social chat. I must say I found him to be a most agreeable fellow from our first encounter, as indeed did John. It was a strange trick of fortune that when I told John to have a thorough medical examination before setting off for Latvia, it was Nathaniel Ross to whom he went, who then became your Douglas's father-in-law. I'm sorry you won't be able to come with me but you'll be on the scent in Cornwall with Martha on Wednesday. It's a shame, but when you report back from your western and southern wanderings, I'll be able to tell you all about Douglas and Rachel from Nathaniel's point of view. So much for my call to him.'

Lorna looked a little disgruntled if not a trifle suspicious. 'I wish you had waited until I was awake. I'd quite like to have spoken with Nathaniel myself. He might have some wise words to say about my disturbed sleep patterns. Maybe I should have had a check-up before embarking on this southern safari with Martha. I'm sure Nathaniel would allow me a family discount.' She gave Daniel a knowing smile before continuing. 'In fact dear, I'm not convinced that you've been on top form since we looked into that volcano. If we both have a proper check I can ask him about a possible "two for the price of one" deal.'

'Don't you dare,' said Daniel, disquiet in his voice. 'I look in my shaving mirror and see a picture of health – for my age anyway. And I thought the "Greensward Off To Sleep" technique had cured your problem. What's more, as a Yorkshire-man I'm bound to question any special offer of "two for one" and ask if it would be brass well spent.'

'Have it your way then,' replied Lorna. 'But the next time Douglas and Rachel come to visit, we must invite Nathaniel over as well.' She gave Daniel a knowing wink. 'As for the expenses of medical examinations, do remember that I'm a Lancashire lass, not constrained by your brass anxieties. In fact, although we're only newly married – or perhaps because of that fact – you have no idea how rich I might be. I could own a diamond mine for all you know but I choose not to wear my diamonds except in my dreams.'

Daniel sensed that an awkward moment had passed by and Lorna's qualms were allayed.

He laughed. 'That's good, and it all goes to show that after such a long wait I didn't marry you for money. You might be a multimillionairess for all I care. "*Amor vincit omnia*" as Julius Caesar said.'

'Oh, really!' said Lorna. 'You and your Latin quotations. I fear your homework has let you down. Not Caesar, but Virgil who wrote in Eclogues "*Omnia vincit amor, et nos cedamus amori*. Love conquers all things, let us too yield to love."'

'Just before we do,' grinned Daniel, 'slip into your diamond encrusted rubber gloves, Love, and pop the kettle on. Too much Virgil makes a man thirsty. If there's a slice of wedding cake left, I'm prepared to share it – otherwise it'll still be in its tin at Christmas.'

It was while pouring a second cup of tea that Lorna chose to strike a more serious note in the conversation which until then had been the usual inconsequential chat about matters of minor importance.

'I can't forget my dream about John's aunt Aino. What are we going to do about her?'

'You ordered me to "check it out" – your own words,' said Daniel. 'Actually, [he drew the syllables out] you said "Damnit, man! Check it out, of course" The first time you have ever called me, Damnit.'

'No, no,' laughed Lorna. 'You misinterpreted my intent. I was echoing your famous word to Sambo when you acquired your infamous nickname. Rest assured, you're just my Daniel. So, any progress on the Aino front while I've been away?'

'Only sort of. The first night you were away I tried to dream my way into our Latvian conundrum – without any success. And then – a flash of inspiration I like to think – I rang the Latvian embassy and spoke to a delightfully helpful and understanding, young-sounding lady by the name of Cirponis. She was very optimistic about the prospect of digging up John's roots. I had the impression, right or wrong, that the embassy was well accustomed to dealing with queries such as mine. The upshot is that I am to telephone the embassy in a week's time and speak to Miss Cirponis again. Fingers crossed. Incidentally, she didn't think a trawl through S.S. records, such as they are, would throw any useful light on the matter when I made the suggestion. I very nearly told her that I knew the S.S. would never have attributed the disappearance of Lutz, the sniper who murdered Uncle Zigrids, to an enraged Janis Kalējs wielding a shovel.

'If we do feel committed or even honour bound to go to Latvia to see aunt Aino what language can we use?' asked Lorna. 'You're no linguist, Daniel and I don't suppose you picked up any Latvian from John over all the years you knew him.'

'Quite wrong,' said Daniel with something akin to a smirk. 'John gave me some "dog commands" in Latvian in case Baggins should have ended up in my care. I've lost them – which no doubt doesn't surprise you. The only word I can recall is *lernem* which means "slow down" or "gently". John talked to his engines when tuning and that was his main instruction. Baggins knows *lernem*. One solitary phrase, a road sign, does stick in my mind because it used to make me laugh. I can't spell it, but phonetically it is *lairnem patiltoo shah oodens apoksha* – it means, "Slow down, bridge ahead with water beneath". There you are, I know you'd smile. But don't worry about it. I'm pretty certain that your German will be easily understood and I will help by keeping quiet.'

'Thanks a lot,' said Lorna, 'for a very dubious vote of confidence in my rather rusty linguistic abilities. But, I have a funny feeling that I won't be needed. I could be wrong.'

'I hope you're right,' mused Daniel. 'It could be a *patiltoo* too far.'

CHAPTER XIII

Res Ipsa Loquitur

(The matter speaks for itself)

'Your Volvo is such an easy car to drive and so comfortable to relax in as a passenger,' said Martha as she and Lorna wandered, barefoot, along the beach at Bude, 'that I think we could have managed the distance from Yowesdale in one day. What do you think? It was a bit of a luxury spending a night in Worcester.'

'I'm inclined to agree,' said Lorna. 'The Volvo always brings a smile to my heart because, as a means of getting from A to B it was definitely Matthew's baby. A work colleague of his owned a Volvo estate car which he used to take his family of wife and four little children camping on the Med. He modified the space behind the front seats so that when converted it became a flat bed with storage beneath. Seat belts were not compulsory in those days and a lot of equipment was carried on a roof rack. The family would go Dover Calais in the evening, put the kids down to sleep – a bit like sardines in a can – then motor down to somewhere near Saint Tropez overnight, only stopping to take black coffee. It wouldn't be allowed nowadays. So that's why I now have Matthew's Volvo. I sometimes wonder what happened to that family. The father must have been crazy. But you're right – it is a pleasure to drive – and I feel sure now that we won't need Jake to come down to West Sussex to help with our return journey. Let's see how we go. It's half past twelve now. How's your appetite? This sea air has made me quite peckish.'

'Me too,' said Martha. 'Surprising really, because we both had a magnificent breakfast. I fancy fish and chips to take away; we can find a bench on the seafront and watch the waves as we eat.'

'And then we'll drive inland and find our B & B in Tamarel. That should give us plenty of time to go walkabout.'

Approaching the village of Tamarel along the leafy Cornish lanes, it was simple for an unskilled map reader to locate the church of Saint Barnabas. The slender church spire was visible from a distance of two miles as Lorna and Martha made their way eastward from Bude.

Lorna, in the passenger seat, suggested that as the church was so prominent in the landscape they could follow their noses straight there, have a look around and then find the B & B.

'It's Grantchester all over again,' chuckled Martha as she climbed out of the driving seat.'

'What do you mean?' asked Lorna. 'Am I missing something love?'

'Rupert Brooke of course,' smiled Martha. '"Stands the Church clock at ten to three?" and all that.'

'And is there honey still for tea?' chimed in Lorna.

They were quiet for a few moments as they, separately, remembered their salad days at Cambridge which included the obligatory cycle ride of a few miles out to Grantchester to try to understand Rupert Brooke's exquisite if sometimes trite poem, "The Old Vicarage, Grantchester."

The path leading from the roadside pavement to the south facing main door of the church was heavily encrusted with moss, lichen and flat, tapestry-habited weeds. The building was encompassed by a lawn, formed from coarse growing grass, which had not seen a mower blade of any sort since the summer of the previous year.

'What an appalling mess,' commented Martha. 'It's a good thing we didn't bring Daniel. He'd have had forty fits just walking up the path. I never really believed the old adage about judging the gardener by the state of his lawns – some say hedges – but this beggars belief.'

'But it's not the vicar's job to mow the lawns or weed the path. You of all people know that Martha,' said Lorna. 'The down to earth work in the parish is the domain of the churchwardens and the P.C.C. This state of affairs suggests an absence of "the workers", as the unions used to call them.'

'You could be right,' replied Martha, 'And yet can you imagine Jake allowing this to happen? He would have dug a grave for a burial if he had to – and so would Daniel.; Something's very wrong here – let's look inside.'

Lorna tried the doorhandle. The church was locked up and the church clock still stood at ten to three.

'Who was it that said, "time is money?"' she asked. 'We've just wasted a lot of money in petrol, with the cost of bed and board to come. Let's adjourn to our lodgings and do something constructive like having a cup of tea if the landlady is sympathetic to our thirsty circumstances.'

'Good thinking,' said Martha. 'What's more, I can't see us needing to be veiled for this assignment. We might well pump more information out of our landlady – if she's a long time resident or native of Tamarel – than we could even glean from working our way into a church that has more than an air of closure about it.' She paused for a moment before continuing. 'If she asks, why are we here? Do we use our little fib from Ravensrigg about examining our ancestry?'

'We may as well. It would display a measure of consistency and save us inventing one more white lie – something which I don't enjoy apart from my firm belief in Father Christmas.'

Within an hour, Lorna and Martha could be seen in the garden of their landlady, enjoying an impromptu Cornish Cream Tea. They had landed on their feet in finding the equivalent Cornish counterpart to dear Violet Rose of Tupshorne – a rich mine of local information and gossip if invited to chat about the great and the good of Tamarel. And the bad.

It was Martha who raised the subject of the church of Saint Barnabas by enquiring quietly if the church had a set rota of opening times during the week. Clothed in such innocent terms, the question opened a veritable floodgate of vitriol and recrimination. Quite unwittingly, Damnit had hit the information button when he booked this particular B and B for the two investigators.

Demelza Heniot's house sign made a statement. Carved out of a fine chunk of Cornish granite, it was incised with a single word – TRELAWNYS. Miss Demelza Trelawney had been born in the home of her ancestors and could trace her lineage back to the hero of Cornish folklore. The same Trelawney hands that had built her house generations ago had been responsible for the building of the church in Tamarel.

Lorna and Martha listened with growing fascination as Demelza poured out a frightening litany of bitter complaints: a fascination enhanced by the charm of her Cornish burr. From the outset, she refused to refer to the sole source of parochial Armageddon by either his title or his name. 'That Foul Fiend' was her chosen epithet for the man with no name inhabiting the vicarage – he who had managed to alienate all those members of his flock who were responsible for and justifiably proud of the donkey work involved in keeping the parish vibrant and healthy, both in spiritual and financial terms. Man, or woman, management and human relationships were glaring omissions from the fiend's *modus operandi*. Devilish incompetence overwhelmed all the good offices and intentions of the Saint Barnabas faithful as, one by one they deserted their place of worship. Demelza's brother, the late Henry Trelawney, with whom she had shared her cottage since the death of her husband, Herbert, had been the senior general jack of all trades at Saint Barnabas' church, ready and willing to undertake any job from emergency plastering to repointing the exterior of the building. He took his turn on the brass cleaning rota but fought shy of helping with the floral decorations unless it was harvest festival time when his prize winning vegetables would draw gasps of admiration from visiting tourists. Unlike Daniel Greensward, he had never aspired to wielding the wand of a churchwarden but the mowing of the church lawns and maintenance of the grounds were his prerogative and would have made them members of the same brotherhood. Demelza said that the Foul Fiend had treated Henry with such lack of respect that after much heart-searching he felt he could no longer carry out his duties, not even for the love of God. The very idea of being in the same room as the wolf in sheep's clothing was anathema to him so he relinquished all his voluntary duties, told the fiend that in two time-flown years he had turned the house of God into a hellhole and in future he could mow the lawns himself. Henry had died two months later and Demelza laid the cause of his death squarely on the vicarage front door mat which should have borne the inscription 'Keep Out'. A select group of parishioners had, according to Demelza, approached their diocesan bishop in a covert attempt to have the Fiend relieved of his incumbency duties and evicted from the vicarage. Hopes and expectations were dashed as the deputation were given to understand that only a gross misdemeanour on the part of the vicar or a total, one hundred per cent boycott of the church by its congregation would trigger off the process for his dismissal. The vicar was fully aware of what had come to pass and from that time never left the vicarage except to conduct the minimum number of church services.

Both Martha and Lorna found it difficult to stifle a chuckle when Demelza invoked the spirit of her famous ancestor, Bishop Trelawney of Bristol, by declaring that if he was alive he would have taken a horsewhip to this particular miscreant and thrashed him out of the county, or made a bonfire of him. Then came the final, damning insult. That Foul Fiend was nothing but a grockle when all was said and done. Mystified, Lorna asked what a grockle might be only to be told, with a grin, that she was; a stranger in an alien land. Martha did allow herself a laugh at this reply, telling Demelza that if ever she was to leave Cornwall for Yorkshire she'd be nowt but an off-comed-un – same as a grockle in another language.

Later on that evening, in the privacy of their room, Lorna and Martha discussed the information that Demelza had divulged to them.

'There's no point in our staying in Tamarel any longer,' said Martha, conviction in her brief statement. 'God alone knows how the man, the Foul Fiend, made the short list.'

'Must have rigged or rejigged his references,' suggested Lorna rather simply. 'One thing is certain – if he were to make it to Tupshorne nobody from here would come in a coachload to cheer at his induction. The locals would be far too well occupied dancing round a celebratory bonfire topped by an effigy of a grockle. But you are right. We must move on and change our itinerary. Grockles like you and I are mistaken in thinking we might have ancestors hereabouts – so the sooner we reach West Sussex the better. Demelza will still be paid in full for our booked stay although I wonder if she deserves it after linking us with the Fiend under the term 'grockle.' Sounds like some kind of racial discrimination to me. Never mind! Do you think, with a little cunning, we could somehow inveigle her into letting the vicar know that her two lady guests from Yorkshire had made a swift departure? He might, just might, put two and two together.'

'Don't count on it,' said Martha. 'I suspect that he is inured to a hint of that kind. Now that we know what we know about him, you realise we are in a perfect position to thwart his aspirations.'

'How do you mean,' asked Lorna, 'apart from reporting back to H.Q. that this applicant is a W.O.T. – a waste of time? What are you suggesting?'

'A bit of not too well disguised subtlety. First thing tomorrow–' Martha broke off. 'No. A head-on approach. Let's be brave. We can find, surely, a vicarage telephone number in the local monthly mag, the Tamarel Telltale. I saw a copy on the coffee table in the sitting room. Ring him now and say we are family researchers wishing to have a quick browse through any parish records available in church and ask if he would be so awfully kind as to open the church for us first thing tomorrow morning – before we leave for West Sussex.'

'And if he is too busy?' queried Lorna.

'Then I shall mention that wonderful term which opens every door – "the going rate for research" – and my Coutts Bank cheque book that lowers every drawbridge.'

'Really,' said Lorna with unfeigned surprise. 'You've pinched my trump card.'

'Just a justifiable white lie, given the circumstances.'

'No need to lie, Martha. I've brought my C.B.C.B. with me. Flash it at the church door, say "Open Sesame" and "Abracadabra" for instant satisfaction.

'Now you're pulling my leg,' protested Martha.

'No, I'm not, as a matter of fact,' replied Lorna. 'It's something I don't broadcast and even Daniel isn't wise to it – yet – so mum's the word, please.'

'That's fine by me,' said Martha, sounding somewhat relieved, if you're quite sure. But we can't let the Fiend profit from our red herring.'

'Absolutely not,' stated Lorna. 'I shall make out the cheque to the Churchwarden or Wardens of Saint Barnabas, Tamarel. It might help them a little bit. You ring the vicarage now and when you've finished I'll ring Daniel to tell him of our change of plan. Fingers crossed, the Fiend with swallow the bait, hook line and sinker.'

The vicar answered the telephone so quickly that Martha was quite taken aback and thought perhaps that he had been awaiting a prearranged call from someone else. Her surmise was then fortified by his apparent efforts to terminate any developing conversation at the earliest opportunity. Lorna, listening, was intrigued and amused as Martha raised the questions – the answers to which she could only guess at.

The vicar was unimpressed by the pitiful tale of two widows in search of antecedents, no matter how far they had travelled to reach Tamarel. To open the church first thing in the morning was totally out of the question because Thursday was his day off inviolate, a habit he was disinclined to change. His mood altered as in reply to Martha's crucial question he coolly enquired about the current fee structure with regard to examining parish records as research documents. By this time, Lorna also had her ear to Martha's telephone and was able to whisper that the going rate was £200 an hour. Hearing the swift intake of breath at the other end of the line, Martha knew that her arrow had struck gold and the Fish was on the hook – bait taken.

The vicar would be at the church door at nine o'clock the following morning to welcome them to Saint Barnabas and dig out any documents that might aid their search. They could take all the time in the world and he would dance attendance on them from time to time throughout the day, all the day.

When Lorna rang Daniel to tell him what had transpired she feared he was about to pass out such was the explosion of merriment at home in Tupshorne.

As Martha was drifting off to sleep she remarked, dreamily, that Lorna's diary for that particular day would merit a mention in the Church Times! In the darkness, Lorna smiled to herself before murmuring that the morrow could not come too soon.

Demelza Heniot was disappointed that for some undisclosed reason her two guests were leaving early. Although she would be in receipt of full payment for their expected length of residence at Trelawneys it was not in her nature to accept something for nothing. Her brief contact with this pair of grockles from the North had been rather enjoyable and in a well meant gesture she invited them to return at any time in the future to use up their three days of B and B credit. She was aware that they had persuaded the Foul Fiend to open the church for their benefit but was puzzled as they bade her farewell. Both her guests were heavily veiled and stank to high heaven, quite literally, of lavender perfume. Knowing their destination, she nearly suggested that extract of garlic would have been a better choice.

With the church clock still stuck on ten to three, the two fragrant ladies were waiting at the door at five minutes to nine when the Fiend arrived. The charm offensive opened.

'So sorry to keep you two ladies waiting on this beautiful morning.' The voice was deep, sonorous and mellifluous: the delivery was unctuous in the extreme, oily enough to calm the most troubled waters. 'How I wish that my dear parishioners were as polite with their punctuality as you two undoubtedly are.'

Lorna, electing to fight fire with fire, smiled broadly behind her veil. Suddenly, and independently of Martha, she felt free to elaborate on their cover story and to let her imagination run riot. Whoppers can be so enjoyable.

'My sister, Lady Virginia, and I are great admirers of Louis XVIII who in his infinite wisdom stated, *"L'exactitude est la politesse des rois."* Our gracious queen is also a believer that, "Punctuality is the politeness of queens." But we tend to err on the early side, sometimes embarrassingly so – like this morning. It's so kind of you to open the church for us, especially on your day of rest – bless you!'

Martha joined in the duplicity, once she had stifled a chuckle with a well worked chesty cough. 'I was forever telling my brother John, the bishop of Auckland, to take a day off at least once a month. He never did, of course. He was a big lad all his life was our Little John. Then when he made it to the see we called him "Little Auk". He died young, became extinct in ornithological terms, so we lovingly referred to him as the "Late Great Auk."' The vicar glanced at each perfumed veiled visitor in a vain attempt to penetrate their undoubted aura. Were they perhaps a trifle wacky?

'Perhaps the bishop doubted the book of Genesis,' he ventured. 'Personally, firmly I believe and truly – as the famous hymn has it – that after six days busy with creating God took a day's rest. And if that's good enough for Him, it's good enough for me.'

'That is as maybe,' remarked Martha, acidly. 'But you, yourself, are in no position to question the beliefs of the "Late Great Auk." Unlike Saint Barnabas' church here, whatever his cure, whether as a junior curate or high in the episcopate, my brother John's church was open to all of God's children all day and every day. God never sleeps, you know, so it doesn't cost money to get Him out of bed.'

The Foul Fiend scented trouble and moved quickly to divert the barbed criticism aimed at him. 'Everyone to their own interpretation of things,' he said. 'If you would care to wander round the church, I'll open up the vestry and bring out the registers and records, such as they are, for your perusal.'

'Don't bother,' said Lorna, with brutal brevity. 'Lady Virginia and I received a telephone call during breakfast this very morning from our genealogy tutor, the gist of which was that there's nothing here in Tamarel. "Wild goose chase," was the phrase he used. I thought to ring you but decided that it would be churlish to put you off meeting us, particularly since you were prepared to sacrifice your day of rest for the pleasure of encountering a brace of dishy old widows. So we'll just sign the visitors' book before we go, append an appropriate comment, and leave you to mow round your church – now that you're here you may as well make yourself useful.'

'But what about the fee due for making the records available, even if your tutor warned you off? £200 was mentioned,' whined the Fiend, all charm gone.

'Absolutely spot on,' said Martha. 'We arrived at least five minutes early for our nine o'clock appointment. That is minus five minutes. It's now five past nine. That is plus five. Add these together and it is evident that we have not been here at all. Time to go, Lady Rose. Adieu vicar.'

'I want my money,' demanded the Fiend.

'I have a cheque in my pocket,' responded Lorna. 'It is the genuine article and I will hand it over to you after we have filled in the visitors' book and are safely outside this chill-struck hellhole you call your church.' Once more in the sunlight, Lorna passed over the cheque. The priest scanned the details and protested vehemently. 'Fifty pounds – payable to the churchwardens. That's an insult.'

'It is indeed,' smiled Lorna, sweetly. 'You don't deserve a penny of it. Your poor churchwardens can put it towards upkeep of the grounds if they wish. If any part of it ends up in your pocket, we'll be back. Kindly ask your churchwardens to send a receipt to my bankers. Their address is on the cheque – Coutts, London is probably all the information the Post Office needs. And as for you, you useless shepherd of the flock, a bit of advice in modern phraseology – "Get a life," or "Get stuffed," even.'

'Amen to that,' added Martha, with mocking piety.

The vicar watched the visitors leave the church grounds before retreating inside his church for no other reason than to examine the visitors' book. His worst fears turned from conjecture to concrete as he scrutinised the two entries.

The first one read, XXVIII-VI-MMI. 0910 hours. 'How very kind of you to open the church for me on your day of rest. Lupus in fabula. Era Virginia Aquae. Middinside. N. Yorks.'

And the second, 28/6/2001 9:10 a.m. 'Seek the intellect behind the veil. Do look me up when in Yowesdale. A lean fee is a fit reward for a lazy clerk (Proverbs). Lady Rose Waters.'

'Lupus in fabula – talk of the devil–,' said the Fiend to himself. 'Insolent bitch.' There were no other entries for the whole month of June. He ripped out the offending page and tore it to shreds, uttering profanities the while. The Creator heard every word.

CHAPTER XIV

Venerunt, Audiverunt, Excesserunt

(They came, they heard, they scarpered)

Et Venerunt, Viderunt, Laboraverunt

(And they came, they saw, they beavered away)

Martha was at the wheel as they left the parking place outside Saint Barnabas' church.

'Would you drive back to Demelza's for me?' asked Lorna.

'Sure' said Martha. 'Why, have you forgotten something? I did double-check our room before we left.'

'No, it's not that,' replied Lorna. 'I've had an idea. Do you suppose that dreadful apology for a priest will pass on my cheque to his churchwardens?'

Martha thought for a moment before answering. 'No, I don't. He'll want to erase any evidence of our visit. I wouldn't mind betting he's torn the vital page out of the visitors' book already. Why do you ask?'

'Well,' said Lorna, drawing out the vowel sound, 'if that cheque fails to clear my account within one month, here's one grockle will demand the reason why. Mrs Heniot, bless her, is bound to know the names and addresses of the churchwardens, if I ask for them. You won't know, but I've made a habit of keeping a little sheet of carbon paper in my cheque book for occasions such as this. The next cheque in the book is a carbon copy of the one I left with the Foul Fiend, except for the number which has to be different.'

The Volvo drew up outside Trelawneys.

'What then?' questioned Martha.

'Then,' said Lorna, 'we'll have him. I'll send another cheque to the churchwardens, accompanied by a letter from my solicitor, explaining that since I had not received an acknowledgement of my first cheque, a request I made to the vicar, and on checking my bank account it was evident that it had not been presented then I had to assume that the vicar had lost it soon after he had received it at ten past nine on Thursday, 28 June. The entry in the visitors book would confirm that, under the name of Lady Rose Waters from Yowesdale. It won't matter whether or not the relevant page is there. Either way, the Fiend will be revealed as a mere mortal fiddling with potential church revenues. And that, my dear Lady Virginia Waters, is a gross misdemeanour of the first water.'

Martha laughed. 'You talk about Daniel's propensity to be devious. I think you've just out-devied him.'

Demelza was surprised to see the pair return so soon and insisted on them having coffee and a biscuit before they went off once more – this time with the information they needed concerning the Saint Barnabas churchwardens.

As they passed the village boundary sign, Lorna now driving, Martha turned her head to look behind them to read the impressive stone-mounted announcement – Welcome to Tamarel. 'Welcome to Tamarel, indeed,' she snorted, laying stress on the last word. 'Such a lovely sounding place name. It reminds me, in its utterance, of James Elroy Flecker's gorgeous poem, "The Golden Journey to Samarkand", in that you can imagine it as one more oasis on the Silk Road from China to Europe.'

'Steady on,' said Lorna, 'Samarkand is my territory.'

'How do you mean?' asked Martha, sensing that there was more to Lorna's remark than could be explained in so few words. There was a serious tone to her voice in spite of the lightness of delivery.

Lorna's reply was swift. 'I researched the Silk Road for my doctorate. It was the principal plank of my thesis and probably the most enjoyable part of my higher education.'

'I never knew you'd picked up a Ph.D,' said Martha, with considerable respect detectable in her statement of ignorance. 'Does Daniel know?'

'No, he doesn't and I'm happy to keep him in the dark on that particular issue. There's quite a lot of things in my past of which he is blissfully unaware – and I appreciate the fact that some of his personal history is not divulged to me unless it happens by accident. I suspect it's the secretiveness of an almost lifelong bachelorhood. He'd have made a wonderful priest, never betraying the secrets of the confessional. In many ways, it is a not unappealing trait even if at times it is a source of irritation.' She laughed. 'Just don't call me Doc!'

It was Martha's turn to laugh. 'I'll give you notice before I do – don't worry. I won't ask why and I'm sure you'll have a good reason. End of subject. Now back to today. When we change drivers we should be about halfway to Wrensdown and ready for a bite of lunch. Have you registered the fact that because we've left Tamarel so early we've no lodgings booked for tonight? Daniel's careful planning of our itinerary is now in a state of utter confusion. We can dispense with our overnight stop near Salisbury. That was scheduled for Monday 2 July. We're four days to the good.'

'Right,' said Lorna. I had sort of noted the shift in our timetable. We can address the problem over lunch and I'll ring Daniel when we've decided what to do. I'm prepared to bet that the Foul Fiend of Tamarel has already notified the Archdeacon of his sudden disinterest in the vacant vicarage of Tupshorne – but Daniel won't know yet.'

'We don't need to wait until lunch to discuss the matter,' said Martha. 'We can thrash it out as we drive and have it cut and dried by the time we sit down to eat. How's that for practical thinking? I'll have a look at the road atlas to see where we might stop for a bite.'

Two hours later they stopped for a lunch break in a small village to the west of Salisbury. Lorna, scout and map reader in the front passenger seat was taken with the name of a very pretty inn sited back from the road. The large inn sign swinging in the gentle breeze, proclaimed it to be the "Queen and Kindle" and featured a tortoiseshell cat nursing her five kittens. 'This will do nicely,' said Lorna. 'My grandpa was a great admirer of tortoiseshells.'

After placing their order for food, Lorna telephoned the B and B in Wrensdown and explained to the owner that their travel plans had altered, owing to circumstances beyond their control, and that they would be in Wrensdown six days earlier than expected. Was there any chance of a vacancy at the B and B ahead of schedule?

The landlady was sorry that she could not accommodate them as the B and B was fully booked up but if it would be of any help she would ring around other similar establishments who might be able to put them up at short notice. Give her half an hour and ring her again and she felt sure that she would have a satisfactory answer for them.

At the coffee stage, three quarters of an hour later, Lorna rang again to learn that a new arrangement had been put into action. The

Wrensdown vicarage had a vacancy, in a twin bedded room complete with *en suite avec un bidet.*

Lorna's face was a picture. 'We can't say No,' she mimed to Martha, who was listening in to the brief conversation. 'What a good thing we decided not to disguise ourselves as nuns – and I don't suppose we shall be able to hide behind our veils as we trot out our little white lies.'

When, that same evening Lorna rang home to High Ash her opening words were, 'Daniel, dear, you're not going to believe this, but…'

On leaving the "Queen and Kindle", Lorna and Martha, in a state of shock bordering on panic talked over the scenario that was opening up in front of them. Their pooled imaginations came up with all kinds of ideas about how or why a vicarage might become a bed and breakfast business.

They realised that they were unaware of the lady vicar's marital status. Was she holding down two jobs, both operating out of her vicarage? House for duty even? Perhaps there was a 'partner' of some kind dealing solely with the B and B. Was there any law within the Church of England that decreed, 'Thou shalt not operate thy vicarage as a bed and breakfast.' Martha was sure that none of the Ten Commandments mentioned B and Bs as such but provision was made so that on the seventh day sheets and bath towels would not be changed nor would beds get made. Lorna then wondered if she had misunderstood what she thought she had heard over the phone. Could it be the 'Old Vicarage' that was now a B and B and the vicar lived in a modern, purpose built, 'New Vicarage?'

'I can see us going home early,' said Martha.

'How do you mean?' asked Lorna. 'We've four days in hand now.

'Well, if it really is the vicar's vicarage, we can't be any closer to our quarry, can we? Depending on just how much face to face conversation we manage to have with her, our united and much vaunted feminine intuition will tell us all we want to know. We shan't even need to witness her performance in church if we pick up all the vibes, good or bad, that will be apparent in her home.'

'If that's the case, then we must be ready with a good story to explain our presence in Wrensdown: otherwise we shall have her own feminine intuition to cope with. Let's pray that she might be among those unusual priests whose noses are not trained to smell a rat.'

The arrangement with Mrs Kent, their original Wrensdown

landlady, was that they would drive to her house to make her acquaintance over a cup of tea and a bun, and she would then give them directions to their new lodgings. This proved to be a quite excellent entrée to the parochial world of Saint John the Divine in Wrensdown since Mrs Kent was honorary treasurer of the church. Lorna and Martha were amused by the similarity between this lady treasurer and their own Violet Rose – the common denominator was a great sense of humour married to a social conscience. She also baked a very fine scone.

Over tea, the conversation never flagged, largely because Mrs Kent was a genuine chatterbox, capable of putting on a one-woman-show for anyone willing to listen. As the two investigators made their way to Saint John's vicarage Martha remarked that Mrs Kent had divulged so much relevant information on the vicar's situation that they could well have set off for Tupshorne there and then. Lorna agreed wholeheartedly. She was becoming increasingly bothered with the pretence of the whole mission as they slipped deeper into a morass of fibs and half-truths. In so many ways, the task that they had been set, through a variety of fortuitous occurrences, had turned out to be ridiculously simple, even downright easy. The only minor challenges they had encountered were all to do with Daniel's carefully arranged and rearranged travel plans. She wondered if the homeward journey would be so trouble free.

'All of a sudden, I think I've had enough of this strange charade and the sooner I'm home, the better. I reckon the only thing that we haven't learned from Mrs Kent is what the "vicaress" looks like. I'm homesick. Let's go home tomorrow. How about you?'

'It's your car, dearie,' said Martha. 'If you want to go then we go. Another thing – you probably have more than enough data from our three visitations to produce a fascinating yarn. The Wrensdown end of things would make a good story on its own. According to Mrs Kent, this vicar is a saintly Christian lady married to an agnostic: an absolutely lovely man, somewhat older than she, who up until their marriage had been a leading light in the murky world of weapons manufacturing before he actually saw the light. What else do we know?'

Stop the car a minute,' said Lorna. 'Are there times when it's possible to have too much information? I'm sure I've heard that said. Let's just collect our thoughts before we meet this "saint."'

Martha drove into the nearest available parking space. 'Right! I've my mental jotter at the ready,' said Lorna, 'so you can start the process – one thought at a time. Off you go!'

'He's quite a lot older than she. I think Mrs Kent said the difference was nearly twenty years. Could be important.'

'Noted,' said Lorna, 'and no children so far. That could mean anything.'

'A big Victorian vicarage with seven bedrooms – built in the expectation of housing a typically large Victorian ménage. So – no kids, no servants but enough accommodation for a B and B,' said Martha, 'which the husband runs single-handed. And sometimes it serves as a *pro tem* refuge for some of the disadvantaged in society. Interesting.'

'Mrs Kent reckoned that despite his agnosticism, his B and B business was a grand example of Christian outreach. Quite some change of direction from being an arms dealer. It sounds to me as if this vicar's better half is the Wrensdown equivalent of Minerva Ossian up in Ravensrigg.'

'I might echo Daniel's remark about the Ossians, at this point,' said Martha.

'Why, what was that?' asked Lorna. 'Was it sharp enough to make the pages of my book?'

'Definitely,' said Martha. 'When we had finished telling our tale of the Ravensrigg enquiry. Timothy Walsh said "Sounds good," but Daniel added, rather caustically at the time I thought, "Sounds too good to be true". It will be interesting to hear his comments on this Wrensdown set-up when we get home.' There was a pause for silent contemplation before Lorna suggested that it was time to make their way to the vicarage and meet their host – and perhaps his wife, their target, the saint of Wrensdown.

It was never in their destiny to meet the saint of Wrensdown, the Reverend Hazel Mears. Hardly had Lorna and Martha arrived at the vicarage, to be greeted by their oh so charming host, Roland, than their introductions were interrupted by the sound of a telephone ringing. Roland Mears excused himself to answer the call. The telephone conversation was brief and he returned to his guests in a state of shock and agitation before sitting down in a chair by the front door.

'*Aequam servare mentem*" thought Lorna. Something serious must have occurred and Daniel's maxim was uppermost in her mind. Roland took several long, deep breaths before speaking. 'I'm sorry ladies. That was Chichester hospital. My wife has been involved in a road accident while driving back from a meeting at the cathedral and the doctors are telling me to hurry over to the intensive care unit without delay. We've only one car between us. I'll have to ring for a taxi.'

Ever practical, Lorna Greensward took command within seconds of sizing up the situation. This parish visiting by herself and Martha which had begun as something of a game, had turned to comedy at Ravensrigg, farce at Tamarel and now threatened to become a tragedy. Daniel had always feared something might go wrong and now it had. 'I'll drive you there. You're in no fit state at this moment even if you had a car. My sister-in-law and I will just leave our cases in the hall for the moment and if you have anybody else in residence Virginia is well up to coping with them until we get back. No time to waste.'

Roland sat still for a few more moments before nodding his head in dumb resignation. Then, drawing on his emotional reserves, he smiled before answering.

'Mrs Kent didn't tell me that she was sending round two angels. I fear I'm not equipped for this turn of events.' He rose to his feet. 'Thank you. I can't protest against commonsense. Please make yourself at home Mrs…' He gave Martha an enquiring look.

'I'm Virginia, and your chauffeuse to be is Rose. We're both Waters, known in the business as the Two Tonics.'

'I'll just grab my jacket from the kitchen and be at your car in two ticks. Oh, your room is Number Four – turn right at the top of the stairs and it is facing you at the end of the passage.'

'Would you mind if I called you Roland?' asked Lorna as she eased the Volvo out of the vicarage drive on to Vicarage Lane. 'At times like this, personal terms are important.'

'By all means,' said Roland, 'and may I call you…or should it be Tonic One, or Tonic two?'

'Rose will do for now,' answered Lorna, with a subdued chuckle. 'I like Christian names. If I have to complete a form that requires me to state my "forename", I have no hesitation in crossing "that" word out and inserting "Christian name." My knowledge of European history tells me that Roland, nephew of Charlemagne, was a crusading Christian.'

'You're very direct,' said Roland, 'but it is only a forename and perhaps inappropriate for this aging agnostic who just happens to have a well qualified Christian wife and calls a vicarage his home.' In the company of this lady with a sympathetic ear and an obvious air of commanding practicality, he was beginning to relax.

Lorna sensed the challenge in his words and rose to it. Without either of them knowing the true gravity of his wife's injuries, this was a window in time when mortal man's feeble efforts at retrieval and healing would be revealed as inadequate.

'Were you married in church?' she asked.

'Yes, we were. It seems like a lifetime ago – at this particular moment.'

'So you made your marriage vows in the presence of a god you didn't believe in. Why?'

'It's what suited me at the time. Lots of people do it, you know – and I'm agnostic not atheistic so I wasn't really lying under oath.'

'Maybe not – just splitting hairs for your own ends, as I see it. Dissembling for the occasion. Split hairs are a curse.'

'We were in love, as much then as now. I had found my soulmate.'

'An interesting word in the mouth of an agnostic because it has spiritual connotations unconnected to any creed.' Lorna broke off abruptly and paused before speaking again. 'We're nearing Chichester. Presuming you know your way to the hospital, would you just give me directions. Left, right or straight on will do. I'll drop you off at the main entrance, and then find a parking space. When you feel it is time to go, you will find me waiting for you in the hospital chapel as I pray for your wife. And you can be sure that back at the vicarage my sister-in-law will also be at prayer. You must know that your wife has held you in her prayers every day of your married life. You are alive and you don't know if she is. This is your personal Road to Damascus.'

After parking the Volvo, Lorna took the opportunity to telephone Martha to tell her not to wait up for her. Then she rang Daniel to explain what had happened to his meticulous route planning. She felt that whatever support for Roland would be forthcoming from the Saint John's congregation, Martha and she had been sent by a higher authority. She was reminded of Hamlet's words to Horatio. 'There are more things in heaven and earth, Horatio, than are dreamt of in your philosophy.' Daniel was strangely subdued during their phone conversation, a quietness that Lorna ascribed to the fact that he might have been missing her. She did know that he had been to see Nathaniel Ross but Daniel chose not to tell her that the visit was not only on a social footing but also involved a medical check, the results of which had given him cause for concern. Daniel, for his part, whatever his state of mind, was cognisant of the fact that the sole contender for the vacant living of Saint Michael the Archangel in Tupshorne would be the Reverend Reuben Ossian of Saint Thomas's, Ravensrigg. Had all the scheming by the Magnificent Seven been a waste of money? He thought not. If Reuben, at interview, was as good as Lorna and Martha had found him to be in his parochial work, the vacancy would not need to be re-advertised. The Foul Fiend of Tamarel had been unveiled as a proverbial 'wolf in sheep's clothing' and withdrawn his application. And as for the Reverend Hazel Mears of Saint John the Divine in Wrensdown, he closed his eyes in concentration and prayed.

It was nearly two o'clock in the morning when Roland found his way to the chapel and sat down next to a very sleepy Lorna. Placing a reassuring arm across her shoulders, he uttered eight vital words – 'she's come back to me, thanks to you' – adding, 'now I believe in miracles.'

Lorna, tired out and hungry after her prayer and enforced fasting vigil, lay down on her bed, fully clothed, afraid that she might be beyond sleep. Martha spoke in a whisper. 'Tell me.'

'She's pulled through, thank God,' said Lorna and promptly fell asleep so quickly that Martha's final remarks went unheeded.

'The vicarage kitchen is fantastic – so state of the art there's even a prayer desk, so I used it. I'm thinking of coming out of retirement to do B and B.' She smiled to herself in the dark, knowing full well what Jake would have to say about that. 'Night, night, Lorna dear. Today we have played a blinder.'

In the morning, Martha was busying herself in the kitchen by seven o'clock. The six other overnight guests were surprised to be served breakfast by a new chef who definitely fancied herself in the apron usually worn by their host, Roland Mears. As a fund raising exercise for the church, initiated by Roland, the apron was printed with an imposing line drawing of the church of Saint John the Divine. Every kitchen in the parish sported at least one, and for all the waiters in the two Wrensdown restaurants it was an essential item of workwear.

It had been Martha who the previous evening had told the other residents about the Reverend Hazel's potentially fatal accident and she was very relieved to serve breakfast along with the news that the lady vicar was pulling through. All the guests, even those who should have made an early start after breakfast, waited for Roland to surface in order to offer their sympathy to him and their best wishes to the vicar for a speedy recovery.

Roland came down to breakfast at half past eight to be followed ten minutes later by Lorna, her hair still wet from the shower. The traumatic happenings of the previous fifteen hours were beginning to assume less nightmarish proportions.

By a quarter past nine the dining room had emptied except for Lorna and Martha – Roland was occupied in the kitchen – and over a leisurely final cup of coffee they discussed their next course of action.

'I think we are needed here for another day,' said Martha.

'We don't know what kind of emotional backup is available to Roland right now, but if he is of a mind that in some way our prayers have helped to bring his wife out of intensive care, then another twenty four hours should see the completion of what has turned out to be a rescue mission.'

'Has it occurred to you, as it has to Daniel,' said Lorna, 'that because of this unfortunate accident to the Reverend Mears, Reuben Ossian is the sole candidate and will have a walkover, or perhaps I should say a "walkin" to Tupshorne vicarage?'

'Yes, I had given it some thought,' replied Martha. 'If you ever doubted that God works in mysterious ways this simplification of the selection procedure should banish all doubts – that is unless the earthly powers that be decide to postpone the interviews, or even worse re-advertise the vacancy.'

'Heaven forbid,' said Lorna rather sarcastically, 'after all our investigative labours that would feel like a kick in the teeth. So much for working in mysterious ways. We both liked Reuben and his Ravensrigg situation. Let's hope that his official interview will chime as sweetly with the panel as his chance encounter with thee and me did.' She paused for a moment in thought before continuing. 'So it's homeward tomorrow, and today we'll play at B and B and helping Roland out in any way that we can. Right?'

Roland appeared in the doorway between the dining room and the kitchen, a tea towel slung over his left shoulder.

'Did I hear my name mentioned?' he asked.

'Talk of the Devil!' said Martha, smiling. 'We were just agreeing that today we are at your service in any way that we might be of help, and then tomorrow we will leave you in peace.'

'Put like that, an' in such a charming way an' all, it would be churlish of me to refuse. My main problem for the moment is transport.

I rang the accident repair garage a few minutes ago to learn that our car is not, as I feared it might be, a write-off. The car insurance policy does cover me for a loan car while ours is mended but I doubt that will happen immediately.'

'So that's our assignment for today – the Wrensdown taxi service,' said Lorna. 'You will be anxious to get back to the hospital as soon as we can take you. We two "angels" will enjoy window-shopping in Chichester while you visit your wife, and I have never been inside the cathedral so that is a must. The Normans did such things rather well. Let's establish the priorities.'

Lorna was moving into bossy mode. 'Get on to your insurance company now, to fix you up with an approved car hire firm. Then it's off to hospital for you. With luck, there might be a car firm in Chichester in league with your insurance company – we'll see. When you feel that your bedside presence is no longer required, ring us on our mobile and we can maybe meet for lunch somewhere. If you think that an afternoon visit is called for – O.K. We can always manage some more window-shopping, can't we Martha – Rose?' She very quickly corrected her slip of the tongue.

Even so, Roland sensed that if angels were blessed with wings he may have just witnessed a slight ruffling of feathers.

'You speak as if you have personal experience of the situation in which I find myself at this moment. I won't ask how or why, but for sheer down to earth practicalities you certainly take the biscuit, and as a sensible sort of a chap – I accept.'

'Quite right, too,' said Martha, 'and this time it's my turn to drive.'

Just as Lorna had suggested, Roland met them for lunch after his morning hospital visit and nearly floored them by saying that Hazel, his wife, would quite like to meet the two lady guests who had come to the rescue of his sanity and his business. It appeared that Hazel's sense of humour was unaffected by her accident as she wondered if either of them, or both, fancied standing in for her at the services on the coming Sunday: angels were rare in Wrensdown. As one, Martha and Lorna realised that in this special case, if they were to meet the still seriously injured third candidate for the vacancy in Tupshorne they would not be able to keep up the pretence any longer, either veiled or unveiled, and sooner or later they would be having a very awkward interview with the Archdeacon. The Magnificent Seven, the Dream Team, would become the Perfect Nightmare. Gracefully, they declined the invitation by suggesting that meeting two strange women could set back her recovery but they also promised to keep in touch and when in the area again the vicarage B and B would be their first port of call, not that nice Mrs Kent's place. It was at that point that Roland told them that Hazel should have been going up to Yorkshire in about ten days time to an interview for a new post. 'We'll never know now if she would have been successful,' he said with an air of resignation. 'Mind you, I'm not sure the vicarage would have been my B and B cup of tea – not big enough.'

Lorna and Martha were close to tears – but everybody knows angels do not weep.

CHAPTER XV

Quis Facit Per Alium Facit Per Se

(He who does things for others does
them for himself)

A loan car was made available during the course of that same afternoon, courtesy of Roland's car insurance company and a two vehicle convoy was to be seen motoring from Chichester homewards to Wrensdown vicarage.

In the early-evening Lorna rang home to High Ash to confirm that she and Martha would be back in Tupshorne in time for a late-tea the following day – Saturday – subject to average travelling conditions.

Next morning, after giving Roland a hand with serving breakfast to the other guests, the two intrepid investigators packed their cases and made as speedy and decent a getaway as they could manage. Neither of them signed the visitors' book before leaving the vicarage – a decision made in an attempt to safeguard their anonymity. The only true fact that Roland could attribute to his two charming and supremely helpful visitors was that they hailed from Yorkshire and in gratitude for their timely support in his time of need he refused to charge them for their two nights bed and breakfast, stating that in all fairness he should have been paying them to stay. Lorna knew that it would be pointless to argue with him because he was absolutely right in his sentiments. Martha ventured to say that when his reverend wife was fully recovered, they might find a suitably large enough vicarage somewhere in Yorkshire where Hazel's pastoral skills and his missionary hospitality would enjoy a free rein. She would be watching the 'Appointments in the Clergy' column in the Daily Telegraph with heightened interest. Immediately after waving off his two angels, Roland went indoors, making a beeline for the visitors' book. It was usual for the book to be left open, an unspoken invitation to guests to sign in as they passed through the entrance hall. It was closed. On opening it, he found an envelope containing two fifty pound notes.

Written on the highly fragrant envelope was a brief message, 'For H's future travel expenses – only. *Bono animo esse.* Two Tonics.' He smiled to himself, having a rough idea of how the Latin would translate and sure that Hazel would confirm it as being something like, 'Be of good mind.' He was still smiling as, envelope and money tucked into his wallet, he set off for Chichester hospital once more. Later in the morning, prompted by his lady vicar wife, he made the crucial telephone call to the appropriate diocesan authority responsible for the Tupshorne appointment – a serious road accident involving the Reverend Hazel Mears would prevent her from attending the selection panel meeting scheduled for Tuesday 10 July.

Lorna and Martha were over halfway home when Martha, who as non-driver at the time and enjoying an early-afternoon snooze, came to with a jolt.

'Are you all right,' asked Lorna, 'that was a rather sudden awakening? Not a bad dream, I hope?'

'Well, yes and no,' said Martha. 'I was dreaming of Roland.'

Lorna giggled. 'After such a brief acquaintance?' she teased. 'I did wonder after hearing his name when you were talking in your sleep last night.'

'Fibber,' said Martha, 'I don't sleeptalk. No! You and I had gone to the hospital with him and met Hazel. It was a flittingly brief dream with time for a single question. Had he notified the archdeacon about her accident and so her absence from the selection meeting? End of dream and I woke with a start. What do you reckon?'

'I'm not sure,' said Lorna, turning over the question in her mind. 'There are ten days to go before the interviews. I think her rate of recovery, if his report of yesterday afternoon is to be believed, would indicate that she will ask him to do the necessary. Could be he's done it already without being asked. I do hope he appreciated the liberal dose of perfume I put in that envelope. If she gets a whiff of it, Hazel might worry about angels, lavender scent and her husband. Questions might be asked.'

'I'm sorry that we didn't meet her, you know,' said Martha. 'It wasn't going to happen though, given the circumstances. And yet, from talking to Mrs Kent – at some length, as I recall – and being of considerable help to Roland in his time of trouble, I feel we came as close to knowing her, short of seeing her in the pulpit, as we could.'

'Absolutely. I fancy she might have given Reuben Ossian a run for his money,' said Lorna. 'We'll never know now, but if, for whatever reason she may have, she makes it to Yorkshire at some time in the future, I hope our paths cross. Our lavender perfume will be long forgotten.'

'Thank God for that,' said Martha with an audible sigh of relief. 'Now I can go back to sleep'

It was a quarter past six when the Volvo nosed its way through the High Ash gateway and drew to a halt a few yards to the left of the main door. The dogs, who had been told already of the impending return of the wanderers, came out like a black surfing wave, tails awag and barking a furious glorious welcome. Miss Bindle, Jake and Martha's black beauty, was the first to reach the car, closely followed by Damnit's Baggins, while Lorna's Rauch, still a pup and not too sure what all the fuss was about, was hot on her dam's heels. And then a fourth dog, known as Mrs Swann's hairy lurcher, appeared – in no hurry at all. 'Oh, Sprottle!' cried Lorna. 'What's brought you here? Where's your master?'

'Right here, mother.' It was Douglas, now standing in the doorway with an arm around Rachel's shoulders. 'We've given ourselves an impromptu long weekend in Yowesdale.

By this time, the stay-at-home five members of the Magnificent Seven had joined the canine welcome committee and, greetings exchanged, everyone went in for the late-tea waiting them on the kitchen table.

Sipping her second cup of tea, sometime later, Lorna whispered her reservations to Daniel. 'I don't believe for one moment that Douglas and Rachel came up here on the spur of the moment. He's up to something, I'm sure.

'So what price your much vaunted feminine intuition?' said Daniel, conspiratorially. 'I'll give you a clue as to my own suspicions. All I know is they're not staying overnight in Yowesdale. After tea, they're off to visit Nathaniel in Preston, then returning here tomorrow. Have you noticed how your lovely daughter-in-law is positively blooming?'

'No?' questioned Lorna, in semi-misbelief. 'You mean?'

'I mean nothing,' countered Daniel, 'and I don't claim any of your intuition. It all adds up. It was bound to happen sooner rather than later. She suspects, they wonder if, she checks, doctor confirms. Keep it secret? Share the good news. Mum and Dad top priority. First opportunity and here they are.' He broke off – then, 'Don't move, Darling – it's action stations – Rachel's just put a very firm hand on Douglas's forearm.'

As if he had been awaiting a cue from Damnit, Douglas suddenly raised his voice, commanding the attention of people and dogs alike by addressing them all. 'My dear Mama, Mrs Damnit,' he grinned at Daniel, 'knows me well, or at least well enough to say that I'm never one to act on impulse. She suspects our arrival here, unannounced, is more than just a courtesy, family, out of the blue visit. She's right as usual. It's all Rachel's fault and she will now fill you in.'

'Well,' said Rachel, 'we've been broadening our education at evening classes. Douglas has majored in apiculture and I've become a poultry specialist. We know all about the birds and the bees and should receive our diplomas around Christmas with the arrival of a cygnet. Douglas will answer any questions.'

'Told you so,' crowed Daniel, as Lorna gave way to tears of joy and relief. 'Next stop Preston. Nathaniel will be thrilled to bits. He'll be searching for his little book of Jewish names.'

Praise, congratulations and good wishes showered down on the very obviously delighted couple. All the usual polite questions were asked as well as one or two of a more saucy nature. Answers were given with grace and humour. No, they did not know whether the baby would be a girl or a boy. No, they did not wish to be informed in advance. Yes, they were happy to know twins were not on the delivery note. Eventually, the parent oriented concerns having been given a thorough airing, the time came for Rachel and Douglas to make their goodbyes and set off to tell her father the good news.

'So now we can get down to the serious stuff,' said Timothy. 'The Magnificent Seven are in session. Perhaps Martha would like to kick off and so give Lorna a little longer to draw breath after learning she's expecting her first grandchild.

'I'm not so sure,' said Martha. 'It's Lorna who has kept the diary of our far flung adventures and who has been reporting back to Daniel from time to time – so you stay at home five will have a fair idea of what's been happening. With suitable embellishment and as much literary licence as you could wish to employ, Lorna's diary is the basis of quite some tale. Obviously, we've discussed the whole affair as we've journeyed from pillar to post and come to the same rather precipitate conclusion. If the Reverend Reuben of Ravensrigg interviews satisfactorily, the job is his. The vicar of Tamarel should never in a month of Sundays have been ordained according to the lady hostess of our B and B. In fact, she stated that Tamarel would be a better and much happier place for Christians if that "Foul Fiend", as she referred to him, had been burnt at the stake.'

At this point in Martha's narrative Lorna decided to break in. 'We met, face to face, with both Reuben Ossian, and "That Foul Fiend" whose proper name, if we ever knew it, we don't remember. You know already that Reuben could have charmed us two old birds off the trees. Now we can reveal that the Fiend would have needed a shotgun to fetch us down – and we are all aware that he will not be coming here to be interviewed next week. We shot HIM down! As for the third candidate, now ruled out of contention by her serious road accident in which she could well have died, we have to base our opinions on information gleaned from the Mrs Kent who should been our B and B hostess before passing us on to the vicarage.'

Lorna paused for a moment before asking Martha if she would care to carry on.

'There's not a lot more to say, really,' said Martha. 'We thought that Mrs Kent was Wrensdown parish's answer to Violet here in Tupshorne.' She grinned at Violet. 'She was the church treasurer, must have known everybody in the parish, was a right chatterbox and her scones would have given yours a run for anybody's money, Violet.' Violet was very impressed with this report, nodding at Martha with an air of amused indulgence. Martha continued. 'Mrs K. described the Reverend Hazel Mears as a saintly Christian lady. That said it all: one woman's opinion of another. As for her husband, an agnostic retired arms dealer, using the spare vicarage bedrooms for purposes of Bed and Breakfast – we liked him very much, perhaps because we found ourselves in the unusual position of being able to help a complete stranger whose wife had come so close to meeting her Maker. We acted as his personal taxi service and kept his other guests well fed and watered until he had pulled himself together after coming close to collapse on hearing of his wife's road accident – and Roland knew that we prayed so very hard for Hazel's safe return from Death's door. Our prayers were heard on high, Hazel pulled through and somehow we turned into two visiting angels. We're not sure about this, but we do think that, without being angelic, we were sent to Wrensdown not as fact finders – more as a pair of Good Samaritans. And Roland was deeply appreciative of the way in which we picked him up and helped to heal his shattered world.'

Lorna spoke again. 'That's about all we can come up with, I'm afraid. The way things have turned out, our efforts might be deemed a waste of time, never mind the money involved but Martha and I are agreed that for us it has been an unforgettable experience, never to be repeated. We may be feeling a bit jaded at this moment, after our long drive, but if you have any questions let's deal with them now.'

Violet and Muriel began to speak at the same time, before Muriel deferred to the treasurer.

'Do you think it was a worthwhile exercise?'

'On balance, yes,' answered Lorna. 'Travel is said to broaden the mind and in this case, whether we like it or not, we learned something about the human condition in general and three individuals in particular. We must have discovered some facts that will probably not become apparent at interview.'

Jake was next. As the retired vicar of St Michael the Archangel he spoke with some diffidence. 'Now that you are both safely home, I wonder if it was fair or kind of us to send you on such a mission but you have carried it out with some *panache*. I have just one question to ask, and it rather puts you on the spot. Is Reuben Ossian up to the job? If you answer, "yes", we have to face up to the fact that the Archdeacon might wish to postpone the whole idea of interviews until the Reverend Mears is fit to attend; or even to re-advertise the vacancy. That must not be allowed to happen. It could all depend on one single interview. If the Arch is favourably impressed then Ossian is home and dry.'

Martha laughed. 'He'll do all right. Lorna and I wanted to kidnap him and bring him back with us. What really swung it for me was that she said Reuben reminded her of you, dear. Enough said!'

Muriel joined in. 'That is what is known as "a ringing endorsement."' It was her turn to have a humorous dig. 'Do we really want another Jake?'

Quiet up to this point, Daniel erupted with a great guffaw. 'I said at the very start that this man sounded too good to be true. If he's being likened to Jake, then I was right.'

They all laughed at this – Jake more than anyone. He well recalled Timothy telling him how Damnit had destroyed, quite brutally, the other priests who were his rivals for the St Michael's cure of souls. Damnit carried on – serious now. 'I was half hoping that the lady would make it – me being a firm believer in the concept of women bishops – but if the Ravensrigg reverend merits the endorsement of our covert investigators I'm comfortable with that.' He looked directly at Timothy, his fellow conspirator and churchwarden. 'So if you, Timothy, are with me on this, between us we will make certain sure the Venerable One looks no further. How about it?'

Before Timothy could reply, Lorna cut in. 'That means you will need to bring Mrs Minerva Ossian into the equation somehow. It was made very clear to us that if Reuben Ossian was king of Ravensrigg the principal gem in his crown is Minerva Jemima. I presume she will be accompanying him on the parochial walkabout even if she is not party to the interview.'

'I'm with you all the way, Damnit,' said Timothy rather grandly. 'The Venerable, unaware of our prescience, shall bow to our will.'

'And as for Minerva Jemima,' murmured Violet, 'leave her to me. I'll find out what makes her tick and why she should be the jewel in the Ossian crown.'

'I do hope that she's not too blinking bright,' added Muriel 'A decent polish, I can appreciate but I really don't want to be dazzled. "Diamond bright, diamond hard. Shade your eyes. Be on your guard," my mother used to say.'

'I think,' said Martha, 'that when Lorna and I observed her in church that Sunday, with her two youngsters, we were impressed by how solicitous the parishioners were when asking her about Reuben, absent ill. Their concern was matched by the calm smiling reply she gave. She doesn't dazzle – she glows with warmth. More ruby than diamond.'

'Point taken,' said Muriel. 'I'll put my sunspecs away.'

Jake rejoined the discussion Since his earlier intervention he had been content to listen, weighing up the various facts which might have had a significant bearing on the situation – especially so, now that the contest barring intervention by the Archdeacon, had turned into a one-horse race. 'Violet intends to find out just what makes Minerva tick. If we rule out her, Martha and me, who of the remaining four is offering to find out why she "glows like a ruby?" Putting on my canonicals, may I remind you of the book of Job. "The price of wisdom is above rubies." And Proverbs asks, "Who can find a virtuous woman? for her price is far above rubies." Personally, I think it's Lorna's cup of tea particularly since she has already experienced the glow that she has described, without actually speaking to her. How about it, Mrs Damnit?'

'I can't wait,' said Lorna. 'Goddess of Wisdom, here I come.' The informal meeting broke up soon afterwards.

Unwinding over a dram of Glenmorangie at the end of a long and busy day, Lorna asked if Daniel's old acquaintance from his High Ashes days was still coming to lunch on the morrow.

'Yes, as far as I know,' answered Daniel. 'I'll be interested in what you make of him.'

CHAPTER XVI

Ecce Minerva, Ecce Sapientiae Diva

(Watch out! Here comes Minerva, goddess of wisdom)

It was Sunday, the first day of July, and despite all Damnit's careful arrangements to spread Lorna and Martha's travels over eighteen days, for the reasons already detailed, their investigations had been completed in half the time.

When Jake realised that Lorna and Martha would be back in Yowesdale on the day before Silas was expected for lunch, he decided to see his contract through as resident chef at High Ash and provide food for those of the Magnificent Seven who were on the original list of diners, namely himself and Damnit and now augmented by the early return of their wives. Lorna and Daniel would bring Silas back from church and he and Martha would lay on lunch for five. 'Easy as pie,' he thought. That was until Martha awoke with a raging headache coupled with a sore throat, and definitely unfit to dine at Damnit and Lorna's.

Jake was all sympathy and precious little comfort. 'Seems to me,' he said, 'that in spite of hiding your face behind that veil when in the presence of the Reverend Ossian, his 'flu germs didn't observe the accepted protocols. And there was I believing that lavender perfume was the equal of a 'flu jab. Would you like a cold compress or a hot water bottle to help ease the aches?'

'Don't be silly,' said Martha. 'It's over a week since Lorna and I departed Ravensrigg. I hope she's all right. Thinking back a day or two to Wrensdown, one of Roland's guests was a bit under the weather with the sneezes. She must have breathed on me when I was dishing up at the breakfast table. You'd better keep your distance or you'll be next. As for me, two aspirins, a mug of beef tea and a bowl of vanilla ice cream will suffice.'

'I think that a really cold flannel might help the fevered brow,' said Jake. 'Freshen you up a bit.'

'Go on then,' said Martha, sensing that Jake was now trying to play a nursing game. 'I'll be fine, by and by, as long as I have plenty to drink. And you mustn't worry about me, while you're busy cooking and chatting over at High Ash.'

'I'm sure Lorna would understand if I backed out of my commitment, to tend to my dear old wife,' said Jake.

'Less of the old, if you don't mind,' smiled Martha. 'I'm sure she'd cope but you'd miss out on meeting this old school friend.' She cleared her throat gently before continuing. 'After all, that's what this lunch is all about. I do hope you like him. Daniel obviously didn't take fright when they met.'

'He was hardly a friend,' said Jake, 'being about four years junior to Damnit and me. That was important then, but all this time later the difference is insignificant. I am prepared to like him even if it's only to please you.'

'That settles that then,' said Martha with a sigh of relief. 'Bring me a light lunch back with you in case I regain my appetite by teatime.'

'Consider it done,' said Jake.

As a churchwarden, Daniel was in church an hour before the Eucharist was set to start. Every little detail had to be checked before service began and nothing was left to chance. He took his responsibilities seriously.

Silas arrived with fifteen minutes to spare; just enough time for Spotty to fix him up with the promised cassock, suitably lengthened, and to introduce the guest tenor to the rest of the choir.

Lorna, unusually for her, was late for the start of the service arriving in the middle of the first hymn. She joined Daniel in his churchwarden's pew, quickly explaining that her leaving home had been delayed by a 'phone call from Douglas.

'They all right?' queried Daniel, *sotto voce*.

'Yes, O.K. More later,' said Lorna. 'Nothing to worry about. Is He here?' referring to Silas.

Daniel nodded his head imperceptibly in the direction of the choir stalls. 'Can't miss a hop-pole at twenty yards.'

Regaining her composure after her late arrival, Lorna glanced over at the choir. At that very same moment Silas looked up from his music to check on who it might be that had sidled in late to join Damnit, and

Lorna found herself, even at a distance, eyeing the charming sidesman from St Thomas's Church, Ravensrigg. For one fleeting moment she wondered if she detected an amused flicker of recognition in Silas's eyes before deciding that she was imagining things, safe in the knowledge that her face, veiled when they had met nine days earlier, would not have aroused his interest. Sinking to her knees on the hassock at her feet, under the pretence of uttering a silent prayer until the hymn came to an end, she took stock of what had come to pass.

It was too much of a coincidence to expect that the presence of Silas from Ravensrigg was anything other than a spying mission on behalf of Reuben Ossian. Why were the two men singing from the same hymn sheet? Silas had not been birdwatching for the last week: he must have been monitoring the parochial behaviour of the good folk of Tupshorne in Yowesdale. How very fortunate that Martha was unable to lunch at High Ash today – veil or no veil, Silas might have stumbled across a half-truth when introduced to two ladies, one of whom turned out to be the wife of the previous vicar of Saint Michael's. As things stood, Silas would be ignorant of the fact that his own cover was blown while hers was, for now, intact. That situation could alter during the course of the afternoon.

The Communion service proceeded smoothly up to the sermon – partway through which Lorna dug out a pencil from her handbag and wrote a brief statement on the back of the service sheet before passing it surreptitiously to Daniel. Four words said it all as he read, 'Silas is Ravensrigg sidesman.'

Short written questions and answers took up the rest of the sermon and all the clear space on their two service sheets.

On paper the conversation was silent.

'When did you realise?' wrote Daniel.

'Immediately you nodded towards him.'

'What does it mean?'

'He's spying for Reuben.'

'What's the point?'

'Same as the Seven. Digging for pertinent information.'

'He's been in the area a week. Could be writing a book.'

'I doubt it. He looks far too bright for that. We can feed him lots of misinformation over lunch.'

'You go home before me, and brief Jake. He'll love it. I'll bring Silas with me after I've seen everyone out of church.'

'Don't tell Timothy just yet,' was Lorna's final comment.

'You'll need your finest Freda Fazackerley voice for the rest of the day. Silas's musical ear might be your undoing,' was Daniel's signing off.

The sermon came to an end without either Daniel or Lorna having the faintest idea what had been preached at them.

Forty minutes later, Stephanie Potts played her favourite retiring organ voluntary – her own setting of 'All that hath life and breath, sing to the Lord,' from Haydn's Creation. The singing of her choir today, augmented by Silas the tenor troubadour had been an inspiration. Any newly appointed vicar was going to be impressed by a choir in such good heart and voice. Perhaps the tenor would come birdwatching again – the sooner the better.

Lorna left the church immediately the service ended, choosing not to stay for the convivial cup of coffee-with-biscuit that followed. Daniel readily understood the reason without being told and apologised to Silas for her sharp exit, explaining that she was rushing home to check on the chef. The introductions would have to wait.

Arriving home at High Ash after a brisk walk verging on a dash, Lorna went into her kitchen to be confronted by Jake wearing the apron depicting the church of Saint John the Divine, Wrensdown – a souvenir of her own and Martha's visit to the West Sussex parish. 'Suits you,' was Lorna's comment. 'It's a good thing it hasn't come from Ravensrigg because I've rushed home from church to apprise you of the fact that Ravensrigg has already come to Tupshorne.'

'What on earth does that mean?' asked Jake. 'It sounds Shakespearian.'

'Well, we don't have much time to prepare for the advent of Silas, the sidesman who so courteously greeted Martha and me at the funeral we attended at Saint Thomas's, Ravensrigg. He must be the Reverend Ossian's spy in Tupshorne – birdwatching my eye! Daniel, you and I will have to do our best to avoid any mention of what is happening with regard to the current state of the interregnum and hope for the best.'

'Would it be best if you disappeared now and went to see how Martha is, so leaving us three Old Ashesians to discuss what has happened to the world since we were schoolboys? It would take you out of the espionage equation straight off and if anyone is going to put their foot in it, it would be Damnit or I.'

'I'll take the risk,' said Lorna. 'If I keep my mouth shut for most of the time, particularly when we're eating lunch, then I can find something to do in the garden while you lads recall your childhood memories. I'll make it clear to Daniel that lunching at High Ash doesn't include an evening meal as well – and in that respect I don't think, from my previous encounter with Silas that he will outstay his welcome. He can always come again. Daniel's worried that Silas might recognise my voice, so I will need to polish up my Blackburn undertones for the afternoon.'

Lunch was fun. Lunch was prolonged. The conversation flowed without ceasing and even Lorna had to join in from time to time when addressed directly by Silas. The word interregnum was never on the topic menu and the town of Ravensrigg might have been a figment of the Greenswards' imagination.

Daniel had introduced Lorna to Silas as she welcomed them both at the front door. 'Lorna, dear, this is Silas Beaune – just one more relic from Jake's and my schooldays.'

'Delighted to meet you,' responded Lorna. 'I'm sorry I had to dash off straight after the service but I had to check on our visiting chef, whom you may or may not remember as Jake Drake at High Ashes.'

Jake chose this moment to appear from behind Lorna and stepped forward to shake Silas's hand. The Wrensdown apron had been consigned to the hook on the larder door.

'Good Heavens!' said Silas. 'Damnit never said he had his captain of cricket living nearby. I'm quite overwhelmed. When did you swap your cricket bat for a carving knife?'

'I didn't,' said Jake. 'I laid down my bat and picked up my Cross instead. I'm the recently retired vicar of this parish where you've stumbled across Damnit Greensward. I followed in Sambo's footsteps. Pleased to meet you again after all these years.' All three men beamed at each other with the pleasure of knowing that after such a long time the mere mention of Sambo's name gave them a common brotherhood.

'By the way,' said Silas, as they drifted through the hallway towards the sitting room, Lorna in the lead, 'I'm Silas Kinnon now. No longer Skinandbone. I dropped the surname Beaune when my father deserted my mother. I kept the Kinnon bit – my mother's maiden name. Enough said, I think.'

Hardly were they seated, Jake, Damnit and Lorna on chairs and Silas on the settee when, their lunch break over, two boisterous black dogs rushed in. Baggins jumped straight on to Silas's lap and Rouch leapt on to the spare seat next to him – both dogs anxious to make sure that their guest's face was washed before lunch.

'Crunch time,' thought Damnit. 'This will test his credentials. *Quis me amat, amat et canem meam.'*

'Oh, I say,' cried Silas with delight, grabbing each dog round their shoulders and hugging them together as they continued with their ritual cleansing. 'What a welcome. Have you a spare one I can take home with me?'

Lorna was cross. 'Come down, you naughty dogs. Just push them off Silas. I'm so sorry – you'll have to believe me when I say they've never acted like that before!' Quickly, she realised that in her displeasure she had spoken in her normal voice and without the overlay of any Lancashire accent. And in that moment, she suddenly remembered that she and Martha had exchanged very few words with Silas, and those in hushed tones, at the funeral service in Saint Thomas's Church Ravensrigg, when he had ushered them to a suitable pew. The chances of his remembering their meeting of nine days ago would be negligible. Or so she thought.

Silas was not in the least bothered by the overfriendly approach of the dogs but gently pushed them down off the settee. He smiled, a trifle wistfully thought Lorna. 'If my late wife was here with me your dogs would still be on the sofa. They know a dog lover when they smell one. I'm only surprised they've taken so long to find me.'

'Don't flatter yourself,' laughed Damnit. 'Lorna must have put their midday meal down just before coming to greet you. No need to tell you, grub trumps newcomers every time.'

By the time Silas set off for home, just after four o'clock, he had divulged precious little information about himself, in general terms, and his connection with the Ravensrigg church was never mentioned. After his departure, Lorna, Damnit and Jake took note of what they had learned. In no particular order they picked out any salient features of the wide ranging and often inconsequential chat that had taken place between Silas's arrival and his leaving, and Lorna jotted down their findings as a kind of post script to the tale of the travelling researches of Virginia and Rose Waters.

Silas Kinnon was clever but quiet except when singing. Parisian born, his native language was French but he spoke fluently in English, German, Spanish and Italian. He had studied Architecture at the Sorbonne and Milan and admitted in a self-effacing manner that he did have something of an international reputation by the time he had retired in the mid-1990s.

Katharine Kinnon, his adored mother, had died in Lausanne, Switzerland in 1983, aged seventy. In that same year Silas had changed his name by deed poll, dropping his father's surname Beaune, and taking British citizenship.

Early in 1966, aged twenty eight, he had married Magdalene Marienburg, an international interpreter from Basel, who for part of her time as a language student had been under the tutelage of his mother. And like Katharine, she was no mean singer. Magda, as she was known, had produced a son two weeks before Christmas. He was to become something in the sphere of social services but Magda had died six months before Katharine Kinnon – struck down by an obscure tropical disease contracted in Zaire to where she had been seconded as an interpreter in negotiations taking place between President Mobutu and the neighbouring African states. Life had been a challenge.

Eventually, in retirement, he had gone back to his mother's roots to live in the north east of England in the village of Eglingham, a few miles away from Alnwick.

Lorna posed the final query to Silas, by asking if within his world of an architect he had any special field or fields which exercised his abilities more than the others in such a wide ranging profession. Silas's answer was interesting. A singer from an early age and coached by his mother he had learned how to project his voice in almost any auditorium. A lifelong interest in the acoustics of public buildings still held his attention – acoustics was still a subject shrouded in mystery, an inexact science.

There was a surprise for Lorna as Silas thanked her for such warm hospitality. They were walking together towards the roadside gateway of High Ash – Jake and Damnit were following a few yards behind. Silas inclined his head from his great height and in his best voice suited to a sidesman spoke a few carefully chosen words. 'I'm delighted to have met you again, today without a veil. I'm not blessed with x-ray eyes but my ears never play me false. My acoustic sense. You also use Aphrodite perfume.' His eyes crinkled up in fun. 'That was my Magda's favourite – so much more subtle than lashing of lavender I think.'

Lorna coloured slightly before responding. 'I'm reminded of a James Bond villain's remarks about encounters. "Once is happenstance – twice is coincidence – a third meeting is enemy action." Tread carefully, Monsieur Beaune.'

'Of course I will,' murmured Silas with a chuckle. 'I've not had such fun for years.'

'What's been such fun?' queried Damnit as he and Jake caught up with the conspirators.

Silas lied. 'Birdwatching for a week in lovely Yowesdale. I've enjoyed it so much in so many ways, I'm tempted to move if I can find a suitable bachelor pad.'

'If that's the case,' said Damnit, 'a few words in the strictest confidence – keep away from Brickshaws Estate Agency. I'll say no more. Let us know if you're serious and if we can help we will.'

'I might hold you to that,' said Silas. 'Today's excellent lunch, for which many thanks, has been the icing on my birdwatcher's cake.'

As they waved goodbye to Silas, Jake chose the moment to muse on his own arrival in Tupshorne as a motherless child at the end of 1944. The little market town had from that time been his second home, visiting the Greensward family. Daniel's mother Emily had been his substitute mother figure. No wonder he had come home to become vicar of Saint Michael the Archangel. And now Silas, fifty seven years later, had fallen under the spell of Yowesdale – that is if he was to be believed in his expression of the chance of coming to live in the dale. 'Wait and see,' he thought. Damnit was amused by Silas's parting sentence, no doubt picked up from the local Yowesdale inhabitants during the week of watching birds.

'See you soon.'

Nine days later the greeting party of the parochial church council of Saint Michael the Archangel, Tupshorne, was standing on the church steps when a Lexus rolled on to the little car park specially reserved for visiting dignitaries. Daniel Tiltstone Greensward, churchwarden, stepped forward to welcome the Reverend Reuben and Mrs Ossian. Reuben introduced himself and Minerva to the little band of local worthies. Then the driver opened his car door and stepped out.

Reuben spoke. 'I persuaded my father to play chauffeur, just for today. May I introduce Silas Kinnon, my favourite architect and amateur ornithologist. He may look familiar.'

CHAPTER XVII

Spectatum Veniunt,
Veniunt Spectentur
Ut Ipsae

(They come to see, they come to
be seen themselves)

'Oh my,' gasped Stephanie Potts, before anyone else could speak. 'My guest tenor of two Sundays ago. How amazing.'

'And how interesting,' remarked Violet drily, very much under her breath before upping the sound level to add, 'Lovely to meet you – all three.'

'I'm not stopping,' said Silas. 'I'm off to the Yowe to see if I can catch sight of a pair of kingfishers I saw near the Middinside bridge. See you soon.'

'Hang on,' said Timothy Welsh. 'I'm sure we can find a spot of lunch for a chauffeur. You'd better do the parish round with us, never mind your birdwatching. We'll not insist on your appearing before the Bishop and the Archdeacon. That's scheduled for 2:30.'

'I'd be in the way,' said Silas, 'and I'm sure Reuben doesn't need his dad to hold his hand.'

'Nonsense,' replied Reuben, 'you might learn something that you don't know already. And you're not one to turn down a free lunch.'

Wrong on the first count, thought Damnit. He's done the tour already, probably several times in the course of his recent visit. Only the vicarage would have avoided the scrutiny of this eminent architect.

'So be it,' said Silas. 'I shall be interested to see the layout of the vicarage. Victorian vicarages were often built on the whim of would-be architects. Have you managed to keep the garden straight since Jacob Drake went?'

'Wait and see,' answered Damnit. 'That's where you're having lunch. With the church hall reduced to ashes, it seemed sensible to make use of the empty vicarage. You can make yourself useful while you wander round eating your sandwiches. I know for a fact that the raspberries need picking.'

Minerva joined in the schoolboy banter. 'Leave the picking to me. They're my favourite fruit. I presume it's a question of pick one – eat one, or more.'

Daniel smiled at her. 'I think you'll find that, if everything has gone according to plan, the canes are bare of fruit and with luck there's a big bowl of raspberries in the middle of the kitchen table waiting for us to add cream, or in my case sugar and cream. Martha used to whip up a fantastic raspberry mousse.'

'Who is Martha?' asked Minerva.

'The last vicar's missus,' answered Violet. 'Not an easy act to follow.'

Minerva noted the comment as, indeed, she identified just who it was that had made it. This was a personage worth cultivating, the church treasurer and a potential power broker. She undertook to ingratiate herself with Violet, not knowing that it was Violet of the Magnificent Seven who had vowed to find out what made her tick.

The pre-lunch tour of the parish began with the church and finished at the vicarage. Any neutral tour guide might have been interested to note that the Reverend Reuben said very little while being shown round. If there were any queries that could have arisen, he already knew the answers as a result of Silas's reconnoitring and he was content to chat about life in general rather than parish life in particular. It was left to Minerva Jemima to enliven the proceedings, mostly at the instigation of Violet, who started off on the right foot by asking about the Ossian children and the forthcoming addition to the family. Quite unwittingly, Violet had flicked the switch that turned on Minerva's inner fire. The family was her *raison d'être*. For her part, Minerva, without resorting to honeyed words wormed out of Violet all kinds of information about the affairs of the parish that Silas would never have picked up during his week in Yowesdale. Not only was Violet the church treasurer: she was a highly competitive baker, a very keen cottage gardener and as for jam making...It amused her to learn that this lovely old lady had played childminder for Daniel Greensward when he was a little boy, before he went away to school in 1943 and it was obvious that she still doted on him.

Lunch at the vicarage was a convivial if rather makeshift affair. In the absence of any furniture except for kitchen fittings, Timothy and Damnit had scraped together enough camping chairs, together with a couple of tables, to accommodate a total of twelve people. Muriel Welsh and Freda Alderwood who were not members of the reception party were responsible for laying on a splendid buffet lunch, the highlight of which was Muriel's signature dish, raspberry flummery based on the vicarage garden fruit.

Daniel had a personal question for Silas: a question that had bothered him since Silas had been introduced by Reuben on their arrival. He picked a moment when they were isolated together in the garden. 'How does father Kinnon equate to son Ossian?'

'With difficulty,' admitted Silas. 'We had a serious disagreement when I dropped my own father's name of Beaune. Reuben was only seventeen at the time and had never even seen or heard his grandfather Marcel Beaune. I was very surprised, even shocked by his reaction, because as my only child he was the apple of my mother's eye and he worshipped her. In hindsight, which we all know is perfect, I ought to have known how damaged he was after losing his mother and grandmother in the same six month period. I thought I knew my son better, but if anything I was more shattered than he and failed to pick up the signs of the depth of his distress. I became Silas Kinnon and he remained Reuben Beaune.'

'So why the change?' asked Damnit. 'Did he suddenly discover that too much burgundy was not good for his liver?'

'No, not at all. In fact, he only drinks beer – in all its many manifestations. No. What happened was, and this was quite unknown to me, his first term reading Theology at Durham University he decided to trace his grandfather. To cut a long story short, he discovered a despicable character, Marcel, alive and well and living in Basel with his fourth wife. They never met or communicated in any way and Reuben was able to understand why I had disowned my father. He told me all about the sorry tale coupled with an apology, not that an apology was necessary, and then his Kinnon sense of humour kicked in with a homonymic force. Beaune, or Bone as in 'skeleton' which translates into Latin as *OS*, plural *OSSA*, he played around with the word and came up with a new surname of Ossian. In his deed poll declaration he is Reuben Kinnon Ossian.'

'You couldn't invent a story like that – truth stranger than fiction,' said Damnit in admiration. 'That is something that hasn't come to light in our enquiries. We know of Minerva Jemima and I'm tempted to ask how she came by those names. Maybe later.' He stopped speaking, abruptly. 'The Bishop has just spotted us,' he whispered, 'and he's coming over.'

'Just one quick question before he reaches us,' said Silas. 'Who was Lorna's scented lady friend up in Ravensrigg?'

'Can't tell you now. It's classified information, like a whiff of perfume on the breeze.' Daniel addressed his bishop. 'I hope you appreciated the raspberry flummery, Bishop. Our caterers took the liberty of asking your good lady if a flummery was ever on the Bishop's Palace menu.'

'It was delicious,' replied the bishop. 'Knowing you of old, Daniel Greensward, I have to presume that you were referring to pudding and not the due process of selecting a new incumbent. It wouldn't be the first time that your innocent air belied some mischievous intent.' The bishop looked from one man to the other before continuing. 'Do I gather that you two have met before today?'

'Our scholastic paths crossed for just two terms at prep school in 1947,' replied Silas. 'Damnit was the hero who saved this little French new boy from a bramble thicket. We met again purely by chance only recently.'

'Some hero!' said Damnit. 'I'd forgotten all about it until Silas reminded me.' He glanced at his wristwatch. 'It's time we were going to High Ash, Bishop. The P.C.C. thought my house was a suitable venue for interviews. If you want to kill a bit of time birdwatching, Silas, go down to the Tupshorne sewage works – you'll see enough swallows and swifts to last a lifetime.'

The Archdeacon opened the proceedings by stating that it was most unfortunate that owing to circumstances beyond diocesan control there was only one candidate for interview, the Reverend Reuben Ossian. If for any reason or reasons he appeared to be unsuitable for the vacancy in Tupshorne, the P.C.C. must say so. The post would per force be re-advertised at the earliest opportunity. The Bishop then said a short prayer, asking for Divine guidance in their deliberations, before inviting Reuben to come into the Greenswards' sitting room to confront his destiny.

Reuben's *curriculum vitæ* was subjected to a searching examination. Any probing questions were answered promptly and without prevarication. Here was the sole candidate speaking confidently from a position of strength and addressing the panel with respect. A most convincing performance thought Timothy, and so polite.

Then the conversation turned from specifics to generalities as the floor was thrown open to a form of 'Any Questions,' or 'Any Other Business.'

'If you have any questions to ask of anyone here Reuben, now is your chance,' said the Bishop.

'Thank you, Bishop,' said Reuben. 'I can't really think of anything to say other than that I know what is expected of me and I feel that I can step up to the mark. Walking round the parish this morning and meeting so many parishioners, I was made very aware that there is a large pair of shoes to be filled and a hard act to follow.' He smiled at the little group on whom his immediate future depended before speaking again. 'I'd rather the post was not re-advertised just because I'm the sole survivor from the short list. I'm sure that the parish finances are healthy enough to stand the cost of a new search but it would not be money well spent. That means that I can count on the vote of the lady treasurer at least.'

'How right,' said Violet. 'And I would be happy to know your take on fund raising activities whether or not you end up in Tupshorne.'

Timothy asked if Reuben was committed to what Timothy regarded as fringe activities such as special services for pets and their owners.

'If it becomes apparent that there is a demand for that particular kind of Christian outreach, I would be very happy to oblige. Some years ago, in Ravensrigg, I introduced a special Palm Sunday service that mirrored Jesus' donkey ride into Jerusalem. There is a Donkey Sanctuary in a neighbouring parish that will supply as many donkeys as we might need. I like to think that a few of the disciples also knew a donkey owner. We put sand down the central aisle and it became obvious that the donkeys thought they were back in Scarborough. After two years of donkeys only, a handful of parishioners asked if they could bring their household pets along. I wasn't too keen on pet snakes at first and you can't deny church entry to a Praying Mantis. It has become Palm and Pets Sunday service.

I'm always pleased to be asked to bless a house or home when new residents move in.

It boils down to the fact that if the Spirit moves anyone to seek, through me, a blessing on their endeavours, as long as it is legal I feel duty bound to attend. I've not been called upon to carry out an exorcism as yet but I'm open to offers.'

'Have you received training in ritual exorcism?' asked the Archdeacon.

'Yes, I have as a matter of fact. About six years into my priesthood. I think a refresher course might not go amiss.'

Violet spoke up. 'Your credentials, as presented, are quite impressive and I can think of one or two of our Tupshorners who might benefit from a gentle bit of exorcism. Have you any weaknesses that you might care to admit to at this late stage? I don't mean women or booze, more like what one might call a ministerial gap, a chink in your armour of light.'

Reuben thought for a few moments before replying. 'In my previous parish, that is prior to Saint Thomas's Ravensrigg, one of my churchwardens, in a moment of rare frankness said, "You're a right people person vicar – right for anyone under seventy." I don't know why it is but I have to say that I'm in my element from the cradle to middle age. I work at it and I think I'm improving. At the moment, I'm fortunate in having a first class backup team when it comes to relating to those who are no longer young. With respect to all here and to those members of the welcome party who are not in this room, the majority are pensioners and you will have been charmed by Minerva, my wife, and Silas Kinnon my father. In the words of a famous song of many years ago – "If the right fist doesn't get you, then the left one will."'

'Nice one,' said Violet. '"And everybody knew you didn't give no lip to Big John". If appointed, do we assume that you will be bringing your backup team with you. Minerva has little choice in the matter, but your pensioner father does. Your young family are surely well settled in Ravensrigg and leaving would be something of a wrench. Does Minerva have any reservations? Will your father transplant successfully?'

'He's prepared to and he's always ready to as well. He's forever gazing into estate agency windows when on his birding breaks, wherever they take him. He's an architect – bricks and mortar of any kind, he finds fascinating.

As for Minerva Jemima, my muse, she is a daleswoman, Ilkley born and bred. If she can't live in Wharfedale, Queen of them all, she'll settle for being next door in Yowesdale.'

'The Empress of the Dales and home of the world's finest cheese,' chipped in the Archdeacon with some enthusiasm. 'Has anyone a final question?'

'I've several,' said Damnit.

'Oh no,' thought Timothy. 'Damnit's going to prick his bubble and we'll be back to square one.'

'But I'll content myself with one,' continued Damnit. 'It's not your usual kind of question, Reuben, but I would like your thoughts on suicide. Does it matter this side of Heaven?'

'That's a bit deep,' said Reuben. 'Do I detect a torpedo aimed at me amidships?' He looked at the Bishop. 'Must I answer, Bishop? Surely this is highly unusual or irregular. I fear my opinions may well be in conflict with those of yourself and the Archdeacon.'

'If so, so be it,' replied the Bishop. 'It is a brutal question at such short notice and presumably this particular churchwarden is intent on upsetting this selection applecart.' He looked at Daniel Greensward with grim disapproval. 'Earlier this very afternoon in the vicarage garden I alluded to your capacity for making mischief, Daniel. May I ask you the same question? "Does it matter this side of Heaven?"'

'Yes it does, Bishop,' said Damnit, belligerently. 'It's a serious issue in any society and I need to know how much it matters in the eyes of Reuben here. This interview process has been an easy passage for our sole candidate. I am a dalesman and I am suspicious of near apparent perfection. I expect an answer.'

'I make no claims to perfection,' said Reuben, showing a flash of temper. 'At least your words and those of the Bishop have allowed me pause for thought. This is to be my final answer and it is brief. Judaism, Islam and Christianity all frown on suicide in the expectation that there is no place in Heaven for those who choose to end their earthly life. Where is the compassion in that, I ask you? When I was a boy I remember being told that real seamen never learn to swim in the belief that the sea will claim its own. Real drowning can be quick so I understand. So if life on this earth becomes not worth living, tell your Creator you're coming home early. The Prodigal Son broke all the rules, admitted his many misdemeanours, and was not turned away by his father. I'm just a simple kind of chap and that is my simple kind of answer to such a barbed question. Now is not the time and neither is this the place to pontificate on suicide bombers, assisted suicide, multiple suicide, pacts *et cetera*. Relatives of suicide victims are themselves victims and I hope you will agree with me on this at least, Mr Greensward, that they deserve all the Christian compassion available this side of Heaven. Have I disarmed the missile you fired at me?'

Daniel nodded, sagely. 'To me, that's an awful lot of sense in a few brief sentences. Thank you. For a moment there, I thought I was hearing the voice of my old headmaster Sambo, Samuel Bone whom your father will surely remember as an early mentor and source of wisdom.'

'I think we can call it a day, a good day,' said the Archdeacon. 'Would you care to go and find Minerva. No doubt she's with Lorna – probably in the garden. The rest of us will remain here a little longer to discuss what we have heard and I expect that we shall come up with a decision. Watch the chimney for smoke.'

The decision was not long in coming. The Bishop made his opinion clear, echoed by the Archdeacon, that to re-advertise the post would be a pointless exercise. 'I think you have your man for the job. Does anyone here disagree?'

Damnit, for all his truculence, was in no mood to contradict his Bishop on the issue. In the same way that Lorna and Martha had been beguiled by Reuben during their brief visit to Saint Thomas's Ravensrigg, Reuben, Minerva and Silas, as chauffeur, had charmed Bishop, Archdeacon and all with whom they had met since their morning arrival at Saint Michael the Archangel in Tupshorne.

'It looks like we have *"nem.con."* Bishop,' said the Archdeacon. 'Could we just confirm that with a show of hands?'

Timothy Welsh, with a sigh of relief, was the last to raise a hand. Thank God, Damnit had opted to refrain from being at his destructive best.

'I think that our prayers, uttered over the past months, have been heard,' said the Bishop. 'Thank you, all of you, together with those behind the scenes who have worked so hard during the interregnum to keep this parish in such excellent shape. May you go on from strength to strength under your new shepherd. Just one small thing, while I think of it – as a P.C.C., would you be so kind as to drop a line of comfort and consolation to the Reverend Hazel Mears in Wrensdown. She may yet find herself up North sometime in the future. Do not waste a postage stamp on the vicar of Tamarel who has given no reason for his decision to withdraw from today's event at such very short notice. In due course, I intend to notify the bishop of Truro of such discourtesy.

Now, assuming that Reuben Ossian accepts this appointment and the usual arrangements go according to plan you may expect to attend his licensing as priest-in-charge on Tuesday, 11 September.

Your Archdeacon will attend the Eucharist next Sunday to inform your congregation, which leaves you with four days to keep tight-lipped.

Daniel, would you care to invite Reuben, Minerva and Lorna to join us – oh! and Silas Kinnon if he's back from visiting the sewage works?'

Lorna reversed the invitation by indicating that afternoon tea was awaiting everybody in the dining room and so it was there that Reuben Kinnon Ossian agreed to be the vicar elect of Saint Michael the Archangel, Tupshorne in Yowesdale.

The Bishop and the Archdeacon took their leave immediately after tea.

Timothy and Daniel discussed removal dates with Reuben and Minerva, mindful of the fact that Helen and Troy would need to be introduced to their new school at the beginning of term. The last week in August was suggested as the ideal time.

Minerva raised the subject of the nearest maternity hospital which might expect her patronage come the end of September.

For his part, Silas announced that he would put his Eglingham house on the market the next morning. He already had his eye on a suitable bachelor establishment, a converted barn on the edge of Tupshorne. Its architecture intrigued him. The Ravensrigg trio were on their way home shortly before 6:30. Two children would perhaps ask where they had been.

CHAPTER XVIII

Manus Manum Lavabit

(Hand will wash hand. [You scratched my back, now I will scratch yours])

At ten o'clock the following morning, the eleventh of July, the telephone rang at High Ash.

Lorna answered. 'Hello. High Ash.'

'Hello. And how is my favourite fragrant lady today?' It was Silas.

'Much happier than this time yesterday, thank you,' said Lorna. 'And you?'

'Very pleased that the two-way dirty tricks campaign has achieved such an excellent result. I'm contemplating writing a book about it all. Would you and your veiled anonymous fellow sleuth care to collaborate?'

'Not a chance,' chuckled Lorna. 'You've missed that particular boat. I looked at three very different priests – you only visited one vacant parish. Mind you, it could be fun to compare notes, but only after you've moved. Your chance rediscovery of Daniel and appraisal of him would make interesting reading for me.'

She broke off from her facetious remarks. 'I'm sure it's Daniel you want to talk to anyway. He's right here next to me, washing up the breakfast pots so he knows to whom I'm talking. He's just taken off his rubber gloves and he's all yours.'

'Morning Silas,' said Daniel, 'what can I do for you? Your family played a blinder yesterday. You deserve the day off.'

'We need to talk,' replied Silas in mock dramatic fashion. 'And the sooner the better from my point of view. It may be to our mutual advantage.'

'You make it sound urgent,' said Daniel. 'Perhaps you should have stayed in Tupshorne last night and let Reuben drive home.'

'It crossed my mind but too late to act so soon after Reuben accepted the job. It's not a matter of life and death but I have so much to talk about and I know that you are just the man to talk to.'

'You flatter me,' said Daniel. 'Unless you are talking personal affairs, I am bound by courtesy to include Timothy Welsh, my fellow churchwarden, in any talk affecting parish admin. Is that understood?'

'Absolutely,' said Silas. 'But you are my starting point in personal terms and then the field can be opened up to Timothy and no doubt others just as soon as you may think fit.'

'The mystery deepens,' said Daniel. 'Is Reuben involved in it at this stage?'

'No, not at all. He has no idea what I have in mind and it might turn out that he could have little interest in my thinking. I could be wrong though.'

'Right,' replied Daniel, seizing the initiative and anxious to short-circuit a conversation that was going nowhere. 'Whatever it is that is exercising your mind, you obviously don't wish to talk about it over the phone. Do we arrange a meeting halfway or must it be on Tupshorne soil? As it happens, I'm free for the rest of the week.'

'Tupshorne would be ideal, bearing in mind that my new concerns belong there. Can I come tomorrow, treat you and Lorna to a bite of lunch in town somewhere? It won't matter if she hears what I have to say and any comment she might feel like making would be interesting and welcome.'

'What a splendid offer,' said Daniel, 'and if you can make it to High Ash for eleven o'clock, expect coffee.'

'I'll be there,' said Silas and rang off. For a moment he wondered why Daniel had not asked him for an inkling about the reason for his returning so soon to High Ash.

Having replaced the handset, Daniel turned to Lorna. 'You overheard all that, I hope. He wasn't giving anything away and I had the impression that, had I enquired he wasn't inclined to elaborate further on his wish to discuss something. Any thoughts, dear? He seems almost anxious to involve you.'

'Blackmail! I reckon,' said Lorna, thinking quickly and speaking slowly, 'I reckon he's set on telling the Archdeacon all he knows about the Tupshorne Ladies Investigation Bureau unless we cooperate with his wicked plans. He doesn't need money, that's for sure.'

Daniel roared with laughter. 'You and your imagination. I can hardly bear to wait for your book to come out, with all its fictional embellishments. High Ashes boys weren't cut out to be blackmailers. Safe crackers, yes – but that's another story involving Albert Prince of sweet and blessed memory. You forgot that Silas was spying as well, so he wouldn't want to blow the whistle on himself, would he?'

Lorna gave an impish chuckle. 'Try another tack. Silas is a highly presentable widower, younger than you by about four years and looking at least ten years less than that. You being a mere man are not as well attuned to detecting the gleam still alive in Silas's eye as Martha and I are. He met me here two Sundays ago, realised I was one of two perfumed ladies at Herb's funeral, then was stunned to find that this "widow" had a husband – you. One down and one to go. Perhaps I should warn Martha.' She chuckled. 'And Jake too.'

'Funny you should say that. Yesterday, just before the Bishop joined Silas and me in the vicarage garden, Silas asked me who your scented lady friend was. My answer was that I couldn't answer because it was classified information. As for that twinkle in the eye – surely it's something all High Ashesians have in common. But coming down to earth again, when I said that Timothy had to be involved in whatever it was that he had in mind, he, Silas, immediately concurred and included anyone else – presumably the P.C.C. – who may be interested. So I think it must be something parochial and we shall have to wait until this time tomorrow to find out.'

Lorna pursed her lips before commenting further. Then, with a twinkle in the eye delivered her summing up. 'He's up to something and he's in a hurry. I suspect this suggestion of materials parochial on his part is a red herring. Silas is a very attractive man – Martha and I, two lovely ladies and respectably married, were acutely aware of his charisma. There was absolutely no reason for him to join our church choir for just one service. What age would you say Miss Stephanie Potts is?'

It was Daniel's turn to chuckle.

'I didn't know, I'd married a *shadchan*.'

'A what?' demanded Lorna.

'A *shadchan*,'retorted Daniel. 'It's a Yiddish word. Put the kettle on – the ability to produce a decent cup of coffee is the prime requirement of a matchmaker. You can get a little practice in before Silas arrives here in about twenty four hours.'

Damnit Greensward took a direct approach from the outset, even before Silas could take a sip of coffee or nibble at a biscuit.

'The floor is yours Silas. What brings you back to Tupshorne so soon? It can't be birdwatching this time.'

'No – definitely not that. A great deal has happened since I first encountered Lorna at a funeral service nearly three weeks ago. And

I'm sure that you will both be amused to know that following their appearance at the Sunday service, when I arrived back at Saint Thomas's after my week in Yowesdale all the talk was of the two veiled lady visitors reeking of lavender. My time here was not wasted and now that Reuben is to become priest-in-charge I shall be moving to Yowesdale from Eglingham where, as of this morning, my house is up for sale. The point is this. When I lunched with you and Jake that Sunday when I joined the choir for a one-off, just before our farewells I jested that I was tempted to move if I could find a suitable property. I was prophetic then and with Reuben's advent I have given in to the temptation. Now, if I could find a property this very day I would still be looking at perhaps a two to three months gap before I could move in. Do you agree?'

'I certainly can't disagree,' said Damnit. 'The way the property market is just now, the gap could well be longer – I'm assuming you will need to sell your current house first. I'm not sure if wise architects and bridging loans are compatible.'

'This prudent architect, in all modesty, can afford to fund a bridging loan but it would be in the best interests of no one.'

Lorna broke in 'So what would, Silas? I think you have a cunning plan – right?'

'No cunning,' declared Silas. 'Walking round the vicarage garden two days ago I couldn't help but notice that the P.C.C., with the best will in the world, was having a problem with garden maintenance. That raspberry flummery we had for pudding was superb – but who is going to prune out the fruited canes? They'll need doing, probably next week. The vicarage is in an excellent state of repair considering it hasn't been occupied since the end of September last year. A lick of paint here and there wouldn't go amiss. Let me live in the vicarage and I will deal with the garden and any touching up of the décor that is necessary. I don't mind camping in the house for six or so weeks until the Ossians move in. I'll even pay rent.'

Silas paused for a moment to let the impact of his offer sink in before continuing. 'I have to say that Reuben and Minerva have no idea what I am up to today. If in the meantime, I have not found a property for myself, I'll clear out of the vicarage before they move in. How's that – everyone's a winner?'

'Timothy Welsh will be wowed,' said Damnit. 'He's been organising the maintenance crew. It would relieve me from mowing the lawn too.

But not for one moment can I see the Archdeacon giving his blessing to such a scheme.'

'Daniel, dear,' said Lorna, 'the Archdeacon never knew about the Tupshorne Magnificent Seven and their underhand detective work. There's your answer. If he ever finds out that you've had a squatter in the empty vicarage for a few weeks before being evicted by mutual consent, you can put it down to Saint Michael's charitable outreach. As for you Silas, you're as devious as Daniel. Who gave lessons on Deviousness, or should it be Deviosity, at High Ash?'

As one, both men replied, 'Mrs Askey.'

'I'll talk it over with Timothy as soon as I can. He might see some sense in your proposals. Have you anything else up your architectural sleeve, Silas?'

'Yes,' joined in Lorna, 'you've come down here at such short notice that it would be naïve of me to think there is nothing else on your agenda.'

'I've not handled this very well,' replied Silas, a trifle ruefully. 'It was my intention to open with an entirely different topic from that of my own property and removal questions. They are secondary to my prime reason for coming down to see you and I will come back to that in a moment. After talking to you, Damnit, on the 'phone yesterday I took your point that Timothy must be consulted about anything to do with parish affairs so I had the temerity to invite him to lunch with us. Muriel is otherwise engaged. I should have told you first thing – it would have made more sense – then I could have raised the vicarage business over the soup course. I'm getting muddled in my old age.'

'I don't think so at all,' said Lorna, 'you're just muddying the waters a little by getting to Daniel first. All will become crystal clear by the time we arrive at the coffee stage. It seems to me that you are procrastinating in spite of an apparent wish to hasten your moving plans. I repeat my last question. What else is on your agenda that you now say is your principal reason for this speedy return to Tupshorne? Words of one syllable would be acceptable.'

Silas rose to his feet and smiled at her before answering. 'A simple, direct question Lorna, deserves a matching reply – and our lunch is not far away. I've booked a table at the Ram and Raddle.

My motivation for being here is as follows. Briefly, I first came to Tupshorne on a scouting mission. Purely by chance I met Damnit, my hero from High Ashes who freed a desperately unhappy little French boy from a giant bramble bush. As a new boy that Lent term, I wasn't physically bullied as such because Sambo never tolerated that sort of conduct but little boys, and for that matter girls as well, can be unthinkingly cruel to something or someone that they perceive to be foreign. Damnit, four years my senior, was the first boy to show me kindness and in doing so, quite literally, threw away his cross country championship trophy that he had won – in record time I was told later – in 1946. I never forgot the champion who released me. I even began to speak English and was at last accepted by my peers.'

Lorna looked at Daniel who was sitting, open-mouthed, staring at Silas, as if in a daydream. She knew, because Daniel had told her about his asking of Reuben his attitude to simple suicide, that Reuben's use of the word 'compassion' in his reply had convinced Daniel the selection panel had found the right priest to follow Jake. And here was Silas as a witness to Daniel's own compassion, exhibited before he had attained teenage.

'I'm here now to grasp the opportunity, I hope, to repay in some measure your act of kindness of over fifty years ago,' continued Silas. 'Saint Michael the Archangel stands in need of a new church hall to replace that destroyed by fire. Let me be the architect. Public buildings have been my special sphere of operation. I would waive all fees.'

The silence in the room was so utter that a feather dropping on the carpet would have been heard and it was Silas himself who was the first person to break it. He cleared his throat.

'Would you like me to repeat my offer?'

'Yes please,' said Daniel. 'I wonder if I can believe what I think I heard. For just a second there I had a flashback to when I acquired my nickname of longstanding. You won't know Silas but I swore at Sambo during a Latin lesson back in September, 1942. Sambo said, "Did I hear what I think I heard?" He'd heard me say "Damn it," and it stuck.'

Silas smiled as he replied. 'Well, you and Lorna did hear what you thought you heard. Let me be the man to rebuild your church hall.'

'Well, I'll be damned,' said Lorna, much to Damnit's amusement. 'I wonder what became of that bramble bush. It should be nominated as a place of pilgrimage.'

'I don't know about damnation but it's certainly a bolt from the blue,' said Damnit. 'To whom it may concern, I say, "I accept" with alacrity.' I can't wait to see Timothy's face when you tell him over lunch.

There is an awful lot of difficult detail to discuss and I know that in this kind of situation there will be many hurdles to clear and hoops to jump through.'

'Lunch at the Ram and Raddle could be the start of something big. From past experience, the diocesan authority might turn out the biggest bugbear,' said Silas, ' – even a major headache.'

'Amen to that,' intoned Daniel. 'Let's shake on it and then go to lunch. One vital thing that you don't know Silas is that the church hall land belongs to me. But that is another story.'

CHAPTER XIX

Aut In Veniam Viam
Aut Faciam

(I will either find a way or I will make one)

Lunch turned out to be a very exciting meal indeed. The menu was short on inspiration, the food somewhat tasteless, the service desultory and the cut flowers on display throughout the Ram and Raddle feeling the heat of a very warm July day.

Timothy Welsh was waiting at the bar when Lorna, Damnit and Silas joined him. As the first arrival, he insisted on buying the first round of drinks. Although Silas had been the one to invite him to lunch, Timothy was under the false impression that Damnit was the instigator of the meeting and it was to him that he directed his opening question.

'So Daniel, there must be a good reason for you to scramble an old fighter like me. What's the urgency?'

'The urgency doesn't lie with me,' said Daniel. 'It's Silas who is concerned with the present state of the vicarage.'

Timothy took umbrage. 'I can't see that it's any of his business, begging his pardon.'

'Sorry,' said Damnit, 'I don't think I worded that at all well. I should have said that he fancies being the vicarage caretaker until Reuben and family move in. Silas can explain it all – it's quite clear really. Over to you Silas.'

Timothy listened with some admiration as Silas outlined his reasons for wishing to occupy the vicarage for a few weeks. Without being selfish, it was obvious that his maintenance team could be stood down immediately. As for the matter of a spot of cosmetic decoration, he was sure the P.C.C. could afford a few cans of paint or whatever it took. He enquired whether or not Minerva would like to turn one bedroom into a nursery for the new addition to the Ossian family arriving in late-September. Silas said he did not know the answer but if his plans on vicarage squatting were approved he would ask Minerva about a nursery and any colour scheme she might have had in mind.

Timothy was rather taken with Silas's offer to pay rent, teasing him about the exorbitant rates that might be charged for a six-bedroomed consecrated vicarage – payable in cash to the churchwardens and not a word to the Archdeacon who might wish to get in on the act. Had such a ruse ever been perpetrated before, he wanted to know?

'Naughty, naughty,' said Lorna. 'Don't put such ideas into Daniel's head – he's very gullible you know and always on the lookout for a fund-raising opportunity: even hare-brained schemes get an airing.'

Daniel smiled indulgently. 'Getting down to brass tacks, Silas, your suggestion – or suggestions – merits my personal approval. Houses, and particularly decent-sized ones, tend to deteriorate, however slightly, if unoccupied for any length of time. I doubt the Archdeacon would be bothered. I say "let's get on with it" and may "mum" be the word.'

'Me too,' nodded Timothy. 'Perhaps from the very start of an interregnum, every vacant vicarage should have an occupier installed, rent free, until a new appointment is made. I can just see a life of being a serial no-rent rectory occupier being very attractive to a certain type such as a countrywide camper *manqué*.'

'I don't see Silas applying for that lifestyle,' said Lorna. She looked enquiringly at Daniel before continuing. 'In fact, if your own property disposal takes a bit longer than you expect at this moment, Silas, I'm sure we could find a bed for you at High Ash. In the meantime, living in the vicarage is a great idea. If it was any of my business, I'd say "move in today."'

'How very kind of you. Thank you,' said Silas. 'Will it be necessary to put my ideas to the P.C.C.? I'm not past pitching my tent in the garden if it would help?'

'I don't think so,' said Timothy. 'The next few weeks will fly by very quickly, mark my words. Several councillors are on holiday right now following the selection meeting and if we were to call an emergency meeting we might not raise a quorum anyway. What do you reckon Damnit?'

'It's purely a matter of property management during an interregnum – very much the domain of thee and me as churchwardens. We'll 'phone the other P.C.C. members, on holiday or not, and tell them straight what we have decided. Violet's the only person who must be told, because the bills for paint *et cetera* will be her concern as treasurer.'

'I would of course expect to pay for fuel and water,' said Silas, 'especially if I'm to be living rent free.'

'Again,' said Lorna, 'it's not my business, but it seems to me that someone who makes no charge for his labour when decorating the vicarage should have all extraneous expenses wiped off the slate. It wouldn't amount to much because if we let it to be known among the congregation that the decorator needs feeding, Silas won't be doing much cooking. *Ergo* – no cooking, no fuel bill. The senior choristers will be queuing up to host a fresh tenor with Stephanie in the lead.'

'That's that taken care of then,' said Timothy. 'You can go back to Ravensrigg – no, to Eglingham, – pack a couple of cases and move in tomorrow. Now, was there anything else on the agenda this lovely day?'

'Silas Kinnon, Part Two,' said Damnit, smiling broadly. 'Prepare yourself for a not unpleasant shock, Timothy.'

Silas addressed Timothy. 'If I'm to get back to Eglingham tonight, pack my bags and return tomorrow, I'd better be brief. Daniel and Lorna only learned about this earlier this morning when I talked about it shortly before coming here for lunch.

First and definitely foremost, I am an architect and although retired from my one-time international practice, my reputation in the field of public buildings construction is still rock solid. End of personal blowing of trumpet.

A few weeks ago, as you now know, I came here to Tupshorne on a spying mission on behalf of my son Reuben and his family. Seeing a kingfisher was a lucky bonus. I saw the ashes of a church hall recently burnt down. By an extraordinary coincidence I met Daniel Damnit Greensward, a man who as a senior prep school boy was the first person to show a little French boy a kindness that I have never forgotten. We were school contemporaries for two terms only in 1947. It has taken fifty four years for me to repay an important debt of honour. For me, Damnit threw away a school championship cross country trophy. It may not have been very valuable in 1947, in cash terms, but all these years later in my eyes that trophy has acquired enormous sentimental value. Pay back time has arrived. I would like to be the architect responsible for the planning and rebuilding of your church hall – and that would be entirely free of charge.'

'Well, I'll be damned,' said Timothy, echoing Lorna's words of earlier that day. 'You provide us with a new vicar, act as vicarage caretaker and handyman for a few weeks and now this. In modern parlance, I find it hard to get my head round it. I presume you've already broached the subject with Damnit?'

'Just before we left High Ash to meet you at the Ram and Raddle,' said Damnit. 'I accepted immediately. I can recognise a gift horse when I see one, just as I am sure you can.'

'Sounds too good to be true,' said Timothy. 'Now who do you think was the last person I heard using that particular expression, Damnit? There's no doubt it's a fantastic proposition but I fear the diocesan authority might not see it that way. It's interesting though because you own the ground the hall was built on. Does Silas know that?'

Lorna was on the point of answering the question as Timothy paused very briefly before continuing. 'I'm sorry Silas – don't misunderstand me. Not for one moment do I doubt your *bona fides.* My first reaction is to agree with Daniel and accept your splendid and generous offer. Then I see the pitfalls that will have to be negotiated. I suggest that we agree to accept in principle what is proposed, sleep on it, mull it over and meet again to discuss it when Silas is ensconced in the vicarage.'

'That's fine by me,' said Silas, 'and Damnit has told me of his title to the land. That alone opens up new lines of development, strengthening your hand when dealing with the diocesan office, something I'm not unfamiliar with. By all means think about my offer, treat it like a pebble, throw it in the parish pond and watch the ripples.'

'More like a hot potato,' observed Lorna, 'but I'm not too sure that Daniel should sleep on it. His dreams have a habit of upsetting the applecart or should that be dropping the chip pan? Am I right, dear?'

'Don't tempt me,' answered Daniel. That's one factor that is an unknown in Silas's book. As Sambo might have said, *'Manus manum lavabit.'*

Silas nodded in agreement.

CHAPTER XX

Occasionem Cognosce

(Spot an opportunity)

Walking homewards from the Ram and Raddle, Lorna surprised Daniel with a seemingly innocent question.

'Have you ever contemplated leaving High Ash?'

'What sort of a question is that?' asked Daniel, bemused for a moment. 'It's not crossed my mind since I moved in eleven years ago. No! I tell a lie. I did think about it, briefly, after Bethan's death. She and I were joint owners but we made a few basic alterations before she, not long widowed, came up from Maidenhead. The changes meant that although we shared the house, she could be as independent as she wished with her own quarters. That was that – I stayed put – and just as well because the nest was reasonably attractive to Mrs Swann when she visited me. And the rest, as they say, is history. The garden suits me at the moment, yet I can foresee a time when its proper maintenance could become a problem as I age. But why do you ask?'

'I just wondered,' said Lorna. 'I've always fancied living in a farmhouse but short of marrying a farmer it's not going to happen. I suppose it's a pipedream like that of a staid old motorist hankering after a flashy sports car.'

'Or an eminent architect who never gets around to building his own house,' ventured Daniel. 'You do know, My Love, that if you had stipulated living in a farmhouse as a condition of your marrying me I'd have given you one as a wedding gift even if it meant robbing a bank. Is it too late?'

'That will not be necessary,' said Lorna, 'and if you're intent on robbing a bank you'd need help from Albert Prince, master locksmith, but sadly deceased. I'll bear your offer in mind though.'

They paused for a moment in their walk, looked at each other and enjoyed a mutual chuckle before Lorna spoke again.

'While we've got Silas in thrall to his knight in shining armour of 1947 perhaps we ought to buy a farm, you can burn it down and he can plan a modern rebuild for us. I mean, just think of the church hall.'

'What? Me an arsonist?' said Daniel. 'How could you even think of such a thing?'

'Because Mrs Askey instructed you in deviousness and there's nothing I wouldn't put past you if you cared to put your mind to it – so there!'

'In truth,' said Daniel, 'I've never struck a match in anger.'

'How about in cold blood?' murmured Lorna softly.'

'Your fervid imagination is running away with you,' said Daniel. 'So much excitement in Silas's corner has produced quite an adrenalin rush – we'll need an early-night to recover.'

'Agreed,' said Lorna. 'It has been fun though, hasn't it? It reminded me of a childhood game my parents played with me. Perhaps they even invented it for my entertainment. It had two titles, both as precursors to a bout of storytelling, "Imagine," and "Suppose If". You would have excelled at it.'

'I might have,' agreed Daniel, 'but I'd have had to give best to John Smith, my marvellous Latvian friend whom you met in your dream of a few weeks ago. He was the raconteur supreme. Which reminds me – I must get hold of a copy of Max Herrick's book when it is published. It should be out later this year I think. "John Smith – Storymaster Supreme," as recounted to Max Herrick, ought to make the bestseller lists as well as feature on "A Book at Bedtime". Janis Kalējs could recount his tales in four languages. He even spun yarns to Rolls Royce engines running on the test bed – and that is why they run so quietly waiting for a plot to unfold.'

Daniel smiled in happy remembrance.

Damnit knew perfectly well that however early an early bedtime turned out to be he would have difficulty in going to sleep. Silas's offer of free professional services was fizzing in his head like a fuse on a firework. Deciding to take the puzzle into his world of dreams, he recalled hearing the voice of Albert Prince as he relinquished Albert's ashes into the mouth of Mount Etna's volcano. Both he and Lorna heard the words 'See you sometime – not bedroom seven – but in the Prince Collection.'

Albert's 'Prince Collection' of locks and all the paraphernalia associated with the art and artistry of a master locksmith was located within a special section of the National Museum of Engineering and it was to there that Daniel dreamed his way. He found Albert at his old workbench, mixing a batch of 'Prince's Emperor Wax (for a right royal impression),' a special product that he had perfected in 1995. Albert spoke without bothering to look up from the task in hand, 'Hello, Daniel – I've been expecting you for some time. Come and have a stir of the wax and tell me what has stirred you into such action that you need my help and or advice. You'll have to hurry as I'm not here for long.'

Daniel told him everything as quickly as he could, cutting out any superfluous information, from the burning down of the church hall to Silas's offer of expertise in the rebuilding. In an afterthought, he even reminded himself that the hall ground belonged to him.

Albert's answer as he began to fade away was succinct. 'You'll be awash with money, Daniel. Do not let it drown you. Think big.' He was gone.

Daniel turned to leave the room and came face to face with his beloved prep school headmaster, the Reverend Samuel Bone. 'I heard it all,' said Sambo. 'Somehow, you must make your confession to Jake before your time is called. Fire is like anger – all consuming. If the money doesn't drown you, the fire under the crucible that you find yourself in will melt you. List to the voice of the singer. Trust Silas.' With a swish of his cassock, Sambo vanished. Daniel sensed a third presence. 'Where are you, John?' he whispered.

'Behind you, Damnit, as usual,' replied John. 'Don't turn round, just listen to me. Use the water, don't drown in it. It is your genie in the bottle. Heed the women.' Damnit knew that John had been and gone.

At breakfast the next morning, Lorna asked Daniel if he had enjoyed a good night's sleep.'

'Not bad at all, thank you,' he said. 'And you?'

'Yes, pretty good once you had ceased tossing and turning and dropped off.'

'Sorry about that. I remember pondering for a while on the church hall situation – that must have accounted for my agitation. It'll sort itself out before long. I'd value your input as soon as you like to make it.'

'Give me until teatime, dear,' said Lorna giving Daniel her best enigmatic smile. 'I'll have a grand plan worked out for you entirely free of charge.'

'I can't wait,' said Daniel. 'Would you like me to take the dogs out for the day, well out of your way while you machinate – nice word that. Fix me up with a picnic and we'll leave you in peace.'

'That's a good idea. Be back by six o'clock and you can tear my machinations to shreds while we have scrambled eggs on toast. It'll be the girls' teatime as well.'

Baggins and Rauch shot out from under the breakfast table where they had been lying listening to the chat. Daniel's 'dogs out' had alerted them to the possibility of physical exercise, but Lorna's 'girls' teatime' was a siren call for two black Labradors ever intent on the next feast.

'Ouch!' said Lorna, still wearing her bedroom slippers. 'Do mind my feet, you clumsy things.'

The dogs padded out of the room and made for the back door, close to where their leashes were hanging on hooks.

'Seeing our two so keen to go out for a walk, why don't you ring Jake and offer to take him and Miss Bindle with you. I know that Martha's recovered from her bad head of last Sunday and a few hours without Jake will do her the world of good. I can make up two picnics – one for you and Jake – and one for me and Martha. So while you're tramping over the moors I can join Martha for as long as it takes us two ladies to decide what to do about the Silas situation.'

'Excellent idea,' agreed Daniel. 'I'll ring right away. We could take the moorland road towards Skipton, have a walk on the wild side, then go onto the Skipton Canal Basin and check on the state of the Bethdan before returning home. Jake will be intrigued by the architectural turn of events. I can pick his brains while you conspire once again with Martha.'

Lorna looked out of the window. 'It looks as if the weather forecast might be right for once. Tell Jake to bring a change of clothing – for all your waterproofs you're going to get damp and sweaty. Just one more thing, if you have to curtail your walk and get to the Bethdan early give Barney Hammond a buzz – your marine engineer friend at S C A...'

'S C A M P S,' finished Daniel. 'The Skipton Cycle and Motorcycle Parts Shop. Why should I bother Barney, he'll be at work?'

'Precisely,' said Lorna. 'Ask him to service Moll. You said we were due for a little canal cruise in September. You'll be cross if your motorbike isn't in good order. I'll put some stale cake and a drop of milk in with your picnic – you invite Barney to tea on the Bethdan – then he can take Moll back to SCAMPS with him.'

'You'd make a marvellous P.A.,' said Daniel 'unpaid of course. Your word is my command, dear wife. I've not seen Barney for a while and I don't think he's ever met Jake. If he's free for tea and stale cake it will be a hilarious meeting.'

And so it came to pass.

The two fragrant ladies met, discussed and reached certain conclusions, all in good time for Daniel's return.

Three black bitch Labradors were exercised, soaked in the process, vigorously towelled dry and settled down to sleep in the back of Trollop, Daniel's Toyota RAV4. Two old friends walked their dogs in a downpour before changing into dry clothing to meet another old friend of one of them on the narrow boat Bethdan, moored in the Skipton Canal Basin.

Moll, the Honda 90 motorbike, went to SCAMPS for an engineering health check.

In the bright sunshine of the late-afternoon two men and their three dogs motored back to Yowesdale, happy, tired and hungry.

'So,' began Daniel as he settled down to tackle the promised scrambled eggs on toast, 'what kind of a day have you had?'

'I've enjoyed a brilliant day – exciting, even exhilarating if the truth be told.'

'Such enthusiasm,' said Daniel. 'Do I detect a slightly provocative nuance in the truth about to be revealed?'

'Not really,' answered Lorna, 'but you remember when we were coming home from the pub yesterday I confessed to having a yen to live in a farmhouse?'

'Yes, I remember,' said Daniel, 'and I suppose today being today you've been out and bought one off the shelf, and now you expect me to drive round and burn it down.'

'How did you guess?' said Lorna. 'I don't want to rush you but as I've not signed any papers yet I'm not in a position to take out fire insurance. It'll take a little time to set up the bank robbery.'

'Now I've heard it all,' said Daniel with an indulgent air, joining in with what he perceived to be a tall tale. 'Tell me you're not leaving me so soon. We've only been married a few weeks.'

Lorna brought him down to earth mischievously but gently. 'Don't fret, dear. It's perfectly true, although I have no intention to abandon you to rattle round High Ash – I'm too comfortable by half living with you.'

'I'm totally mystified,' said Daniel with mock resignation. 'Enlighten me. Has Martha been leading you astray?'

'Let's take our final cup of tea into the sitting room, settle down comfortably and all shall be revealed,' said Lorna.

The rain of earlier in the day had passed over and given way to an evening of sunlight streaming in through the westerly facing window as they sat down to talk about Lorna's day with Martha.

Daniel's eyes widened as Lorna began. 'I don't for a second imagine that you and the other principals concerned will heed what Martha and I have come up with. We realised that obstacles might crop up to derail our plans. That is par for any course.' She extracted a sheet of paper from a hip pocket and began to read, elaborating as she developed each point.

'Point one. You own the church hall site. It's valuable.

Two. Martha is adamant that the hall itself has for some time been too small for its purposes. Late-1800s– OK, early-twenty first century, US.

Three. Sell the hall site for residential purposes or better still, to maximise any potential profit, develop the site under your own steam and be prepared to recompense Silas out of those profits for any fee earning work that you may ask him to perform for you. It is, at this point anyway, the church hall rebuilding that Silas has offered his services for – free of charge.

Four. Pray that the Almighty Insurance Company will allow the fire insurance payout to be used for building a new church hall – or part of it at least.

Five. Graft the new hall on to the north wall of the church.'

Daniel interrupted her. 'There's not enough space there for anything, even on the scale of the old hall, never mind a replacement of a significantly larger size, which as Martha so rightly says is needed.'

'Correct,' said Lorna. 'Now comes the twist. We toyed with the idea of extending the church to the north over any available ground,' – she smiled 'that would cut down on your mowing activities now you're getting so old – only teasing, dear; then we would incorporate the main body of the church building into a kind of hybrid church hall when required The chancel itself could be screened off during secular events.'

'Not a cat in Hell's chance,' stated Daniel. 'the diocesan authority wouldn't stomach that.'

'Which is just what Martha and I expected,' said Lorna. 'So at eleven o'clock we called a tea break, after which we read the tea leaves in each other's cups and came up with our own interpretations. The outcome of our deliberations became obvious. Martha told me something that I didn't know about – the extent to which the huge fundraising effort of Jake's last nine months in office had exceeded its target. No less than £29,000 which the P.C.C. thought would refurbish the church hall with plenty to spare. Then it was Violet who dashed their hopes. Your treasurer said that the diocese would not countenance the spending of any monies raised for the church fabric to be siphoned off for any other purpose. End of story.'

'Is that it then?' said Daniel. 'You gave up?'

'Gave up?' laughed Lorna, 'not blooming likely. Thinking caps donned once more, we decided on a change of tack. Build out to the North as in our Point Five, sequestrate and or screen off the chancel – ditto; replace the pews with the finest and most comfortable stacking chairs we can find; all to be paid for out of the fire insurance money plus some of the excess from last year's fundraising spectacular. That way, you'd end up with a really "churchy" hall with the altar thrown in as an optional extra.'

Daniel gave a big sigh that descended into a minor groan. 'Clever, I have to admit but no more spacious than your earlier idea. And there's no substitute for a proper church pew with a classy hassock. You'll have to think again.'

'We did! We did!' cried Lorna. 'Martha thought I was having a brainstorm or a revelation even, Violet like. It was like looking into a crystal ball. As the swirling mists cleared, I could make out a rough field covered in docks, thistles and brambles. Then out of the ground there arose a large dilapidated farmhouse enclosed by all kinds of exotic looking trees. The house and the weeds vanished in a flash, the trees dwindled in number before a new building resembling a gigantic mushroom appeared in the landscape. It was over in seconds before Martha asked if I was all right. Of course I was – I'd seen the future – again Violet like.'

'I wish I could,' muttered Daniel. 'Whatever it is, your flight of fancy has left me grounded. So what is the future?'

'Point Six was Martha's domain. I hadn't realised that Freudian psychology was a minor slice of her graduate pie and she interpreted my dream with practised ease. With the church hall gone and little prospect of creating a new, larger one by any means on the church site, we must look elsewhere – in a run down landscape – to produce a rapid growing building : hence the mushroom.

First the revelation, then the miracle. The farmhouse of our chitchat yesterday afternoon was the key to everything. So with Martha's help, I contacted several agricultural estate agents, looking for a farm up for sale, in Yowesdale. By teatime, I had bought one. You are bound to know it, as a stretch of its perimeter is shared with the northern boundary of the church.'

'What? Not Lambkinfold, Harold Miller's place? And you've bought it?' said an incredulous Daniel.

''fraid so,' said Lorna. 'One more indirect casualty of the Foot and Mouth outbreak apparently. You might have noticed when you've been mowing the grass at the back of the church that Lambkinfold was becoming something of a wasteland – not my words, I assure you.'

'But Millers weren't affected by F and M,' said Daniel. 'Yowesdale kept free of it, God alone knows how. But Winnie died about two years ago and Harold must have found life difficult since. The threat of F and M would have been the last straw, no doubt.' He stopped abruptly, before continuing. The penny purchase had finally dropped. 'You've bought Lambkinfold. What on earth for? You said only yesterday you weren't moving.' He was shocked. 'Where's the money to come from? Dilapidated and run down or not, that farm is as desirable as Naboth's vineyard and worth ten times as much. We can't expect to get a mortgage at our age. Get real, for Heaven's sake.'

'Do I detect a note of exasperation, dear?' asked Lorna. 'I said that I had bought the farm – I means ME, not US.'

CHAPTER XXI

Lucri Bonus Est Odor Ex Re Qualibet

(Wherever it comes from, money
smells good. *Juvenal*)

'This has to be a dream, surely,' said Daniel, partly to himself, 'a massive property deal and I am not involved – or consulted for that matter. Is there anything else that I am not party to? Like how on earth you're funding such a purchase? I know you sold your Cambridge house for a handsome figure but when trading that for a two hundred acre farm there'll be a considerable shortfall. Are you expecting me to sell High Ash? Even if we achieve a decent price it won't make up the difference when put in the balance against Lambkinfold Farm.'

'Just cool down, dear,' said Lorna soothingly. 'I told you yesterday, I'm too comfortable by the half, living with you at High Ash. I don't intend to occupy the farmhouse – ownership is enough. Does that reassure you?'

'Sort of,' answered Daniel. 'You must know by now that if you wanted me to sell High Ash, I'd do it. If such a move would make you happy, I'd even consider living in a cave. But what about the money?'

'The money. Yes. Now that is another story. You and I are both fully aware of the fact that, for reasons best known to each of us, we have secrets that we do not share. The secrets of the confessional perhaps – I don't know and I don't suppose it matters that much anyway. Sooner or later the truth will out. We respect each other's secrecy. Do you remember, just before Martha and I set off for Tamarel at the end of June we had a rather flippant conversation about us having medical checks with Nathaniel, as in "two for the price of one". As a Yorkshire-man you questioned whether or not it represented good value for money. I replied that as a Lancashire lass I wasn't worried about brass. Remember?'

'Yes, I remember all right,' said Daniel, 'and you also said that you

didn't wear diamonds except in your dreams, or words to that effect.'
He paused. 'Where is this all leading? The suspense is killing me.'

'Please don't die too soon, dear. The diamonds were never the stuff
of dreams – I won the National Lottery.'

Daniel was stunned, open mouthed for a few seconds before
recovering his powers of speech. 'Why didn't you tell me?' he said,
before adding 'But you don't even do the Lottery.'

'I don't need to, thank you very much,' said Lorna, 'after I scooped
the jackpot. And as for telling you about it – you never needed to
know about my financial affairs so you didn't ask.'

'Apart from picking the right numbers, how did it happen?' asked
Daniel, 'and when?'

'Matthew had no time for gambling of any kind. "A mug's game",
was his firm conviction. I was quite happy to know that a few pence
of my weekly "investment" went to the charitable Heritage Fund and
he was content to humour me on the subject. He was twelve years
older than I, and being a practical, pragmatic man expected to die
before me. He made every possible provision for my personal comfort
and wellbeing when confronted with widowhood. I suppose most
married couples joke about the widow being better off without the
husband – we certainly did. It was in the week before he died that
my numbers came up. We both knew that he was dying and not far
from death. I was in turmoil wondering whether or not I should tell
him about my colossal stroke of luck in case, putting it bluntly, the
excitement finished my darling Matthew off. I did, of course, and
through his constant pain and fears he laughed until tears ran down
his cheeks. Laughter, the best medicine! He smiled through the tears
before speaking. He said that all of our life is one gamble after another
and none bigger than marriage, a special race we'd won with flying
colours. And now I'd become as rich as Croesus, without any effort
and without any need, "Call on your wisdom, My Darling. Take all
the time you need and then place your bet on the future." Those were
his last words. That was nearly four years ago and I know you will
understand if the memory brings me to tears even now. Some wounds
never fully heal.'

Daniel sat quietly, sending wave after wave of unspoken sympathy
to envelop Lorna as she struggled to control her emotions. Five
minutes passed before he felt it was the right moment to break the
silence that followed the cessation of her gentle sobbing. He became
aware of the ticking of the clock on the mantelpiece and counted to

sixty. Until then, they had been sitting in separate chairs either side the window. He rose to his feet and crossed over to her chair, digging a handkerchief from a trouser pocket as he went.

'Here we are, dear. Have a good blow – it's a clean one this morning.' He proffered her the hanky and carefully helped her to her feet.

Lorna dried the remains of her tears, blew her nose loudly enough to break the tensions of the moment, took the deepest breath of her life and gave out a prolonged sigh. Then she spoke once again.

'It's been the hardest of secrets to keep and I'm so relieved to share it with you now. What happens next is out of my control. Tell me what I have to do.'

'Classic riposte,' joked Daniel – never prone to panic. 'Chin up and put on a smile for me. The answer lies in the soil. So we'll go for a walk round the garden: I'll bring secateurs with me and you can command me which roses you would like me to cut for you. They are all fragrant varieties. There's plenty to choose from. I've not had roses in the house since Bethan died. Why, I don't know – it wasn't a deliberate decision. Would you be kind and fill the rosebowl – it was a favourite of my mother. While you're doing that, I'll gather some lavender, drop it in the blender and while we share the calming vapours with our dram of Glenmorangie in hand we'll sit close and put the world to rights.'

'You're impossible,' said Lorna. 'I feel much happier already with the promise of roses. That's enough for me, thank you. Forget the lavender. I know it's a calmative in herbal terminology but compared to you it's a stimulant.' She gave a little giggle. 'You won't know it, but Aphrodite is Silas's favourite perfume, a potent reminder of Magda, his late wife. He hasn't forgotten the two lavender sodden ladies whom he encountered in Ravensrigg.'

Daniel foreshortened any evening discussion relating to church, hall and farm matters by declaring that it would be a wise move to wait for Silas's arrival and acquaint him with the changes in the situation. He was prepared to trust Silas just as Sambo had said. His dream was coming true in the most dramatic fashion. Albert, Sambo and John had warned him not to drown in money, and John had told him to heed the women.

Yet, he was not ready to confess anything to anybody. Drifting off to sleep that late-evening, Daniel whispered to an equally sleepy Lorna, 'You didn't say how much your jackpot was worth.'

'Nor I never did,' said Lorna. Contented, she smiled and slept.

CHAPTER XXII

Terra Incognita

(Unknown territory)

The next morning Lorna was up early and waiting at the breakfast table for Daniel who was roused from his slumbers by the powerful aroma of freshly percolating coffee.

'Help yourself to cereal,' called Lorna. 'I'll produce fresh toast when you're ready. Your apple juice is waiting here on the table. Come as you are.'

He padded through to the table clad in dressing gown and slippers, washed but as yet unshaven. 'So, how is the farmer's super-wealthy wife this beautiful morning?'

'Lovelier than ever before, and still popular with Coutts Brothers – I hope.'

'Right,' said Daniel, drawing out the vowel sound with thoughtful hesitancy. 'Another little drip of trickling truth to go with the gush of the Lottery. Anything else to declare Mrs G? Like who else knows about this fortune of yours? I think I need to know everything about it before I drown in my wife's wealth – or, even worse, make a fool of myself in my ignorance. I have the feeling it's an enormous sum – exactly how much doesn't bother me. I'm sure it's not hidden under the mattress or in a trunk under the bed, so where is it?'

'In a charitable trust that I set up with the help of my financial adviser. There are three trustees, myself, Douglas and my Cambridge solicitor. I intend to appoint Rachel as a fourth when I get round to it, and at some stage I shall look for a fifth suitable board candidate about the same age as Douglas and Rachel. I would invite you on board except for your age – my old man – but I can use all your wit and wisdom without calling a meeting of trustees. And you come free.'

'Charming,' said Daniel with an amused air. 'Board trustee or not, I call that a vote of confidence. Thank you. There is one angle to all this secrecy that gives me pause for thought however. I have no doubts regarding the absolute integrity of your trustees but I have to ask how you expect or hope to hide the true identity of the new owner of Lambkinfold Farm.'

'Not a clue,' said Lorna, 'at least not at this early stage. If you have any ideas please tell me. We might need to concoct some kind of a tale to satisfy local curiosity. You're a good one at producing a smoke screen – that I do know.'

'I presume,' said Daniel, choosing to ignore the reference to his ability to muddy the waters, 'that this Trust of yours has a title that can be used as a genuine front to any scheme which may present itself or any scheming that we may be called upon to put in train.'

'Quite so,' replied Lorna. 'It has been quiescent since I set it up, but it is registered as the "Swannery Trust". I think that Silas Kinnon is going to enjoy any dealings he may have in the future with Swannery. Just wait and see.'

'How right you are,' observed Daniel. 'I had a vivid dream the other night involving Sambo. He told me to listen to the voice of the singer and to trust Silas. Sambo has never let me down.'

'We shall see,' remarked Lorna, 'Silas will soon be upon us. I can hardly await his arrival. I wonder how long it will be before he bumps into Martha in the local supermarket, hears her voice and sees her unveiled face. Do you remember that lovely ballad with the opening line "It seems to me I've heard that song before?"'

'It's from an old familiar score,' answered Daniel in his finest crooning mode. 'I know it well, that melody. Of course I remember it – we used to dance to it when we were at Cambridge. That, and "Moonglow". How you put up with my forever treading on your toes I'll never know but dancing with you was a part of the magic of my salad days until you decided that this humble engineer was not for you. Oh, the power of nostalgia! You must have regretted it ever since.'

Lorna snorted in mock derision. 'I'm making up for it now. I've been living with you for nearly a year and you've yet to take me dancing. Now, there's a thought. When the new church hall is finished we should hold an inaugural dance and you can invite me to take to the floor as the first couple to do so. How's that for an offer you can't refuse?'

'Well, at least it gives me time to take some dancing lessons. This aging engineer's moving parts are a trifle rusty and maybe it's time I mastered the foxtrot. I wish we had some idea of how long it will be before I can gather you into my arms, sweep you off your feet and carry you onto the dance floor.'

'Who's getting carried away now, you old romantic?' laughed Lorna. 'Dancing lessons, Weight Lifting sessions, whatever next? But seriously, much of the timetable is going to hang on Silas's handling of the various planning hurdles we shall have to negotiate.'

'Or skirt round,' added Daniel. 'I have heard tales of planning committee members receiving sweeteners for favours rendered – not in our local authority I have to admit. But you never hear of Parochial Church Councils resorting to bribery – corruption maybe – and bribery works best on a one to one basis if the bond of secrecy is to be maintained. I know that I could afford the underhand dealing at a pinch, but by the same token I also know that you would never countenance the idea. Greasing of palms is for engineers only.'

'Now it's my turn to surprise you, my dancing partner. Sambo taught you to *"Aequam servare mentem,"* Panic Not. And you don't. My Latin teacher's pet quotation was a bit of Ovid – *"Exitus acta probat,"* The End Justifies the Means. If Ovid was right, and he generally was, I'm confident that the Swannery Trust would make the necessary funds available – to you personally – and consider it to be money well spent. Think of a coin spinning after being tossed up on the cricket field. It has two faces. Heads or Tails. Loyalty or Betrayal. Trust Fund or Fiddle Fund. Just one more gamble.'

'Ovid was wrong,' said Daniel firmly.

'Of course he was,' said Lorna, 'and I loathed my Latin teacher whose favourite English phrase was "Get that into your thick skull," enforcing it with a quick clip round the ear. No nostalgia there!'

Daniel laughed. 'It's a funny thing, you know, but the older I get the more I enjoy a good nostalgic wallow. Doctors and policemen were so much older when we were young and summers were always warm and dry – especially when I was in my youthful cricketing prime.'

It was Lorna's turn to laugh. 'And now Silas arrives on the scene, still happy with the memory of his High Ashes hero – the unforgettable Damnit Greensward. The stage is set. The backdrop features a church set against a background of farmland. Enter a new hero, Silas Kinnon.'

'To be accompanied by his faithful squire, Reuben,' added Daniel with amusement.

Two days later Silas was to be found dossing down in the vicarage. The date was Monday, 16 July, 2001. The two day interval had enabled Lorna and Daniel to liaise with Timothy and Muriel Welsh and Violet Rose, to explain the involvement of the Swannery Trust which had decided to buy Lambkinfold Farm. At that stage, none of them had any idea what future plans the Trust would be seeking to hatch with regard to the estate but early consultation with the church authorities would be high on the agenda. Daniel, without mentioning Martha's name, said that it had been pointed out to him that the old church hall had been, for a long time, too small to be of much practical use in the local community. As the sole owner of the site, he had decided to veto any well intentioned if misguided suggestion of rebuilding the hall there. He had been of the opinion that if the Almighty Insurance Company would agree to pay out the fire insurance policy without quibble there was a good case to be made for using the money to extend the church itself, so creating a new hall, complete with new furnishings. But not any more.

'Bright Boy,' said Violet, with ill-disguised sarcasm. It'll give us less room to swing a cat than we had in the old building. We'll be back to square one. That is unless Mr Kinnon lists miracle worker among his many undoubted attributes.'

Lorna decided that now was the moment to reveal that she was the principal pen in the swannery. 'I had a dream,' she told them, 'a quite crazy dream, that Martha kindly interpreted for me, the upshot of which was that I should buy a farm. I won't bore you with the details except to say that the run down farm and dilapidated buildings metamorphosed into a fresh landscape and a building that grew so fast I thought it was a mushroom. Obviously it wasn't. So I'm following a dream without really knowing quite where it will lead me. I may be acting on a wild impulse, akin to a hunch but I'm utterly convinced that Silas is of a mind to leave his mark on Saint Michael's.'

Much frank, rigorous and vigorous discussion took place and Lorna was amused when Muriel Welsh took it upon herself to summarise. She was unprepared for Muriel's opening words.

'For a Lancashire lass, Lorna, you are an absolute gem. Damnit should have been called James, after his father. Never mind "Damnit," he's the perfect "Lucky Jim". I can foresee some rare sparkle brightening up our petty parochial affairs when you get together with Minerva Jemima described by Martha, not so very long ago, as the glowing ruby in Reuben's crown.' Muriel paused for a few seconds to collect her thoughts before continuing. 'We've just about talked ourselves to a standstill. So can I as a peripheral member of this August body recap and state what I perceive to be our consensus. Silas must join the parish electoral roll and is to be co-opted as a member of the P.C.C. with special responsibility for planning in general and a new church hall in particular. Damnit has made it quite plain that he has his own agenda with reference to the hall and insists on informing Silas of such. Personally, I think it only right and fair he should be party to whatever Silas gets up to, architecturally speaking, because it was Joseph "Tiltstone" North, his great-great-grandfather who was responsible for the building of our church, the only church in the world to have a Tiltstone. Need I say more?

'I think you've pretty well said it all,' agreed Violet. 'From my vantage point in the counting house I will undertake the task of keeping the P.C.C. informed of the state of play in our game with the A.I.C. I'm confident that they will pay out in full – sometime, and I don't anticipate that they will have any objection to the money being spent on the building of a new hall on a fresh site, just so long as we continue to insure it with the A.I.C.

One final thought from me, forsaking my treasurer's hat, and this is directed at Daniel. We shall have a new vicar in a few weeks time. Don't expect him to be unconcerned about any plans you might have for tinkering with the fabric of Saint Michael the Archangel – and, by association, a brand new hall. You and Silas must seek his opinions and his approval every step of the way. That will be easy for Silas to accept, being his father – I'm not too sure though about you Daniel.'

Violet looked at Daniel, searchingly. 'I would still love to know how the church hall managed to burn down when you were honeymooning. So convenient for all concerned.'

'Act of God, perhaps, Violet, in answer to your many prayers as I am given to understand if my husband is to be believed,' suggested Lorna.

Daniel roared with laughter. 'Which Archbishop was it who said that the power of prayer beggars belief?'

'Geoffrey Fisher,' replied Lorna, quick as a flash. 'But he was Bishop of Chester at the time, as I recall.'

'Thank you, dear,' said Daniel. 'I knew I could rely on you to provide the answer. And as for Reuben, Violet – my powers of persuasion shall prevail – or else. Who was it who said he who pays the piper calls the tune?'

'In this particular case, it has to be Burns. But please don't quote me on it,' said Lorna, reliable to the end.

CHAPTER XXIII

Magister Artis Ingeniique Largitor Venter

(The teacher of art and the allocator of genius is the belly [Necessity is the mother of invention])

By the time of his licensing as priest-in-charge on 11 September, Reuben Ossian and his family had already been resident in the vicarage for two weeks.

Silas had abandoned his camping lifestyle on the day before his son and family moved into the vicarage. During his six weeks residency he had accomplished all that he had set out to do when he offered his services as a handyman. The garden was so immaculate that, highly impressed, Damnit suggested that he might be persuaded to allow Silas to take a turn with the mowing of the church lawns. There was no higher accolade he could bestow. Silas's reply was polite but non-committal and certainly surprised Damnit.

'If your two veiled lady investigators had stayed another day or two up in Ravensrigg, there's a chance they might have had a peek at Reuben's garden – except that it wasn't his. If the garden was more than just tidy, it was all down to me – the under gardener acting under the instructions of the mistress of the house. It amused me that at interview time your panel, Bishop and all, did not enquire of Reuben if he was in any way daunted by the prospect of coping with such a large vicarage garden. I like to think his answer would have made you smile – something along the lines of "Not me, Damnit! That's Minerva's province. She's the head gardener." And so she is, my horticultural director – a well qualified botanist with a special interest in dendrology.'

Daniel did indeed smile at the allusion to his own nickname. 'I'm not sure if Bishop and all would have a clue about dendrology. Something tells me it has to do with rhododendrons. Am I right? It's all Greek to me.'

'Clever boy,' said Silas, 'partly right. It's Greek for sure. Rhodon means "rose", as in pink and Dendron means "tree". Anything you might like to know about trees – ask my daughter-in-law, Minerva, Roman goddess of wisdom.'

Silas's house in Eglingham was sold within a month from the date it was put on the market: bought by a high-powered executive of a global pharmaceutical firm with a manufacturing facility in Northumberland. All relocation expenses would be taken care of by the company, obviating any problems or complications which might have arisen if the sale and purchase of the property had been subject to a chain. Completion was scheduled for the last week in October. In the meantime, immediately he was informed of the acquisition of Lambkinfold Farm by Lorna in the guise of the Swannery Trust, he postponed any plans he had for buying a Yowesdale cottage in favour of renting a small modern town house in Tupshorne. He had a powerful hunch that an upheaval in the town's property market was imminent. Feathers would fly if a fox found its way into the swannery. Lambkinfold could turn out to be a minefield providing a veritable field day for any planning authority wishing to flex its muscles and the signs were ominous when correspondence from the authority was signed, not by Mr A. Fox but by Mr A. Wolff, Chief Planning Officer. Alarm bells could be heard to ring. Violet's dealings with the Almighty Insurance Company were plain and simple. The full sum of the fire insurance claim was paid out on the agreed understanding that it would be spent on a church building – somewhere. The company recognised the need for a larger capacity hall than could be accommodated on the original site, owned by Daniel Greensward.

The Diocesan Planning Committee had other ideas which Daniel, at his charitable best, described as downright daft and they were all discredited and dismissed. First of all, the Committee tried to insist that the new hall should be erected on the same site, only giving way when the self-styled Saint Michael the Archangel Restoration Team, Inspired, Exacting and Spirited SMARTIES for short – pointed out that it was essential for any new hall to be much larger than the old one in order to meet the demands of the twenty first century.

Next it was mooted that Daniel Greensward, the owner of the land which until Violet's earlier revelation everybody presumed to belong to the diocese, should honour the original intention of his great-grandfather George Greensward and gift the plot to the diocese to dispose of in any way it might think fitting in the current circumstances. Daniel sent for his high horse and mounted. Nobody, with the possible exception of Lorna, was going to tell him what to do with his newly acquired estate. Also, tongue in cheek, he intimated because it amused him greatly to do so, that it must have been ordained from on high that such a handy plot would fall to his lot in the fullness of time, a mere one hundred and thirty five years to be precise. A scheme was then advanced with a view to extending the church itself to the northern boundary of its grounds and turning the whole edifice into a multi-purpose building incorporating an altar on wheels that could be rolled out when required. Silas, donning his architect's hat, put the kibosh on that idea stating bluntly that such flights of fancy were based on the premise that the church would lend itself to such a conversion and that such a presumption was entirely false.

It was Reuben, who on examining the preliminary sketches of the possible extension observed that the increase in floor space when compared to that of the old hall would be next to negligible when taking into account the provision to be made for toilet facilities and kitchen arrangements that would measure up to the demands of the Department of Health and Safety. And as for the thought of an altar on wheels being hidden away from sight from one church service to another – over his dead body.

Stalemate had been reached. The SMARTIES had, in effect, dismissed all plans submitted by the Diocesan planners because they had scrapped their own earlier plans for the same reasons. Inspiration, in spite of the SMARTIES title, was lacking. The Diocese hardened its stance concerning the whole affair and declared that if Tupshorne wanted a new hall the town could fund it from the local community that needed it so badly, but unless such a building together with any ground it might be built on was presented to the church as a gift without any strings attached, it could not be called the Church Hall of Saint Michael the Archangel. And that was that.

Damnit Greensward was furious. Once he had achieved his target of burning down the church hall, the last thing he had expected was downright boneheadedness from those in authority. It was Lorna, of course, who came up with the oil to calm his troubled waters and who, ignorant of his solo star performance as an arsonist, reminded him of some of his father's words of wisdom although she had never had the pleasure of meeting James Greensward. 'Just calm down, dear,' was her opening command. 'Anger does not become you – it shortens your life and is the most lethal of the seven deadly sins. Do us both a favour. Remember your heart and remember that it's a long time since you were my fiery red-headed young man. I prefer the rather distinguished looking grey-haired model.'

Daniel knew she was right and he smiled in recognition of the fact. 'I take your point, dear. You sounded just like my dear old dad giving me a lecture. His final words on the subject were, "Don't get angry – get even." The trouble is, at this moment, I can't see a solution to the problem of being without a church hall despite all the best efforts of the SMARTIES. Perhaps I should consult Jake. What do you think?'

'Not unless you've something to confess,' said Lorna. 'I am sure – well, we know – he knows all about SMARTIES existence and for one reason or another has quite deliberately refrained from offering an opinion. Let's leave it at that. One more thing, I don't think you will find the answer or any answer in your private dreamworld – it may cause complications. It's only that I have a germ of an idea of how we might now proceed but I need to talk it over with Martha first – woman to woman – before I put the germ under your microscope to decide if it is worth culturing or not. Incidentally, I'm not aware of you and Silas putting your heads together seriously as yet on the subject of what sort of a hall might be conjured up. When I consult with Martha, you can break new ground with Silas. With luck, and more importantly, God's blessing, we two will sort out this unholy mess to the benefit of the whole Tupshorne community. Who knows? Even our diocese might learn something from the phoenix that will arise from the ashes. Wait and see.'

'Wait and see, indeed,' retorted Daniel, somewhat ruefully. 'Our initial excitement, generated by Silas's offer to provide architectural expertise free of charge, has quietly dissipated. Here we are, at the end of November, no further forward than we were when the wretched hall was reduced to ashes. I'm starting to wonder if it's worth the candle. Enthusiasm can be such a frail abstract.'

Lorna gave her husband an impish grin. 'A penny candle I presume. Violet will be intrigued to learn what started the fire. I don't suppose a little candle, caught up in a blazing inferno, leaves any residue at all.'

Serious once again, she set about restoring Daniel's usual positively cheery outlook on life. 'Come on you old misery. Look on the bright side. "*Bono animo esse*" as Julius Caesar might have said. Be of good heart. It's been a remarkable six months starting on the day we married – the beginning of a fairytale.'

'And all downhill since,' ventured Daniel.

'Nonsense,' replied Lorna. 'Let's look at the facts. You, yourself, a dusty crusty old bachelor said your honeymoon was worth a forty year wait.

Somehow – and it had to be with Divine Guidance – we've found a seemingly worthy successor to Jake. You've discovered a very useful acquaintance from your early schooldays – a musical architect, no less.

The new vicar's wife presents her husband with a baby boy on the feast day of Saint Michael the Archangel.'

'Very clever that,' said Daniel, brightening up a little at the thought. 'Divine Deliverance do you think? Should have been christened Michael but no doubt we'll get used to Ajax Achilles Agamemnon. I don't expect Reuben and Minerva to have any more children. Do you? You can't improve on a triple-A rating. By the way – going off at a tangent – how is the book progressing? You've not been burning any midnight oil for quite a while.'

'I was wondering how soon you'd notice,' replied Lorna. 'Since the tragic accident to Hazel Mears, vicar of Wrensdown, I seem to have lost that initial spark that fired my early enthusiasm. Her brush with death highlighted the basic trivialities of my and Martha's enquiries up to that point. I'll work something out sooner or later but just now I don't feel inspired. By the way, you know how careful we all have been to keep shtum about the activities of our Magnificent Seven, I quite forgot to tell you that after the Archdeacon preached at last Sunday's service, he enquired of me in what I perceived to be a rather knowing way how my book was coming on. Playing for time and praying for time to collect my thoughts, I asked him to which book he might have been referring. Imagine my relief when he said the latest one about the Wars of the Roses.' She laughed. 'I could have kissed him, but refrained, choosing to tell him that it had been finished some time before our wedding.

And so, putting things into their proper perspective, and not forgetting that I've bought a farm that I don't know what on earth to do with, the planning difficulties we've experienced will turn out to be a minor hiccup and not a major headache.

Let Silas sort out you and your aspirations while Martha and I look into our crystal ball. I have an idea that we may find Minerva there.'

Discussion over, Daniel announced that with the help of the dogs he was going into the garden to prune the blackcurrants. The task would be finished in time for the dogs' tea and by then he would be ready for a reviving cup of tea himself.

As Daniel approached the currants, secateurs and saw in hand, the house telephone rang.

Lorna answered. Nathaniel Ross was on the line. 'Hello Nathaniel. How nice to hear you. Are you after Daniel?'

'Not on this occasion, Lorna, thank you. I must speak with the chatelaine herself and beg a favour.'

'Ask away. I'm in granting mode at this very moment.'

'This is a bit cheeky of me, I know, but Rachel tells me she and Douglas are coming to you and Daniel for Christmas. Please may I come too. The baby is due just about then and I might come in handy – midwives can be scarce at Christmas. There's nothing I like better than to polish my F.R.C.O.G. I delivered Rachel so why not her baby if I am fortunate enough to be on hand when her time comes.'

'That would be wonderful. Of course, you are most welcome to come for Christmas. I should have thought of it in the first place. Knowing what I know now, if you had been somewhere near when I managed to produce Douglas, I might have had more children. But it wasn't to be.

So do Rachel and Douglas know about this conversation?'

'No. I didn't wish to presume on your kindness in case you already had a houseful.'

'Kindness be blowed. It'll be a pleasure – and don't tell them you'll be here. Come the day before they do, then you can open the door to greet them. Such a lovely surprise might bring about another arrival.'

'Understood! Many thanks. And how is Daniel at the moment? It's a few months since I checked him over.'

'You examined him?'

'Yes – very thoroughly at the time. He told me you were away with Martha. You didn't know?'

'I certainly did not know. Did he pass his MoT?'

Nathaniel clammed up.

'I'm sorry. It never occurred to me that he might not have mentioned such a matter to you. Entirely unintentionally I have broached patient confidentiality I'm afraid you must ask that particular question of Daniel.'

The dogs rushed into the house in search of their meal as Daniel called out from the back door, 'Is the kettle on?' swiftly followed by 'Who's on the 'phone?'

'Yes. Kettle's on the hob and it's Nathaniel on the 'phone. He's joining us for Christmas with Douglas and Rachel,' replied Lorna, still holding the phone. Then, addressing Nathaniel, she bade him a slightly nervous goodbye before pushing the subject of Daniel's health to the back of her mind. No mention was made of it over tea.

CHAPTER XXIV

Salus Populi Suprema Lex Esto

(Let the good of the people be the chief law [Cicero])

Later that same evening Lorna rang Martha and offered to treat her to lunch next day – a little outing to Skipton was to be neither undertaken lightly nor alone she said.

'I'd be delighted to go to Skipton on any day but tomorrow,' said Martha. 'Jake will be out all day at a jolly for retired clergy – well hardly a jolly – something to do with utilising the talents of those who have a smidgen of life left in them and how those talents may best be deployed. There's certainly life left in my old dog as yet. So he has the car for the day and it was the ideal opportunity for me to have the central heating system serviced. The engineer should arrive any time between nine o'clock and noon. The check-up usually takes about an hour. So Skipton's out, I'm afraid.'

'Right then,' said Lorna, short and to the point as usual. 'Change of plan. I'm coming for coffee. I need to pick your brains and with luck a coffee break will suffice.'

Martha chuckled. 'Oh me of so little brain that it can be picked over in the time it takes to drink a mug of coffee. You might do better to consult a gypsy fortune teller. Of course you're welcome for coffee. Eleven o'clock suit you? Then, unless the service engineer finds a fault that takes her into overtime, you can treat me to lunch at the Ram – it's only just down the road.' She broke off for a moment before continuing. 'If it's the usual lady engineer, I'd be perfectly happy to leave her in the house while we lunch. Miss Bindle will be at home and they know each other well.'

'Done,' said Lorna. 'As you've mentioned Bindle, shall I bring Baggins and Rauch then we can walk off any excess lunch in the afternoon?'

'Just before you ring off, might I enquire what it is that I will need to train my brain on? A little notice possibly could stimulate the grey matter.'

'Didn't I mention it?' said Lorna. 'I would value your ideas and opinions on what I should do with Lambkinfold. It's a blank canvas to me, and I'm no artist.'

'I see,' said Martha. 'I'll crack open my teabag after breakfast and we can read the tea leaves as we sip our coffee. Don't be late. But what about Daniel? If we're not off to Skipton, he might fancy escorting us two lovelies to the Ram.'

'Not a chance. With luck, he should be treating Silas to lunch somewhere and comparing notes on how to break the *impasse* that has brought the plans for a new church hall to nought. I'll update you in the morning. One last thing. You still haven't met Silas since our Ravensrigg exploit. I'll rectify that situation fairly shortly so dig out your veil and the lavender perfume. Enlightenment beckons. See you in the morning.'

Damnit made a similar call to Silas, drawing a blank. The architect had booked already a seat on a coach trip from Tupshorne to Chester for the morrow but would be happy to confer the day after. The Sandpiper in Leyburn where Daniel and Lorna had held their wedding reception could expect two gentlemen for lunch.

'So what did you learn from reading the teabag fragments?' Lorna enquired, halfway through her first cup of coffee.

'Sweet nothing,' laughed Martha. 'I should have known that a shattered teabag yields little but a sloppy sort of silt. However, we're drinking ground coffee at this very moment so when we've supped up you pour the grounds from your cup into my cup, I'll swish them round a bit and we can proceed from there. I'm sure we'll be able to draw the same conclusions, whatever we use, be it coffee, tea, cocoa or rice pudding.'

It was Lorna's turn to laugh. 'Let's try it with tapioca.'

The prospect of reading anything into remains of a sedimentary nature vanished into thin air with the sudden arrival of a triple helping of black Labradors. Miss Bindle had heard Martha's laughter and came rushing in from the garden, chased by Baggins and Rauch. The first two dogs avoided the coffee table: not so Rauch who, fully grown at fourteen months old, had the build of a four-legged black battering ram with a kennel door in its sights. Lacking the weight and four-square solidity of a kennel, the table went for six that might have been rated two or more on the Richter scale, tipping the coffee cups on to the floor and scattering the biscuits beyond salvage. The dogs took no notice of the coffee grounds as they vacuumed up the digestives and custard creams with practised ease before eventually obeying orders to 'Get out.' The bump as the coffee table tumbled and the ensuing uproar brought the lady gas service engineer dashing into the sitting room and almost tripping over the dogs as they made a hasty exit. Martha and Lorna were still shaking with laughter as the engineer took in the scene of chaos.

Martha was the first to recover her equilibrium. 'Do you do carpet shampooing as well as gas heating installation servicing?' she asked the engineer.

'No, but I know a man who does,' she replied, echoing the catchphrase of a well known television advertisement of the time. 'My brother, Andrew, also known as 'Andy Andy Anyjob Anywhere Anything for Money.'

'Oh, I like it,' said Martha, 'quintuple A rating. I'll remember that for the next emergency. Luckily this coffee catching mat is machine washable.'

'I'm terribly sorry for Rauch's misdemeanour,' said Lorna. 'Put it down to youthful exuberance. It'll be a few years before she matches the serenity of Bindle or Sprottle. I hope Douglas brings her at Christmas. Sprot will more than give Rauch the runaround. Her greyhound genes are definitely dominant.'

'I blame Bindle – she arrived first,' said Martha, 'and you can bet she had the lion's share of the biscuits. Bang goes our coffee grounds research though. Would you like a cup of instant? At least the crockery is intact even if the biscuits have disappeared.'

'Maybe not. My cup was nearly empty – bar the dregs, thank you. Are we ready to give my property poser an airing? Now the mumbo-jumbo has been ruined by our dogs I'm ready to listen to you and how you might re-interpret my brief vision. I've bought the farm as it stands but there's not a mushroom shed in sight.'

'You may not like what I have to say, but I have to say it,' said Martha, mysteriously. 'Since you acquired Lambkinfold, all St Michael's plans to rebuild a church hall have ended up in the shredder – that is common knowledge in Yowesdale. As I see it, the building that, in your dream, appeared growing like a mushroom on your farm-to-be is the new hall arising phoenix like not from the ashes of the old hall but from the wasteland. You mentioned trees being in your dream – all kinds of exotic looking trees, you said.'

'That's right,' said Lorna, 'and most of those vanished as the building grew larger. Is that significant?'

'It could be,' replied Martha. 'Tell me – did your Matthew have any interest at all in trees?'

Lorna pondered the question for several seconds before answering. Martha was unravelling for her the deeper complexities of a brief encounter with the supernatural. 'No, not trees as such, that you might plant in your garden or as part of a forest. He had a fascination with wood that began when his carpentry lessons at school introduced him to the world of marquetry and his father gave him a treadle operated fretsaw. The choice pieces of furniture that I brought to High Ash when I married Daniel were all made by Matthew. When he died, for reasons that I can't begin to explain, I tried to dispose of anything that reminded me of him – photos, books, clothes, the rings we had exchanged, his wood working tools, recorded cassette tapes featuring his voice – I did keep a few items for Douglas. My grief was so unbearable, it nearly destroyed me. You may ask why I kept the furniture. That was an oversight. There must have been some kind of commonsense mechanism in place that said I would have nothing to sleep on, sit on or eat off. With that in mind, Daniel has been nothing short of incredible – the manner in which he has welcomed Matthew's beautiful legacy to High Ash. All other memories are in my head.'

Martha looked at Lorna who was visibly upset by her recollections of Matthew's passing. Her next question could be key and in framing it she took her time: the time needed for Lorna to recover her composure.

'That's Daniel for you – a man for all seasons. "Cometh the hour – cometh Damnit," to coin a phrase. Just one, and I hope final question. The decorative art of marquetry demands the use of wood of many different colours. Was that the aspect that fascinated Matthew?'

'I'm not absolutely sure about that,' mused Lorna, turning the thought over in her mind, 'but I think so. If you can recall the Great Gale of October, 1987, that destroyed fifteen million trees – some of those trees were rarities in the Royal Botanic Gardens at Kew with heartwood of colours never seen before in British marquetry. Matthew was one of the lucky cabinetmakers who acquired what he referred to as his sack of rainbow logs. You will have had a fair number of drinks at High Ash that were placed on our coffee table – the one covered with a sheet of plate glass.'

Martha interrupted. 'Don't tell me – rainbow logs! It must be worth a fortune. Unique!'

'Unique yes, but only of sentimental value. Give it another couple of hundred years, then who knows. The tabletop is solid oak inlaid with a kaleidoscope of colours, all wood sourced from the gale. As for weight, I don't think Rauch would budge it.' Lorna gave a little smile. 'Matthew had his own private joke about it. If you really want to know which woods went into the design, you'll need a decent torch – crawl under the table, turn on to your back and scan the underside of the top. Every tree species is incised there, highlighted by the application of Indian ink to the incised letters. Does all that nonsense help your further interpretation of my dream?'

'Indeed it does,' said Martha, 'but I have to put myself in your shoes to explain what I find. Imagine that I am you. I own quite a sizeable farm, contiguous at one point on its perimeter with the boundary wall of my local church.

My local church stands in need of a new hall. My busy market town lost its meeting room years ago. So, I give a piece of my land away to someone who fancies putting a building on it that will satisfy the requirements of my whole community, provided that the plans merit the approval of the local authority. I fear the Green Belt Regulations. The rest of my farm I still don't know what to do with except that it will involve trees or wood in some way.

I shall discuss this with my husband in whose opinions I have complete confidence. Over and out!

Back in my own shoes now, I see that it's lunchtime. The Ram awaits our arrival.'

Hardly had Martha finished talking than the service engineer made it known that she had finished her assignment and was waiting for Mrs Drake to sign the official worksheet before leaving for her next appointment. Although the Ram was only a short walk from the Drake's cottage, Lorna put all three dogs in the back of her Volvo estate car so that, following lunch, they could drive up to the moors for the promised walk.

Speaking through her first mouthful of shepherd's pie, unsurprisingly the Ram's star dish of the day and every day, Lorna expressed her admiration for and satisfaction with Martha's explanation of her dream.

'I'm so impressed with your quite masterful interpretation –

"mistressful" sounds even better don't you think? My next move will be, as you in my shoes decided, to involve Daniel in some kind of a property deal. When teatime comes round, I'll clue him in on what we settled over coffee. He's conferring with Silas tomorrow about how they can break this logjam that is preventing progress of any kind with the powers that be. I don't want to talk about it any more just now. Let's enjoy our lunch and then have our walkies before the light goes.'

'My word,' said Daniel as the dogs ran into the house through the open doorway, 'that's what I call timing. I've just put your grub down. Is the mistress with you?'

The two black beauties disappeared into the kitchen, much too keen on their food to bother to reply.

Lorna followed. 'Yes, the mistress is here and if your timing is right you'll have a kettle on the boil. I'm home for tea, and bearing a packet of crumpets.'

'That's what I call telepathy,' said Daniel. 'I lit the fire in the sitting room not long after you left for Middinside. I expect the dogs are there already, toasting their chests. I hope I can find the toasting fork.'

'It's in a drawer in the kitchen along with the rest of the cooking utensils, I think,' said Lorna, not altogether convinced. 'If not, it might be with the barbecue gubbins at the back of the garage. I'll look, while you brew up and persuade the fire into toasting mode.'

'So,' asked Daniel, part way through his first crumpet, 'how did things go with Martha? Problems solved?'

'Not completely,' replied Lorna, 'but she pointed me in the right direction. That's for sure. I have decided...'

'Oh! Have you indeed?' interrupted Daniel. 'That sounds promising. Are you buying another farm?'

'Don't be facetious, dear. It doesn't become a churchwarden of your advanced years. As I said, I have decided that the Swannery Trust, subject to planning permission being granted, will make available land for the erection of a Tupshorne Community Hall on Lambkinfold.'

'Well, I'll be...'

'No, you will not,' retorted Lorna, 'well, at least not yet because I've not finished. This means that the diocesan office will no longer be involved and the "developers", for want of a better word, will be able to call the building whatever they like – nothing too provocative, I hope, but I do think "Archangel Hall" sounds rather grand. I can foresee problems relating to Green Belt policy. In the end it may all come down to the geology of the farmland and the power of local community support.'

'Well, I'll be blessed!' said Daniel. 'Were you thinking I was about to say something else and stand in danger of having my mouth washed out with soapy water? "Blessed" Greensward sounds too saintly for me. To be serious though, if say "thank you" it isn't enough. I'm lost for words.'

'Then don't say a word,' said Lorna, 'not now. By the time we have our first dance in the new hall I know you will have thought of something choice to say. For now, the Swannery Trust has given you the means to break the logjam, as I like to call it. Tell Silas tomorrow that the way is clear for the two of you to pool your imagination and change the Tupshorne landscape for the better – and for the common good.'

'I'm sure we'll come up trumps,' said Daniel. 'By the way, when a logjam bursts like a broken dam, what do you suppose happens to the logs?'

'They will end up on some lucky person's fire.'

CHAPTER XXV

Dux Femina Facti.
Nota Bene

(It was a woman who took the lead.
Consider that!)

On entering the Sandpiper, Damnit was agreeably surprised to see that Silas had arrived already and was seated at a corner table commanding a view of the doorway as he came in. He was surprised even more to note that Silas was not alone but had a little baby on his knee. Minerva Jemima had accompanied Silas, bringing with her Ajax Achilles Agamemnon.

'Well, what a treat,' said Daniel, not in the least fazed by the presence of the unexpected. 'I hope that isn't Guinness in Ajax's bottle that you're brandishing there Silas.'

'It's Ouzo, very dilute,' answered Minerva, 'and it works wonders when it comes to rearing a contented baby. The Greeks know a thing or two about anise – in a herbal context that is. Only joking, Damnit. I wouldn't expect you to know that aniseed is good for nursing mothers with regard to milk production. So if you want to impress the young Ossians a gift of aniseed balls is a surefire bet.'

Silas gave a low chuckle at this educational statement. 'She's a mine of information is my daughter-in-law, Damnit and it's not all trivial. I hope you don't mind me bringing her along with me – and Triple A is a champion sleeper. Minerva might possible bring a little wisdom to our lunch conference.

'I'm delighted,' said Damnit. 'You wouldn't know this, but I am under strict instruction from another world that I should pay heed to the women – somehow. I always listen to Lorna, unless I'm asleep, so I'm perfectly happy to hear what you might care to contribute to the solving of our challenging problem, Minerva dear. But for now, let's establish our priorities and order our lunch which is on my slate today. I'm feeling in a generous mood. Lorna has lit the lamp at the end of the tunnel.'

As the three picked away at their starters, Damnit apprised his guests of Lorna's decision to open the Lambkinfold acres to change of use, subject to the appropriate planning approval.

'That,' said Silas, 'is fantastic news. For some time I have thought of such a move as the most obvious way forward but it was not my place to suggest it to the new landowner. My prayer has been answered. I wonder what prompted Lorna to make the offer.'

'You musn't laugh,' answered Damnit, 'but she had a remarkable dream which her very good friend, the second lavender-scented lady, whom I'm sure you will remember, interpreted for her in the finest of Freudian terms.'

'Aha!' said Silas. 'One day I shall meet her again – I hope.'

'You will. You will,' said Damnit, 'and that anon, I can promise you. But I should warn you that she is long married. As a matter of fact, you may, all unknowingly have come face to face with her in the Market Square – lavender perfume long gone.'

'Point taken,' said Silas, smiling at the mention of a fragrant memory. 'Now to serious business. I need to know all about your personal ideas on what kind of a new church – in parenthesis – hall you have in mind. You've had enough time, methinks, since the old one went up in smoke to have thought up something to interest this humble architect. So fire away.'

'Right,' said Daniel. 'I do like your choice of words. First off, I'm going to sell my highly desirable plot on which the old hall stood – that is after I have built a new dwelling house on the same spot. That way, as the developer, I intend to maximise any profit that is to be had from such a venture.'

'Do you have a potential buyer in mind at this very early stage?' enquired Minerva showing interest for the first time.

'No!' replied Damnit, abruptly, 'but I expect your father-in-law to design the house to the very highest specification – in which case it will sell like a solitary hot cake. A beautiful phoenix shall arise from the ashes.'

Silas almost choked on a mouthful of bread roll. 'Where on earth did you dream that up?' he exclaimed. 'I've brought the plans of Phoenix House with me. They're in the car. Drawing up or should I say designing a new build for the site has been an autumn exercise that I set myself.'

'So that's the reason you've been renting since you moved out of the Vicarage,' said Minerva. 'You sly old fox!'

'No, no,' expostulated Silas. 'It was purely a task for a hypothetical situation. You see, I've never lived in a house of my own design until…' He stopped. 'Consider Phoenix House sold, Damnit. Your solitary hot cake shall be on my personal plate at a fair price. Have you, yourself, any special features that you would like to see incorporated into my "ideal home?"'

'Only one,' said Damnit, seriously. 'I insist on there being a Tiltstone to connect the cellar with the floor above – the ground floor. A cellar exists already.'

'Consider it done,' said Silas. 'I'll see if I can fit it on the precise spot where the fire is thought to have started.'

'How exciting,' said Minerva with a chuckle. 'Us Ossians will look forward to coming to stay with Grandpa Kinnon in his ultra modern house with a Tiltstone. I presume that it will be a working feature, not just a replica.'

'Because it was invented as a form of emergency exit, it is imperative that it is fully functional, even if never operated,' said Daniel, 'in the same way that a miner's safety lamp, by law, must always be perfect. Imitations are illegal. Will you have any difficulty in constructing a Tiltstone, Silas? I know for certain that the classic example in Saint Michael's church is in perfect working order following the repair to the slab which was fractured in the heat of the fire which must have been started accidentally by John Smith. There's nothing particularly complicated about it. In fact it's something I could probably manage myself, never mind asking some ancient architect to produce one – if you get my drift.'

'If I can see it, then I shall be able to copy it,' replied Silas. 'You can show me just how it works – as in, "Tiltstone demonstrates the Tiltstone," probably the first time it's been used since its installation in the mid-1860s, I should think.'

'I wouldn't know about that,' said Damnit, fingers firmly crossed on hands hidden by the tabletop. 'You do realise that as a would-be property tycoon I shall be looking for a top price deal on this occasion – no special treatment on account of the old school tie that binds us. To be blunt, I need the money because I intend to spend it, every penny, on whatever kind of a new hall we can raise on Lambkinfold, subject as always to planning permission and my approval of your plans. At least, with you designing your own Phoenix House you won't have any exorbitant architect's fees to pay.'

It was Silas's turn to laugh – at his own expense. 'I'm beginning to wonder why I let you free me from the dreaded bramble bush. Never fear – your Yorkshire bluntness is an admirable trait not to be measured against sharp practice. I know that you know that I will pay only a fair price and no more. Now you can tell me what you have in mind for the new hall. I must say Lorna's suggestion of Archangel Hall has a definite ring to it – something special depending on which Archangel takes your fancy. So, fire away – again.'

'I have drawn up a list,' stated Damnit, a trifle pompously, 'but having secreted it in a jacket pocket, I've driven over here wearing a different jacket. Silly me! I'll just have to dredge my memory and test my powers of recall. Maybe you could use the reverse side of the menu Silas, if you feel like jotting anything down.'

'I can do that,' said Minerva, 'I used to be a good note-taker, and unlike my dear father-in-law I can read my own writing.'

'How kind,' responded Silas. 'I knew you would come in useful sooner than later.'

'Good,' said Damnit. 'Priority number one – the hall shall have a Tiltstone and that of itself demands a cellar or basement which will require digging out.'

'Problem number one,' said Silas. 'What if the site selected has solid rock under it at shallow depth?'

'I wondered about that. We'd soon find out the answer with the help of Y.Q.C. – that's the Yowe Quarry Company. If there is stone to be had, odds are it's limestone, and Frank Flint would tell us pretty sharpish of its quality: whether or not it was fit for building or fit only for road base purposes. We might be able to make use of it either for Phoenix House or Archangel Hall itself – or both, depending on the amount of excavation that is necessary to create decent sized cellars. There's a bonus to be claimed if we are lucky enough to find ourselves on a rocky outcrop.'

'Wow!' said Minerva. 'I am impressed by the very thought. When the time is right, I'll get Reuben to lead us all in praying for stone. We know that faith can move mountains. But why this desire for large cellars?'

'For storage purposes, mostly,' said Damnit. 'There's never enough space above ground unless we went for a sprawling building and I don't see the planning folk being happy with that. As a community resource, I envisage the cellar as a place for keeping theatre props, extra chairs and tables that may be needed, perhaps changing facilities for entertainers *et cetera*. With carefully planned access, some maintenance machinery could be kept there although I would not go so far as treating it as an underground car park.'

'Slow down, Damnit,' pleaded Silas. 'Minerva's running out of menus. I presume all the energy supply controls, fuse boxes and the like will be in the cellar as well.'

'Certainly. Which leads me directly to priority number two – The environment. I expect you to allow in your plans for all feasible features that may be beneficial to both the economic and environmental health of the enterprise. See what you can do in the way of harvesting rainwater, heating from geothermal ground sources, generating power from the sun and, at a pinch, using wind power. Heaven knows we get nearly as much wind as Wensleydale.'

'Problem number two,' said Silas. 'You would not want all of those elements. I use the term "elements" as in the sense of fundamentals referred to in ancient philosophy – Earth, Air, Fire and Water. You can collect the warmth of Mother Earth: our friendly fireball, the Sun, will provide solar power: clouds may not give as much rainfall as we expect, year on year, so recycling of grey water could come into play. We're fortunate that Yowesdale air is so pure but don't expect it to power wind turbines round the clock. However, with a new build on a virgin site we shall have every chance to be cooperating with the environmental concerns of planet Earth. Next item Damnit!'

Ajax, asleep until then, woke up feeling hungry and demanding to be fed. The peace of the dining room was disturbed for a short time until Minerva decided to carry him out to Silas's car and pacify him with nature's own, already fortified with a drop of anise in Minerva's breakfast fruit juice. She apologised to Silas and Damnit for her need to abandon her secretarial role.

'Don't fret, m'dear,' said Daniel, using his most avuncular tone. 'I'm just about through anyway. What else I have to say is right up Silas's street and he is quite capable of making mental notes.'

Minerva gone, Damnit resumed. 'I'll be brief, Silas. I want this hall to be a blessing on our Tupshorne community. The auditorium at full size, should seat four hundred people – at a pinch – for serious concerts of all kinds, dances, wedding receptions and the like. In between times, I need your undoubted expertise to engineer a system of space dividers, false walls – call them what you will – that when deployed will reduce the size of the auditorium to something more intimate, suitable for the meetings of the smaller local clubs or societies. There will be a permanent theatre stage complete with dressing rooms for the cast of any strolling entertainers who wish to tread the boards. The dressing rooms could double as committee rooms, in between times.'

'You don't want much, do you Damnit. You must have been hatching these ideas for years.'

'I agree that it is a big ask, Silas, and your arrival on the Tupshorne scene has been a catalyst. As for my ideas, they have come to me only in the recent months since I burnt the hall – sorry, a slip of the tongue there. Although the fire was the answer to Violet Rose's prayers, she still seems to hold me, absent on honeymoon in Sicily, responsible. The age of miracles is not past, you know. I'm almost finished, you'll be pleased to learn.'

'Just as well. Minerva's on the move, probably anxious to get home in time for Helen and Troy coming home from school.'

'Three very quick final points. One. A sensible car park to remain as rural as possible with grasscrete underfoot and plenty of shade trees – maybe – no, definitely several parking spaces having permanent overhead shade for motorised kennels. Two. Top notch kitchen facilities for hosting anything from a charity coffee morning to a full blown banquet. Lorna told me about your superb kitchen in Ravensrigg Church Hall.

My last and by no means least wish is that the hall should be a desirable venue for a civil wedding ceremony. I think the time will come when it will be possible to get married in your own backyard if that's the way you want it, and that without the blessing of Almighty God.'

'I don't like the sound of that,' remarked Minerva who by now had come close enough to catch Daniel's last statement. 'It may depend on the size and indeed the ambience of the backyard you're talking about. I can vaguely remember a song from my father's record collection – he was a great fan of Sammy Davis Junior. The words that stick were "You may go to the East, go to the West – someday you'll find happiness and I guess…"'

Silas sang as he joined in. 'Dum did um, dum did um, dum did um Back in Your Own Backyard.' He broke off. 'It was a sort of upbeat, updated version of, 'There's no place like home.' There has to be something to be said for celebrating the great events of one's life in a place where you feel most comfortable.'

'That's as maybe,' retorted Damnit, 'but it wouldn't do for me. My point, in this case, is that with Archangel Hall within a stone's throw of the church of Saint Michael the Archangel, couples marrying in church may well opt to hold the wedding reception in the hall. The other side of the coin is that those who tie the knot in the hall may "see the light" and process over to the church to be properly blessed – the icing on the wedding cake I like to think.'

'Next, you'll be wanting a cloister from hall to church. Cloisters is very expensive,' offered Silas with a smile. 'It can be done though, especially if we have enough stone. I'll plan the feature as an optional extra. Stonemasons love cloisters.' He paused. 'Sorry Minerva, it's time to go.'

Walking to the cars which had been parked in the market place, Minerva apologised for having contributed little to the discussion.

'Nonsense,' said Daniel. 'They also serve who only stand and wait as I understand it. Your time will come.'

'Has Lorna any idea what she intends to do with the rest of Lambkinfold?' Minerva asked. 'Apart from a pretty substantial farmstead and many yards of dilapidated dry stone walls, it's a blank canvas.'

'I think she's waiting for a sequel to her original vision that prompted her to buy the place,' replied Daniel. 'Nothing's forthcoming as yet.'

'Right,' said Minerva Jemima. 'I'll ring her up for an appointment. I think my time has come.'

CHAPTER XXVI

Peccavi

(I have sinned)

Halfway home from Leyburn in Wensleydale to Tupshorne in Yowesdale, quietly motoring across the watershed, Trollop suddenly gave one guttural cough from deep within her engine – no more. Then she proceeded serenely on her way. The moment of alarm gave Daniel a jolt and he was aware that his heart had missed a beat, reminding him of his last visit to consult Nathaniel Ross when Lorna was absent with Martha on their fact-finding mission. Nathaniel had not been too impressed with his overall state of health and had said so in unequivocal physicianly terms. Trollop had just served him with a gentle reminder.

Two miles further on, after negotiating several potentially dangerous bends, Daniel guided Trollop into a roadside parking place, opened the glove box and helped himself to a couple of antacid tablets. A touch of indigestion did not surprise him – lunch at the Sandpiper had been comprehensive and, yielding to temptation, perhaps he had overindulged. Chewing on the tablets, he seized the opportunity to take stock of his own progress with regard to the provision of a new hall, having managed at some distance to burn down the old one. Since his dreamland visit to glean some wisdom from Albert, Sambo and John several things had happened that lent credence to his initial confidence that all would be well.

Albert had told him that there would be much money and that he should not drown in it but think big. Lorna had proved to be the source of the money and, personally, he hoped that his own instructions to Silas about the plans for a new community hall would prove ambitious enough to satisfy Albert's exhortation.

John had ordered him to heed the women and surely he had listened to Lorna, with Minerva also now about to involve herself at the behest of Silas. John also told him to use the water, presumably the same money that Albert had referred to, telling him not to drown in it. It was somewhat puzzling that John had called the water his genie in the bottle. Which bottle, he had no idea – and what if the genie was an evil one!

Sambo's assessment of the situation was disturbing. Jake would die of shock if he was to make any form of confession.

As the very best of friends for approaching sixty years Jake was well aware of how very secretive Damnit could be. In ancient Greece, he would have been a classic example of Stoicism which taught the wisdom of remaining calm and indifferent to the fickleness of fortune, pleasure and pain. It had been Sambo himself who in a Latin lesson dedicated to notable phrases had introduced his pupils to a choice gobbet from Horace, *'Aequam memento rebus in arduis servare mentem'* abbreviated to *'Aequam servare mentem'* and translated as, 'Remember to keep a cool head when in trouble.' Daniel had taken 'A.S.M.' as his motto for life, together with the High Ashes Preparatory School motto emblazoned on the school shield *'Meum verbum mea vita.* My word is my life,' and he thought that confession should be limited to the confines of the deathbed.

What else was it that Sambo had said? He had echoed in the first instance the words of Albert Prince in warning him not to drown in the money: then to beware of melting in a fire of his own making. He could make no sense of it. Could it be that Sambo was threatening him with the fires of Hell, should he fail to make his confession?

Contemplation over, he started Trollop's engine, thanked her for bringing him down to earth by reminding him of his own mortality, and then drove home to High Ash.

Lorna met him at the front door, alerted to his return by the excitement of Rauch and Baggins.

'You're a little later than I expected, Daniel. Minerva rang me about half an hour ago after arriving home. She was of the opinion that you and Silas had an excellent lunch and a most productive discussion. She thinks that she may have some interesting thoughts to share on what the Swannery Trust might do with the rest of Lambkinfold if or when a new community hall is built somewhere on the site. So after tea, I'm off to the Vicarage to consult the oracle and, with a bit of luck, cradle the baby.'

'Silas must have been driving faster than I,' replied Daniel. 'He doesn't appreciate the views that are to be had from our Rav. His Lexus is a marvellous motor but a trifle too low to the ground for me. I stopped at the top of the watershed to admire the view and to review how our plans might be working out. Trollop enjoyed the brief rest.

No doubt Minerva told you that she was taking down minutes on several menu cards. And I can say that Ajax was angelic. He's a bonny lad for a three month old. We hardly knew he was with us until he woke up and let it be known that it was his lunchtime.'

Lorna set off to walk to the Vicarage at seven o'clock, leaving Daniel to his own devices. The wake-up call that he had received on his way home from the Sandpiper needed to be answered and as soon as he heard the front door close he sat down at his desk, took out some notepaper from the top drawer and began to write.

My dear Jake, the boon companion of most of my years in this world, under orders from Sambo, I have decided , before it becomes too late, to unburden myself of my more serious misdeeds. When I consulted Nathaniel Ross in the summer while Lorna and Martha were carrying out their business for the Magnificent Seven he was not pleased with my state of health, principally because I told him that when I consigned Albert's ashes into Etna's crater I was conscious of my ticker having a little flutter. Lorna and I, at the time, put it down to the altitude and the heat emanating from the crater. Nathaniel pooh-poohed that idea and was of the opinion, after examining me, that my personal volcano could blow any time without warning.

Lorna knows that I went to Preston, ostensibly, for a meeting, hastily convened, of the trustees of the National Blacksmiths' Museum. I regret that that was a lie, told to cover my tracks in case my medical threw up any concern the like of which I would not have wished Lorna to know or worry about. She believes that my call on Nathaniel was purely social – in fact a courtesy call while in the area. Nothing unusual or suspicious about that – after all, Nathaniel is the father-in-law of her son.

It seems to me that a goodly number of people who appear to be prominent in our modern day society for one reason or another, when asked if they fear death reply in the negative. Bully for them, I say. And though I am in no way a society animal, I agree. But when asked about the fear of dying I suspect the answer would be different. Dying can take a long long time even for those who believe in a Heaven and can hardly wait to get there. Joseph-Ignace Guillotin, a physician no less, certainly had a sharp edge to his thinking. I would not wish to linger or be a burden to anybody. But I would die happy if I could live long enough to witness the official opening of Archangel Hall. A good name d'you think? Lorna's suggestion of course.

Forgive my rambling on! You have to know that Sambo, in one of my famous dreams, ordered me to tell you all about my sins. You will not deny me absolution and forgiveness even if you read this when I have gone. Now re-read my first sentence.

And so I begin. You are the only person – that is unless you have told Martha (and I don't think you have) – who knows where the £12,000 came from that was stuffed into the hole-in-the-wall safe at the back of the church: and you also know that I made use of the Tiltstone to hide my comings and goings from the cellar into the nave. Half the money, £6,000, I stole from Gary Brickshaw the estate agent. It was my revenge for the time when sister Bethan and I were negotiating the purchase of High Ash. Brickshaw was well aware of how much Bethan wanted the bungalow, and in a roundabout kind of way he demanded an extra £6,000 – in cash – on top of the original asking price on which we had agreed and shaken hands. He broke his word. Bethan would have been shattered if the deal had foundered so I stumped up the six grand, cash down, and she never knew. It was just as well because had she known of Brickshaw's extortion racket she'd have told him where to go. Now – you will remember my uncanny talent for reading a combination lock, first exhibited on Tell's tuckbox at High Ashes, a gift that never deserted me.

Damnit paused in his writing before continuing.

This letter of confession is becoming too lengthy which is not my intention. Cackle will be cut and précis will follow.

When you appealed from your pulpit for donations to a fund to put St Michael's to rights, I decided to have my £6,000 back from Brickshaw. With Albert's covert help and my own subterfuge at the golf club, I made a copy of the estate agency's entrance door key. I tricked Gary, in his innocent stupidity into revealing the burglar alarm code. I deposited £6,000 cash with Gary as a bond of 'good faith' (!) that I was intending to move from High Ash. That little manoeuvre of mine was too late in the day for him to bank it and I will never know why he didn't take the money home. I got lucky! Such a horrid phrase. Fortune is said to favour the brave and it seems strange, even now, that I was banking on the chance that he would leave it in his office. I suppose banking might be close to betting in terms of Ethics. But I am not a born gambler as well you know.

However, I drove Tottie over to Skipton to my narrowboat, returning on Moll the motorbike in the dead of a foggy night to 're-acquire' my money from Brickshaw's safe with its fancy combination lock. It was so simple, although I did come off Moll when trying to avoid a flock of sheep waiting for me in the middle of the road across the high moor as I 'molled' it back to the canal basin. Gary had to honour the receipt he had given me for my 'bond money,' out of his own pocket – his insurance against office theft stipulated that there was a £500 limit on cash held on the premises. Nothing else was stolen: only Gary and I knew about the money. He would have worked out that I had righted the wrong he had done me over the purchase of High Ash. Just how I did it, only you now know. Nobody was hurt.

Now to the burning down of the old church hall – still an unsolved or unexplained incident. Violet Rose let it be known, at the time John Smith accidentally set fire to the church itself, that if it had been the hall she would have dashed round with her bellows to give the flames a helping hand. She seems to be convinced that this humble churchwarden was responsible even though Lorna and I were honeymooning in Sicily. It is an incontestable fact that at just about the time the fire was starting in Tupshorne I was dropping Albert's ashes into Mount Etna. That was a remarkable coincidence – a rare sort of contemporaneous spontaneous combustion – given the fact that I had no control over the precise day when I arranged for the hall to burn down. Once again, nobody was hurt as I committed the crime of arson at a distance of over 1600 miles if one is to believe a migrant crow. The method that I used was based on rudimentary physics. Cast your mind back to when Lorna hurt her ankle and her arm. Martha came over to High Ash with a bunch of flowers from the vicarage garden – a gesture of good cheer. She found a crystal glass jug to show off the flowers. I told you at the time that the jug, when filled with water to a critical level became a magnifying glass when left in the sunshine and that it had set table mats alight on two occasions. That was why it had been relegated to the back of the vase cupboard – where she found it.

Cackle cutting time again! I took the ewer to the church hall cellar where I had arranged on a rickety old table some crumpled up newspaper and the cheap paint and turps that were scheduled to be used to redecorate the hall when I returned from the honeymoon. The exterior door of the cellar faced south and the half dozen or so small glass panes in the top half were blacked out with paint. I replaced one pane with clear glass, but then blacked it out with vinyl tape. Twenty minutes or so before our wedding, you may recall that I crossed from St Michael's to the hall – to use the loo, I told you. And so I did. But I went into the cellar, also, and topped up the water level in the glass jug to the vital line – it was already lined up to catch the sun's rays and focus that power on the paper under the decorating materials. Before exiting the cellar I ripped off the vinyl tape to allow an inquisitive little sunbeam a shot at the water jug magnifying glass. A few days later the sun obliged me while Lorna and I were atop our honeymoon volcano. I repeat – nobody was hurt for which I thank God, deo gratias as Sambo might have said. Violet Rose has

had her prayers answered and the profits of the Almighty Insurance Company
have not experienced a seismic shift so far as I know.

I have nothing else to add except to make it clear that, 'I did it my way,'
without corrupting or involving anyone else. I ought to have some sense of
guilt, I know – but I have more a feeling of joy because what I have done has
been for Saint Michael the Archangel in Tupshorne, the community in which
I am rooted. I hope that Michael will see things 'My Way.'

And they say that friends do not have secrets between then!

Bless you, Jake. You, who have been one of the major lights of my life.

Bono animo esse et aere perennius.

Daniel

He re-read the letter before placing it in an envelope, addressed to
the Reverend Jacob Drake. In turn, that envelope was placed in a
larger one, with a covering note requesting his solicitor to put the
letter together with his will. As he wrote the name and address of the
solicitor, he wondered if he had done the right thing. Of course, he
would only find out at a later date which itself might be sooner or
later. Such is life – or death.

Rauch and Baggins were unamused to be roused from their
evening slumbers to be walked to the nearest postbox where Damnit
posted his letter to his solicitor.

Lorna's evening with Minerva Jemima unfolded like a magical
stair carpet – one step at a time from the bottom of the staircase up a
short flight that before she left to return to High Ash had changed into
a flight of fancy soaring on the wings of Minerva's wisdom.

Lorna began by recounting in detail the brief but vivid dream that
she had had and how its interpretation by a friend had resulted in
her buying Lambkinfold Farm on behalf of the Swannery Trust and
offering a plot of land from its two hundred acres for use by the whole
community of Tupshorne. Beyond that, she had no idea what to do
with the remainder.

'I'm no Freudian psychologist,' said Minerva, 'but it seems to me
that half your dream has been explained and, indeed, acted upon. It's
the trees – exotic looking you said – weeds and brambles that need my
attention. Do you know anything about arboreta or arboretums if you
prefer it that way?'

'Only that the word means a place where trees grow' replied Lorna.
'Shame it's such an ugly sounding word.'

'Precisely,' said Minerva, 'but that is what your fancy trees dream feature is about. You need to replace sheep with trees – lots of them, of all shapes and sizes if you are allowed to. Trees are poetic, not ugly.'

'Allowed to?' queried Lorna. 'I like the idea right away. Everyone knows we need more trees so what's to stop us creating a small forest in Yowesdale?'

'Change of use from sheep farming, that's what,' said Minerva. 'The agricultural powers that be don't often approve of tinkering with the *status quo.*'

'So how do we proceed from this point? I'm sure I heard some kind of a rumour when the outbreak of foot and mouth disease was over, the government said it was no bad thing in farming terms because the sheep population had been unsustainably high for some years, resulting in overgrazing. Not that such an idea was of any comfort to a sheep farmer when flocks had been destroyed. Now could be just the moment for a change. Brazil clears its rainforest – Yowesdale replaces it. How's that for a compelling argument?'

'Not bad at all,' said Minerva, smiling broadly. 'But I've had another idea. An arboretum doesn't maintain itself – it requires regular upkeep and that costs money.'

It was the moment for Silas to enter the discussion. He had walked round to the Vicarage in order to collect a couple of the menu cards on which Minerva had made précis notes during the lunch at the Sandpiper and which somehow had ended up in Ajax's carrycot. He came into the room in time to catch Minerva's last remark.

'Regular upkeep that costs money – what's that all about?' he asked.

'An arboretum we're planning for Tupshorne,' said Lorna. 'It can't possibly be self supporting for some years. I fully understand why. What can we do about funding it right from the start? Any ideas Silas? I haven't a clue where to begin.'

'I'm full of ideas,' laughed Silas, 'all to do with either drawing plans or good gardening practice. Daniel will have told you all about my plans to build me a house on the old hall site – Phoenix House it would have been, arising from the ashes.'

'Would have been?' asked Minerva. 'I thought you had the situation cut and dried at lunchtime. That's a mere five hours ago. I thought at the time that it seemed a bit precipitate. How right I was! So what's changed?'

'My approach to the drawing board,' replied her father-in-law.

'After I brought you and Ajax home this afternoon I drove round to Lambkinfold Farm, camera at the ready and expecting to find the place empty. It wasn't. I was met by Harold Miller, the previous owner, who was all packed up and ready to move out tomorrow. I knew his name from a conversation with Damnit and so was able to introduce myself to Harold without too much awkwardness. He was the very height of courteousness considering the unfortunate timing of my call. Before the light failed, he showed me round the farm buildings and then we had a mug of tea as he gave me a guided tour of the house itself. A delightful fellow.

The upshot to all this stems from the fact that I had no idea of the size of the farmhouse itself, and when you add in the buildings, to an architect the whole lot shouts out 'conversion, conversion.' Forget my Phoenix House – Daniel can do what he likes with it – I want to live in part of a newly converted barn, (plans by S. Kinnon) and along with other like-minded people of refined taste pay an appropriate rent to the Swannery Trust for the privilege. That would be as steady an income stream as you could wish for, once full occupancy has been achieved. But it wouldn't provide you with any start up funds for an arboretum. Maybe the Trust could help out.'

There was silence for a few moments while the impact of Silas's new plans sunk in. Minerva then spoke. 'Let me get this straight. You are suggesting that the Swannery Trust could and might set up the arboretum on land that it already owns. Personally speaking I think that is too much to ask. I can see the attraction of using the rental income from a farmstead conversion to cover the ongoing upkeep of the planting, perhaps even with a little to spare as the arboretum matures over the years. As a botanist with more than a passing interest in dendrology I have a fair idea of the cost of young trees and the expense involved with establishing them – things like labour, stakes, treeguards – perhaps a special 'starter' compost and in Yowesdale we will need the best windbreaks we can find and get them planted tomorrow! Now, I'm talking too much. It's your baby, Lorna – over to you.'

'Some baby!' said Lorna. 'the obvious scale of the project is in danger of whelming me over. I need a drink.' She treated Silas and Minerva to a beaming smile of satisfaction. 'In fact, it's time I was going home. Thank you, both, so much for your input provided at such short notice. Now I need to sleep on it before taking a firmer grasp of what we have discussed. Minerva, we need another meeting to discuss how we go about getting our ideas out of the garden of rose-tinted spectacles into the modern jungle. If we give ourselves a couple of days to mull things over, would you like to bring Ajax for mid-morning coffee and biscuits at High Ash – say about ten o'clock. I'm sure he won't object to us talking arboribusiness. It's a Friday and as far as I know, Daniel should be free as well and may like to sit in – or even join in our deliberations. You'd better stay for lunch while we're about it, and tell Reuben there'll be a mess of pottage for him if he cares to roll up about one o'clock – that's unless it's one of his fasting days.'

'He'll be there, no fear,' replied Minerva Jemima. 'A free meal is the ace of trumps when anyone needs a top card to break a fast. I won't need to drag him.'

'He's his father's son,' observed Silas, with a chuckle.

CHAPTER XXVII

Commune Bonum

(The common good)

It was morning coffee time on Friday, the thirtieth day of November and the sitting room at High Ash was occupied by three generations of humans and two generations of black Labrador retrievers. Ajax Achilles Agamemnon Ossian was fast asleep in his carrycot. Baggins and Rauch Greensward were fast asleep, sharing with some difficulty the same dog bed which was placed strategically and most comfortably in front of the woodburning stove. In the warmth of the room, it was not expected that baby and dogs would take any part in the discussion.

In his capacity as master of the house, Daniel asked if he might 'sit in' on the return fixture, as referee – as if one was likely to be required.

'Certainly, you can,' agreed Lorna with mock severity in her tone of voice, 'just so long as you don't interrupt. "Sit in" as "chair" but we don't expect a squeak out of you.'

'I know when I'm not wanted,' said Daniel, 'so I will lay on the coffee, before I take Ajax for a spin in his pram – if that's O.K. with you Minerva.'

'Consider yourself to be appointed to an honorary grand-uncleship. He's due a nappy change shortly,' replied Minerva, then batting the phrase back, 'if that's O.K. with you.'

Lorna laughed. 'There's a first time for everything so they say. This would be verging on the miraculous. The ancient bachelor engineer marries in June and within six months is expected to change a nappy. Ajax won't mind being fitted with a fresh oil filter.'

Daniel rushed away to the kitchen, the laughter ringing in his ears.

The dogs never stirred until as Daniel re-entered the room bearing the coffee tray there came a gentle knock at the front door and Martha Drake let herself in. Chaos reigned briefly while the dogs went through the exuberant ritual of welcoming an old friend, asking why Miss Bindle was not accompanying her mistress.

'That's good timing,' said Daniel. 'You must have homed in on the aroma of coffee.' Then, seizing the moment, he decided that the time had come to unveil the true existence of the Magnificent Seven of Saint Michael the Archangel. 'Martha, dear, as the wife of the previous vicar, I'd like you to meet Minerva Jemima, the wife of Reuben Ossian, our new vicar.' As he spoke, he almost imperceptibly nodded his head to Martha and gave her a wink by way of an invitation to abandon any previous pretence.

Martha understood, raising an eyebrow by way of acknowledgment. 'I'm delighted to meet you and to be introduced, officially. I have to confess that I have seen you before and even on several occasions since you moved into the vicarage – always in the Market Place on market day.'

'Of course,' said Minerva, 'it's only a few weeks ago when I saw you in the market and asked a parishioner standing next to me at the fish stall who you were. "The wife of the previous vicar" was his answer. And I'm very pleased to meet you as well. Am I to understand that we may have met before without my knowing?'

'Got it in one!' said Lorna, joining in the imminent unveiling. 'Silas, Reuben and yourself have known for some time that I and another unknown woman travelled up to Ravensrigg to find out what kind of a priest might fancy himself as vicar of Tupshorne. Martha was that other woman – like me, heavily veiled and reeking of lavender.'

Lorna turned to Daniel. 'I hope you've brewed enough coffee to cater for a cup for Martha, if she can spare the time, and we three can tell Minerva all about the Magnificent Seven of Saint Michael the Archangel.' She stopped. 'Silly me, Martha. I, or we haven't asked what has brought you to High Ash this "oh what a beautiful morning" – to borrow your phrase Daniel.'

'I've come to beg a cup of coffee – what else at this time of day. And so to my unveiling – after coffee that is.'

'Come, come now ladies,' said Daniel, 'this is too good a chance to miss. Coffee, confession and conciliation fit together very well. Get them out of the way and then Martha can add her penn'orth to your ideas about Lambkinfold and its future place in the community. You three witches can stir the cauldron while I prepare lunch. Martha simply must stay to lunch because Reuben should be here as well about one o'clock. And now I'm going to ring Silas to summon him to lunch.' He laughed as Lorna, Minerva and Martha looked at him in disbelief, before continuing his rationalising of the situation. 'Silas is the final piece in this jigsaw puzzle and I happen to know he's been dying to meet Martha – the lavendered lady behind the veil. I can hardly wait to see his face.' Again, he paused. 'You won't want me around while you come to any conclusions, so when I've rung Silas I'll walk the dogs for want of something better to do.'

At the sound of the phrase 'walk the dogs,' Baggins and Rauch awoke from their slumbers as if they had heard the last trump and charged towards the back door where their leashes were hanging from their personal hooks. 'Bacon and eggs for six when I get back. Just remember this though, *"Commune bonum"* must be the key to all your endeavours.' Those were Daniel's parting words as the dogs barked their demands to go a-walking from their waiting post at the back door.

Lorna smiled indulgently. 'I hope you like B and E, Minerva. I know Martha does. For Daniel it's his signature bachelor's dish and it works every time. Take X rashers of B and Y number of E, smash them all together and fry. You add your own salt and pepper.'

'It's true,' said Martha, 'but Lorna omitted to say that he does shell the eggs first. Perhaps I should have brought Jake with me – my personal master-chef.'

'Yes, you should,' replied Lorna. 'You may as well 'phone him now to tell him you're out for lunch and either he can starve or feed himself or drag himself over here for an impromptu feast. And I'll lend him my apron.' A sudden thought struck her. 'But you've got the car. That means he'll need to walk or hitch a lift from Middinside.'

'No, he won't,' said Martha. 'It's he who has the car. He dropped me off here and then went to call on Violet. He should still be there catching up on local scandal.'

'Right,' said Lorna, a note of decision in her next pronouncement. 'It's going to be B and E for, let's see, me Daniel Minerva Reuben Silas Martha and Jake. That's seven. We've room for eight. I'll ring him at Violet's and tell him to come bringing her and further supplies of bacon and eggs – and a stale loaf if he can find one and we can all indulge in some decent fried bread.'

Telephoning done and invitation list completed, the three women sat down in comfy chairs round Matthew Swann's beautiful coffee table which for Lorna was a source of inspiration now that Minerva had interpreted that part of her dream which Martha had failed to understand.

The stage was set for Minerva. 'I've had a stroke of luck,' she said. 'Would either of you know where the nearest arboretum is? It's not far away.'

'Easy,' said Martha, 'it's Thorp Perrow in Wensleydale. I know, because for several years the Saint Michael's Sunday School youngsters have enjoyed a summer picnic there. It was an initiative begun by Jake, admittedly with Daniel's support, and all to do with their prep school, High Ashes and Daniel's house High Ash. The truth of it is that Jake had a vision his first summer up at Cambridge. Sitting on a bench beneath a tall tree in the college garden he acknowledged his calling to the priesthood. That tree was an English Ash.'

'That,' said Minerva, emphatically, 'is fantastic! I'll explain just why, a bit later.'

'No, no,' said Lorna. 'Tell us now. I'm intrigued. The Ash tree in Scandinavian mythology is called "Yggrdrasil", the tree of life, knowledge, time and space. It was unbelievably important, binding together with its roots and branches the three worlds of Heaven, Earth and Hell. What's more it was evergreen.'

'Well,' replied Minerva, 'it's a trifle convoluted, the explanation. But everything I have been pondering on is beginning to add up and make sense. Forget the arboretum for a moment and think "Ash". I have something to add to your Jake's reverie under a tree all those years ago, Martha. The time will come when our world as we know it today will run out of fuel, be it oil, gas or coal. That is an inevitable and unarguable fact. Fossil fuel is not renewable. If we are not prepared, as a nation, to access our vast coal deposits or put our faith in nuclear power we will become dependent on other countries for our sources of heat and light.' Minerva stopped to draw breath.

'Have you noticed the gradual rise in the number of woodburning stoves in recent years? Many of them come from Scandinavia and they burn just about anything. And which is the finest log of all?'

'I know a little poem, all about logs,' said Lorna.

'So do I,' said Martha, 'by that famous poet, Anon.'

Then, both together, they answered, 'Ash.'

'Can you remember between you the particular compliments paid to the Ash?' asked Minerva. 'There are three in the particular version of the poem as I know it.'

'"Ash new or Ash old is fit for queen with crown of gold,"' quoted Lorna.

'"Ash wet or Ash dry a king shall warm his slippers by." That's the last line, I'm sure,' said Martha. 'So which is your third extract?'

'An echo, really, of Lorna's line,' answered Minerva. '"Ash green or

Ash brown is fit for queen with golden crown." So when a lumberjack eyes his logpile, Ash is number one – top of the logs you might say.'

'You've lost me now,' said Lorna, slightly baffled. 'Surely one Ash tree doth not an arboretum make.'

'No!' said Martha, seeing the light, 'it maketh money.'

'Got it in one,' said Minerva. 'Maketh money to fund the arboretum and yieldeth wonderful timber for fine furniture, tool handles – never mind logs for fuel. I did my homework yesterday, bearing in mind that Daniel had made it perfectly clear from the off – never mind his *"Commune bonum"*, as he went out earlier this morning – that all our endeavours should benefit the whole of Yowesdale.' She glanced at her wristwatch, gave a start and looked at it again. 'I'm talking too much – as usual – and the lunch party will be here before we're really ready.'

'Don't worry about that,' said Lorna. 'In the present circumstances, as long as Ajax is catered for in all his needs, the adults can jolly well wait.'

'Jake jolly well won't wait,' giggled Martha. 'Is Reuben the same, Minerva? Jake's dear Reverend father could be quite tetchy when hungry. Perhaps it's a priestly common factor.'

Minerva joined in the merriment. 'All I can say is that Reuben fasts twice a month and twice a month I keep out of his way. "Like a bear with a sore head" is the phrase that comes to mind. So I will now be as brief as I can before the men – and Violet descend on us.'

Silas is pushing on with his plans for a new parish stroke community hall, a new house where the old church hall used to be and his ideas for turning the Lambkinfold farmhouse together with its farm buildings and barns into several dwellings to be available for rent. The rents should go a long way towards funding the upkeep of an arboretum. So that takes care of that. Arboretum! I have been in touch with the owners of that delightful arboretum at Thorp Perrow. They are very happy to be consulted on any aspect of establishing an arboretum and even suggesting that their curator may well have some words of wisdom to offer as well. As a botanist, my contacts in the sphere of dendrology could prove to be useful. Daniel said, in so few words that meant so much, "Think of the common good". Anything we do, up to a certain point, must involve the whole town and that means every household will need to have pointed out to it the benefits to be gained from our efforts.'

'That would be nigh on impossible,' interjected Lorna, a trifle glumly. 'I do believe in miracles, but this...'

'This won't call for a miracle, Lorna dear,' said Martha. 'Minerva Jemima can see the future and is quite obviously full of optimism. It all ties in with what our Ravensrigg landlady told us during our visit. Do you remember her description of Minerva when we asked if the Reverend Reuben Ossian had a secret weapon, the source of his success as a parish priest?'

Lorna smiled at Minerva as she answered Martha's direct question. 'At the risk of making you blush, Minerva, we were told that you were the jewel in Reuben's crown. Please carry on and reassure me who am of little faith.'

'Oh dear!' said Minerva, 'I don't deserve such a testimonial – and I'm not about to ask where you were lodging. That's a stone best left unturned. However, back to business – the business of logs. Plan out the arboretum with its essential shelter belts *et cetera* over roughly half of your acreage. Then plan your logging operation with a view to providing fuel for all the wise folk of Tupshorne who will be investing in woodburning stoves if they don't already own one. Invite every member of our community, man woman and child to buy a little sapling to be planted in their name in the plantation and let each one have a plan of the site, as a certificate, showing where their personal tree is growing. Saplings are not expensive in the first place, in fact they're downright cheap, and you will also be able to claim a more than useful government grant towards establishing an almost limitless source of renewable energy.

As a central plank, so to speak, of the actual arboretum establish a selection of Birch species and cultivars that given time will grow to become recognisable as a National Collection. There are several notable collections in existence already but none further north than Shropshire. Birch trees thrive in this locality and birch sap is the source of a rather fine wine. Need I say more? We'd need to ascertain if one particular species, when bled, produces more sap than another and plant a stand of however many it takes to support a winery.'

'Further income,' ventured Lorna. 'You really have been busy with your homework. I've had a few sips of birch sap, unfermented, and must say it was most refreshing. One of Matthew's fellow pharmaceutical research chemists was analysing various tree saps, to compare the amount of some special acid that is found in willow trees with other trees that have it in their sapstream. That was when I sampled the birch juice. It was all to do with aspirin, as I recall.'

'Spot on,' said Minerva, 'but I'll not bother you with the plant chemistry involved except to say that the acid is salicylic; a willow is a Salix and yields more of the acid than a birch. My father was afflicted with rheumatic fever in his mid-teens and told me that he was treated with "salicylates" which looked like, and he thought might have tasted like horse piddle.'

Martha and Lorna hooted with laughter.

'Maybe that's what fired your interest in botany,' suggested Martha.

'We'll never know,' smiled Minerva. 'I wasn't born until about twelve years later, by which time the effects of the "willow water" must have worn off. It's a good story though. Dad was also a maple syrup addict and the liking is definitely in my genes. In fact, I'm only sorry that the North American Sugar Maple doesn't appreciate our climate otherwise we could be founders of the Archangel Maple Syrup Company and plan an acre or two *ex arboreto* – further income as you might say, Lorna.'

Minerva stopped talking and took a deep breath. 'That's me done,' she said;. 'What might the Swannery Trust have to say about my little scheme? It's a lot to take in, I know.'

'The Trust is amazed,' said Lorna, 'or even flabbergasted to be honest. As chairman of the Trust I am truly impressed to the extent that I would be delighted if you would consent to join the board. I've been looking for a fifth trustee for a while. You don't need to give me an answer now. Think about it. But, for the moment, and before everyone rolls up for lunch, have you any idea how we can persuade the Rural Affairs Ministry to permit a change of use from a sheep farm to a business based on trees and tree products, alcoholic or not?'

'Well,' replied Minerva, drawing out and elongating the vowel, 'I have taken to heart Daniel's exhortation "*Commune bonum*. For the common good", and turned it on its head. It is obvious that your Swannery Trust is bent on being a serious benefactor here in Yowesdale. To get your plans, and Silas's plans as well for that matter, over the hurdles that stand in the road leading to official approval you must have the overwhelming support of the whole community. Tit for tat. The Trust scratches the community back and surely deserves the reward of a responding pat on the back. We must assume or even presume that the future of Lambkinfold Farm will be what we wish it to be. So let all Tupshorners who are offered the chance to buy a sapling Ash, also be requested to sign a petition supporting the change of use relating to the farmland and Silas's building development plans. Actually, there would be two petitions – one arboretum orientated, the other for bricks and mortar – and I can't see any planning committee resisting a very sensible proposal underscored and countersigned by what we hope will be the entire populace. And that is what I call, *"Commune Optimum,"* the Best, not just good.'

'Phew,' said Martha, otherwise lost for words.

'That was a virtuoso performance,' said Lorna, lost in admiration. 'Have you written it all down somewhere?'

'Certainly not,' replied Minerva Jemima. 'A lot of it was off the cuff and developed like a snowball rolling downhill. But I'm confident that if you like what I've said, then we three witches will be able to recall most of it between us.'

'Let us pray,' said Lorna, quite out of the blue.

'What on earth's the matter now?' asked Martha – a frisson of alarm in her voice.

Minerva, Goddess of Wisdom, read Lorna's thoughts before Lorna could reply and answered Martha.

'Lorna is praying that our beautiful Ash trees are not visited by something as deadly as Dutch Elm Disease. We'd better get all Yowesdale on their knees – it's the finest insurance I can think of.'

Ajax Achilles Agamemnon awoke from his slumbers and demanded his mid-day feed. A timely intervention!

CHAPTER XXVIII

Nunc Accelerabimus, Scriptor Et Dramatis Personae

(Now we will all get a move on)

The prospect of letting Damnit cook bacon and eggs for eight was more than Jake could bear and once he had conducted Violet into the sitting room to join Lorna, Martha and Minerva, he set to in the kitchen, clad in Lorna's apron. There was no audible protest from the displaced chef who was content to set the table, a task for which he was well suited only because he knew where to find the cutlery.

Silas was the last person to arrive for lunch and on entering the sitting room was gently 'collared' by Minerva and Reuben each taking an elbow and propelling him across the room to meet Martha Drake, unveiled and free of any reek of lavender perfume. Reuben had been introduced earlier on his own arrival and been slightly bemused to discover that the only member of the Magnificent Seven of Saint Michael the Archangel whom he had not met turned out to be the wife of his predecessor in Tupshorne vicarage. Was it any wonder that the other six had never divulged the identity of Lorna Greensward's partner in crime?

Minerva spoke. '*Beau-père,*' she said, 'I know that you met Jake Drake in this house when you were reconnoitring for Reuben. This lovely lady is Jake's wife, *sans voile et sans parfum de lavande. Elle s'appelle Martha.*'

Silas looked down at Martha. 'Are you quite certain *belle-fille?*' he said, questioning his daughter-in-law. 'The height is right but I need to hear the voice.'

'But I have heard you sing in Ravensrigg Church,' replied Martha, 'and neither of us has altered in the intervening five months.'

'That's the voice,' said Silas, 'I'm sure Jake won't mind,' and inclining his head bent over and gave Martha a kiss.

An aproned Jake walked into the room just in time to hear Silas's statement and to see him bestow a kiss on Martha's cheek.

Silas saw him and called out 'I'm repaying a good turn Jake. I'm convinced that without a favourable report from these two ladies of a very distinctive bouquet the Kinnon-Ossian clan would even now be in Ravensrigg – and I like being here! So it's three cheers for the Magnificent Seven.'

'Ay-men,' said Damnit, with feeling.

Lunch passed by in a haze of friendly badinage and relaxed bonhomie. Much of the conversation was concerned with Christmas Day and the generalities of Christmastide. Violet, the oldest person present, was her usual ebullient self, enjoying the cheeky deference accorded to her on account of her age. She had not forgotten her declaration of some months earlier that it would be her task to find out what it was that made Minerva Jemima tick and just why the good folk of Ravensrigg looked upon her as the jewel in Reuben's crown. She really was a gem and she sparkled – but, observed Violet, not today; today Minerva was in musing mode, pondering on something even more important than Christmas and waiting for the right moment to arrive before giving voice to her thoughts.

Eating over, Lorna enquired if anyone would care for a cup of coffee. Only Minerva declined the offer, but she insisted on helping Lorna to prepare coffee for seven. On their return to the sitting room, each carrying a tray, Violet perceived what the matter was that had been preoccupying Minerva's mind during the meal when it was Lorna who provided the explanation sitting down to enjoy her cup of coffee.

'You will all be aware by now that Minerva, Martha and I have been discussing what might be done with Lambkinfold Farm, in the long term, now that it is owned by the Swannery Trust. To be brief, because Minerva has to be home shortly to greet the children, I as principal trustee have invited her to join the board with immediate effect. Thank goodness, she has agreed because I have decided that she is the person who on behalf of the Trust should mastermind – or should that be mistressmind? – the development of Lambkinfold as a community project while liaising as closely as possible with Daniel and Silas, not forgetting Reuben, on any vague chance that Saint Michael's might benefit from some or even any cooperation at all with the activities of the Trust.'

Lorna took a few sips of her coffee before she continued. 'I've nothing else to say really, at this moment, except to ask Minerva if she would like to give you an idea of what she has in mind. Believe me, she wasn't christened "Minerva" for nothing.'

'You're too kind,' said Minerva, smiling directly at Lorna. 'But I promise that I shall do nothing without consulting you every step of the way. You are captain of this new ship about to launch and I can be first mate.

It's time I was going, so I'll leave you with a thought. It is essential that any plans or schemes that we come up with and which will require approval by the powers that be ought to have the backing of everyone in town. If possible, each application must be signed by all Tupshorners who can write their name or make their mark. I will see to it.'

CHAPTER XXIX

Licet. Quando?

(Is it allowed. When?)

The deadline for submitting material for the December issue of the local monthly magazine, 'Tupshorne Times, Tidings and Tittle-tattle' or 'The Five Tees,' as it was affectionately known, had passed while the eight diners were enjoying B and E at High Ash. Minerva knew that she was out of time even as she returned to the vicarage, accompanied by Reuben. Ajax was not forgotten. 'Have you anything urgent that you need to attend to in the next few minutes?' asked Minerva of Reuben.

'No. Nothing pressing,' replied Reuben. 'Polishing this Sunday's sermon is not high on my Friday agenda. Is there something you need help with?'

'I've overrun Five Tees' copy deadline at lunchtime. Do you think, in your highly esteemed position as vicar, you could, on my behalf, ring the editor and beg an indulgence of twenty four hours. I think you know her well enough by now to have the cheek to ask a favour. All I need is a few hours to collect and commit my thoughts to paper, run the article past Lorna and deliver it to the editor. I doubt if she will be doing any editing until Monday. Would you do that for me? You see, I have this strong conviction that although the Swannery Trust is the prime mover in this whole business, Saint Michael the Archangel ought to have his finger in the pie somewhere, and you and I are part of that finger, like it or not!'

'Consider it done,' said Reuben. 'And by the way, our Archangel is more likely to have his sword in the pie so I'll make the 'phonecall sharpish like.'

Ten minutes later Reuben had sweet-talked the editor into extending the deadline to nine o'clock on Monday morning, the third of December. She understood immediately the thrust of the article that Minerva was about to contribute and its potential importance in communal terms. It would feature prominently as a stop press item. At that stage, the editor was not in a position to foresee that the national press would pick up the story shortly after its publication in the Five Tees.

Realising that space in the Five Tees would be at a premium, Minerva attempted to make her submission in the form of a letter, paring down the information to the bare minimum in a succession of terse statements aimed principally at Tupshorners but with the expectation that the wider reaches of Yowesdale would wish to be involved.

The letter ran as follows:

Dear Reader,

You will have learned already that Lambkinfold Farm, Tupshorne has been acquired, in its entirety, by the Swannery Charitable Trust. Amidst the many wild rumours circulating, you may be seriously concerned about the intentions of the Trust and what the future holds for Lambkinfold.

Fear not, keep calm and be reassured that the Trust has the future well-being and prosperity of the whole area at the heart of its plans. In due time the Trust will solicit the support of the community when applying to the planning authorities for permission to implement any changes they wish to make on the Lambkinfold Farm Estate.

Architect's plans are at an advanced stage for a community hall to serve as a multi-purpose venue, able to accommodate up to four hundred people at any one time. The construction of the building will be in traditional style with a typical stone outer shell but the interior will incorporate many 'state of the art' features and will include an ultra-modern kitchen facility. The main room will have a theatre stage and be able to host drama and music events. In sympathy with the church of Saint Michael the Archangel there will be extensive cellars, or a basement, beneath the hall which the Trust expects to be built within a stone's throw of the church, and the architect is charged with incorporating a Tiltstone linking the cellars to the ground floor above. Provision of a car park has not been forgotten.

The Lambkinfold farmhouse together with the associated farm buildings will be converted into several dwellings using the services of the same architect responsible for the community hall and any income accruing from the renting out of the properties will be used at the discretion of the Trust for the benefit of the estate and its further development. As regards the agricultural land of Lambkinfold, the Trust has very ambitious far-sighted plans. It notes the inevitability of the eventual exhaustion of the world's fossil fuel reserves. At the same time, the careful inspection of data concerning imports, especially those from Scandinavia, reveals a significant increase in the number of U.K. dwellings installing wood burning stoves. Logs from managed tree planting provide a totally renewable source of energy, becoming available ten or so years from the original establishment. Accordingly, the Trust intends to plant up to one hundred acres, or just over forty hectares in modern parlance, with trees suitable for coppicing to produce logs for our community – at a fair price. The dominant indigenous tree in Yowesdale is the English Ash, closely followed by the Sycamore, an alien possibly introduced by the Romans. Both produce excellent logging timber and will be core to the operation, alongside an investigative trial of Eucalypts with a view to finding a species that will enjoy our dale and yield a vast amount of timber.

Birch trees also thrive in the dale and all those who have enjoyed a glass of birch wine will understand why the Trust intends to establish a commercial block of Birch to give the sap essential for a successful winery. The remaining hectarage will be devoted to the creation of an arboretum or, perhaps to be more accurate, a woodland park which, once the timber business comes on stream in ten years time, will be open to the general public to frequent at their leisure. There will, at some stage, be enough space for a campsite for use by scouts, guides and other youth movements.

The Trust will actively seek out all possible sources of funding both for the building of a new hall and the provision of trees for the arboretum and the logging project. To that end, in the coming January every private home and business in Tupshorne will receive a visit from a member of the Trust soliciting donations for the trees to be planted – £5 for a logging tree and £25 for an arboretum tree to be dedicated to the donor. A certificate of grateful acknowledgement will be presented for each tree. After a minimum period of ten years, when the logging begins, all log certificate holders will be entitled to two free sacks of logs every year in perpetuity. What an investment! But do not lose your certificate. The deal will be on a basis of 'NO CERTIFICATE – NO LOGS.' Accompanying the tree offer will be two forms which we hope you will sign to indicate your support for the Trust's plans to provide a hall and woodland park for your community.

Finally, the Swannery Charitable Trust intends to name the community hall 'Archangel Hall' and the arboretum 'Archangel Park' in recognition of the initial driving force behind our plans, a churchwarden of the church of St Michael the Archangel – Daniel Tiltstone Greensward.

Signed. Minerva Ossian (for the S.C.T.)

The Vicarage, Tupshorne.

Minerva read the letter and was horrified to see that it was far from brief: in fact it was far too long and in danger of failing to make the desired impact. In horticultural terms, her epistle was in need of severe pruning and for once she could not see just where to begin. Help was very close at hand and by the time Reuben had finished with his blue pencil the length of the letter was reduced by a quarter.

The next day Minerva, on showing the revised draft to Lorna for her approval, had to confess that it was the hand of Reuben that had produced the finished article when Lorna complimented her on such a comprehensive analysis of the situation in comparatively few words. Then, endorsing the content of the letter, Lorna of High Ash, Tupshorne, countersigned it in her capacity as chairman of her own Swannery Trust. With tongue in cheek and in recognition of the tribute paid to Daniel in Minerva's final paragraph, she suggested that perhaps the last three words should be altered to, 'the notorious Damnit Greensward.'

The letter was published without any further redaction. Christmas had come early for the Tupshorne community.

CHAPTER XXX

Placet Et Fugit Tempus

(It pleases and time flies)

If it could be said that the 'Archangel Project' had a ring to it that suggested a debt to the sheer brass neck of its planners, Minerva grasped it by the scruff. By the end of January, she had visited every building within the bounds of Tupshorne distributing the information pack and planning permission forms soliciting the support of all who cared to be involved in the community initiative – and Ajax Achilles Agamemnon went with her every inch of the way, in his pram, sometimes pushed by Reuben who tagged along in support. He recognised missionary zeal when he saw it and by association he understood that by accompanying Minerva he was fulfilling part of his pastoral duties within his parish.

Many questions were asked of Minerva and all were answered with conviction and sincerity. Not all of the questions were concerned with tree culture and she had to answer quite a number on behalf of the sleeping Ajax, unaware of the admiring comments aimed at his baby beauty.

It had been Lorna's earnest intention to share the burden of distribution with Minerva but in the run-up to Christmas complicated family matters demanded that her priorities be re-assessed. Rachel's baby, a boy, arrived two weeks earlier than expected, catching everybody on the hop. Without being prompted, Daniel insisted that Lorna should go south to be with her daughter-in-law and son to help out with her first grandchild. Lorna did not need a second bidding and, when Rachel was discharged from the maternity unit, was at the wheel of her Volvo ready to drive Douglas and his newly enlarged family homewards.

The arrangements for the grand family Christmas get-together at High Ash were thrown into chaos. Originally, knowing that Rachel's baby was due just about Christmas, Lorna was quite comfortable with the thought of shopping for festive fare, and decorating the house and Christmas tree in good time for the arrival of Nathaniel three days before the day itself. That date would have been Saturday, twenty second of the month, with Douglas and the pregnant Rachel pitching up the next day. The good ship High Ash should have been dressed overall for a happy and glorious Christmas with High Admiral Lorna at the helm, wearing her seasonal holly and ivy printed pinafore.

Damnit assumed command with the practised ease of a man who had always subscribed to his childhood Latin maxim *'Aequam servare mentem'* – Panic not. This *'Omnium horarum homo'* – the 'man for all seasons' was in his element.

The early birth of Rachel's baby, while not life-threatening was not without some minor complications and Lorna decided that her 'extra pair of hands' would be better employed in helping the young Swanns with their new cygnet until, in convoy with them, she could return to Tupshorne on the Sunday before Christmas, the day originally scheduled for their arrival. Sprottle was overjoyed to see her, and until the entire household set off for Yowesdale Lorna's visit meant daily walkies times two. Travelling around in Lorna's Volvo estate car was just like old times for a hairy lurcher bitch no longer in her youth and the journey up north was canine heaven ending in a reunion with Miss Bindle, Baggins and Rauch.

True to form, Damnit coped magnificently in the absence of the power behind the throne, Lorna. Nathaniel arrived on the Saturday to find High Ash in a state of high alert, vacuumed, dusted, washed down in places that needed it and decorated for Christmas. Even the dogs' bedding had been put through the 'heavily soiled' programme on the automatic washing machine. His greatest coup, however, was the appointment of a top chef, someone he had known for a long time, to take on the duties of cooking the Christmas turkey. Jake and Martha had been invited to lunch at High Ash, joining the Greenswards and Swanns, and meeting for the first time Rachel Swann's father, the eminent physician Nathaniel Ross, né Rosenbaum, a child survivor of the Buchenwald Nazi concentration camp. Damnit gave Jake notice that with Lorna absent until two days before Christmas Day he might as well bring his personal apron and roast the turkey for all. There was a mischievous hint that if Jake felt unable to comply then there would be no lunch at all. That's what friends were for and Jake should never forget that it was Damnit's mother, Aunt Em, who had taught him to cook long before he received his call to the priesthood. Jake laughed before reminding him that Aunt Em had also made sure that Daniel qualified as an expert peeler of potatoes and preparer of Brussels sprouts, and more besides.

When Lorna had agreed to Nathaniel's self-invitation to Christmas at High Ash and so conspiring with him in the chance of delivering Rachel's baby, she had been looking forward to seeing the surprise on the faces of Douglas and Rachel when Nathaniel opened the door on their arrival. Such high expectation went by the board as soon as Rachel went into labour early.

Immediately Nathaniel learned of the early advent of his first grandson, he rescheduled, with a certain degree of difficulty it had to be said, all of his pre-Christmas medical appointments. Not all his patients were pleased to be offered a fresh date in the New Year – skiing holidays for some had to give way to the powerful draw of the maternity ward. Nathaniel's private secretary had to be at her personal and most persuasive charming best, juggling the new appointments and so enabling him to fly down to London the day after Rachel's return home from hospital. The young Swann's nest boasted only three bedrooms and so it was Grandpa Nathaniel who booked in for a couple of nights at the nearest inn, grateful that there was no call for him to share the accommodation with an assortment of oxen and asses. After his brief stay, it fell to Lorna's lot to drive him to the airport for his return flight to Ringway, as she insisted on calling Manchester Airport. The greater part of any conversation over the previous two days had been devoted to baby talk – to baby, with baby, over baby and about baby. Only as they were saying their goodbyes before he made his way to the departure gate did Nathaniel enquire casually about Damnit's present state of health.

'Daniel never complains,' replied Lorna. 'I do know that sometimes, after a more strenuous walk than usual with the dogs, he'll have a good long soak in a hot bath in an effort to pre-empt the inevitable onset of the aches, pains and stiffness of his advancing years. I think the time might have arrived when he should invest in a suitable ride-on mowing machine for his self-imposed task of keeping the church lawns in tip-top condition.

'Did you ask him about his visit to my consulting rooms?' enquired Nathaniel, sharply but quietly.

'No, I didn't,' replied Lorna. 'Although I am his wife and have known him since our Cambridge days, he still remains an intensely private man – perhaps something to do with his being almost a lifelong bachelor. I well understand that you cannot divulge any information to me, so I will wait patiently until he chooses to tell me. Maybe he never will.'

Nathaniel winced.

Damnit had no plans to tell anyone about his state of health, this side of the life hereafter. A live confession was not in his bag. Whatever had transpired during his rigorous medical check-up with Nathaniel was of no consequence when he suffered his second heart attack as he was carving the Christmas turkey, isolated for a couple of minutes in the High Ash kitchen. The Christmas guests were seated at the dining table, watching the covered dishes of vegetables as they cooled down and waiting the dispensation of sliced turkey hot from the carvery. For a few moments in time there was absolute silence in the dining room as they heard the unmistakable sound of a carving knife being honed on a steel. The ring of metal on metal was akin to an incantation prior to the casting of a spell. Nathaniel broke the reverie by standing up and announcing that he would go and fetch the dining plates as Daniel carved the bird. He reached the kitchen open door just in time to witness the dropping to the tiled floor of the heavy carvers as they slipped from Daniel's grasp. The clatter of steel on stone roused those still sitting at table but unlike Nathaniel, who was on the spot, they did not see or hear Daniel as he slumped to the floor uttering the strange sound of a suppressed groan.

Nathaniel the physician was in his element. Thwarted in his earlier avowed intent to help at the birth of Rachel's baby boy, he was now in the right place at the right time to apply the vital first aid to Daniel as Lorna summoned an ambulance. He, Lorna and Jake – in Lorna's Volvo – escorted the ambulance to the Airedale Hospital, leaving Martha and the others to salvage what they could from a Christmas feast for which they had lost any appetite. Douglas assumed carving duties immediately and by careful husbanding of resources was able to ensure that when Daniel left hospital nine days later his first meal, home at High Ash, was one of Jake's favourite dishes, a very tasty fricassée of turkey. Jake knew that one of Damnit's ideas of Heaven was the plentiful availability of 'sauced-up' meat. As a young lad, his aunt Em, Daniel's mother, had taught him the secrets of *une fricassée épicée* based on the regular supply of wild game easily collected on the moors above the Yowe.

Reuben and Minerva, together with Helen, Troy and Ajax came for a quick lunch to welcome Daniel home and sample Jake's recipe.

They came and went again with some despatch, not wishing to tire the patient newly discharged after the drama of Christmas Day.

'You've given me an idea, Jake,' said Minerva as they were leaving.

'How's that?' asked Jake. 'Is it a gem of an idea or a directive from on high. You're full of ideas – it's a mystery to me how Reuben keeps pace.'

'He indulges me – it's as easy as that,' smiled Minerva, 'but my idea stems from the lunch you've just dished up. No wonder Lorna gives you the run of High Ash kitchen, given the chance. It's a mystery to me how Martha copes with you – there's nothing worse than an insufferable cook. Mind you – I enjoy a bit of mystery.'

'Simple,' said Reuben, joining in the banter, 'she loves him in spite of. So what's the latest idea?'

'Fricassée. in a word,' replied Minerva, 'or if you need three words – *fricassée de gibier* – Roadkill.'

'Now you've really lost me,' said a baffled Jake. 'Never mind my chef's *tour de force*, let's have the idea in words of one syllable in English, *s'il vous plaît*.'

'Tricky, but I'll try,' chuckled Minerva. 'Get on and build new hall. Find or buy a big deep freeze that we will use to hold game found dead on the road and brought in by aides and paid for with a few pence.' She was forced to halt the flow of words. Game birds qualified, along with hare and deer but rabbit was disyllabic. 'Oh, hang it!' she said. 'I will undertake to prepare it all – with a bit of help from my lovely butcher whom I shall charm with the magic of my mint sauce to accompany his spring lamb – not for nothing am I named Minerva – and he can butcher the venison for me. I'll *fricassée* the lot and serve it up for any Tupshorners who care to attend the Grand Opening of Archangel Hall. Charge a fiver a head to cover the cost of vegetables, stroke spuds and rice *et cetera*, with a few pence to spare.' She paused again. 'How's that for a germ of an idea?'

'That's an epidemic idea. Saints preserve us!' said Damnit who had come to the gateway just in time to overhear Minerva Jemima's plans for the roadkill of Yowesdale. 'It'll be biblical in scale – the Feeding of the Two Thousand – and the diners will have to bring their own plates and cutlery. You'll need two days at least and several sittings. And do not expect me to do any washing-up.'

'I was expecting no such thing,' said Minerva. 'I suggest that the Bishop and the Archdeacon be invited to the Inauguration. I believe it was Milton Friedman who coined the phrase, "There ain't no such thing as a free lunch." And I'm sure that Reuben and Jake will agree that all gentlemen of the cloth, whatever their rank, are naturals at washing-up.'

'Amen,' responded Damnit, Jake and Reuben simultaneously.

Ajax Achilles Agamemnon awoke from his slumbers with a howl.

'Can we go home now?' asked Troy 'I need to go to the loo.'

'Me too,' said Helen, 'and I can't wait.'

'Pop inside again,' said Lorna with a smile. 'You both know where it is. Ladies first of course!'

CHAPTER XXXI

Cave! Ecce Aquarius!

(Watch out! Here comes the waterboy!)

Two years and ten months after Lorna's prophetic dream, in May 2004 Damnit contacted the National River Authority to ask if they had any idea how much water, to the nearest million gallons, might pass per annum under the Yowe Bridge where the river Yowe flowed by Middinside, updale from Tupshorne. The bridge was the site of the installation that monitored all things to do with the river's ecosystem. The Authority came up with a figure, averaged over the previous five years, and asked Mr Greensward, most politely, the nature of his business when enquiring after the flow statistics. This being an apparently harmless telephone conversation, Damnit stifled a chuckle before replying that he was in the early stages of carrying out a feasibility study with regard to generating hydroelectricity from the waters of the Yowe. The voice of watery wisdom on the other end of the line gave him explicit instructions about what he might do with his feasibility study before the 'phone call was terminated – and that, abruptly.

Daniel typed the information into the speech that he was destined to deliver at the opening ceremony for Archangel Hall. The mere mention of the word 'statistics,' when taken out of context was always good for a laugh. Approaching three years of however many million gallons of river water flowing by Tupshorne was a measure of the time required to build Lorna's dream from its original vision to the swivelling of the Tiltstone in the architectural fantasy of Daniel Tiltstone Greensward, courtesy of Silas Kinnon and Minerva Jemima Ossian.

In the preparation of his speech, Daniel set out to review the entire process of development from the submission of plans, through the execution of the work involved to the moment when the madam chairman of the Swannery Charitable Trust would turn the key in the lock of the main door into Archangel Hall for the first time.

Looking back with the incontestable value of hindsight, it appeared to an outsider that the saga of the good ship Archangel had been plain sailing from commissioning to its launching and maiden voyage. Hindsight is never better than when combined with the deployment of rose-tinted spectacles but Daniel's personal précised account owed more to a microscope or a magnifying glass. His observations, some of them tongue in cheek, were of the 'warts and all' variety – small warts with never a carbuncle in sight.

After his second heart attack, it was inevitable that Lorna learned the truth about the reason for his consultation with Nathaniel at a time when she was away from Tupshorne investigating the suitability of potential occupiers of Saint Michael's vicarage. He confessed, somewhat shamefacedly, that he was frightened of an existence in which he might persist in a vegetative state; a burden on all who might love him for what he had been once upon a time. Following obligatory cardiac repair surgery, he was assured by Nathaniel that the Grim Reaper would have to bide his time at least a few years longer. As his recovery proceeded and he heeded sound advice, there was no reason why in a few months time he would not be back to his old routine exercise regime based principally on walking the dogs. Come the end of April, he was indeed to be seen busy mowing the lawns that surrounded Saint Michael's. Some things in life never seem to change but in this case he was at the controls of a ride-on mower – a gift to the church from the Swannery Trust. Even so, ever pragmatic, Daniel invited Silas to learn the intricacies of a simple mowing operation which had been his custom to carry out on alternate Wednesdays throughout the growing season. The greater width-of-cut of the new machine reduced the four and a half mile walk behind the old mower to a comfortable forty minute ride on the new model which came supplied with two pairs of ear-defenders. Minerva caused great amusement when she presented Silas with a well travelled Walkman to replace one pair of the defenders. The good folk of Tupshorne were long accustomed to hearing Damnit Greensward whistling as he mowed the church lawns – now they became reconciled to the sound of Silas singing along to the accompaniment of Luciano Pavarotti on his 'Rideman' as Damnit insisted on calling it. By mid-summer a strange pattern of grass behaviour became apparent. It was Lorna who reported, with some conviction, that the grass grew greener and faster after being whistled at. Nobody was surprised when her opinion was dismissed out of hand by the Food and Agriculture Organisation as being fanciful.

Although Nathaniel Ross was not involved in Daniel's medical treatment, post cardiac arrest, he kept his own watching brief. In August, there was another family reunion at High Ash which also allowed Lorna to convene a meeting of the Swannery Trust. With the Trust in session, Nathaniel found himself alone in the High Ash rose garden when Daniel interrupted his reverie.

'Mr Ross,' said Daniel, with quiet, smiling formality, 'might I have a private word?'

'Of course, Mr Greensward,' replied Nathaniel, so preserving for the moment at least the niceties of the consulting rooms. 'Are you troubled, Damnit?'

'Not seriously,' said Daniel, 'it's just that I have been toying with the idea of leaving my mortal remains to medical research. I have already made arrangements or left instructions for the "recycling" of any of my useful body parts after my death. Lorna knows about that.' He stopped for a moment before continuing.

'Which reminds me that I need to alter my will which if scrutinised right now takes no account of my getting married last year – an event that has created some loose ends that ought to be tied. However, back to brass tacks, do you think this old cadaver would have any future on the dissection bench?'

Nathaniel gave a long sorrowful sigh, masking some kind of inner torment. 'You're asking the wrong person, I'm afraid Daniel. In a nutshell, I have history as they say.'

'You've totally lost me,' said Daniel, puzzled. 'That's a strange answer to a pretty simple question. What on earth has history to do with dissection?' Hardly had he uttered the question when he realised the extent of the gaffe he had made.

The sudden depth of the silence between the two men was unfathomable until Nathaniel spoke again. 'Don't kick yourself Daniel. You are far from being the first to make the link between Jewish history and Nazi human vivisection, and I wonder sometimes why I am still prone to be upset by a purely unwitting reminder of my own origins. You, quite innocently have put your finger on the very reason why I vowed to become a physician. You may know already that as a baby boy with his mother, by a miracle I survived Buchenwald. I'm not sure how old I was when mother told me that father was just one of six million Jews exterminated by the Nazis. Then at my Bar Mitzvah I learned the truth – he had been murdered in a hospital operating theatre – one more bungled medical experiment without the mercy of anaesthesia. In that moment I knew Medicine was my destiny.

Now, in answer to your question, I tell you this. My body goes to medical research as soon as my soul vacates it. In fact, I firmly believe all medics should donate their bodies on death for the benefit of those who would be surgeons in their own time. Leave your own past for someone else's future. You won't be turned down, I assure you. Just make sure your funeral director has a big enough pickle jar to accommodate you! Only joking.'

Damnit laughed. 'I think you know that John Smith ordered me to place his ashes under the "spreading chestnut tree" at the National Blacksmith's Museum. He was brought up never to waste a thing. Great man!'

He lowered his voice, 'Would the body of a suicide be acceptable to medical science, I wonder?'

'I'm sorry,' said Nathaniel, 'I didn't quite catch what you just said.'

'You weren't meant to,' replied Daniel with brutal finality. 'I was merely thinking ahead – I mean aloud.'

The response to the circulars and the petitions delivered throughout Tupshorne and beyond was positive in the extreme. In statistical terms, ninety two percent of those who received the forms returned them to the temporary headquarters of the Swannery Trust based at the Saint Michael's vicarage and every one of the signatories endorsed the far-sighted intentions of the Trust.

The very idea of investing a fiver for a period of ten years with the solid prospect of a guaranteed annual return in apparent perpetuity caught the imagination of the local populace: yet it wanted even more. Walter Sheepshanks, the bank manager, was not the only recipient of the arboretum information to look into the logging business as an exercise in arithmetic. The questions he asked himself were, 'How many trees – give or take the odd thousand – would be required to plant up one hundred acres of land, assuming a reasonable depth of soil over the whole area?' And, 'Whom did he know that could provide him with the answer?' He had a suspicion that the Swannery Trust had not got round to such an important piece of homework. How wrong he was! A brief telephone conversation with Minerva revealed his suspicion to be groundless and gave his calculator brain a severe headache. She talked of her forester friend in Scotland, a fellow member of the Dendrology Society: she talked of metric measurements, hectares and tonnes: she stated that at a planting distance apart of two metres, forty and a half hectares could accommodate one hundred and one thousand two hundred and fifty saplings. The establishment of shelter belts in strategic places and suitable service tracks through the plantation would reduce the number required, but by a comparatively insignificant factor such as one and a quarter percent to give one hundred thousand saplings on forty hectares.

Walter was astounded by the simplicity of the equation. In conversation with many of the bank's clients, it became clear that if they were to be persuaded to buy a wood burning stove they wanted more than a 'measly' two bags of logs every year and a minimum of ten might be acceptable. He conferred with Lorna and Minerva in a private meeting at the bank and together the three thrashed out a completely new deal which was aired in the next month's issue of the Five Tees. In essence, the initial offer was replaced by a second that was more generous within certain limitations, but beyond those boundaries, the sky was truly the limit – well – a limit of one hundred thousand or thereabouts. All the villages and market towns of Yowesdale were included in the scheme which invited subscribers to buy as many saplings as they wished at a price of five pounds each but only the first two 'whips' qualified for the precious certificates entitling the donors to five free sacks of logs per certificate per annum. Donations beyond the first two would be treated as being without any strings, or sacks, attached. Walter pointed out that the system was open to abuse in that the 'bags o'logs' certificates would become a currency in Yowesdale and possibly the neighbouring dales as the dalesmen, especially those who had no interest in burning wood, wised up to the sure fact that in ten years' time logs would cost a fiver a bag and sell on their two certificates for anything over fifty pounds. As a bank manager Walter was looking forward to the day when he might be asked the question, 'How many euros to the bag o'log?'

The February issue of the Five Tees, when looked upon in terms of pebbles in ponds, caused many a ripple and one unusually large ripple, likened to a micro-tidal wave, washed up a most unexpected visitor on to the Welcome mat of High Ash. Lorna was unaware of the gentle tap at the front door until alerted by the excited barking of Rauch and Baggins responding to the new sound of bare knuckle on wood – normal callers rang the doorbell which was perfectly obvious, attached to the right hand door jamb. The dogs thought that the knock had come from the garden, perhaps a pigeon bouncing off a window, and rushed outside through the open back door in the hope of retrieving something, dead or alive. Then the doorbell rang. Lorna opened the front door to be greeted by the sight of a man, very alive, lying flat on his back, roaring with laughter and fending off two very friendly but overinquisitive black bitches. For only a moment, she was lost for words before calling the dogs to order with the simple word 'sit' and helping the stranger to his feet.

'You poor man, I'm so terribly sorry. Are you all right?'

'Never better,' was the reply from the still chuckling stranger. 'I'm a black lab man myself, dyed in the wool you might say. Would you care for the name of my private dry-cleaner – not cheap but first rate?'

Lorna was taken aback by the tenor of the remark until she realised that the chuckle in the voice was matched by the twinkle in the eye. 'Don't worry,' she said. 'Dry clean, be blowed. I come from a long line of washer women. Strip off and I'll have you back on the road in no time at all. Now, just whom do I have the honour of addressing? Your sense of humour reminds me of my husband.'

'May I take that as a compliment?'

'You certainly may. I presume it's he you've come to see but I'm afraid you've drawn a blank, Mister…?' She paused, unable to complete the unfinished question and looked him quizzically in the eye.

'Sam. Sam Keld,' he replied. 'Samuel, the prophet – Keld, a water-source.'

He gave Lorna the benefit of what a schoolmaster might have termed a cheeky grin. 'All us Kelds, on the spear side, are born dowsers, water diviners – in our spare time that is. You must be Mrs Lorna Greensward, the lady of High Ash, and it's you I've come to see. I think I could be of service to you.'

Lorna gave up. 'Perhaps you'd better come in and have a cup of something warming. It's cold out here standing on the doorstep.' She spoke to the dogs, so obediently still sitting. 'Come on girls. Bring Mister Keld in and we'll introduce him to the water taps.'

Walking into the kitchen Sam said, 'Now I know you the washer woman, and you know me the dowser, who are these black beauties?'

'Rauch, she's still a pup really, is a wedding present from my husband when we were married last June – and Baggins, his dog, is Rauch's dam. As a declared black lab man, do I gather you have one, or even several, at home?'

'Sadly, no. I had to say goodbye to my old Zebo eighteen months ago. She was my tenth and definitely the last. My long-walking days are over since it was confirmed that I am suffering from *annodominitis* – wear and tear in English. I mustn't complain – no one wants to listen. Now, as for names, Rauch is a new one on me but Baggins has to be from Cheshire like me.'

'Or Lancashire, like me,' said Lorna. 'In fact, she's half Durham, half Yorkshire. And Rauch translates from German as "Smoke." So tell me what brings a Cheshire Cheese to my door, uninvited?'

'Although I live next dale – Grassington to be precise – I always receive a complimentary copy of the Five Tees. The page devoted to gardening month by month is absolutely first class. Professor Compost who writes it really knows his onions and this very day he's come to see you in his capacity as an unsung tree man. Professor C. O'Malley Post adores black Labradors and trees.'

'Now I think I've heard it all,' said Lorna, incredulity in her voice. 'I'm just sorry Daniel, my husband, isn't here to meet you professor. Where exactly in Cheshire do you hail from? I can feel a revelation coming on. Don't let me down.'

'I'm a Knutsfordian. Is that what you wanted or expected to hear?'

'Yes. And you are a galanthophile. Am I right?'

'Absolutely! O'Malley loves his snowdrops as much as he knows his onions. How could you know that?'

'Feminine intuition with a touch of serendipity. If I add two and two together, invariably I end up with four. On the way home from our honeymoon in Sicily, our driver Colin Blunden a friend from Daniel's years at Rolls Royce, took us on a brief detour through Knutsford, down the road where Henry Royce had lived. He rhapsodised over the seasonal sea of snowdrops planted along the grass verges, by an unknown man whom he thought had retired and moved to somewhere in the Yorkshire Dales. I even speculated at the time that we might meet, but not quite as soon as this – Mister Snowdrops. You've found me. Now what? To be blunt – what do you want?'

'Blunt?' laughed Sam. 'Pretty sharp, I'd say. I really should apologise, I know, for landing on you out of the blue. So I do.' He stopped to take a deep breath before ploughing on. 'I want to be your very first A.A., unpaid of course. How's that?'

'A A as in "automobile" or A A as in "alcoholic?"' queried Lorna, mystified.

'Neither,' said Sam. 'I hope that you are looking at an "arboretum assistant" – first class. I know trees – I know all about the machinery you'll need to nurse and maintain them – and, perhaps the most important factor, I'm "Cosh" qualified.'

Lorna giggled at his earnestness. 'That sounds to me like a conviction for "assault and battery". I'm familiar with the wisdom of the statement – a dog, a woman and a walnut tree; the more you beat them the better they be – but with a cosh? I think not.'

'You're right. It's an acronym for "Control of Substances Hazardous to Health". In the early years of establishing your trees from first planting it's imperative that you prevent any competition from other plants or a potentially crippling attack by insect pests. That's where COSHH comes in – my speciality – safe chemical control.'

'Now I'm out of my depth,' said Lorna. 'I'm only a mere historian who had a dream about trees which when interpreted by my botanist friend, Minerva Ossian, our vicar's wife will in God's good time turn into the reality of the Archangel Arboretum.'

'I bet your dream didn't feature a man like me pottering about amongst the trees.'

'If it had, he would have been my first husband – that's for sure. Although an amateur, he was highly skilled in the art of marquetry. You'll appreciate what I mean if I show you a coffee table that he made. It's in our sitting room, and is another good excuse for planting trees.'

Sam Keld marvelled at the intricacy of the pattern, inlaid on the table top, and asked Lorna if she could name the different trees represented by the various colours and grains.

'Not offhand,' said Lorna, but if you really want to know, you'll need to lie on your back under it and with the aid of a decent torch read the answers incised on the underside. Such was Matthew's sense of humour – he always maintained that the best way to study the stars required you to lie supine.'

'That's quite a story,' remarked Sam. 'It's given me a little idea – unless you've already thought of it. In which case, feel at liberty to tell me to mind my own business. Maybe a section or sector of your arboretum could feature trees noted for their importance in marquetry. You might even call it "Matthew's Marquetry Wood." Or if you want to capture the imagination of future generations plant a maze of box bushes or yew – both great subjects for turnery as well as marquetry. I'm sure you would enjoy picking a suitable title from the words Magical, Mystery, Matthew's, Marquetry, Maze. And kids love a maze.' He smiled. 'You must forgive my flight of fancy – I get carried away too easily. I'm sorry.'

'Don't be,' laughed Lorna. 'I believe in the virtue of being prepared to think the unthinkable. This concept of an arboretum is my personal magical flying carpet with Minerva Jemima Ossian my two i/c at the controls. Climb aboard.'

She paused for a moment. 'May I assume that you have time on your hands? If so, let me take you over to Lambkinfold and you might get a feel for the place. If Minerva's at a loose end, I'll give her a ring to see if she can join us. You will have an opportunity to chat to Ajax Achilles Agamemnon – he's beginning to talk – should have been christened "Precocity"'

'I'd love that,' said Sam, 'and if it's all right with you, I'll bring my hazel rod with me and make a dowser out of Ajax.'

Walking along a rough farm track, Sam pushing the pram, Ajax bouncing up and down as the springs took the strain of the uneven surface, Lorna explained that they were standing roughly on the site proposed for Archangel Hall.

Sam spoke quietly, hardly interrupting Lorna, 'I can sense water. Would you take Ajax for a moment, Minerva, and pass me my trusty bit of hazel?'

Until that moment, Minerva had been using the wand as a normal walking stick even though, in overall length it was more of a staff. She proffered it to Sam, holding it in both hands flat across her open palms and horizontal to the ground in a manner that suggested the handing over of a ceremonial sword. Before he could grip it, the rod trembled so violently in Minerva's hands that she was unable to prevent it falling to the ground.

'Well, I'll be damned – pardon my French – ' said Sam, open-mouthed with shock and looking at Lorna as he spoke. 'You didn't tell me the Swannery Trust had its own resident water diviner. That impromptu performance confirms my assertion that we're treading water you might say.'

'Sorry to spoil the moment,' said Minerva, 'I was only joking.'

'You might think that you were joking,' remarked Sam thoughtfully, with stress on the words 'you' and 'think'. 'But I'll bet you a pound to a penny that if you now bend to pick up the rod, it will recoil at your touch until you grasp it firmly. Try it and see. I know you've got water there and your fumble with dear old Moses, my dowsing rod has confirmed it. It'll be a spring.'

Moses did not fail to backup Sam's assertion about the presence of water and when the time came eventually to begin the excavation of the cellar for Archangel Hall a particular problem arose. Reuben, Minerva and Lorna were enjoying a light lunch with Silas at his cottage when a telephone call came through for Silas in his capacity as self appointed site manager for the building development, from the foreman in charge, who was none other than Frank Flint, prime mover and production director of the Yowe Quarry Company.

'We've hit a snag, Mr Kinnon,' said Frank in a tone of voice that suggested that the end of the world was nigh.

The front door bell rang – just one ding.

'Can you hang on a moment Frank, – I've someone at the door?' said Silas as Damnit eased his way in, knowing that he was expected.

'It's all right – the someone is expected,' continued Silas. 'So what's up? Don't tell me you've struck oil.'

'No such luck, I'm afraid,' replied the foreman not given to looking on the bright side of life – ever. 'We've hit water – gallons of the stuff.'

'You've hit water?' said Silas, echoing as well as questioning the foreman's report. The echo was loud enough to alert Minerva who like many a vicar's wife was blessed with a sharp sense of hearing, a most useful attribute when employed on the parochial stage. She joined her father-in-law by the telephone.

'Yes,' replied the foreman, bluntly.; 'What do you want me to do about it?'

Minerva entered the discussion. 'Don't sound so surprised *beau-père*. I told you ages ago that I'd found water, quite by chance, when I was handling Sam Keld's divining rod for the first time in my life.'

'So you did,' said Silas. Then, talking into the mouth piece, he spoke to the foreman. 'You probably heard that Frank – my daughter-in-law saying she knew about it already. Give me a few minutes to think about it and I'll 'phone you back a s a p.'

'Don't take too long,' said Frank, a shaft of humour appearing in his voice. 'It's running crystal clear and my crew are drinking it like it's the elixir of life. I'll give you thirty minutes while we break for lunch.' He rang off.

'Did you catch that last remark?' said Silas addressing Minerva. 'What do you make of it?'

'A massive profit is what I make of it,' she replied, as Damnit appeared at her elbow.

'An intriguing eavesdrop, I do declare,' he said. '"A massive profit" suggests a touch of money for old rope. Am I right?'

'The quarrymen have just found the underground water source that Sam Keld's dowsing rod pointed out to me so dramatically when Lorna and I first introduced him to Lambkinfold. In terms of oil exploration it sounds like a "gusher" and whether or not you call the stuff "black gold" or "Texas tea" it's a valuable commodity. And so is spring water. Think Buxton, Malvern, Evian and Perrier. Let's have it analysed and if it comes up trumps for purity – no nasty bugs – and interesting mineral content, so long as the spring continues to flow unceasingly then the Archangel Aquifer is a real moneyspinner.'

'Hang on a mo,' said Damnit. 'Let's not get carried away by the tide.'

'I must ring Frank back with some sort of directive,' said Silas. He stroked his nose between his thumb and forefinger. 'If, as he reported, his gang are lapping the water up as if it is was nectar and they then go down with some dreaded lurgy we'll know the source is polluted. They may be sick as dogs already. I've come across the problem before but although the water was potable the potential well ran dry within seventy two hours and that was that. I'll tell Frank to carry on for now, pray the men aren't ill and if we have to pipe the water away at a later stage we will.'

Damnit had been listening carefully before speaking again. 'The chemistry will decide for sure whatever the rate and continuity of flow. We could end up with a spa to rival Harrogate or a bottle of water that would be better than anything imported – or, thinking big, the Yowesdale Olympic Pool. But it's just occurred to me that a 'phone call to Harold Miller might throw some light on the matter. Would you mind if I use your 'phone Silas?' Harold's still in the area and will have kept his old Lambkinfold number.'

'Sure,' replied Silas. 'You know where it is – on the low bookcase in the hall. The phone book's right by it.'

And a most interesting conversation ensued. For the price of a local call, Harold opened the door to a wealth of water by uncapping the well of Lambkinfold Farm. He remembered well the day when mains water was piped to the farm for the first time, and the day following that saw the removal of the little well house, the levelling of the well curb and the placing of a massive stone slab over the source itself. It had never run dry, never failed any pollution check and, said Harold, if and when he arrived at them Pearly Gates and the Water of Eternal Life tasted half as good then he might be persuaded to stay. It was obvious to Harold that the activities of the quarrymen had disturbed the Lambkinfold spring, away from his old farm buildings and Damnit should know, sooner rather than later, that if so desired and without official sanction it would be feasible to sink a modern borehole and extract any amount of water – up to several thousand gallons a day or a week – he could no longer recall the precise data involved but there would be enough and to spare for any proposed development on his old land. Harold closed the conversation by wishing Damnit well and expressing the expectation that when any borehole was up and flowing he would be receiving a complimentary forty gallon drum of water once a month – and he would collect it!

Daniel relayed the information to the others while they were drinking a post prandial cup of coffee and all agreed that if everything in the development project flowed smoothly there was money to be made from the sinking of a borehole – and in the long run a lot of money. The water extraction would come on stream years ahead of the logging business and prove to be a profitable investment in keeping with the ethos of Lorna's Swannery Trust. Nothing surely could be more environmentally friendly than pure water.

The sense of euphoria in Silas's sitting room was quite palpable. Self-satisfaction almost to the point of downright smugness permeated the atmosphere: all given substance by the undeniable fact that the plans and good intentions of the Swannery Trust together with the input of Silas and Daniel had cleared all the planning hurdles. The sole objector to the idea of siting the Archangel Hall within a stone's throw of Saint Michael the Archangel's church had been the diocesan authority but it withdrew the objection when Daniel explained that because the new hall, like it or not, would be licensed to conduct marriage ceremonies, how very nice it would be if the newly-married happy couple could stroll across to Saint Michael's for a quick blessing. To that end, Silas, the architect added an open-sided cloister or colonnade to his drawings to link Archangel Hall with the Archangel's church. Violet, as church treasurer, threw her weight behind that particular proposal, pointing out that the final fundraising effort of Jake Drake's vicariate had thrown up a surplus of £29,000, over and above the money required for essential building repairs. The church could afford to fund its fair share of colonnading. It was at Timothy Welsh's subtle suggestion that Reuben had invited the Bishop to attend the opening ceremony of Archangel Hall and confer a blessing on the building before he could qualify for a free cup of tea. Daniel was convinced that a few choice Episcopal words in the ears of the diocesan planning committee worked the necessary miracle. But the Bishop had already elected not to confess to his chaplain that he had given way to temptation. The siren call of Minerva Ossian's *Fricassée de gibier* had reached him on the wind well in advance of Reuben's official invitation and game was his Achilles heel! Daniel had then calmly proceeded to prick the bubble of euphoria.

'I'm sorry,' he said, 'I can't go along with it. Borehole, yes! Water, yes! Money, no!'

'What's got into you? said Lorna sharply. 'You have to admit that it makes sense – certainly in economic terms. Have you been dreaming again?'

'Put so simply,' replied Daniel rather wistfully, 'the answer is "yes". When you dreamed up your arboretum just after you'd bought Lambkinfold, I also had a dream – my last as it so happens, involving John Smith, Sambo and Albert. Albert told me not to drown in money. Sambo told me to listen to the voice of the singer and to trust Silas. But my dear friend, Janis Kalējs of Latvia, the giant John Smith set me a puzzle that I have worked out only in the last few minutes. Albert said, "Don't let the money drown you". John said, "Don't drown in the water. Use it". Then he added, "It is your genie in the bottle". He was equating water with money in terms of value and use to the community. What he meant was, don't turn water into money.'

Damnit paused and looked pointedly at Reuben before continuing. 'I'm sorry Reuben if my strange dreams appear to sit uncomfortably with my position as a churchwarden. I just count myself lucky that my three mentors in another world have never played me false. And both Lorna and Jake know it. But if you can interpret for me what John was getting at, talking of my "genie in the bottle", then you're a better man than I – and all that jazz.'

'Of course I am,' smiled Reuben. 'It's simple. I've heard Jake talk about your John Smith with genuine Christian affection, probably or partly to do with your mutual admiration. No harm in that, but Jake did pass an unsolicited comment on John's accent which he said on occasion could be described as execrable. What you heard in your dream was not "bottle". He said it was your genie in the "borehole" If you will now allow me to share in your imagination with an added biblical slant, from time immemorial the populace have always gathered round the village well, or the village pump to call to mind a song taught me by my father.'

'And I learned that song from Sambo; so you will know it Damnit and so will Jake,' said Silas.

'That's it,' said Daniel excitedly. 'The genie is the community spirit to be set free when the well is uncapped. A free source of water for the new hall, but leave it at that. Design me an impressive fountain feature Silas, at the well head and put your signature on it. Then we'll have a Tiltstone at one end of Archangel Hall and a Kinnon at the other.'

'With pleasure,' said Silas, with a beatific smile. 'And now I'll 'phone Frank back to tell him that everything is sorted.'

'Truly,' said the Reverend Reuben Ossian in his finest pontifical vein, 'if one might rewrite a line from Saint Luke's gospel, "The wellspring from below hath visited us" and Damnit is saved from a watery grave.' All those in the room laughed at Reuben's deliberate misquotation except Lorna who was unamused. Turning to Daniel she murmured, 'Pity the wellspring forgot to bring a cheque book.'

'You're absolutely right, My Love,' replied Daniel, just as quietly, 'but in terms of *commune bonum* the wellspring's credit card has a limit of infinity.'

'That may well be,' said Lorna, 'but don't forget that the Swannery Trust owns the land and if at a later date I decide to tap into the aquifer with a profit motive, I surely will. And that's that!'

CHAPTER XXXII

Res Ipsa Loquitur

(Matters speak for themselves)

Lorna and Daniel breakfasted early on the day that Archangel Hall was opened officially. It seemed appropriate that after all the undoubted excitement of applying the final touches, man and wife were at liberty to enjoy a leisurely first meal of the day and recall how their dreams had come true thus far.

The conversion of the farmhouse and its outbuildings had been completed for some time and the dwellings that resulted were all yielding a satisfactory and acceptable rent. Lorna had decreed that the Lambkinfold Farm well should remain capped. She had a long-held conviction that if a ruined barn was never to be used again for its original purpose, then it should be dismantled and the site grassed over. This opinion was anathema to the agricultural powers that be and it took all the persuasion of Sam Keld allied to Minerva's applied wisdom to permit two of the barns to be taken down and the stone to be carted away – not too far on the two hundred acre farm – to be re-erected and grafted on to a third barn, all three made good and fit for the purpose of housing all the machinery that in time would be needed to service the demands of an arboretum. A fourth barn turned out to be a bat roost and although it looked as if it had been hit by a bomb it was absolutely bombproof when under assault from those who might wish to restore it. In terms of restoration, bats truly rule the roost.

Special permission was also required to remove many yards of drystone walling from where such walls were bound to hamper the establishment of new trees in both the logging plantation and the arboretum itself. At the instigation of the Swannery Charitable Trust, the Otley and Yorkshire Dales Branch of the Dry Stone Walling Association was approached and invited to check over and repair or rebuild, where necessary, all the retained lengths of dry stone wall using stone salvaged and selected from the walls no longer needed. The O.Y.D.B. were swithering about the commitment they would have to make until, during the course of a 'phone call from Minerva and Sam Keld to the Branch Chairman Sam mentioned that the Trust was concerned that all teams operating on the site, whether construction workers, plantsmen, scouts and guides – even the obligatory building inspectors, should not be expected to work on an empty stomach and to that end a mobile canteen had been commissioned to provide good wholesome Yorkshire food and drink on demand and free of charge for as long as it might take to complete the several projects involved. The swithering ceased abruptly! Copious mugs of tea and a mountain of bacon butties were a *sine qua non* for the good folk of the dry stone walling persuasion.

Some of the stone salvaged was of the right nature and quality to be used in the cladding for the external walls of the new hall. The remainder of the stone needed for the hall came from the excavation of the cellars – the same excavation that released the genie in the borehole or 'Bottle,' as it came to be known, after Silas had designed, in acknowledgement of Damnit's dream, a well head that resembled a crown cork for a gigantic beer bottle.

Just like marriage, the creation of an arboretum is, as Saint Paul might have written, commended to be honourable among all men: and therefore is not by any to be enterprised, nor taken in hand unadvisedly nor lightly; but reverently, discreetly, advisedly, soberly and in the fear of God; duly considering the causes for which arboriculture was ordained. To that end, Minerva, in close consultation with Sam Keld, took all the help and advice she could glean from many sources of expertise in tree culture and then stamped her own imprint on parts of the arboretum. With feeding of wild birds in mind, she created the principal windbreaks along the south-westerly boundary of Lambkinfold to be entirely of fruit-bearing trees and their pollinators where necessary. Lorna seized on Sam's idea of having a section devoted to trees of use in marquetry and cabinet-making as a lasting reminder of her first husband Matthew Swann. Sam himself insisted on presenting a tree which he had discovered in 1976 and named after his elder brother Ezekiel Keld, a truly upright man. This particular field maple grew upright, like a typical Lombardy poplar but in autumn in turned from green to fiery red. On hearing about it Damnit was inspired to suggest a section given over to trees of a similar habit, and there are many to choose from, that could be sited somewhere between the Archangel Hall and the Church of Saint Michael the Archangel, so linking the church bell tower with the campanile shaped trees. The concept appealed to Silas's architectural soul and he named it, with Damnit's blessing, Spires Corner. But it was Sam who had the final word on Spires Corner when he pointed out to Lorna that the planning committee, in a rare display of wisdom, had insisted that the car park, like every other car park above ground, never a thing of beauty should be well planted with trees to counter the dull monotony created by rows of cars parked on quite a large expanse of hardstanding. Lorna agreed that if the narrow crowned trees were dispersed in and around the car park then the aims of both planners and arboretum designers would be achieved but she expressed concern that the result would look like a dark square fruit cake with lines of green candles atop in a regular pattern – nearly as boring as naked tarmac dotted with cars. Minerva the botanist and Sam, the nurseryman assured her that upright, or in horticultural parlance 'fastigiate' trees might resemble anything from a pencil to a skyrocket, a corncob to a Doric Column, a smokey bonfire on a windless day or a squashed ellipse standing on end: evergreen or deciduous, the potential variations were limitless. Lorna was convinced and it seemed apt that in the local Yowesdale pronunciation the car park became Spires Carner.

Lorna was intrigued by the persona of Sam Keld, the man who had landed on her front doorstep like a gift to the arboretum from the Gods to complement the wisdom of Minerva, the precious ruby in Reuben's crown. He was a true 'man of the trees' – so much so that when he talked to them even Daniel remarked that they lifted up their leaves and listened. He tended to be quiet, sometimes wistful. His thought processes were rigorous and he never joined in a conversation until he had something to say that might be worth hearing. His puckish sense of humour was pure Damnit and they hit it off from the start. In fact it was Daniel who remarked to Lorna that he could not fathom out how she had unearthed such a gem. It transpired that Sam's wife, Harriet, had died a few months before his old dog Zebo and apart from his dedication to the Grassington cricket club he had no serious ties to Wharfedale. Once his offer of becoming an A A, serving under the banner of the Archangel had been accepted, he reasoned that a move to Yowesdale – even to Tupshorne – made sense in so many ways, and he sold his Grassington cottage. By the time that Silas's conversion of the Lambkinfold farmhouse had seen the completion of the first dwelling, Sam was ready to be the first tenant. It was one of his interpretations of heaven on earth to be living on the job, right in the middle of an arboretum. He brought with him another tree for the arboretum, to be planted where he could watch over it from his new abode. The only specimen of its kind on planet Earth, it was a Lime tree with brilliant red twigs and very finely, deeply incised leaves. Its shape was that of an elongated rhombus standing on end. He asked Lorna and Minerva if they would care to name the tree as they were the prime movers in the Swannery Trust's arboricultural aspirations. Perhaps Archangel Raphael or Gabriel sounded good suggested Sam. Not good enough though, stated Lorna and Minerva. So they declared it to be *Tilia platyphyllos* 'Sam's Diamond', a real gem of a tree. Damnit fancied calling it 'Tiltstone'!

The planting of an arboretum is not unlike the building of Rome – not done in a day. The wide range of tree species are to be acquired over several years.

When the opening ceremony took place, the basics of deer fencing, rabbit wiring and dry stone walls were complete. The shelter belts had been put in place as soon as the last staple was hammered into the last netting post. The transplants in the forestry plantation were next, followed by the Birch saplings intended to provide sap for the winery. The planting up of the Matthew Marquetry Wood was half finished – some tree species proving difficult to locate.

Sam Keld let it be known that he hated the word 'arboretum.' Such an ugly word for a thing of beauty, he said, and was surprised when Silas Kinnon agreed with him, wholeheartedly but for a different reason. 'There's no music in the word "arboretum", stated Silas. 'Angels and Archangels positively suggest "singing" in a euphonious way. Arboretum sounds quite the opposite.' And that was how Archangel Hall became set within the bounds of Archangels Park and Sam Keld changed from being an AA to an APAA, an Archangels Park Administration Assistant.

Phoenix House had been built and sold at a considerable profit.

The Lambkinfold Farmhouse and farm buildings had all been converted and rented out to happy tenants: among them Silas and Sam.

The planting out of the Spires Corner trees had to be left until the last, waiting for the final touches to be put on the car park before the landscapers waved the builders on their way. It is a well known axiom in the world of landscape gardening that just like oil does not mix with water it is unwise to put plantsmen in the garden to play football with builders – except those who are, as mentioned earlier, of the dry stone walling persuasion.

The chairman of the Planning Committee cut the white ribbon across the main gateway into the Archangel Complex. This was something of a pretence because he was late to arrive and the Spires Carner was already half full.

The local M.P., with Sam's help, planted the final token tree on the Carner.

Lorna, hand in hand with Minerva turned the key of the main door into Archangel Hall. Silas switched on the Kinnon fountain and as the general public wandered into the main auditorium Damnit Tiltstone Greensward, having hidden in the cellar a few minutes earlier, activated the Tiltstone swivelling mechanism and appeared to rise as if through a stage trapdoor in the finest traditions of the pantomime arrival of the wicked witch.

The Bishop was rather taken aback by this sudden demonstration of the abstract power of a Tiltstone in action but he was not surprised to see it was Daniel Greensward play acting, much as usual. Accompanied by Reuben Ossian and Jake Drake, a special guest for such an important Tupshorne celebration, he was soon in his element. He blessed the new hall, he blessed the fountain, he blessed the colonnade that linked the church to the Archangel Hall. Finally he conferred what Silas referred to as a Blanket Blessing on the head of everyone present, those who had found something better to do with their time and all those who, at the bidding of the Swannery Trust had worked so hard to achieve such a marvellous amenity for Tupshorne and the wider reaches of Yowesdale. As the last Amen died away into silence the Bishop realised that he had quite forgotten something vital to the success of the whole enterprise and he proceeded to utter a special benediction for the benefit of the trees in the plantations and the park. Above the general mumbling from the assembly, the fervent 'Amen' from Lorna and Daniel Greensward was heard loud and clear.

Radio, Press and Television had an absolute field day.

By teatime Daniel felt drained.

CHAPTER XXXIII

Tres Viri: Duae Canes: Una Navicula

(Three men: two bitches: one boat)
With grateful acknowledgement to
Saint Jerome K Jerome the Blessed

Not many days after the inauguration of Archangel Hall fell the third anniversary of Daniel and Lorna's wedding.

'Let's go mad and celebrate such an important date,' announced Daniel, a mere twenty four hours ahead of the official day, June the second.

'What on Earth's brought this on?' asked a slightly mystified if not apprehensive Lorna. 'I'm surprised you have even remembered – and in such good time too. In fact, I am very impressed. Are you proposing to bring me my breakfast in bed or is that too much to expect?'

'If you like,' said Daniel, 'and that would be a good start to the day. Anything else you might have in mind?'

'Off the top of my head, no. I need notice of your grand designs, one of which you are about to tell me all about. So fire away.'

'Well, I thought first of all, a ritzy picnic with all the trimmings would fit the bill. The weather forecast looks kind – that is why I was waiting before broaching the subject with you.'

'Hang on a moment! I'm not good at "ritzy" picnics and aren't we getting a bit long in the tooth for such foodie trysts à deux?'

'Shame on you!' laughed Daniel, 'suggesting my teeth are beyond sweet romance. This is what I had in mind. Not à deux but à quatre. You know Jake and Martha's Luke and family are due from New Zealand at the month end and we won't see much of them for a few weeks. So I thought we could turn the clock back to our university days of so long ago when one unforgettable summer – I suppose it must have been 1950 and counting – the four of us on several occasions took a punt out on the Cam and enjoyed a picnic, the very memory of which can still make my mouth water.'

'That,' said Lorna, 'was Martha's forte – even back then she managed to rustle up your "ritzy" picnic.'

'Actually,' said Daniel, 'I thought I would treat us all to a ready prepared picnic – you know, napkins an' all – from Skipton Skoffit who specialise in providing fancy grub for any occasion. I've heard they're very good – top nosh.'

'So have I. In which case, I'll be happy to join you,' said Lorna. 'At the very least you will manage to avoid the washing-up. And where do you intend to take this little trip down our Memory Lane? If you're getting the food from Skoffit's, the obvious thing is to take the Bethdan and pootle down the canal – and she's far more comfy than any punt ever was,' she gave a little chuckle, 'and as I recall, you are more proficient at the Bethdan's tiller than you ever were on the end of a quant. Punts don't have a loo either.'

'You've a point there,' said Daniel. 'But no! In all my Yorkshire life, I've never taken a boat out on Semer Water and I'm pretty sure Jake hasn't either. We can picnic on the shore and take it in turns to have a little row on the lake.'

'That sounds wonderful to me,' said Lorna, heaving a sigh of relief. 'We'll take the dogs as well and lots of towels.'

'I wasn't intending to swim. Were you? It'll be jolly cold and none of us carries much blubber.'

'Funny man!' said Lorna. 'Towels is for dogs. Just one more thing, can we invite Silas? It would be a nice gesture and it will create some amusement for Martha and me, his two lavender doused ladies, to see the three schoolboys playing on the sand – or perhaps it's shingle.'

'Splendid idea,' agreed Daniel, 'and Silas will be pleased to be free of any washing up. Maybe we could go out for dinner in the evening – the five of us – and invite Reuben and Minerva if they can find a baby sitter at short notice.'

Lorna pursed her lips in a moment of cogitation before speaking again – a hint of mischief in her voice. 'If we celebrate in the evening, we could invite Stephanie Potts to join us. I don't suppose you've noticed how over the past few weeks she and Silas have become much more at ease in each other's company. There's more to our church choir than meets the eye.'

'That choir has a lot to answer for,' replied Daniel, with mock gravity, 'but I have to confess that perhaps because I'm a non-chorister I haven't been aware of Cupid drawing back his bow but if he has – and in that respect I have to bow to your well documented feminine intuition in such matters as affairs of the heart – I hope the arrow strikes gold. By all means, we can invite Stephanie – she always looks as if a good meal wouldn't go amiss. Shall we book a table for six at the Sandpiper Inn in Leyburn – they did us proud for our wedding reception?'

'Your arithmetic's up the creek,' said Lorna. 'Didn't they teach you anything at High Ashes? We'll be eight not six if everyone comes. You ring the intended guests and when we know numbers I'll 'phone the Sandpiper. You know – I'm really looking forward to our anniversary. I'm sure it'll be another day to remember.'

How right Lorna was. Indeed it was to be a day to remember and impossible to forget.

The weather forecast for the picnic had been accurate. Warm sunshine beamed down from a clear blue sky on the five picnickers, sheltered from the distinctly cool breeze blowing across the surface of Semer Water by an old terylene windbreak that Damnit had thrown into the back of Trollop as an afterthought. For a surcharge, Skoffits had delivered the complete picnic package, chilled boxes for the food and drink, vacuum flasks for hot drinks together with two large groundsheets and matching sized blankets – all to High Ash by mid-morning. It suited Lorna to provide crockery and cutlery from a picnic basket which had been a wedding gift on the occasion of her first marriage. Trollop accommodated the lot along with Baggins and Rauch.

Silas had driven out to Middinside to collect Jake and Martha. Miss Bindle was feeling her age and the effects of the rheumatics, so elected not to join the other younger, boisterous dogs swimming and dashing through the shallows.

The two carloads met in the lakeside car park, and alighted – dogs first of course – gathered up the picnic containers, rugs and dog towels, and walked for about a hundred yards along the shore to a likely spot to pitch the wind break.

The wondrous repast provided by Skoffits would have fed six hungry young men at the very least and on the low nearby hillside, not many yards distant one such young man looked on with envy. He had wolfed his own packed lunch two hours earlier, several miles back. Benbo Beaumont was engaged in a long haul fitness hike, part of his training schedule prior to an Autumn crack at the International Three Peaks Challenge. Accompanying him, also with an eye on the lavish picnic provender was his faithful hiking partner Bilbo Beaumont, also known as Stupid, his exceeding handsome black Labrador dog.

After lunch, Lorna and Martha smothered themselves with suncream and stretched out on the rugs to soak up anything coming their way that might raise their vitamin D levels. The three men at Damnit's instigation set off for the boat landings to hire a rowing boat. They were all familiar with the famous quotation from Kenneth Grahame's delightful tale 'Wind in the Willows', 'There is nothing – absolutely nothing – half so much worth doing as simply messing about in boats,' and were anxious to find out if there was any truth in it.

Damnit decreed that he would take first turn at the oars. The breeze had stiffened and the surface of Semer Water was becoming slightly choppy but not alarmingly so. The rowing boat was about fifty yards offshore from their picnic spot, within easy hailing range of the sunbathers, when he felt that he was tiring and decided it was time for a change of oarsman.

The watcher on the hill saw the rower ship the oars and stand up as one of the other men also half rose to his feet. In what seemed like a flash in eternity, the little boat capsized and all three men were flung into the cold waters of the lake with a loud enough splash to alert Lorna and Martha. The boat floated away with the quickening tide, out of the reach of the floundering men, shouting out in distress as the chill bit into their limbs. A cloud began to hide the sun. One of the women on the shore appeared to order two black dogs into the water on a retrieving mission. At which point Benbo sent Bilbo down the hillside with the single command – 'fetch' – before rushing down himself to try to help the stricken men in such extreme difficulties.

Lorna took stock. What would Daniel do if in her shoes at that moment? *'Aequam servare mentem,'* his watchword, 'Panic not,' came to mind immediately. She seized her mobile phone and rang for an ambulance. With Benbo's help, the three dogs brought the bodies ashore and then lay down exhausted by their own efforts. Rauch looked at Bilbo and asked Baggins who the magnificent stranger was. 'He's your dogfather,' said Baggins the Beautiful. 'We only met once when I gave my old master the slip. You can just make out his torn ear where I bit him in all the excitement. Then you arrived nine weeks later. And he's still handsome enough for me!'

Bilbo Beaumont gave a tired wag of his tail, quietly wondering if all three had earned a Canine Victoria Cross.

Not for the first time in history was Semer Water in Raydale a scene of tragedy. The few roads that ran anywhere near the lake were little more than narrow country lanes quite unsuited to a normal emergency service vehicle when speed of access can mean the difference between life and death. The Yorkshire Air Ambulance Service was alerted and a rescue helicopter scrambled within minutes of receiving the S O S from Lorna's mobile 'phone.

The promise of a day to remember had gone horribly wrong and there would be no celebratory anniversary dinner for eight at the Sandpiper over in Wensleydale.

In the early-evening Lorna insisted that Martha should come to High Ash, bringing Miss Bindle with her. In the same way that Lorna had come to Daniel's home to rest an injured ankle, so came Martha now in urgent need of a port in the cruellest storm of her life. Daniel's sister Bethan's old room was once again a safe haven.

Miss Bindle joined Baggins and Rauch in sharing their queen-sized dog bed.

It was after midnight when Martha left her bed in Bethan's room, wandered down the passage and crawled in beside Lorna. In each other's arms they wept until there were no tears left to weep: at which point the arms of Morpheus, Roman God of Sleep, enfolded them both.

Just before slipping away into the Land of Nod, Lorna recalled how Daniel had told her the story of how on returning to school at High Ashes following his mother's funeral Jake had crept into bed with him in the middle of the night and cried himself to sleep – and he had never known him to cry since. How very odd, she thought, here we are sixty years later and a Drake is asleep with a Greensward. This though was no dreamless sleep: through the mist of her own dried tears she could discern Jake talking with Sambo, Albert and Janis Kalējs

She was in Daniel's world of dreams but there was no sign of him.

CHAPTER XXXIV

Lector Benevole, Si Monumentum Requiris, Circumspice

(If you are seeking a memorial,
kind reader, look around)
Wren. Troglodytes troglodytes

Timothy and Muriel Welsh were walking along the roadside footpath that led from the Market Place and would finish, eventually, at the bridge over the Yowe as the main road stretched away in the general direction of Skipton. It was late-morning in Tupshorne on the last Wednesday of August that same year of the opening of Archangel Hall. A slow moving car overtook the pedestrians, reduced speed to a crawl and pulled in to the kerb, coming to a halt a few yards beyond them.

'Not a kerb crawler, surely,' said Muriel, 'in Tupshorne in broad daylight. I don't like darkened glass.'

'Not a chance, love,' answered Timothy with a laugh. 'The car's too new, too clean and too polished, and they are lost. With tongue in cheek may I suggest that at your age...' He suffered Muriel's indignant elbowed dig in the ribs with equanimity if not considerable fortitude.

As they reached the car, the window in the nearside front passenger door was lowered noiselessly and the beautifully melodious voice of the lady in the front seat addressed them.

'Excuse me,' she said, 'I'm sorry to bother you, but could you direct us to Archangel Hall. We've driven quite a long way and I'm hoping you might be locals.'

'Your luck's in,' said Timothy. 'We do live here – have done for years – but really we're off comed'uns from Bolton. Another twenty years and we might qualify for "local."'

'You're here for a wedding,' chimed in Muriel in forthright fashion.

'How did you guess?' asked the lady.

'Simple,' said Muriel, mischievous now, 'your car is very new, very clean and highly polished. And on your lap is a lovely frothy creation of a hat that surely gives the game away.'

'Come on. Get on with it,' broke in Timothy, 'or you'll make these good people late.'

'Sorry,' said Muriel, 'I can go on a bit. My husband is much better at giving directions so I'll shut up.'

'Right then,' said Timothy, 'drive straight on for about two hundred yards and you'll come to Church Road on your right.' He glanced at his wristwatch. 'Being Wednesday morning you'll maybe see an old lad riding on a lawnmower, giving the church greensward a trim and almost certainly whistling as he goes. Then, about sixty yards on there's a wide entrance to a drive on your right with a striking new sign "Archangel Hall and Archangel's Park". Turn in. Big car park. You've arrived. Shall I repeat?'

'No need, thank you,' answered the gentleman in the driving seat. 'Your instructions couldn't be clearer. Local or not, you'd make a fine tour guide – and I can just catch sight of the parapet on top of the church tower.'

Both driver and passenger repeated their thank yous and were on the point of easing away from the kerb when Timothy delayed them for a few more moments.

'By the way,' he said, 'you might know it as "Archangel Hall" now, but to us locals it will always be "DAMNIT 'ALL." But that's another story.'

Donovan Caldwell Leaman Scripsit

XIX·VII·MMXII

Deo gratias